Praise for *Catching the Wind* and other novels by Melanie Dobson

Catching the Wind

"Another captivating weave of great characters, superb storytelling, and rich historical detail from talented wordsmith Melanie Dobson. A story to remind us all that resilience springs from hope, and hope from love."

SUSAN MEISSNER, author of *Secrets of a Charmed Life*

"A childhood bond, never forgotten, leads to a journey of secrets revealed and lifelong devotion rewarded. Readers will delight in this story that illustrates how the past can change the present."

LISA WINGATE, national bestselling author of *The Sea Keeper's Daughters*

"Intricate and lyrical, *Catching the Wind* tells intertwining stories of lost souls and faithful hearts. Once again, Melanie Dobson pens a novel full of fascinating historical detail and characters as real as your best friends—and worst enemies. Engrossing, beautiful, and thoughtful, this is a novel to be savored."

SARAH SUNDIN, award-winning author of *When Tides Turn*

"*Catching the Wind* is a sweeping and beautifully written historical novel that showcases Melanie Dobson's ability to tell a complex and enduring tale—one that will captivate readers with how love transcends the ravages of war."

KELLIE COATES GILBERT, author of the Texas Gold novels

"My heart raced and at times broke as I read *Catching the Wind*. As I've interviewed refugees in the Middle East and Europe, I've heard countless stories of people being ripped away from family, home, and country. I've also heard stories of hope and redemption. And ultimately that is the story of this book, that grace can take us further than we can imagine . . . to a place our hearts feel at home."

TAMARA PARK, producer, director, and author of *Sacred Encounters from Rome to Jerusalem*

Shadows of Ladenbrooke Manor

"Masterful. . . . mysteries are solved, truths revealed, and loves rekindled in a book sure to draw new fans to Dobson's already large base."

PUBLISHERS WEEKLY

"Dobson's latest is a splendid combination of the past and the present, skillfully woven together with an interesting mystery. The fascinating British setting, exploration of family secrets, and hopeful ending create an engaging reading experience."

ROMANTIC TIMES

"[This] poignant mix of historical and contemporary family drama . . . delivers a beautifully redemptive love story that will appeal to a diverse audience of readers."

SERENA CHASE, *USA Today*'s Happy Ever After blog

"Melanie Dobson's magical story of the lives and loves of the Doyle women, and the healing that finally comes for them, is a beautiful tale of the redemption that can happen even when we're not consciously looking for it."

BOOKREPORTER.COM

"For the second year in a row, Melanie Dobson has penned my absolute favorite novel of the year. I was swept into the world of English gardens and intertwined families. Do not miss this novel!"

SARAH SUNDIN, award-winning author of *When Tides Turn*

Chateau of Secrets

"Amazing characters, deep family secrets, and an authentic French chateau make Dobson's story a delight."

ROMANTIC TIMES

"A satisfying read with two remarkable heroines."

HISTORICAL NOVEL SOCIETY

"Intriguing and suspenseful; rich in secrets, hidden tunnels, and heroic deeds—Melanie Dobson's *Chateau of Secrets* weaves a compelling tale of a family's sacrifice for those in need. A beautiful story."

CATHY GOHLKE, Christy Award–winning author of *Secrets She Kept*

CATCHING THE WIND

MELANIE DOBSON

CATCHING
the WIND

Tyndale House Publishers, Inc.
Carol Stream, Illinois

Visit Tyndale online at www.tyndale.com.

Visit Melanie Dobson's website at www.melaniedobson.com.

TYNDALE and Tyndale's quill logo are registered trademarks of Tyndale House Publishers, Inc.

Catching the Wind

Designed by Ron Kaufmann

Edited by Sarah Mason Rische

Published in association with the literary agency of Natasha Kern Literary Agency, Inc., P.O. Box 1069, White Salmon, WA 98672.

Scripture taken from the New King James Version,® copyright © 1982 by Thomas Nelson, Inc. Used by permission. All rights reserved.

Catching the Wind is a work of fiction. Where real people, events, establishments, organizations, or locales appear, they are used fictitiously. All other elements of the novel are drawn from the author's imagination.

For information about special discounts for bulk purchases, please contact Tyndale House Publishers at csresponse@tyndale.com or call 800-323-9400.

Library of Congress Cataloging-in-Publication Data
Names: Dobson, Melanie, author.
Title: Catching the wind / Melanie Dobson.
Description: Carol Stream, Illinois : Tyndale House Publishers, Inc., [2017]
Identifiers: LCCN 2016055744| ISBN 9781496424785 (hardcover) | ISBN 9781496417282 (softcover)
Subjects: LCSH: Women journalists—Fiction. | Missing persons—Investigation—Fiction. | GSAFD: Romantic suspense fiction. | Christian fiction.
Classification: LCC PS3604.O25 C38 2017 | DDC 813/.6—dc23 LC record available at https://lccn.loc.gov/2016055744

Printed in the United States of America

23 22 21 20 19 18 17
7   6   5   4   3   2   1

To Tosha Lamdin Williams

My forever friend and the heroine of a beautiful story.

Thank you for loving me at and through all times.

PROVERBS 17:17

❀

"Better that one heart be broken
a thousand times in the retelling . . .

if it means that a thousand other hearts
need not be broken at all."

❀

ROBERT McAFEE BROWN

Preface to *Night* by Elie Wiesel (1986)

Chapter 1

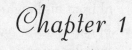

Moselkern, Germany, July 1940

M aple leaves draped over the tree house window, the silvery fronds linked together like rings of chain mail to protect the boy and girl playing inside.

Dietmar Roth charged his wooden horse across the planks, knocking down two of the Roman horses with his toy knight as he rushed toward the tower of river stones. In his thirteen years, he'd become an expert on both knights and their armor. Metal rings were useless for protection on their own, but hundreds of these rings, woven tightly together, could withstand an opponent's arrows. Or sword.

Standing beside the tower, a miniature princess clutched in her hand, Brigitte yowled like a wildcat. As if she might really be carried away by warriors.

At the age of ten, Brigitte was an expert on royalty. And drama.

Instead of an army, Brigitte played with one toy—the princess

Dietmar carved out of linden wood and painted for her last birthday. He liked renaming his knights, but Brigitte never changed the name of her toy.

Princess Adler.

Eagle.

Brigitte thought her princess could fly.

Dietmar drew a tin sword from his knight's scabbard and began to fight the black-cloaked opposition that advanced in his mind. Stretched across the tree house floor was an entire army of battle-scarred knights, all of them with a different symbol painted on their crossbows. All of them fighting as one for the Order of the *Ritterlichkeit*. Chivalry.

He'd carved each of his knights' bows from cedar and strung them with hair from Fonzell, their family's horse—at least, Fonzell had been the Roth family horse until Herr Darre stole him away. Herr Darre was a German officer. And the Roths' neighbor. He was punishing Herr Roth for not bringing Dietmar to *Deutsches Jungvolk*—the weekly meetings for Germany's boys. Brigitte and her father were the only neighbors his family trusted anymore.

Dietmar was too old to be playing knights and princesses, but Brigitte never wanted to play anything else. And Dietmar didn't want to play with anyone else. He and Brigitte had been the best of friends since her family moved into the house across the woods six years ago, playing for hours along the stream until his father built the tree house for them. Their mothers had been best friends too until Frau Berthold died from influenza.

Once, Herr Berthold asked Dietmar to care for Brigitte if anything ever happened to him. Dietmar had solemnly promised the man that he'd never let anything or anyone harm his daughter. Not even an army of toy knights.

He lifted one of his knights off the horse. "Brigitte . . ."

She shook her finger at him. "Princess Adler."

Cupping his other hand around his mouth, he pretended to shout, "Princess Adler, we've come to rescue you."

Brigitte flipped one of her amber-colored braids over her sleeve, calling back to him, "I will never leave my tower."

"But we must go," he commanded, "before the Romans arrive."

She feigned a sigh. "There's no one I trust."

Dietmar reached for Ulrich, the knight who'd sworn to protect the princess at any cost, and he solemnly bowed the soldier toward her. "You can trust me, Your Majesty."

"'Your Majesty' is how you address a queen," Brigitte whispered to him as if his words might offend the princess.

Dietmar knew how to address a queen, of course. He just liked to tease her.

With his thumb, he pounded the knight's chest. "I will protect you with my life."

Brigitte studied the knight for a moment and then smiled. "Very well. Perhaps I shall come out."

Outside their playhouse window, six rusty spoons hung in a circle, strung together with wire on a tree limb. The warm breeze rustled the branches, chiming the spoons, and Brigitte leaned her head outside to listen to their melody. The whole forest was an orchestra to her. The strings of sound a symphony. Brigitte heard music in the cadence of the river, the crackling of twigs, the rhythm of the wind.

Dietmar checked his watch. Only twenty minutes left to play before he started solving the geometry problems Frau Lyncker assigned him tonight. The world might be at war, but his mother still expected him to do schoolwork between four and five each afternoon. Even though everything outside their forest seemed to be foundering, his mother still hoped for their future. And she dreamed of a future filled with *Frieden*—peace—for her only child.

Brigitte leaned back in the window, her freckles glowing like a canvas of stars. "I shall make a wish on this tree, like *Aschenputtel.*"

"Should I capture the evil stepsisters?" he asked.

At times it seemed the threads of imagination stitched around her mind like rings of armor, the world of pretend cushioning her sorrow and protecting her from a real enemy that threatened all the German children. She was on the cusp of becoming a woman, yet she clung to the fairy tales of childhood.

"I want you to capture the wind."

He laughed. "Another day, Brigitte."

Her fists balled up against her waist. "Princess Adler."

"Of course."

Her gaze traveled toward the ladder nailed to the opening in the tree house floor. "I'm hungry."

"You're always hungry," he teased.

"I wish we could find some *Kuchen*."

He nodded. Fruits and vegetables were hard enough to obtain in the village; sweets were impossible to find, reserved for the stomachs of Hitler's devoted. But his mother's garden was teeming with vegetables. He and his father had devised a wire cage of sorts over the plot to keep rabbits away, though there seemed to be fewer rabbits in the woods this summer. More people, he guessed, were eating them for supper.

He'd never tell Brigitte, but some nights he felt almost hungry enough to eat a rabbit too.

"I'll find us something better than cake."

He left Princess Adler and her wind chimes to climb down the ladder, rubbing his hand like he always did over the initials he'd carved into the base of the trunk. *D. R.* was on one side of the tree, *B. B.* on the other.

He trekked the grassy riverbank along the Elzbach, toward his family's cottage in the woods. Beside his mother's garden, he opened a door made of chicken wire and skimmed his hand across parsnips, onions, and celery until his fingers brushed over a willowy carrot top.

Three carrots later, he closed the wire door and started to march toward the back door of the cottage, the carrots dangling beside him. He'd bathe their dirt-caked skin in the sink before returning to battle. Then he'd—

A woman's scream echoed across the garden, and Dietmar froze. At first, in his confusion, he thought Brigitte was playing her princess game again, but the scream didn't come from the forest. The sound came from inside the house, through the open window of the sitting room.

Mama.

The woman screamed again, and he dropped the carrots. Raced toward the door.

Through the window, he saw the sterile black-and-silver Gestapo uniforms, bloodred bands around the sleeves. Herr Darre and another officer towered over his parents. Mama was on the sofa, and Papa . . .

His father was unconscious on the floor.

"Where is the boy?" Herr Darre demanded.

"I don't know," Mama whispered.

Herr Darre raised his hand and slapped her.

Rage shot like an arrow through Dietmar's chest, his heart pounding as he reached for the door handle, but in that moment, in a splinter of clarity, his mother's eyes found him. And he'd never forget what he saw.

Fear. Pain. And then the briefest glimpse of hope.

"Lauf," she mouthed.

Run.

He didn't know if the officers heard her speak. Or if they saw him peering through the window. He simply obeyed his mother's command.

Trembling like a ship trapped in a gale, Dietmar turned around. Then the wind swept him away, carrying him back toward the tree house, away from his parents' pain.

Coward, the demons in his mind shouted at him, taunting as he fled.

But his mother had told him to run. He just wouldn't run far.

First, he'd take Brigitte to the safety of her home. Then he would return like a knight and rescue his father and mother from the enemy.

CHAPTER 2

London, England, 2017

Dear Miss Vaughn,

I received your e-mail and am deeply offended by your implication that my mother participated in some sort of secret Fascist network during the war. I object to your accusations and question the integrity of the entire World News Syndicate for proposing an article founded on lies.

If you decide to pursue this course of action, I will contact my solicitor in London. Fenton & Potts will put an end to this fallacy.

Signed,

The Hon. Mrs. Samuel McMann

Quenby's finger hovered over the Trash icon on her iPad as she skimmed the e-mail one more time, but she flagged it instead. Not that she would forget the woman's message. Her next feature for the syndicate was banking on an interview with the Honorable—and much-appalled—Louise McMann.

Sighing, she closed the iPad cover, and her gaze wandered past the kitchen table in her flat, through the patio's sliding-glass window. Fog veiled the hills and trees of Hampstead Heath like a filmy curtain draped over a production on the West End. Any moment the curtain would lift, revealing the spring flowers and pond below.

Usually the beauty of the view energized her, but this morning she wished she could slip back into bed. Chandler Parr—her editor and best friend—was planning to feature the espionage story next week, but even though Chandler had asked her to focus solely on this article right now, Quenby still had nothing even close to ready for publication.

Her feet slid into her slippers, and she propped them up on the opposite chair, pressing her fingers into the back of her neck. If only she could knead away every tendril of stress that coiled under the skin.

Two weeks ago, without any sort of fanfare, the War Office had released more than a hundred detailed files related to espionage during World War II, held under lock and key by the curators at the National Archives in London. She'd recently written a series of articles on the influx of refugees in England, and a friend at the archives thought she might be interested in the espionage files as well. He was absolutely right.

Few people outside England knew about the seemingly ordinary, even upstanding British citizens who'd supported Nazi Germany during World War II, but hundreds of these sympathizers had been rounded up before or during the war for betraying their country. Many of the newly released files contained information about Nazi spies already known to the public, but she'd found a confidential inquiry into the background and character of Lady Janice Ricker—Mrs. McMann's mother—who'd resided mainly in Kent.

A woman whose story would interest both North American readers and those on this side of the pond.

Lady Ricker was an American citizen who'd married into a wealthy upper-class British family before the war, becoming the wife of an astute Member of Parliament, and according to a memorandum in one of the files, she'd admitted to being sympathetic to the Nazi cause. The British government suspected that her ladyship had assisted the Nazis during World War II, but so far, Quenby hadn't been able to find any documents with solid proof that she'd operated as an *Abwehr* spy.

She'd located the obituary for Lady Ricker in the *Kent and Sussex Courier*. February 8, 1953. Lady Ricker was survived by a son and daughter at the time, but Louise McMann was the only child who remained now. Since Mrs. McMann refused to answer questions, Quenby would contact Lady Ricker's grandchildren to request an interview.

Not that Mrs. McMann wanted the world to know her mother might have participated in German espionage, but she'd thought the woman might be willing to share her family's perspective in the article, even if it was to declare Lady Ricker innocent of the accusations. Or perhaps give a reason as to why Lady Ricker had betrayed her country.

If Lady Ricker was innocent, Quenby would write a story about the difficulty deciphering who was innocent and who was guilty of espionage during World War II. An article about trust and deception and witch hunts—today and in the past—sparked by fear. Chandler might ax her story even before Evan Graham, the owner of World News Syndicate, saw it, but it would be the truth.

She took a long sip of the milky tea she'd brewed an hour ago. In her mind, journalism was a science that educated society about both past and present in hopes of bettering it, keeping people accountable for their actions and informing them about the past so they wouldn't repeat mistakes. In the mind of Mr. Graham, it was more about keeping a dying industry alive and, of course, selling papers. If people stopped paying for news—online or off—Quenby wouldn't have a job.

As president of World News Syndicate, Mr. Graham wasn't afraid of a little conflict. Or a lawsuit. His family had been in the business of news for more than sixty years.

A breeze blew through the park below her flat, curling the fog into strange shapes over the pond's surface. Then a ray of light pierced through it, a spotlight on nature's stage.

Cue the actors—otherwise known as mallards—along with the pods of water lilies that had tucked themselves away for the night. In another half hour, she figured, the curtain would rise on them all, and she'd have to make her way to the office for her own performance during their team's Friday morning editorial meeting.

Right now, she had about as much clarity as the foggy park below. Without the help of Lady Ricker's descendants, there would be no story. And Chandler might unravel in front of the whole team if Quenby didn't have at least a lead.

Her mobile phone rang, and she glanced down to check the number, but there was no ID. Perhaps Mrs. McMann wanted to talk after all.

Quenby rotated her mug so it aligned perfectly along the table's dark oak before answering the call. "Hello?"

"My name is Lucas Hough," the caller explained. "I'm looking for Miss Vaughn."

Standing, she stepped toward the window. "How can I help you, Mr. Hough?"

"Is this Quenby Vaughn?"

"It is."

"I'm a solicitor in London."

Her heart felt as if it skipped a beat or two. Had Louise already contacted her lawyer?

"I have a client who would like to meet with you."

She leaned against the table, the fog-infused shapes over the park shifting below her. "Why does your client want to meet?"

He chuckled, a low, amused sound that startled her. Was he laughing at her?

"I don't find any humor in that question."

"My apologies," he replied. "Most people would inquire as to who wanted to meet with them before they asked about details."

She glanced at the microwave clock. The editorial meeting started in an hour. "I believe I can decipher both the who and why in one shot."

"Indeed," Mr. Hough said. "My client is Daniel Knight."

He said *Daniel Knight* like she should know the name, but she didn't recall contacting anyone with the last name of Knight for any of her recent articles.

"You still haven't explained why your client wants to meet with me."

"Mr. Knight would like to hire you."

She reached for her mug but didn't take a sip. "He wants me to write a story?"

"No," Mr. Hough said. "He wants you to find someone."

She sighed. "Then your client should hire a detective."

"He already has, but none of the investigators were able to find this person for him."

Her mug clasped in her hand, she moved down the narrow hallway, into her bedroom. A stray pair of jeans hung off the side of a woven basket at the end of her bed, and she stuffed them back inside. Laundry would be the first order of business over the weekend. "I'm a writer, Mr. Hough. I find people so I can tell their stories."

"This story is quite remarkable, but Mr. Knight wants to hire you as a researcher instead of a reporter."

She set her mug on top of a book on her nightstand and pulled a pair of clean jeans and a white blouse from the wardrobe, spreading her clothes across the end of the bed. Then she arranged her slippers neatly underneath.

Mr. Hough's secrecy was maddening, but she couldn't resist a good story and had a feeling this man knew it.

"Who exactly is Mr. Knight looking for?" she asked.

"Someone he lost."

Maddening, intriguing, and *irritating*—she mentally added the word to the list. "A child?"

"No." He paused. "His best friend."

Quenby sat down on the bed and leaned back against the headboard. Her floor trembled as the Tube ran its morning course underground. "When did he lose this friend?"

"Seventy-five years ago."

She groaned. "This is crazy."

"Not crazy," he clipped. "Perhaps unusual, but not crazy."

Her head was beginning to ache. If only she could go back to bed and start this day again.

"I'm simply the messenger, Miss Vaughn. My client has done his homework, and he's decided that you are the person he wants to locate his friend."

"Because I'm a journalist?"

"His reasoning is unbeknownst to me."

This time she laughed. "Unbeknownst?"

"I'm sorry," he said without sounding the least bit. "I assumed you understood the queen's English."

She leaned forward, clenching the phone in her hand. He might think his teasing hilarious, but she had no time for this.

"Assuming can be a detriment in both of our professions," she replied. "But then again, I've been assuming that you and your client know I have a full-time position as a journalist."

She heard the clicking of a keyboard on the other end. "Mr.

Knight will pay you a significant amount of money if you decide to work for him."

"I'm not motivated by money, Mr. Hough."

"Miss Vaughn," he said with a sigh, "everyone is motivated by money."

She massaged her temples, tiny circles to clear her mind. He was pushing too hard now, and she didn't respond well to manipulation. Or the condescending tone of his voice. "I can't take the time off work to help your client."

"Before you decide, you should listen to his story."

It was like dangling a sweet carrot in front of her, enticing her to follow. She should tell him no, but perhaps she could mine a newsworthy story over the weekend, something to appease Chandler until the Ricker article was complete. "I can meet your client tomorrow morning at Pret's in Camden Market—"

"I'm afraid that won't work."

She drummed her fingers on the bedspread. "I suppose you already have a plan."

A phone buzzed in the background. "I'll fetch you in the morning at seven sharp, in front of your building."

"Wait—" She moved her feet back over the edge of her bed, onto the rug. "How do you know where I live?"

His laugh grated on her skin, like a pumice stone sloughing away her nerves. If he laughed one more time, she was going to throw him and his queen's English into the laundry basket.

She nudged the lid of the basket with her toe instead and watched it fall over the pile of dirty clothes. For some reason it made her feel better to hide it even though no one could see the laundry but her. "I can arrange for my own ride."

"Pack a suitcase," he instructed. Then he disconnected the call.

Quenby stared down at the screen in her hand, the time staring back at her. 7:32 a.m.

She'd done plenty of crazy things in her stint as a journalist, but she wouldn't be packing her suitcase for this Mr. Hough. Nor would she go with him to some undisclosed location in order to meet a stranger who seemed certifiable, even if he promised her an interview.

The money was just a ploy. A second carrot dangling on the stick, probably luring her right over the edge of a cliff.

She didn't know what these men wanted, but she was certain of one thing—she would be spending her weekend trying to track down someone to interview for her story on the Rickers, not searching for the friend Mr. Knight lost seventy-plus years ago.

CHAPTER 3

——

"You have to go with him," Chandler Parr insisted, leaning back against the L-shaped desk in Quenby's ten-by-ten cube of an office. Her best friend and boss wore a pear-colored blazer and black trousers. Between her fingers, Chandler clutched an unlit cigarette that doubled as a baton.

Smoking wasn't allowed in their building—and Chandler was trying to quit anyway—but she liked to cling to a Kent Blue. To combat stress, she said.

Unbeknownst to her, the staff referred to Chandler's cigarette as her "dummy." Pacifier. And now, thanks to Mr. Hough, the word *unbeknownst* was stuck in Quenby's head.

"I'm not packing a suitcase and leaving London with a man I don't know," Quenby shot back, drumming her three-inch heels on the floor. "Especially one who won't tell me where we're going."

She'd thought Chandler would be amused by Mr. Hough's early morning call, but instead her boss was appalled that Quenby had turned down his request to meet Mr. Knight. Like Quenby was crazy for not driving away with a stranger.

"Rubbish," Chandler said. "You may not know Mr. Hough, but that doesn't mean he's dangerous."

"Nor does it mean he's safe."

"Just because your mum told you not to talk to strangers . . . ," Chandler started. Then she stopped herself, her smile falling. "Oh, Quenby, I'm sorry. I didn't mean to—"

Quenby brushed away the apology with a swat of her hand. "I know you didn't."

And this was precisely why Quenby didn't tell people about her mother. She didn't want them stumbling over apologies when it wasn't their fault. Chandler only knew that Quenby's mother hadn't wanted to be a mom.

Chandler nudged her aside and clicked the mouse beside her computer. "Type in your password," Chandler said, her boss voice prevailing.

Scrivener, Quenby typed. A medieval reminder that her job was to create new stories, not regurgitate ones that had already been told.

Chandler usurped the keyboard controls to search Google for Lucas Hough, and she found him at the law office of Hough and Associates. According to the firm's website, the senior Mr. Hough had been practicing law in London for forty years. The junior Hough probably hadn't struggled a day in his life, slipping easily into the role his family already carved out for him.

Quenby despised the bitterness that welled inside her. She should be pleased for his success, not aggravated. If only Mr. Hough hadn't been so arrogant on the phone.

Another search, and Chandler selected an image from the faces that filled the screen. A man with wavy brown hair and brown eyes, wearing a gray bomber jacket and jeans. In his smile Quenby could almost hear his laughter. The thought annoyed her even more.

Chandler tapped her cigarette on the screen. "Let me introduce you properly to Lucas Hough, one of the most eligible bachelors in London."

Quenby turned away from the screen. This Mr. Hough wasn't like one of the friends her boss attempted to set her up with. Chandler had never even met this man. "He may look nice enough, but it doesn't mean he's safe." She didn't need a mother to explain that to her.

Chandler sighed. "Mr. Hough is a prominent attorney."

"Defending the law doesn't mean he obeys it."

"He's not going to kidnap a reporter," Chandler said, waving the cigarette back and forth in front of Quenby's face. "Go with him. I'll track you on my phone."

"A lot of good that will do if I end up in the Thames."

Chandler pushed away from the desk. "You might get a good story out of it."

Quenby straightened her keyboard and mouse pad. "Speaking of stories . . ." She opened the e-mail from Mrs. McMann and let Chandler read it.

Chandler stuck the cigarette between her lips. "You have more contacts than her, right?"

"I'm e-mailing her grandchildren this morning, and I've requested more files from the War Office. They'll be transferred to the archives on Tuesday."

The cigarette shook. "Evan Graham is not a patient man."

"I'm well aware of that." He had personally called Quenby out twice in their editorial meetings this year to say she needed to dig deeper. Find the stories no one else was telling.

"Go talk to this Daniel Knight," Chandler said as if she were scrounging for crumbs under the fridge. Then she glanced at her watch. "Let's not mention the fate of your article to the team yet. You'll have a break soon enough."

"Lady Ricker's daughter practically threatened to sue the syndicate if I don't drop the story."

"As long as you stick to the facts, she can only threaten."

"I figured Mr. Graham wouldn't mind the publicity."

Chandler put her finger to her lips. "He's in the office today."

Quenby cringed. Sightings of their boss were rare and, on days like today, unwelcome. "He'll ask about my current article."

"I'll cover for you."

Quenby reached for her coffee mug and followed her boss into the meeting room.

❖

Quenby wasn't packed by seven the next morning. Nor was she waiting for Mr. Hough in front of her building. Instead she'd fallen asleep on top of her bedspread, exhausted after a long night of researching the Ricker family.

But her mind didn't rest. Hundreds of puzzle pieces crammed into her dream, different colors and shapes, and she was desperately trying to fit them together on her table so she could see the entire picture instead of a jumbled mess.

The puzzle was almost finished when a loud noise rattled the pieces and they blew out the window, floating like bubbles toward the heath. She saw herself for a moment in her flat, her blonde hair tousled around her face, green eyes pale in the mist. Then she saw the girl with straw-colored hair, the one who often haunted her dreams. This time, the girl was alone on the heath, trying to gather the puzzle pieces in her arms. But no matter how tightly she grasped, the pieces kept slipping away.

Quenby tossed on the bed, knowing it was a dream and yet wanting to help. The girl ignored Quenby, as she always did, and Quenby felt paralyzed in her own body. She wanted to break free. She wanted to—

More pounding from beyond her dream, and Quenby jolted back into reality. Her arms moved again, as did her legs, but even as she sat up, the lonely girl lingered in her mind.

She'd planned to meet Mr. Hough downstairs at seven, sans suitcase, and demand that he answer her questions. It was ten after seven now, and she hadn't even gotten herself dressed for the day.

Before she answered the knock, she stumbled into the bathroom and replaced her nightshirt with a pair of running shorts and a paint-splattered T-shirt. Then she brushed her fingers through the layers of her cropped hair and swished Listerine around in her mouth. With a glance at her ragged T-shirt in the mirror, she reevaluated her attire but decided there was no reason to attempt to impress this Mr. Hough.

Mr. Hough was clearly not impressed. "You were supposed to be ready by seven," he snapped when she opened the door.

"I never agreed to go with you." She looked him straight in the eyes, undeterred by their espresso color that was steaming hot—in the precise Oxford Dictionary definition of the word.

He glanced at the time on his phone and then at the floor beside her like a suitcase might suddenly appear. As if he didn't have time to waste on someone like her. "We're going to be late."

"Late for what?" She stepped out into the alcove, closing the door behind her. Mr. Hough towered over her by at least six inches and smelled like sandalwood and soap. Blast Chandler for making her look at his picture online. Lucas Hough was even more handsome in person.

"Perhaps I should have given you more information."

She crossed her arms. "Starting right about now."

If he was willing to answer a few questions, she might go with him—for Chandler's sake—to hear Mr. Knight's story in person.

"I can't say much, Miss Vaughn. It's my job to protect my clients."

A brick wall, that's what he reminded her of. A fortress of pride and aristocracy that had blocked out the lower classes for centuries, as if the lowers might corrupt them.

"Is your client's friend a man or a woman?" she asked.

"A woman."

"His lover?"

When Mr. Hough shook his head, Quenby leaned back, propping her bare foot on the trim behind her. "You don't think I can find her, do you?"

Doubt flickered in his eyes. "I think the best investigators in London have tried for decades to no avail."

"Is she hiding from your client?"

He glanced at his phone again. "Her last known address was near Tonbridge, on the property of Lord and Lady Ricker."

Goose bumps prickled her arms. No one knew what she was working on except the syndicate and her contact at the archives. Had Mr. Hough somehow discovered her secret, or was it mere coincidence that Mr. Knight's friend lived at Breydon Court?

"Did your client know the Rickers?"

The man's phone vibrated. Instead of answering her question, he checked his text, then glanced back up. "The plane is ready."

She tilted her head, her cool demeanor waning. "What plane?"

Finally he smiled. "You didn't think we were driving, did you?"

Chapter 4

Belgium, August 1940

Cowbells echoed through the valley, somewhere along the border between Germany and Belgium—at least that's where Dietmar thought they were. The evening smelled of wild chamomile, and phlox painted the narrow path a pale-pink color that reminded him of the flowers along the Elzbach near his home.

Brigitte stumbled on a rock, and he reached out to catch her. But she kept walking, her bare toes crushing the summer blooms. The sun had freckled her cheeks, burnt her nose. Her eyes were often red too, tears blurring her vision as they trekked west together.

In her thin arms, Brigitte clutched a cookie tin filled with gold and silver coins. Dietmar carried her shoes and kerchief in the makeshift knapsack he'd tied together from a sheet, but she refused to let him carry her father's box or even to hide it when they slept on the forest floor. The toy princess she kept in the pocket of her cardigan.

The cache of coins in the cookie tin had been useless on their journey, but the box wasn't really about money for Brigitte. It was a piece of her parents, the only piece she had left. He would never ask her to leave it behind.

Dietmar kept telling her that they would see their parents again soon. That it was all a terrible misunderstanding. And as they plodded west, he kept trying to believe his words were true. That one day they would all return to Moselkern.

Herr Berthold had been arrested that same afternoon as his parents, their family's cottage ransacked like the Roths' sitting room. The scene scrolled painfully through Dietmar's head again and again as they walked in silence through the fields and forest.

He never should have coaxed Brigitte away from their tree house that terrible day, back to her home. He'd never imagined that the Gestapo had come for her father too.

He'd wiped up the blood in her kitchen while she was upstairs, calling for her father, but even though she was young, Brigitte was smart. Smart enough to know where her father had hidden their family's money from the Nazis. While Dietmar gathered blankets and a bit of food from the house, she dug up the tin box with a trowel. Herr Berthold had buried it under the pink stars flowering on a magnolia tree, hidden among the threads of roots that crept away from the trunk.

Dietmar had taken Brigitte to his classmate Heinz's house on the other side of Moselkern. After Heinz hid them in the back shed, he explained that the Gestapo was rounding up anyone suspected of feeding the Jewish people still hidden in the area. Someone thought Brigitte's father—a Lutheran minister—was helping them. While Heinz didn't have any information about Dietmar's parents, villagers knew Herr Roth was once an outspoken critic of Hitler and his party of Nazis.

Fear had silenced his father from speaking publicly against the

Führer in the past year, but Dietmar heard his parents' whispers at night, his ear pressed against their bedroom door. They thought Dietmar too young to trust with their secrets, but he hadn't said a word to anyone about their work. Nor would he now.

"What's wrong with helping the Jews?" Brigitte asked Heinz. "My friend—"

"Hush," Dietmar said, squeezing her hand.

He hadn't wanted to be harsh with her, but the way Heinz looked at her, then back at Dietmar, sent chills down his spine. His classmate's eyes were full of suspicion. Scorn. In that moment, Dietmar knew that neither he nor Brigitte would be safe anywhere in Moselkern.

"Wait here," Heinz had said as he backed out of the shed. Then he closed the door.

In the dim light, the image of Dietmar's bruised mother flashed through his mind. And he heard her silent plea for him to run.

He peeked out the crack in the door and saw Heinz glance at the shed before slipping into the house.

Dietmar had to protect Brigitte, but even the shield of a knight, forged in fire, wasn't strong enough to ward off the Gestapo. If someone like Herr Darre found them, he'd force Brigitte to join the *Jungmädelbund*—League of German Girls. And he'd probably send Dietmar to a labor camp.

From the moment they stepped out of the shed, Dietmar never looked back. For almost a month now, he and Brigitte had been running, following the path of the afternoon sun toward England.

They were far from home, yet he knew Germans had infiltrated the land between here and the wide channel that separated Belgium from Great Britain. But if he and Brigitte could get across the water, they could find his aunt in London. Surely his mother's sister would help them.

The sun was beginning to settle behind the trees that flanked them. Soon they needed to find something to eat and a place to rest.

"Are you hungry?" Dietmar asked.

Brigitte shook her head.

"You must be thirsty then." They'd turned away from a stream yesterday and had yet to find more water.

"A little."

"We'll find our way home. One day."

The fading light caught the blue in her eyes and made them shimmer. "As long as we're together—"

He reached for her hand and gently squeezed it. "I'm not leaving you."

The cowbells rang again, their song melding with the breeze, and he scoured the mantle of dark shadows and tall pine trees beside them. A knight may fight with sword and shield, but his greatest duty was to fear God and live by honor. To defend the weak and keep the faith.

"We need some milk," Dietmar said, guiding her toward the melody of bells.

She followed him into the shadows, the pine needles snagging their stained clothing and matted hair. He'd never milked a cow in his life, but how hard could it be? They'd been subsisting on river water and berries and the sausages from Brigitte's house. Sausages they'd finished three days ago. Milk would give them the strength to continue until he found more food.

A parade of light broke through the trees, and on the other side, a dozen tan-and-white cows grazed in a circular pasture before them. Two of the cows glanced up at the children, curious, but then they bowed their heads to return to their feast.

His stomach rumbled from hunger, and he eyed Brigitte's tin. Would she let him use it to catch the milk?

Before he asked, she pointed toward a pail hanging on a post. Quickly he retrieved it and walked toward a lone cow near the trees. Kneeling beside the animal, he eyed the swollen udder and then tugged on the teat.

Nothing happened. The cow didn't even look back.

Brigitte stepped up beside him, an unruly-looking halo bunched on the top of her head. "You're pulling too hard."

He glanced up. "Have you ever milked a cow?"

Her chin inched up. "A princess would never milk her own cow."

"Then it's good I'm not a princess," he tried to joke, but she didn't smile.

He tried milking again, lighter this time, and a few drops of liquid dripped into the bucket. Brigitte clapped her hands.

Someone called from across the pasture. Turning, he saw a man running toward them, a wiry fellow with blotched skin, waving a straw hat over his head. He shouted something again in a language Dietmar didn't understand.

Dietmar sprang to his feet, ready to sprint, but he didn't run. He couldn't leave Brigitte behind.

In seconds the man was beside them, studying their mud-spattered clothing and wild hair. Dietmar stood tall, and Brigitte stepped in quietly behind him. He was prepared to defend her. Prepared to do whatever he must.

Instead of reprimanding them, the man simply asked a question, this time in German. "Are you hungry?"

Dietmar didn't reply.

A stone farmhouse stood beyond the pasture, its sloping roof made of thatch. Smoke puffed out of the chimney and clouded in the orange-tinted sky. He could see the fence around a large garden, the dark leaves ready to harvest. Perhaps they could buy some food from the man.

The farmer pointed back toward the house. "My wife is making a rabbit stew for dinner."

Dietmar didn't see ridicule in the man's eyes, like he'd seen with Heinz. Only curiosity and perhaps compassion.

"You can sleep in our attic tonight."

The stew would strengthen Brigitte—strengthen both of them—as would rest in a safe place. If this house was safe.

"We will eat some stew," Dietmar said.

Brigitte took his hand, and they followed the farmer to the house.

Inside, the man's wife was bent over a copper pot on the stove, a worn apron with a patchwork of colors tied around her wide girth. Dietmar's mouth watered as the spicy aroma from the pot permeated the room. He'd once thought he couldn't eat rabbit, but he had no qualms about eating one now.

The woman's forehead was creased with wrinkles, and sweat trickled down the sides of her graying hair. She spoke to the man in the foreign language as she tugged on the fraying edge of her apron. Dietmar knew some English from his mother, but he didn't recognize any of the woman's words. Perhaps it was Dutch.

"Are we in Belgium?" Dietmar asked.

"*Ja,*" the man replied. He opened a cabinet and retrieved two chipped bowls. "You are fifteen kilometers from the German border."

Dietmar knew Germans occupied Belgium, but he didn't know about the Gestapo. Perhaps he and Brigitte would be protected here.

The farmer filled the bowls with steaming stew and placed them on the kitchen table along with two steins of honey beer. Then he and his wife slipped into another room.

Brigitte sat in the wobbly chair beside Dietmar, silently folding her hands for a blessing before tasting the food. Dietmar forgot that he was eating rabbit. Forgot that he was in a strange house in Belgium. He almost forgot that he was running away.

The stew tasted like the beef soup his mother used to make, full of carrots and potatoes and chopped leeks. It warmed his belly. Reminded him of home.

After supper, the farmer showed them a bathing hut outside. He filled the zinc tub with water, and while Brigitte bathed, Dietmar dragged two straw pallets from the barn and positioned them on the wooden floor in the attic, above the kitchen. Then he took a short bath, not wanting to leave Brigitte alone for long.

Brigitte was already asleep by the time he lay on his pallet. It felt good to have clean skin, to rest his head on a mattress even if it was made of straw. He hadn't slept well in the forest, keen to the noises and shadows around them, but as his eyes closed, he hoped he could rest tonight.

When he woke again, Brigitte breathed peacefully on the pallet beside him. Moonlight slipped through the dormer window, its fingers reaching back into the dusty corners filled with crates and broken furniture. The attic was silent, but someone spoke below them, the voice muted by the floor. He crawled across the rickety floor and quietly opened the door before descending the steps. Near the bottom, he could hear the whispered urgency of a woman's voice even if he couldn't understand her words.

Who was she talking to?

As he peeked around the corner, Dietmar saw the fat hips of the farmer's wife, draped in a green robe that looked ghoulish in the kerosene light. She was alone in the kitchen, the telephone cradled against her ear as she spoke to someone in Dutch.

Then she switched to broken German. "There is a boy here," she explained. "And a girl."

His heart seemed to stop at her words. Last night, he'd thought the woman frightened or vexed at having to share her food. He'd never guessed her to be malicious.

Did the farmer know?

Probably not—judging by her whispers. Either she didn't want her husband to find out or she didn't want to wake their guests. Then again, if the police offered a reward for runaways, perhaps the farmer knew exactly what was happening. Instead of being concerned, he might have used the bait of stew to lure Dietmar and Brigitte into the house.

Dietmar never should have allowed his stomach pains to dull his good sense.

The woman slammed the phone onto the receiver, mumbling something to herself in Dutch. Dietmar turned swiftly and tiptoed back upstairs. Then he shook Brigitte's arm. After the farmer's wife left the kitchen, they snuck down the steps, clinging to each other in the darkness until he unlocked the front door.

Hours later, as he was shoveling leaves and moss into a mound for their bed, Brigitte stared up at the moon above the forest, the bright orb webbed by tree limbs.

"Dietmar?" she whispered.

"Yes."

"Why must we keep running?"

He stopped and looked at the moon with her, hoping their parents could see the light wherever they were.

She tugged on his arm, repeating her question. "Why do we have to run, Dietmar?"

He put his arm around her to keep her warm. "Because my mother told us to."

CHAPTER 5

A pearl-gray castle was pleated into the island's jagged cliffs, the same color as the oyster shells swept along the shoreline below it. From the air, Quenby couldn't tell where the seams of the castle were stitched into the fortress of rock—it all appeared to be one grand monument built by a collaboration of God and man.

The private jet circled above a copse of stone spires on the castle and cast shadows over the white-capped bay and a roof of solar panels implanted on a greenhouse. Beyond the castle, the island was thick with forest, like a layer of moss clinging to stone.

Samantha, the flight attendant, slipped a china cup off the table in front of Quenby. "We're about to land," she said, raising the soft leather seat Mr. Hough had occupied during takeoff. "You'll want to buckle up."

Quenby scanned the hill behind the castle for some sort of

landing strip but didn't see a break in the trees. "Where exactly are we landing?"

Samantha zipped her thumb and finger across her lips. "Sworn to secrecy."

Quenby rolled her eyes. "Mr. Hough won't hear you."

"Don't bet on it," he mumbled from behind them.

Glancing back between the seats, she saw Lucas Hough stretched out on the couch, exactly where he'd been for most of their flight across the Atlantic and then the expanse of Canada. His eyes were closed, his tweed blazer hanging neatly in a closet near the galley. Dark stubble peppered his chin.

According to the profile she'd found online, he was thirty-one years old, only three years her senior. He might call her Miss Vaughn, but she was an American by birth and no one in the States called their peers *mister* or *miss*. From now on, she was calling him Lucas.

The plane jolted in their descent, and she turned toward the front again.

Samantha winked as she passed by one last time. "It's more fun than a roller coaster."

"I never thought roller coasters were fun," Quenby replied, leaning back on the headrest.

In London, ten hours ago, Lucas had given her fifteen minutes to shower and throw a few things into an overnight bag. She might have done it in fifteen minutes if he weren't so bossy. Instead it took her a full half hour to get ready.

After she reluctantly agreed to a plane ride, the driver had carried them off to London City, straight to the waiting jet. No security checkpoints. No lines. When she saw the private jet, a Global 6000, she stopped pestering Lucas with her questions. Time, she decided, would answer the most pertinent ones.

Minutes after they departed, Samantha had served eggs Benedict drizzled with the best hollandaise Quenby had ever tasted. Then there was the blueberry parfait with sprigs of fresh mint and the London Fog lattes made with Earl Grey tea and lavender. She'd tried to pretend she wasn't impressed by the gourmet breakfast or pristine cabin but failed miserably.

Lucas had told her to sleep—and she'd tried—but the golden petals of sunrise trailed them across the ocean, drifting over the snow-crested peaks and fjords of Greenland, lingering on the horizon. The beauty of it was like some sort of mirage. Almost like this Mr. Knight had hired the light to perform for them.

They'd crossed over the entire continent of North America and, according to the GPS on her phone, were now preparing to land on an island in the horseshoe between the coasts of Canada and Washington State, in steel-blue waters called the Salish Sea.

As they flew, she'd tried to track down more information about Mr. Hough's client, but there were hundreds of Daniel Knights listed online. Of course age was a factor, along with income and location, but until now, she hadn't known exactly where this Mr. Knight lived.

Samantha had calmed any fears she had over traveling alone with Lucas, replacing her trepidation with a strange sense of anticipation and a host of questions.

How did Mr. Knight know about the Rickers? Whom did he want her to find? And why had he picked her to do this job?

The plane descended toward a grove of pines behind the castle until it seemed they were skimming treetops. Then the forest opened into a long spray of asphalt framed by green. The plane landed smoothly and stopped near a lone hangar.

Groaning, Quenby pried her fingers from the armrest and swept her hair back into a ponytail.

Samantha pressed a button, and the door on her left opened, the airstairs unfolding onto the runway. "It's almost eleven local time."

"Are you coming with us?" Quenby asked.

The flight attendant shook her head. "But I'll see you tonight. You like scallops?"

"If they're broiled with butter."

Samantha laughed. "How else do you eat scallops?"

"Where I'm from, they eat them fried."

Her fists on her slender hips, Samantha looked insulted. "Nothing fried ever comes out of this galley."

Two men stepped out of the hangar to help them with luggage, and—Quenby assumed—maintenance and fuel before they returned to England.

At some point Lucas had slipped into the lavatory, and when he stepped back out, his blazer was buttoned, hair combed, face apparently shaved. He didn't look up to see if she was ready, his gaze devoted solely to his iPhone as he climbed down to the runway. He'd done his job delivering her to this island. Now, she'd apparently trickled back to the bottom of his priority list.

A metallic gray Cadillac Escalade pulled up beside the plane, windows too dark to see inside. Who needed tinted windows on a remote island? Only someone, she surmised, determined to hide.

Perhaps this Daniel Knight was some sort of Hollywood star or politician, living here under an assumed name. But then why would he build a medieval-looking castle on the cliff? That was hardly inconspicuous.

Perhaps the castle wasn't his after all.

Or maybe Mr. Knight was a mob boss, Lucas Hough his devoted crony. One of her articles in the past year might have offended him, and she would end up in the sea instead of a river.

As she reached the bottom of the stairs, she pulled her mobile out of her handbag to text Chandler one more time.

We've landed on an island near the Puget Sound, middle of nowhere. You're tracking me, right?

Before she sent the message, Lucas reached out. "I'm afraid I'll have to take that."

She pulled her phone back to her chest. "I'm keeping my phone."

"Mr. Knight doesn't allow mobile phones in his house."

"Perhaps your Mr. Knight should meet me right here."

He eyed the plane. "Perhaps you'll have to return to London without seeing him after all."

Her phone still clutched in one hand, she wrapped her fingers around the handles of the bag hanging from her shoulder. So help her, she wanted to clobber him with it.

But somehow Mr. Knight knew about the Ricker family and perhaps the fact that she'd been researching them. Instead of a new story, this interview might be exactly what she needed for her current one.

She held out her phone, and Lucas slipped it into the pocket of his blazer. Then a gray-haired man wearing a black suit and tie stepped out of the Escalade, the buttons on his jacket straining to contain the bulge underneath.

"How are you, Jack?" Lucas asked.

"As good as the day I was born." Jack clapped him on the back. "Mr. Knight's been counting down the minutes until you arrived."

"We had a bit of a delay—" Lucas glanced at Quenby.

"I hope all is well?"

Lucas shrugged. "Well enough."

Quenby turned her attention to the chauffeur. "Could you please tell me where we are?"

"You must be Quenby Vaughn." Jack extended his hand.

Reluctantly she shook it.

"My boss is anxious to meet you."

Cool wind rustled the pine trees beside them, showering the asphalt with needles and cones. "I'm anxious to get my phone back," she said. "And for someone to tell me the name of this island."

"Solstice Isle," Jack said with a smile. "I can't help with your phone situation, though. Mr. Knight confiscates them for almost all of his meetings."

"What is your boss trying to hide?"

"Not hide so much as protect." Jack opened the rear passenger door. "And it's more about the who than the what."

"This woman he's trying to find?"

"Perhaps." Jack motioned for her to get inside the car and Lucas followed her. Seconds later the Escalade pulled away from the plane.

The car's interior might have been plush, but there wasn't nearly enough room for both her and Lucas inside this vehicle.

"Let me text my editor," she said, edging as far away from him as possible. "And then I'll hide my phone until after this meeting."

Lucas eyed her as if he wasn't certain he could trust her with her own phone. So she reached out and snatched his, clutching it at her left side.

He stuck out his hand. "Give that back."

When she refused to return it, he tried to reach around her, but she elbowed him away.

Jack glanced in the rearview mirror. "Children?"

"Give me my mobile," Lucas insisted.

"Not until I contact my editor."

Lucas retracted his hand. "You are remarkably juvenile for a journalist."

"And you're remarkably arrogant, even for an attorney."

Jack laughed. "Do I need to pull over?"

She sent her text to Chandler, then deleted it from Lucas's phone and tossed the thing back to him. He immediately started working on it again.

"Are you exempt from the no-phone rule?" she asked.

He didn't look up. "I don't need an exemption."

"I have to take notes during the meeting."

"Mr. Knight is equipped with plenty of pens and even some paper," he said, his gaze still focused on the screen.

She drummed her fingers together. "Maybe I don't remember how to use a pen."

"It's like riding a bicycle, Miss Vaughn." He stopped momentarily to glance at her. "You do know how to ride a bike, don't you?"

"I don't believe that's any of your business, Lucas."

His eyebrows climbed at the use of his first name, but he didn't reprimand her. What was it about this man beside her that made her want to revert to those awful middle school years when she thought everyone was better than her?

They were from vastly different backgrounds, but no matter her own insecurities, she and Lucas Hough were indeed equals. Grammy Vaughn told her this often during those tumultuous years—every boy and girl was shaped in God's image, equally loved as His creation. Unlike earthly parents, God didn't reject His kids. Instead He offered them a way home.

In her freshman year of high school, with tears in her eyes, Quenby had accepted God's gift of salvation, and His love began to strengthen her. In her junior year, she found theater—or rather, theater found her when the drama teacher asked her to try out for *The Sound of Music*. She'd liked slipping into character, both on and off the stage. God loved her—she knew that—but it was still much safer to mimic a character so others would like her too.

After two years of theater, Grammy encouraged her to pursue journalism, and she discovered that she could lose herself in other people's stories on paper. Unlike roles in theater, there were always more stories to read. More to write.

When she looked out the window, the evergreens reminded her of the dark forest of Fangorn in *The Lord of the Rings*, hundreds of Ents with arms linked together as one so no human could destroy them.

Then the filter of sunlight through them turned into a flood as their vehicle emerged from the canopy of trees.

She leaned forward to talk with Jack. "How many people live on Solstice?"

He glanced in the mirror again. "Including Mr. Knight's staff?"

She nodded. "The entire population."

"There are eight of us."

She leaned back. "So your boss doesn't like people . . ."

Jack shrugged. "He has his reasons."

They stopped beside a stone guardhouse, and Jack keyed a number into a pad. A pair of iron gates opened slowly in front of them, and there was the castle she'd seen etched into the cliff.

A stone tower pierced the sky, and a dozen oval windows were paned with leaded glass. On this side of the castle, a pedestrian drawbridge linked the front entrance to the driveway.

After he stopped the car, Jack opened the door for her. "Mr. Knight said he'd like to meet with Lucas first."

"What should I do while I wait?" Quenby asked.

Jack grinned. "Let your imagination soar."

CHAPTER 6

*E*erie. *Cavernous. Cold.*

The words ticked through Quenby's mind as the housekeeper guided her through a dark-paneled passageway that smelled like vinegar and lemon oil.

Gothic.

That was the word she was searching for—the dark wood reminded her of the Brontë sisters' descriptions of Thornfield Hall and Wuthering Heights.

Was Mr. Knight a hero or villain? More like Mr. Rochester or Heathcliff?

The housekeeper opened a door and ushered her out into a courtyard. In that moment, darkness evaporated in the light, and when her eyes adjusted, she saw a pristine pool in the center of the yard, filled with teal water that bubbled up from a spring. A portico made from creamy-hued rock circled the rim of the open space, wooden benches staggered between its columns.

The housekeeper directed Quenby toward an open doorway under the portico. "Mr. Knight will meet you in his office when he and Mr. Hough are finished," the woman said. "Do you prefer tea or coffee?"

"Tea, please."

She didn't want to climb back down into a cave, but Mr. Knight's office wasn't dark like the passage. Nor did it resemble any office she'd ever seen.

Windows towered up two stories across the room, overlooking the bay, and at the base of the windows was a crescent-shaped desk made of stone, the glass top inlaid with colorful seashells and covered with faded leather binders, a collection of hand-carved fountain pens, and a vintage rotary telephone.

To the left of the windows were shelves of books stacked to the ceiling, a rolling ladder on hand to retrieve the higher ones. To the right were dozens of framed photographs of windmills—old wooden ones amid Holland's tulip fields and new turbines set above river gorges and in the valleys between snowcapped mountain peaks. One picture displayed a brigade of wind turbines lined in perfect formation, water lapping against their foundations, white blades prepped to dance with the breeze.

No visible screens—computer or TV—distracted from the view. No power cords were strung across the wooden floor. No heart-drumming ringtones or honking horns. Just quiet and plenty of space, it seemed, to think. Or as Jack said—let her imagination grow wings and soar.

Her fingers ran across the stiff leather chair behind the desk. She could envision herself sitting right here.

"You should see the view in the wintertime."

Quenby twirled around to see an elderly man stooped slightly over, leaning against a wooden cane. His face was mottled with dark spots, but age hadn't stolen his hair. It was a wild, bushy white, giving him an eccentric Einstein look. Intelligent and absentminded.

His eyes were still on the placid bay. "The storms capture those waves and whip them into a fury."

It was a curious thing to say. "Do you like fury?"

"Controlled chaos, I suppose."

"And how exactly do you control chaos?" she asked.

"People try to fight chaos all the time, but you have to outsmart it instead." He pointed toward an alcove with two chairs and a round table. "At least, the fighting never worked well for me."

She sat in a chair that faced the windows. "You must be Mr. Knight."

"For seventy-seven of my past ninety years."

"And who were you in those first thirteen?"

"A boy who liked to fight."

She crossed her legs. "You've brought me a long way, Mr. Knight."

"Indeed," he said. "Welcome to Solstice Isle."

"I'm remarkably interested in knowing why I'm here."

The door opened and the housekeeper backed into the room, a silver tray secured in her hands. After she set it on the table, she poured each of them a steaming cup of Darjeeling. Quenby added a cube of sugar to hers.

Mr. Knight sipped his tea in silence for a few moments before speaking again. "Has Lucas been a gentleman?"

She stirred the sugar into her black tea. "Define *gentleman*."

"He's a loyal soul, Miss Vaughn."

Her eyebrows climbed. "He's not the least bit loyal to me."

"That's because he sees you as a threat."

"I haven't done anything to threaten him."

"Of course not, but he thinks what I'm asking of you is a threat." His gaze wandered back toward the bay. "In the Middle Ages, knights used to wear heavy sheets of armor, but no matter how strong the armor, it couldn't always keep them alive."

Perhaps it was the long flight or her lack of sleep, but she didn't understand why Mr. Knight was talking about the Middle Ages. Was he comparing Lucas to an armored knight? Or was his proposition one that would threaten her life?

"Centuries ago, the Germans figured out the weak places in plate armor. You can't spear through an iron plate, but there are ways to go around it."

"I'm sorry, Mr. Knight, but what does this have to do with Lucas?"

"The man has spent the past seven years of his life trying to protect me." Another sip of tea. "He thinks what I'm asking of you will pierce my weakest spot."

She leaned forward in her seat. "What exactly are you asking me to do?"

On the shelf beside him was a simple wooden chest, not much bigger than a cigar box. He opened the lid, and she could see a toy figure of some sort nestled within a sheet of white. He lifted the toy gingerly from its bed of cloth and held it out to her as if it were a treasure, flecked with gold.

It was a wood carving of a girl, painted rather exquisitely at one time perhaps, but the yellow strands of her hair were chipped and her gown had faded into an indeterminate color. Quenby turned it over, searching for some sort of marking.

"What is this?" she asked.

His voice was sad when he answered. "It's a princess. Princess Adler. But you should always address a princess as Your Royal Highness."

She tucked Princess Adler back into the cloth. "I'm sure she was a good toy," she said placidly, knowing her words sounded lame. What exactly did one say about a toy far past its prime?

He picked up the princess and cradled her in his stiff hands. "Toys aren't real, Miss Vaughn."

"I am fully aware of that."

"But the girls who play with them are. Eventually these girls grow up into women."

"I still don't understand . . ."

"I've read a lot about you in the past month, ever since your article comparing the *Kindertransport* with the thousands of refugee children now coming into England. You have a passion to help lost children."

"I have a passion for stories, Mr. Knight. Preferably ones with happy endings."

"Because your own story wasn't so happy . . ."

Her gaze flicked up to meet his eyes. "You don't know anything about me or my story."

He tucked the princess back into her bed, then reached for a manila file folder beside the box. Opening it, he began to read. "You like classic British literature and your favorite color is cornflower blue except after a long season of rain—then you prefer pinks and yellows. Your last boyfriend, Brandon Wallace, was an accountant and—" he glanced up—"not a very good one, I might add."

She bristled. Not even Chandler knew about her relationship with Brandon.

"In your free time, you enjoy piecing together jigsaw puzzles, running when you're stressed, and like you've already noted, you're passionate about unearthing stories, including your latest one about the Ricker family."

She looked across the table, trying to glimpse his notes. "How did you find all that information?"

He returned to the file. "Your mother was originally from England, but she moved with her mother to the United States when she was twelve. Your father was half-German, but unfortunately he died when you were four, and then your mother left when you were seven. After your mother disappeared, you moved to your grandmother Vaughn's house near Nashville, and she liked reading the German fairy tales to you. Sadly, she died the week after you left for college."

Quenby stood up quickly, her nerves bristling. "You've certainly done your homework."

He closed the folder. "Our lives are like the jigsaw puzzles you like to put together. All the pieces are out there, but we have to frame it before we complete the inside."

Her heart raced as she stepped back from the table. "Did you hire someone to investigate me?"

He tapped on the file folder. "Just like you, Miss Vaughn, I always do my research."

"Lucas said I was supposed to be investigating something for *you*!" Her voice escalated, but she didn't care. It seemed these men were playing some sort of game around her, using her as a pawn.

Pawns, everyone knew, were disposable. Especially to knights.

"Please sit back down," he said politely. "I'm not trying to insult you, nor will I share the information about your life with anyone, including Lucas."

She eyed the chair but didn't sit. "What do you want from me?"

"I want to tell you a story."

"Just a story?"

He began to look tired. "You can decide what you want to do with the information."

"Will it include what you know about the Ricker family?"

"I haven't investigated the Ricker family," he said. "But our interests seem to intersect at Breydon Court."

She slowly, begrudgingly, eased back into the chair. "I don't want to talk about my mother again."

"I only wanted you to know that I've handpicked you for this assignment, Miss Vaughn. Your past and present are all part of my decision."

Bristling, she leaned toward him. "Who are you trying to find, Mr. Knight?"

"A girl named Brigitte."

"And how did you lose this Brigitte?"

"I didn't lose her, exactly," he replied, his voice dipping down. "Brigitte was taken from me."

Chapter 7

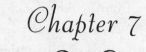

Belgium, October 1940

Hunger etched itself in the crevices of Dietmar's belly. A deep canyon aching to be filled. Rain dripped off the maple leaves overhead, streaking down his greasy hair, seeping through the holes of his jacket, and pooling on his skin. Leaning back, he let the drops pool in his mouth as well before swallowing them.

The rain was *Spaetzle*, slathered with fresh butter and cheese. It was cabbage rolls. Boiled potatoes. Bratwurst. His mother's favorite *Kuchen*, made with candied nuts and fruit.

He rubbed his wet hands over his sleeves, his stomach aching along with his heart. The only food they'd eaten in the past weeks had been gleaned from abandoned gardens along their journey. He'd almost forgotten the taste of his mother's cooking.

Gray twilight clung to treetops, a gift for Brigitte so she could sleep beside him a bit longer. He wouldn't wake her until the darkness enveloped the forest again.

They only traveled at night now, through Belgium's woods and fields, skirting the checkpoints on foot. The English Channel was close; he could smell the salt in the breeze. Somehow they would find a way to cross the water. In a day or two. His aunt would be waiting for them on the other side, and her pantry, he felt certain, would have plenty of food.

He pulled a compass from his knapsack, rotating it until the needle hovered over the NW. Their path to freedom.

More than a month had passed since he and Brigitte had run from the woman who'd wanted them arrested, this compass guiding them. It was a gift from the farmer, he guessed, tucked into his knapsack while they ate dinner. He'd found it the day after they'd run, the compass string looped around a small burlap bag filled with bacon and dried apples.

"Mama," Brigitte moaned, tossing her head on the muddy pillow of leaves.

In her sleep, tears mixed with the raindrops, but he didn't wake her. The reality, he feared, would be much worse than her dream. Perhaps, in sleep, Frau Berthold was still alive, holding her daughter close. Giving her warm milk before bed, sweetened with cinnamon sugar, and tucking a thick, dry blanket over her nightclothes.

They were miles and miles now from home, but Dietmar couldn't stop thinking about the gentleness of his own mother's words, the strength and integrity of his father's life. Both of his parents' decision to choose rightness in a world bent on wrong.

Brigitte cried often for her father at night, but she never spoke about either of her parents when they traveled. So Dietmar told her stories as they trekked through the countryside in the moon and starlight, dodging villages and farmhouses.

He told her about the time he'd caught a frog in the creek and tried to hide it under his bed, about the noises it made all night and his mother's failure to hide her laughter when she tried to reprimand him.

He told her about the fleet of paper boats he'd made to sail down the river, but instead of sailing, the boats turned into aeroplanes, taking flight in the wind. He told her about his aunt living in England, about the two cousins he'd never met, about the kind people they'd meet on the other side of the English Channel.

Sometimes his stories made her laugh. One time they made her cry. But the stories kept them both pressing forward.

Dietmar shivered as the gray light disappeared behind the leaves.

The nights grew colder now, the hours of black stretching long, but they never stopped to light a fire. In the darkness, they kept moving. The trees were changing their colors in this new season, from a wardrobe of greens to autumn hues. He and Brigitte rarely saw the color in the darkness, but he could tell summer had ended by the crunch of parched leaves under their worn shoes, the aroma of woodsmoke in the air whenever they edged around an occupied home. How he wished he could slip inside one of those houses and collapse beside a roaring fire, warm his bones—for that's what remained of him and Brigitte now. They were two shells, their souls caged in by waning skin and tired bones.

During the day hours, they rested in some sort of hiding place. A cave or abandoned barn or—like today—a grove of trees. As the weeks passed, they found more country homes empty, more gardens overgrown. Had the Gestapo whisked those residents away as well?

He didn't mention his thoughts to Brigitte. She'd grown even quieter since autumn had settled upon them, and he feared she was slipping away in her sadness. Desperate, he tried to make her laugh again, tried to rescue her from her sorrow before she drowned in it. But no matter how hard he tried, he seemed to be failing her.

"Brigitte," he whispered, nudging her wet shoulder. "It's time to go."

She moaned again. "Mama?"

He reached for her, pulling her to him like he could be both mother and father, protect and care for her. When she shook him away, he felt her forehead, the back of his hand resting on her skin. It was a fire ablaze. An inferno.

When had she caught fever?

In the distance, beyond the trees, he heard a noise. Then the sound he feared most—barking dogs. His heart started to race.

Brigitte collapsed back into the wet leaves. The darkness. "I'm staying here," she said. "Forever."

He knelt beside her. "We have to go a little farther, Brigitte. Until we reach the channel."

Her eyes closed. "Mama and Papa are waiting for me."

"No," he replied, his heart stricken at the mention of her mother. "They are waiting for us on the other side of the water."

When she shook her head, he tugged on her arm, repeating their mantra. "We must run."

"We've run and run," she whispered. "Yet we never get anywhere." Her body stilled, limp on the ground, an edifice of grief when they both needed wings.

The dogs weren't far now. Their howls resonated through the forest, echoed between the trees.

Was the Gestapo tracking them?

"Please, Brigitte," he begged. They couldn't stop running now.

When she didn't answer, he strung his knapsack over his shoulder and lifted her in his arms.

If she couldn't run, he would carry her.

CHAPTER 8

While Lucas met privately with Mr. Knight inside, Quenby stepped out onto the back patio of the castle, overlooking the white froth of sea. On a terrace below, deck chairs surrounded a tropical swimming pool.

Her hands shook slightly after her conversation with the man inside. A dozen questions sprouted in her mind and then tangled together like the shoots of vine running over the trellis on the patio, blocking the sunlight.

Mr. Knight had told her the story of his childhood, about fleeing from Germany in 1940 and traveling through Belgium with Brigitte. The country was about the size of Maryland—a journey that would take three hours by car today—but he said they'd spent almost two months dodging both Germans and Belgians who feared their occupiers more than they wanted to help two German kids.

He hadn't told her yet how he and Brigitte had been separated. Nor what information his investigators had discovered when they'd searched for her.

If his detectives could find out about Quenby's mother, why couldn't they find Brigitte?

Perhaps she'd gotten cynical during her four years as a journalist, but she'd talked to plenty of people willing to make up a story—embellish a few facts even—to see their names in print. If he didn't seem so averse to the spotlight, she'd suspect that Mr. Knight might be making up a story, seeking attention in his last years.

Then again, Brigitte might be a means to some sort of end she wasn't privy to. Or Mr. Knight's memories of this journey could have altered over the years.

He said he would hand over the file he had on Brigitte and the Ricker family after she decided to search for Brigitte. Other questions she had were for the girl that he'd lost, the most pressing one being, if she was still alive, where had she been hiding for the past seventy-five years?

Maybe Brigitte didn't know that Mr. Knight was searching for her. Or maybe—like Quenby's mother—she didn't want to be found.

Quenby's fingers twitched again at her side, and she lifted her face to bask in the glorious sunshine, something that had evaded London for weeks.

Mr. Knight was correct—the yellow-and-pink strands of a sunrise were her favorite colors this time of year—but how did he know that? How did he know the name of the man she'd dated last year? And most disconcerting—how did he know her mother had abandoned her? She'd thought that story had been buried two decades ago. Never to be exhumed.

In spite of the warm air, she shivered at the memories.

Impossible to love—that's what Brandon had said about her when he'd ended their short-lived dating relationship. And he'd been frustrated with her obsession for work. She might physically leave the office at night, but her mind was always churning, putting together the pieces of a story. *Chewing* was what he'd called it their last time together. Chewing the cud.

Nasty business, this chewing. It drove other people crazy, but it kept her sane. Working on someone else's story kept her from having to reflect on her own.

Leaning against a pillar, she removed an envelope from her handbag. This visit wasn't about her. It was about a girl lost long ago. A girl who'd never seemed to find her way home.

Mr. Knight had given her a copy of a black-and-white photograph. The image was grainy, but there was a girl with braids in the center, a bow over the wide collar of her dress, a ruffle around her hem. She was holding the hands of her parents. Smiling. Her mother's eyes were hidden behind her glasses, but her father looked worried, his lips pinched.

Had Brigitte reunited with her father? Perhaps she had returned to live a quiet life in Germany after the war, taking care of a man who'd been broken in a concentration camp.

Quenby slipped the envelope back into her handbag. Then she descended the steps toward the lower terrace. The patio was surrounded by boulders and a man-made waterfall that cascaded over rocks, into the swimming pool. Water bubbled out of the pool near the rock wall, into a creek bed that trickled across the terrace before pouring over the edge of the cliff.

Quenby took off her sandals and sat on the tiled edge of the pool, dipping her toes into the cool water.

One thing was clear to her—to this day, Mr. Knight loved Brigitte deeply. She saw it in his gaze that kept wandering down to the princess toy in his feeble hand. Heard it in the tremble of his voice as he talked about the girl he'd struggled to keep alive.

His story fascinated her. The journey through an occupied

Belgium seemed impossible, and yet he'd finished it, despite all that opposed him. It would make a compelling feature, but no matter how much she researched—or what she uncovered—there would be no article. Mr. Knight wanted to find Brigitte, but he'd made it quite clear that this story was not for the syndicate.

Any information she found on the Rickers in the process of her search, she could retain for her article, but how could she take on this job and maintain her position with World News? Even if he did pay for her work, she wasn't certain she wanted to partner with a man she knew so little about. A man who apparently knew an enormous amount about her.

She heard footsteps behind her and turned to see Jack, his gaze focused over her head, beyond the stone wall. "If you keep your eyes on the water, you're bound to see one of the orca pods swim by."

"Killer whales?"

"It's a strange name to call them when they're not even whales," he said. "Orcas are actually part of the dolphin family."

She sighed. "Not everything is as it seems."

Jack sat on the edge of a cushioned deck chair, his knees folded up into an awkward sort of platform. "Don't be afraid of Mr. Knight. He is a good man."

"He's asking me to do the impossible."

"I've worked for him more than forty years, and one thing I know for certain, he's an excellent judge of character." Jack stretched out his legs, then scooted the chair closer to her. "He wouldn't ask you to do something he thinks an impossibility."

She lifted her feet, letting the water stream off her toes, back into the pool. Had Jack heard the story of the boy who'd tried to rescue Brigitte? Daniel didn't seem like the kind of person who liked to share his past either.

Her neck craned back, she looked up at the spires towering over-head. "Who built this place?"

"Mr. Knight hired a crew to build it in 1970, but it took them almost ten years to complete."

"Why did he build a castle?"

Instead of answering her question, Jack pointed at the highest tower in the center. "That's the keep."

She examined the gray walls. "It looks like a tower to me."

"The keep is much more important than a tower," he said, smiling. "In the Middle Ages, if an enemy stormed a castle, the residents would either escape underneath it or they'd take refuge up there. Knights could win a battle from the keep."

She studied it again. "And your employer needs one of these because—?"

He smiled again, dimples creasing in his ruddy cheeks. "A fine question to ask him."

She sighed. "Could you tell me what time it is, or is that a secret as well?"

"Two o'clock, Pacific time."

She calculated the hours in her head. "Ten o'clock in London. How long do you think they'll meet?"

"It's different every time," he said, tossing her a white towel. "You have family in England?"

She shook her head as she dried her feet. "Not anymore. I always wanted to visit London, though, so I accepted an internship at a newspaper there during college." She threw the towel into a hamper. "Spent most of my summer grinding coffee beans and running errands, but after graduation, my former boss offered me an editorial job."

"I went to London once, on my honeymoon." He looked back toward the sea. "My wife pretended we were royalty for a week."

"Royalty seems much more glamorous on a TV screen."

"It was the best week of my life," he said, his voice cracking. "We visited Westminster Abbey and Buckingham Palace and got to see the great Hannah Dayne perform in *Gone with the Wind*.

"My Alice lost her battle with cancer two years later. Mr. Knight pulled me off my job and asked me how I was doing. When I told him I wasn't doing that great, he asked me what I thought about moving to the San Juan Islands. It was exactly what I needed."

"I'm sorry," Quenby said, silently reprimanding herself for her gibe about the royal life. She needed to think before she spoke again.

"It's been more than forty years, and I still miss her. She would have loved this island."

"What is Mr. Knight's business?"

The smile slowly returned to Jack's face. "Farming."

She tilted her head. "He must own one big farm."

"It's not your typical type of farming."

Before she could ask another question, Lucas stepped onto the terrace with them, holding out her mobile. "He's decided to trust you."

She snatched it from his hand, afraid he might retract the offer. "Does that mean you trust me as well?"

"You'll have to earn my trust, Miss Vaughn."

Quenby glanced at Jack, at his shoulders trembling, the hand unsuccessfully covering the corners of his lips. The man was laughing at them. "I'm sorry, Lucas," she said, "but you're going to have to earn mine first."

CHAPTER 9

Early Tuesday morning, Quenby rode the District line west to the village of Kew. Then she walked three blocks through a neighborhood of terrace homes with wrought-iron gates and flowers blooming on their patches of lawn.

Instead of residing among the monuments in central London, the National Archives were housed here, hidden between gardens and houses as if the country's heritage was embedded in the hearts of its people. A thousand years of history documented and stored in one building, the immense structure reflecting back on itself in a shallow pool below the entrance.

Inside, she stored her leather briefcase and most of her belongings in a locker on the bottom floor. Her iPad and mobile were dumped into a clear plastic bag that, like a school uniform, equalized all stations of researchers who used these archives—those searching for their family's genealogy, history for a textbook, or information for a news story. Inside these walls everyone was treated alike.

After security searched her plastic bag, she retrieved the stack of files she'd requested, taking them to her reserved seat in the reading room, an octagonal table overlooking a park. The top file on her stack was a faded-green folder, stamped *Secret* in red and held together with orange yarn and plastic tabs. The type across the top read: *German Espionage in the UK*.

The file was filled with transcriptions of interviews, memorandums, and correspondence related to men and women suspected of spying for Germany during World War II. As she skimmed through the records, Quenby typed notes into her iPad about a network of British people helping German combatants who parachuted into Kent or snuck over to England via boat.

Germans, she read, recovered the identity cards and wallets from British soldiers they'd killed or imprisoned, then supplied these personal items to spies sent over the channel to retrieve information or sabotage airfields, machine shops, and factories. Many of these spies were incarcerated hours after landing in England, but some managed to infiltrate the country. Then they'd report back to Berlin via wireless about British defenses and military. Or whether they'd been successful in their sabotage work.

If she was going to write this feature, she needed a compelling new angle that would pique interest today. Like an aristocratic American woman who moved to England before turning traitor. Or perhaps she'd relocated to England specifically to assist the Germans.

Her gaze wandered out the window to a boy and girl swinging in the park below. And her thoughts shifted to the boy and girl in Mr. Knight's story.

Mr. Knight said that Brigitte had been taken from him. Had they made it out of Belgium together? If so, it must have been dreadful living in England as a German during and after the war. No matter their innocence, most Germans were despised in the 1940s. They might have hated Hitler and his regime, but during that decade, they were all considered guilty.

Quenby leaned back in her chair, her eyes heavy from lack of sleep. Mr. Knight's jet had returned her to London on Sunday afternoon, but it almost seemed like the trip to his island had been part of a dream, like she'd never awakened from watching the girl trying to capture puzzle pieces that floated in the heath.

On their way home, the plane had stopped in New York to leave Lucas and his work there. Once they were airborne again, she'd slept the entire journey.

Leaning forward, she checked her e-mail again, hoping one of the Ricker grandchildren might actually enjoy the warmth of the limelight, but none of them had responded to her request to meet. Her next step was to visit Mrs. McMann at her home in Breydon Court, but first she needed to arm herself with more information from the war files.

In the next folder, she found exactly what she was looking for—the transcript of an interview between Lady Ricker and an unnamed interrogator from an advisory committee. Quenby glanced over both shoulders as if someone might be trying to scoop her story, but the other dozen or so people in the room were equally intent on their own research. Still it made her feel better to know everyone around her was occupied.

The interviewer asked about Lady Ricker's upbringing in Philadelphia and about her first husband, whom she'd married in Boston when she was nineteen. Then he began quizzing her about her involvement during World War II.

Q. You entertained many people at Breydon Court during the war.

A. (nod) I entertained people there before the war as well.

Q. Some of these people were known advocates of the Nazi party.

A. Known now, perhaps, but no one ever advocated for Hitler in my presence.

Q. You told a friend once that you despised Jews. A Mrs.—

A. That doesn't make me a Nazi.

Q. Why do you hate the Jewish people?

A. I don't hate them. (fidgets with handkerchief) I was concerned about what was happening in Germany.

Q. Your aunt was German.

A. She immigrated to America when she was six.

Q. Still she would have been an influence.

A. She never spoke about her childhood.

Q. Did you visit Germany with her?

A. Once.

Q. Did you maintain contact with the people you met there?

A. Any contact I had stopped at the beginning of the war.

Q. Several German POWs were employed at Breydon Court.

A. Many of the prisoners from Tonbridge worked on local farms.

Q. Did you help these men?

A. Lord Ricker and I supplied all of our staff with food and shelter.

Q. Did you supply the German prisoners with information as well?

A. Our head gardener spoke directly with them, not me.

Q. Because he spoke German?

A. Yes, he was an asset.

Q. Until he died.

A. One tends to lose their significance after death.

Q. Your gardener had a German grandfather.

A. He couldn't change his lineage, no matter how distasteful.

Q. How did your marriage to Lord Ricker work out?

A. My marriage is no concern of yours or this investigation.

Q. Your husband died in 1944.

A. (nods) Our flat was hit by a doodlebug.

Q. Why was Lord Ricker in London?

A. I can't recall.

Q. You can't recall what your husband was doing the night he died?

A. (No answer)

Q. Was Admiral Drague with you?

A. (stands up) Is the committee finished with their questioning?

Q. We can resume later if you'd prefer.

A. I have nothing more to add to your inquiry.

After the transcript was a handwritten letter from Lady Ricker to a woman named Olivia. The letter was brief and rather impersonal, talking about the weather, gardening, and the health of her baby, who apparently suffered from croup. Quenby took pictures of the interview and letter before turning to the next page.

A profile on Janice Ricker listed her description as five foot six in height with blue eyes and short black hair, curled in a fashionable style. She had been married twice. Her first marriage was to an American businessman who amassed a fortune before they divorced in 1928. As a wealthy socialite, Janice had relocated to England in the 1930s like many other American women who enjoyed London's society. There she met and married Lord Ricker.

Her next of kin included a son born during her marriage to Lord Ricker. And Louise, who was born a few months after Lord Ricker died.

Quenby's mobile phone blinked inside the plastic bag, and she glanced down at the text. It was from Lucas.

Do you have dinner plans?

She read his message twice and turned over the bag. Why was he bothering to be amiable now? She'd text him back later, after she made plans.

At a half past four, she left the study room to return her files. Along the wall were computers to search through the 32 million records available. Slipping into a seat, she decided to search for Brigitte Berthold. Nothing came up in the results, but that didn't mean Brigitte's name wasn't included in another file. Only that there was no archived mention of Mr. Knight's friend.

Someone stepped up beside her. A thin woman in a trouser suit, her hair twisted in a sock bun. "We're closing in fifteen minutes."

Quenby thanked her, and with the plastic bag at her side, she cleared security and descended the staircase to the locker room. The ground floor smelled like cinnamon rolls and coffee, the scent lingering from the cafeteria. Lunch had been an afterthought today, a quick meal of crisps and an apple she'd stored in her locker.

Her phone blinked again: another message from Lucas asking about dinner. She did have plans—a run through the heath and eating take-out sushi on her patio.

Her briefcase secure over her shoulder, she crossed the plaza by the reflecting pool. Then she heard someone call her name from near the car park. Turning, she saw Lucas hurrying toward her, waving a bouquet of peonies and lavender like it was a white flag.

Groaning, she walked faster toward the train station, but he caught up quickly to her side. She refused to look over as she hurried toward the street. "I thought you were in New York."

"I flew back last night."

With a glance to her right, she stepped off the curb. "How did you know where to find me?"

"Your editor said you were here."

She just might wring Chandler's neck.

He held out the flowers. "I couldn't find an olive branch at the florist."

She didn't take the flowers, but on the other side of the street she stopped and faced him. His brown eyes reminded her of a puppy, guilty of stealing his owner's shoes, then chewing them to shreds when no one was around. "What do you want, Lucas?"

"A truce."

"Really?"

"And dinner," he said, glancing at his watch. "I'm guessing you're hungry too."

"Please stop making assumptions about me." She resumed walking toward the Underground station.

He caught up beside her again, the flowers down at his side. "I'm paying."

Of course he was. He probably thought she couldn't afford to buy her own dinner. "I can pay for myself."

"I'm sorry for being so abrupt before—"

She didn't stop walking. "You were downright rude, Lucas."

"Tell you what," he said, ducking under the limb of a tree. "You choose the place and the conversation. Or for that matter, you can choose not to talk at all. I will completely ignore you if that's what you want."

She hiked her handbag up on her shoulder. "Did Mr. Knight tell you to play nice?"

"He really wants to hire you."

"Your job's on the line, isn't it?"

"No, but he's done a lot for me, and I want to help him."

She slowed her pace. How could she argue with that? "I can't linger for hours."

"Nor can I."

He followed her to the station, up the flight of stairs. Sterile lights illuminated the tracks and platform, the board above ticking through arrival times. Her train would be here in three minutes.

"How about Italian food?" she asked.

"Actually . . ." He paused. "I made reservations at the Garden House."

The Garden House was an elegant, award-winning restaurant near Kew Gardens, known for insanely high prices and excellent food. A place she'd always wanted to try, but still—"You said I could choose the place."

"I'll cancel."

She faced him again, people streaming around on both sides of them. "If I eat dinner with you, you'll answer my questions."

"I'll answer anything I can."

"Which probably isn't much."

He flinched ever so slightly before he regained his composure. "Mr. Knight asked me to tell you about the last time he saw Brigitte."

Her breath caught against her will. "What if I decide not to search for her?"

"He thinks you can keep a secret."

The word—*secret*—whistled through her mind, her thoughts jolting back again to that day with her mother long ago, to the secret she'd kept for more than twenty years. Ironic, really, since she searched daily for the truth about other people, often finding men and women who didn't particularly want to be found. Just never the person who'd once mattered most.

Even as she sought other people to interview, she'd refused to seek the truth about her own past.

"Quenby?"

She turned toward Lucas, barely registering the use of her first name.

"Are you all right?"

She nodded slowly.

Mr. Knight was right—she could keep secrets. And whether or not she chose to search for Brigitte, she would keep his story secret as well.

Chapter 10

Belgium, October 1940

The dogs barked again as Dietmar stumbled around a lake, Brigitte lying motionless against his chest. There was still life in her; he could feel her breath in the cold, the heat from her skin.

He ducked into the dark forest, branches scraping his arms and face as he fled.

It would be impossible to escape a pack of dogs, even if she ran beside him now, but the alternative was unthinkable. They'd come so far these weeks, struggling to survive. If the Nazis didn't kill them, they would surely separate him from Brigitte.

She would never survive their treatment, and he—

He didn't think he could bear being torn from someone else he loved.

If the enemy overtook them, they would go down together. Nothing would make him leave her side.

A needle of light pricked the darkness, like the slender shaft drifting through a keyhole. Then he smelled woodsmoke mixing with the salty air.

Was another house nearby? He knew well the risks of seeking shelter, but if he didn't try, he'd regret it.

Instead of running away from the house, he followed the trail of light and smoke.

Brigitte moaned softly, stirring in his arms. "Be still," he whispered, so different from his commands to run.

This time she listened.

The light drew closer, but so did the dogs, the haunting sound of their hunt echoing through the trees. They had to get inside, hide from the animals and the men who hunted them.

But the light in the woods didn't come from a house. It trickled out of a rambling structure built of towers and stone. A fortress of old.

Dietmar rapped on the massive front door, praying he would find a friend on the other side.

A man dressed in a black robe answered his knock, a lantern clutched in his hand and a silver cross dangling from his neck. He glanced down at Brigitte, then up at the flashes of torchlight in the trees.

"Quickly," the monk commanded, ushering them into a great hall. The man shut the door behind them and slid a bolt. Nothing would keep the Nazis out, Dietmar knew, but perhaps the bolt would slow them down.

The monk lifted Brigitte from his arms.

"I won't leave her," Dietmar said.

The monk studied him before speaking again. "Come with me then."

Dietmar heard a knock as they rushed through a series of stone corridors, up into a room with ten beds, six of them already filled.

There was no time to change into nightdress, but the monk took the knapsack from Dietmar's shoulder and tucked it into a closet.

Brigitte, he laid in one bed. Then Dietmar climbed into the one next to hers.

"You must listen," the monk said in German, and Brigitte's head turned toward him. "No matter what happens, keep the covers over your clothing and your eyes closed. The only children we house here are ones who cannot see."

Brigitte's eyes fluttered shut, but as the monk locked the door behind him, Dietmar glanced toward the window. Faint rays of moonlight stole into the musty space, and he saw the faces of the sleeping children around them. None but he and Brigitte were aware of the enemy downstairs.

Yet inside these formidable walls, he felt safe.

He prayed that God would bring them through this night. That He would provide food for their stomachs and nourish Brigitte's empty soul.

When he heard footsteps outside the door, the lock clicking as it opened, he closed his eyes so he wouldn't see the lightning stripes down the collars of men who wanted to take everything from him.

It seemed to him that the entire world was blind to the Nazis' evil scheme.

Tonight he would pretend to be blind to their scheme as well.

CHAPTER 11

A server bustled around the white-cloaked table at the restaurant, interrupting Lucas's story. Quenby uncurled her fingers from the edge of her chair, returning to the clamor inside the dining room, the glare of streetlights filtering through the window.

In her mind, she'd been right there in the dark forest with the children, running from the Gestapo. She could hear the clicking of boots across the cold stone floor, eyes examining the face of each child, awake or asleep.

She couldn't imagine how Brigitte and Dietmar must have felt. Two children trying to survive. Strangers in a hostile country, desperately needing a home.

"Quenby?" Lucas whispered.

She blinked. "What?"

He motioned toward the server. "This gentleman is inquiring about your meal."

"I can return later," the man said, clearly concerned about her mental state.

"No, I—" She scanned the menu. "I'll have the white onion soup and pearl barley risotto."

The server took their menus, and Quenby turned toward Lucas again. "Did the Nazis find them in Belgium?"

Lucas smiled. "I'll finish the story after dinner."

She leaned back in her chair. "I'm not going to leave here before I eat."

"Still," he said, the firelight from their candle flickering on the glass behind him. "It's collateral."

She sipped on mineral water as she studied the man sitting across from her, his dark-brown eyes and the shadow of a goatee around his lips. The arrogance in his gaze had been replaced by something else. Admiration, she might even think, if she wasn't convinced he thought himself elite compared to her.

Perhaps it was still a game for him to win. Mr. Knight wanted to hire her, so Lucas needed to be cordial to her. The second she declined the work—or found Brigitte—his cold shoulder would turn her way again.

In the meantime, she'd regain her own professionalism and return his attempts at friendliness, no matter how feigned. "So you won't tell me any more about Mr. Knight as a boy—"

"In time, Miss Vaughn."

"How about you?" she asked.

He shook his head. "This isn't about me."

"What were you like as a boy?"

"Ornery," he answered. "Inquisitive."

"Annoying?"

The server was over his shoulder, pouring white wine into his glass. Lucas sniffed it, then took the tentative sip of a wine connoisseur, seeming to consider its virtues. For a moment, she thought he might actually send it back, but he nodded his approval before resuming their discussion. "What did you ask?"

"Were you annoying as a child?"

He shrugged. "It all depends on perspective."

"How about the perspective of your parents?"

"Unfortunately they weren't around enough to make much of a judgment. I spent most of my growing-up years at a series of boarding schools."

The exclusive ones, she had no doubt. She almost made a snide comment about the woes of the upper class, but something flashed in his eyes as he took another sip of his wine. Regret, perhaps. Vulnerability.

This time, she held her tongue.

"Do your parents live in London?"

"Yes," he replied. "In Brentford. How about your parents?"

The server placed a bowl in front of her, and she dipped her spoon into the onion soup served with pancetta and a poached egg. The egg bounced in the wake.

Mr. Knight had said he wouldn't tell Lucas about her past, but she'd assumed he would surely learn the worst of it. "I thought you knew—"

"I've read plenty about your career, but nothing about your family."

"My father died when I was four, and my mother—I think I'll have to decline commenting about her."

"Fair enough," he said. "Family can be a tricky subject."

She nodded, dipping her spoon back into the soup. It tasted like peppered bacon and wine.

"They are part of who you are," Lucas said, "and yet sometimes you wish another family was blessed to have a member or two of yours."

She wouldn't wish her mother on any family.

"How about your grandparents?" he asked.

"I never knew my dad's dad, but my grandmother was my best friend." She swirled the water in her glass, watching the bubbles cling to the sides. She and Grammy hadn't had much money, but they had each other—something she'd never taken for granted. "My grandmother loved God and loved Germany even though she had to leave her country after she married. When I was a child, she'd alternate reading to me from her Bible and the Grimms' fairy tales in German."

"An interesting mix."

"She was more like a mom to me than my own mother." The words slipped out of her mouth quickly, as if she were confiding in a friend, and when she saw the startled look on Lucas's face, she wished she could retract them.

"What about your mom's parents?"

"I never met them," she replied briskly and then changed the subject. "Does Mr. Knight have family in the States?"

"None that are still living."

"Did he ever marry?"

Lucas shook his head as the server delivered their main course. She picked up her fork to eat the risotto. "Surely you can tell me about his life as an adult."

He leaned forward, pressing his knuckles together as he spoke. "Mr. Knight has worked his entire life to right this upturned world. He's a generous man who is fascinated by heroes from history, discounting the fact that those who know him think he's a hero as well for his compassion and willingness to help people in need. And he's determined to find out what happened to Brigitte before he passes away."

"What if Brigitte doesn't want to see him?"

Lucas took a bite of mahimahi, spiced with coriander and lemon juice, before responding. "He would be disappointed but relieved knowing that she'd survived the war."

"And if she didn't survive?"

His eyes met hers, steady and calm. "Perhaps we'll withhold that information."

She set her fork beside the plate. "What do you mean 'we'?"

"Mr. Knight has asked me to help with whatever you need."

"But I haven't agreed to look for her—"

"He's convinced that you will."

These men were exasperating. They had certainly piqued her interest, but she hadn't made any promises. Nor would she until after she talked to Chandler.

"I can have an answer to you next week," she said. "In the meantime, I have a story due for the syndicate by Friday."

He leaned forward again. "If I help you finish your story, will you ask your boss for a week off?"

She stiffened. "I don't need your help on my story or any search."

"I spent almost two years trying to help one of the investigators find Brigitte."

"And—"

"We kept smashing into dead ends."

She glanced over at him. "What happened at the monastery?"

"Are you trying to derail me?" he asked, reaching for his glass of wine.

"Trying to put you back on track."

He stared at her for a moment, his glass in front of him.

She shook the hair off her face. "What?"

"I was just thinking," he said, taking a sip of his wine.

"Thinking about telling me the rest of the story?"

"No." The server refilled his wineglass. "I was thinking I was still hungry."

"You're a rotten liar."

He laughed. "Do you really want to guess my thoughts?"

"I wouldn't dare."

"You are a wise woman, Quenby Vaughn."

She shook her head. A wise woman would step away from this story before it consumed her.

"Why did you decide to become a journalist?" he asked.

She hesitated. "The answer is as complex as my family."

"You're nosy?"

She laughed with him. "I suppose that's part of it, but I really like capturing the heart of a story. Digging deep to find what others missed."

He considered her words. "It would be impossible, I imagine, to really capture someone's heart on paper."

"A good writer shows someone's heart by recording their actions."

"Out of a person's heart come evil actions," he said. "That's what Jesus said, in the book of Mark."

She leaned back in her chair, surprised to hear him quote the Bible. "But every good and perfect gift is from above—"

"The book of James."

"Exactly." She smiled. "We each choose between good and bad in our hearts, and our actions follow. The hardest choices are when we don't know if something is good or bad."

"Or someone, I suppose." He set down his glass. "Mr. Knight doesn't want to wait until next week for you to begin searching for Brigitte."

"But it's been more than seventy years since he lost her."

"The matter is quite urgent to him."

She didn't like to be pushed, and yet . . . "I'll let you know in two days."

"He's asked for tomorrow."

She didn't respond, either way. While she wouldn't admit it to the man across the table, she was hooked on the heart of this story.

Chapter 12

The night fog was thick as paste, so dense that Dietmar could rub it between his hands. After a few hours, the monks had awakened Brigitte and him and led them away from the monastery, under this cloak of black sky and haze, until they reached a strip of sand along the channel waters separating captivity from freedom.

In the late hours, after Hitler's men had left, the monks had burned his knapsack and given both him and Brigitte a clean set of clothing, the pockets stuffed with their treasures from home. The monks had no shoes to spare, but Dietmar told them it didn't matter. He'd thought he'd lost Brigitte, but after a warm meal and some sleep, she was walking beside him again, clinging to his hand.

They were stored like fish in the dark hold of a trawler. Wind and waves battered the wooden frame as they motored across the channel, shaking them like glass marbles in a jar. Brigitte vomited her meal on his new trousers, but she didn't say a word. Nor did she cry.

He tried to pretend that the stormy sea didn't bother him. Or the stench and frigid air. England wasn't far now. They would be warm and well there. In England Brigitte would find her strength again.

Several hours later, the rocking ceased, and Dietmar waited, praying they were safe. A fisherman opened the hatch, and he and Brigitte emerged slowly. The fog was clearing in the sunlight, and he saw a desolate beach before them, covered in pebbles.

One of the fishermen carried Brigitte through the water, up to a patch of tall grass. The sharp rocks cut Dietmar's feet as he crossed the beach, but he was grateful to be off the boat.

Turning, he looked back at the strait of water. Searching for dogs, for men in black uniforms and lightning bolts chasing them. But all he saw were waves.

No one would follow them here.

He tried to thank the fishermen in English, assuring them he could find transport to London, but they didn't seem to understand. Minutes after landing, the fishermen climbed back into the trawler, their boat vanishing into the fog.

Dietmar and Brigitte tromped across muddy fields for hours until another fisherman gave them a ride. But instead of taking them to London or the depot for trains, the man left them at a police station.

A constable, dressed in dark blue, glanced between them. There was no red band around this man's arm or iron cross dangling from his collar. "Where do you come from?" he asked.

Dietmar stood tall, hoping he looked older than his thirteen years. "London, mister." Mother once told him to call the men from England *mister* instead of *Herr*. He hoped this man would understand him and direct him to the city.

"And your parents—"

Dietmar's gaze fell to his bare feet.

"I see." He spoke to another officer in English, but his words were a flood, so rapid that Dietmar couldn't decipher one of them.

The constable looked at Brigitte. "What age are you?"

Dietmar felt Brigitte's hand tremble in his.

"She—" he started, practicing the words in his mind before he spoke. "No talk."

The constable's eyes narrowed for a moment, and Dietmar feared he would find out about the boat. That the man would send them back to Germany.

"We need aunt," Dietmar said, trying to be clear.

"What's your name, son?"

Dietmar understood the question, but he couldn't tell the man his real name. His mind raced until he remembered the name of his uncle in London.

"Daniel," he said, hoping it was a good English name.

"Daniel—"

"Knight," he replied.

The man jotted a note into a book.

"Come along, Daniel Knight," the constable said when he looked back up. "And bring your sister. I'll drive you up to Tonbridge."

Dietmar shook his head. "London."

"No children are going to London until the Huns stop dropping bombs, but plenty of boys and girls are being billeted near here. The people in Tonbridge will find you a home until it's safe to return."

Dietmar didn't remember his mother saying the word *billeted*— or *Huns*—but he knew the word *home* well. That was what Brigitte needed most of all.

The man fed them sausage and chips and somehow found them each a used pair of shoes that fit well enough. Then he drove them to the public hall in Tonbridge. Brigitte clung to Dietmar's hand, her fingers trembling as they waited with the other children for a home. Men and women circled the vast room, examining the girls and boys as if they were livestock.

The younger children were led away first from the room, and

then the girls. One couple stopped before Dietmar and Brigitte, but Brigitte recoiled from them, burying her head in Dietmar's shoulder when they tried to speak to her. They appraised Dietmar for the briefest of moments before the woman turned up her nose and backed away.

No one else attempted to talk with him or Brigitte. Perhaps it was because he stank of vomit. Or because he was an unruly-looking boy. Besides Brigitte, only older boys remained in the room.

He reached into his pocket and clutched the knight hidden beside Brigitte's princess. He might have helped Brigitte find safety across the channel, but now he was an anchor that prevented her from sailing any farther. A crutch splintered into a hundred lousy pieces. In order to rescue Brigitte now, he must walk away. Because if he stayed here, standing beside her, no one would ever take her home.

He leaned toward her. "I need to speak with the *Chef*."

"Please don't leave me." Her whisper trembled like her hand, but the return of her speech emboldened him.

Brigitte didn't need him anymore. She needed a warm bed for the winter and good food. She needed a doctor and medicine to make her well again. Here in England, she would recover her strength and her laughter. Her love of princess stories and fairy tales.

Removing the knight, he placed it in her palm, gently folding her fingers over it.

"I'll only be a moment," he lied. "The knight will protect you until I return."

Her gaze rested on the wooden toy as he kissed her cheek, his heart aching. "I will find you."

Her blue eyes were wide when she looked back up at him. "You promise?"

He nodded. "A thousand times, Brigitte."

Her smile shook, but it pleased him to see a glimpse of her joy. "Princess Adler."

"Princess Adler," he concurred. Then he turned rapidly away before he changed his mind.

There was a door beside the stage—a closet—and he slipped inside. In the shadows, he watched the crowd of adults dwindle in the hall. Only four children remained—Brigitte and three boys.

What would they do with the children who didn't have a family to care for them? Brigitte would never survive in some sort of work camp or institution. She needed someone to care for her until she was strong again.

Across the room, the door opened again, and a thin woman entered the hall. The tiny brown-and-cream checks on her coat reminded Dietmar of teeth, a hundred of them snarling at him.

The woman scanned the remaining children and crossed the polished floor toward Brigitte. As she studied Brigitte's hair and eyes, he leaned forward, straining to hear her words.

"What's your name?" the woman asked.

Brigitte didn't answer.

"Are your parents in London?"

Dietmar wanted to rush out and say that she was indeed from London, but if Brigitte refused to speak, perhaps the woman wouldn't suspect she was German. Perhaps she'd think Brigitte deaf as well when she didn't understand her words.

The woman surveyed the hall as if she were considering the options. Her gaze breezed past the remaining boys before resting back on Brigitte. "You need a bath, but I suppose you'll do."

The woman reached for her arm, but Brigitte didn't move.

"Come along," the woman prodded.

Brigitte's head jerked to the right, her eyes searching frantically around the room. Before she turned toward him, Dietmar stepped farther into the closet, wishing he could hear what the woman was saying. Instead all he heard were raindrops pattering on the roof.

In the dark space, he clutched the toy princess in his pocket, silently chiding himself for transferring his care to a woman neither he nor Brigitte knew. But a knight must make the toughest of decisions for the good of those he must defend. He'd promised Herr Berthold that he would protect his daughter, and Brigitte's father would want her sheltered. Fed. Dietmar wanted her sheltered and fed as well.

He'd keep his promise to Brigitte, too. When she was healthy again, when the bombs stopped falling, he would find her. Then they could walk into London hand in hand to find his aunt together.

He glanced back out the door and saw the woman with the tooth coat holding Brigitte's arm near the front door. He slipped up beside the wall and hid behind the long drapery to watch them.

"I'll take this one," the woman said.

A second woman, seated at a desk, asked Brigitte for her name.

"She seems to be mute."

The lady at the desk pushed up her glasses, nodding before scribbling something in a book.

"My name is Mrs. Terrell," the tooth woman said.

"Where do you live, Mrs. Terrell?"

"On Mulberry Lane."

Mrs. Terrell didn't look at Brigitte again. If she had, she would have seen tears pouring down her cheeks, the trembling of her lips. Dietmar's heart burned inside him, longing to rush forward and rescue her again, take her to a safe place. But he had nothing to offer her at the moment. Not even an aunt to help care for her.

Through the gray window streaks in the public hall, he watched Mrs. Terrell open the door to a black motorcar. Brigitte shook her head at the woman, refusing to get inside. His chest aching, he prayed silently that she would go with the woman. Soon they would be together again.

A man climbed out of the driver's seat. Mr. Terrell, Dietmar assumed. He was much taller than Mrs. Terrell, his shoulders as wide as those of the men who'd hurt his mother back in Moselkern. Perhaps he could coax Brigitte into the vehicle.

But when the man stepped toward her, Brigitte backed away. He said something as he grabbed her arm, shoving her roughly into the car.

A family was supposed to feed Brigitte. Give her shelter and medicine and kindness. But this man—he wouldn't be kind to Brigitte at all.

Dietmar spun toward the front door and raced through it, down the steps to the sidewalk.

"Brigitte!" he yelled as the car pulled away in the rain. Her nose was pressed against the back window, eyes weeping with despair. And the depth of her sorrow shot straight through his chest, piercing his heart.

He wouldn't wait until Brigitte saw a doctor or the bombing stopped in London. Somehow he would earn enough money for medicine and food. A safe place where no one would hurt Brigitte. He would find her on Mulberry Lane before nightfall and steal her away again.

"Lad?" a man called out from the other side of the street.

Dietmar glanced both ways before realizing the police officer was speaking to him. This man's voice was gruff, nothing like the constable who'd brought them into Tonbridge.

The man marched through the puddles, water sloshing on his blue trousers as he crossed the street. "Where's your home?"

"London, mister."

"You're far from home."

"Billeted," he said, borrowing the word he'd learned from the constable earlier today, hoping the man would be impressed with his English.

Instead the officer latched his fingers over Dietmar's shoulder. "Come with me."

The moment he looked up into the officer's eyes, he knew he wouldn't be going to Mulberry Lane this afternoon. And perhaps not tomorrow either.

Dietmar's gaze returned one more time toward the road that led away from Tonbridge. In the distance he could see a speck of black piercing the rain. And then it was gone.

"Auf Wiedersehen," he whispered, his heart sick.

Until we meet again.

CHAPTER 13

Quenby leaned back on the leather seat, closing her eyes as Lucas drove his Range Rover through the boroughs of London, toward her flat.

She heard a siren nearby, the sigh of hydraulic brakes on a bus, but in her mind, all she could hear was Brigitte sobbing as the Terrells stole her away. Not understanding why Dietmar had let her go. And the faintest sound, like a rip of a Band-Aid, echoed through her mind as she imagined the two children, the best of friends, being torn apart.

No wonder the guilt haunted Mr. Knight. For months, he and Brigitte had leaned solely on each other, and then they'd been brutally separated like so many during the war. He'd fought long and hard to protect her, sacrificing himself repeatedly for her good. Then he felt as if he'd failed her. And poor Brigitte, she probably thought Dietmar had abandoned her.

Abandonment—Quenby knew what that felt like. A full-blown quake of earth as two plates, once fused together, were wrenched apart. People abandoned those in their care for different reasons, but in this case, Dietmar had no other choice. He'd wanted what was best for Brigitte because he loved her. Not because he wanted to be rid of her.

She pressed on her temples, trying to massage away her own memories. This wasn't about her story; it was about Dietmar and Brigitte.

Lucas said the Terrells had indeed taken Brigitte to their house on Mulberry Lane, located on the grounds of Breydon Court. But none of the investigators were able to find out what happened after Brigitte left Mulberry Lane.

Perhaps it wasn't too late for Dietmar—Daniel Knight—to discover where Brigitte went. Quenby's only fear was what she might find. What if Brigitte died on Mulberry Lane? Or what if this Mr. Terrell or other men abused her when she was a girl? The truth might destroy him.

"You okay?" Lucas asked.

"Pretty wrecked."

"The story wrecked me too."

The safety of home had been stolen from Brigitte and Dietmar during the war. Their family and friends stripped away. They were strangers in a new land, like the children she'd interviewed for her article on refugees.

She slowly opened her eyes. "Where did the police take Mr. Knight?"

"To the Isle of Man, hundreds of miles from Tonbridge."

"The camp for prisoners of war?" she asked.

"It was an internment camp, mostly for German professionals living in Great Britain."

Lucas glanced into his rearview mirror to change lanes. Then he circled his Range Rover through a roundabout and drove north toward her flat.

"Did he tell the police about Brigitte?"

Lucas shook his head. "He was afraid of what officials would do if they discovered she was German as well, so he didn't even try to write her until after the war. He kept her secret, but he prayed every day for her."

They drove up Rosslyn Hill, the trendy boutique shops and eateries closed for the night. She and Lucas had lingered at the restaurant until much too late, closing down the place after eating coconut ice cream and dark-chocolate mousse. And drinking two rounds of cappuccinos. Lucas remained on his best behavior throughout the meal. She still doubted his authenticity, but at least he seemed to realize she was genuine in her concern about Brigitte.

"In retrospect—" he stopped at a red light—"Mr. Knight was treated quite well at the camp, and he was gifted with a brilliant education from some of the brightest German professors and scientists who were also interned there. A Jewish man named George taught him how to generate electricity, and the two of them used a downed German airplane called a *Pfeil*—"

"Arrow," she translated.

"Exactly. They took the propeller from the plane and created wind on the island to help power the camp. They all hoped, of course, that the war would end soon. Mr. Knight busied himself with his reading and work with George, thinking his mother would be pleased with his education when they were reunited. But the months on the island turned into years. By the time the war ended, he was almost eighteen."

The clock on his dashboard rolled over to 11:42 as Quenby processed the story.

It must have seemed like an eternity for Mr. Knight, waiting on that island, not knowing what happened to Brigitte or his parents.

They probably received very little news about the war while they were interned there.

Quenby directed Lucas to turn toward the park called Hampstead Heath. "Where did he go after the war?"

Lucas parked his car outside the weathered brick building that housed her flat. "To live with George and his wife, Letha, in London. It was supposed to be a temporary situation until he found his aunt, but his aunt and cousins had died in the Blitz. The uncle didn't have the resources to help his late wife's nephew."

Lucas opened his door and stepped outside. When she reached for her handle, Lucas moved swiftly around the car, opening the door for her. The night air was pleasantly cool, and she could smell the musty scent of woodland and moss drifting over from the heath. Lucas escorted her up the sidewalk, the bouquet of flowers clutched in his hand again, but he didn't climb the steps leading into her building.

Quenby leaned against the metal railing that lined the stairs, lamplight pouring down over both of them. "What happened to his parents?"

"They died in a concentration camp called Chelmno, long before the war ended, and the Nazis killed Brigitte's father too."

A tear slipped down her cheek, and she silently chided herself as she turned away from Lucas, wiping her eyes with the back of her hand. Seventy years might have passed, but the grief was fresh for her. And it explained why Mr. Knight lived as a recluse in his castle. After losing everything as a child, he must have found security inside the walls. The illusion of strength.

Lucas's voice swelled with emotion, and his grief caught her off guard. Perhaps he was being genuine with her as well. "George and Letha's only son had been an engineer in Hamburg. He lost his life in a gas chamber."

"So much loss—"

"It's horrific, what people can do to one another."

"Did George and Letha adopt Mr. Knight?" she asked, hoping for a glimpse of hope in his story.

"Eventually," he said. "They wanted to relocate to the United States, but he insisted on finding Brigitte first. When his letters to Mulberry Lane weren't returned, Mr. Knight traveled to Tonbridge with George and searched for her until they exhausted their means. George thought she might have been relocated to another country, but it was impossible for them to locate her after the war.

"Instead of keeping their German surname, George and Letha changed their name to Knight as well, and they all immigrated to Washington State. George and Daniel used the technology they'd developed back on the Isle of Man to create new parts for wind turbines. They called the company Arrow Wind."

Quenby wrapped her arms over her chest and rubbed them. "Jack said that Mr. Knight's career was in farming."

Lucas smiled. "Wind farming, to be precise. On the plateaus above the Columbia River at first and then around the world."

"The wind farms must have been successful."

"Quite, but he never got what he wanted most in this life." Lucas leaned against the elm tree on the lawn. "He can't seem to stop thinking about Brigitte, like she might need his help again."

"It's sweet that he still wants to find her, after all these years."

"Mr. Knight is not a romantic."

She tightened her hand around her bag, bristling again. "Perhaps you're the one who's not romantic, Lucas."

In the dim light, his head tilted slightly, and she suddenly felt small standing so close to him. "I'll leave that designation to others."

She stepped up toward the door. "Thanks for dinner."

He held out the bouquet again. "Please take these."

Quenby eyed the flowers in the dim light, their sweet fragrance mixing with the balm of moss and trees. Then she met his gaze. That glimpse of vulnerability had returned, perhaps even a fear of rejection. But he didn't fear rejection from her personally—he probably had dozens of stunning, wealthy women vying for his attention. He was worried that she'd reject his client.

When she took the flowers, he glanced down, retrieving keys from his pocket. "What should I tell Mr. Knight?"

"That I think he's sweet."

Lucas raised an eyebrow. "What should I tell him about Brigitte?"

"That I'll make a decision by tomorrow night."

He smiled. "Very good."

"Even if I decide to search, I can't make any promises that I'll find her."

"He doesn't expect promises."

"What does he expect?" she asked, lowering the flowers to her side.

"That you'll search with your heart as well as your mind."

❀

Mulberry Lane, Tonbridge, England.

Quenby typed the location into Google Maps, waiting for the result on her iPad as she stood by her kitchen counter.

Drumming her fingers on the pale wood, she tried to distract herself from Lucas Hough and the way he'd looked at her in the darkness as if he was trying to read her mind. Her heart was wholly tied up in the plight of this boy and girl, but she needed to keep it away from Lucas.

She'd arranged his bouquet of peonies and lavender in a pale-green vase made of recycled glass. In their four months of dating, Brandon had never brought her flowers, and she'd never desired them. Flowers were a frivolous expense in his mind, a gift that would wilt and fade in days.

Somewhere in her mind, a seed planted pre-Brandon had begun

to grow. Flowers were for special occasions or just because, when one person valued another. People valued her for her work, her investigative skills and writing, not as an individual. Even Brandon had been intrigued by her work until he realized that work was her life. Her own fortress.

Lucas was no different. He'd never bring flowers unless he wanted something from her.

The map loaded on her screen, and she enlarged it. Mulberry Lane was located three miles northeast of Tonbridge, in the Weald of Kent.

She leaned closer, studying the surrounding landscape. On the map, Mulberry Lane ended at the green space that surrounded Breydon Court. According to Lucas, Mulberry Lane used to be one of the roads on the estate.

Did Brigitte know the Ricker family when she lived there? Probably not—a refugee girl wouldn't have the opportunity to socialize with an aristocratic family. But Brigitte had lived on their property. Perhaps their lives had intersected at some point. If so, Quenby could work on her espionage story while helping Mr. Knight find Brigitte.

She searched Kent County's database for a family named Terrell, but there was no listing for them. Even if she found the Terrells, Brigitte might have been sent north shortly after she arrived or shipped off to another country like many of the evacuated children during that era.

Quenby paced around the kitchen table, scrolling back through the notes she'd found in the archives as she walked. When she went to visit Mrs. McMann, she would ask about the Terrells.

Reaching for her mobile phone, she dialed Chandler's number. Her boss answered after the third ring, her voice groggy. "This better be important."

"I didn't think you'd be sleeping."

"It's after midnight, Quenby. Most people are asleep by now."

"I want to go down to Breydon Court, to speak with Mrs. McMann."

"Lady Ricker's daughter?" Chandler asked, sounding much more awake.

"Yes," she said as she slid open the glass door that led out to the patio. "I can take a train down to Kent in the morning."

"I told Evan you were working on a big story. He asked if you could have it done by Thursday."

"I need to get my facts in place first."

"He's more concerned about breaking it before anyone else."

"He should want the truth," Quenby replied. It was a constant irritation, this implication that she should invent facts if she must to gain readership. She would have a story for Evan Graham—and it would be accurate.

"Sort it all out, but do it quickly."

After saying good-bye, Quenby closed her iPad and stepped out onto the small patio. The woodlands around the heath blocked the lights of central London, and she could see the stars over the pond and trees.

The truth was out there, for both the Ricker family and Mr. Knight. She couldn't step away from either story now.

But alway take heed that thou fight

with this mind and hope . . .

that thine enemy once overcome to his shame,

shall never afterward come upon thee again.

DESIDERIUS ERASMUS

The Manual of the Christian Knight (1501)

CHAPTER 14

Silver ribbons of rain streamed across the tower window. Below him, wind churned the seawater into a mad froth. A wave crashed into the cliffs, the spray shooting like white flames up the rocks. It wasn't long past the dinner hour, but the sky was more inky black than gray.

Daniel couldn't remember the last time they'd had a thunderstorm in these islands. Two years ago. Three perhaps. The days and months and years all blended together into a soupy sort of mess in his brain. He could remember the details from seventy years past, but yesterday was often a blur.

A crack of thunder shook the tower floor. Like the powerful, invisible pull of a magnet, the thunder lurched him back to the years he'd spent on another island, far away from here. To the top bunk in his barracks on the Isle of Man.

The roof leaked whenever it rained, cold water dripping in a slow cadence onto his bedclothes. On the nights he couldn't sleep, all he could think about was Brigitte. Sleeping beside her under the trees in Belgium, the leaves dripping on their heads as they dreamed about blankets and bratwurst. Warm fires and hot apple cider. Parents to care for them and their needs.

Coward.

The storm seemed to accuse him again for what he'd done as a boy. Choosing flight over fight. Twice.

George and Letha had told him repeatedly that he'd done the right thing, made a courageous choice all those years ago by escaping Germany and then hiding in the closet of that public hall so a family would take Brigitte home with them. But in his dreams, when he saw Brigitte's tears, her face pressed against the car window, he didn't feel courageous at all.

If only he could have predicted the future. The police who had relocated him to an internment camp. The war that lasted four more years.

He'd prayed for Brigitte, every day since Tonbridge. Prayed that she would be strong, healthy, and loved. That she would know in her heart he'd never meant to abandon her.

The room trembled again from the rage of thunder, and Daniel reached for the wood column in the center of the tower to balance himself.

He'd thought he built a castle big enough for space to breathe, but on days like this, when the memories returned, even the windowed walls up here, with their sweeping views of the sea, seemed to close in on him. On these days, it felt as if he were being attacked from the inside.

The tower of the castle—the keep—was the final refuge in an attack from the enemy, but no fortress of stone could protect from the enemy who crept up from memories, moving stealthily through the entire body, raiding the refuge of one's mind.

He needed to clear the adversary from his head before it took hold.

Slowly he descended the spiral stone stairs, using the banister instead of his cane for balance until he reached the tiled entrance hall. The hall held two suits of armor that he'd purchased back in England, worn centuries ago by knights who were rumored to have fought alongside William Marshal in the twelfth century.

When he was a boy, he'd thought all knights were good, that they'd fought unselfishly to protect others. But he'd learned during his internment that not all of them had fought for what was good or right. Some only wanted to steal away what wasn't theirs.

Even so, he believed in the medieval Code of Chivalry. To fear God and live by honor. To defend the weak and keep faith. To persevere in every endeavor until the end.

A heraldic flag, its fierce lion colored a dark midnight blue, hung over the armor. Autumn leaves dropped behind the animal, seeming to plummet at his roar, and a swath of grass trailed back into the distance under the shower of leaves.

Letha had designed the coat of arms for their family. It meant freedom from evil. The power of the wind. New life. It brought him great honor to hang this symbol of knighthood in his house.

Eileen, his housekeeper, waited by the front door with his trench coat and tweed hat. Long ago, she and Jack used to try to stop him from walking in the rain, but those days were past. Instead of barring the door, she dropped the coat onto his shoulders and handed over his hat.

"It's lightning, Mr. Knight."

"I know."

She opened the door. "Take care."

He breathed in rain as he hobbled toward the front gate, the moisture coating his lungs. Rain clung to the cold wind and splashed his face. He loved the thrust of power to stir the sea. Shake trees. Carry the voice of a child crying for help.

Here in the storm, tears could fall freely down his cheeks, mixing with the torrent of God's grief falling from the sky. On days like this, he thought God must surely be crying over the destruction mankind unleashed on one another. At the sight of His children entrenched in violent bitterness and jealousy, their barbaric quest for power detached from Him.

Daniel leaned against his cane as he moved past the gatehouse, toward a grove of pine trees that battled the wind with its daggers of needles and bark.

A blissful peace had settled over England in the late 1940s and '50s, except in the hearts of the many people trying to find loved ones they'd lost.

After the war, he and George had spent months searching for Brigitte, but they couldn't locate her. Youth today didn't understand a world before social media and mobile phones, before one could search the Internet for a missing person or post their picture on screens around the world. And many people—today and from years past—didn't understand or honor faithfulness. A deep commitment to those you loved, to persevere no matter what. One didn't just forget a lost friend.

He tightened his grasp around the knob of his cane. Every day he prayed that he wouldn't forget her.

Wind channeled between the pine trees, like the current of a river carrying him deep into the forest.

For decades after the war, he'd returned to England to search for Brigitte on his own. George and Letha had pitied him, thinking she must surely have passed away. He knew the realities and yet something kept prompting him to look for her. That quiet, still voice that urged him forward. A voice the assailants in his mind had tried to slay.

But he'd persevered like the knights of old, searching for the lost maiden. Like he'd done back in the tree house long ago. Whenever he returned to England, he would look for her, but the longer he searched, the more it seemed as if he were searching for a specific pine needle in this island's vast grove.

George and Letha both died in 1984. That year he hired a private investigator in London. When that search availed nothing, he hired a second company. Then a third. One of the men he'd hired had come close to finding her—or so he said—but then he'd rammed into a dead end. It had been five years since the last agency closed his file.

Some thought him eccentric to continue this search, but he didn't care. The knight's code was to defend, protect. Long ago, he'd promised to find Brigitte, and he would persevere in this quest until God chose to take him home.

Six months ago, he'd begun an exhaustive search for a new investigator, trying to hire a person who would make this a personal journey instead of merely a professional one. He'd wanted to hire a woman who understood English along with some German. Someone who could think differently from the agency men he'd hired in the past. Someone compassionate, smart, and who knew how to keep a secret.

Someone who knew what it was like to be left alone.

When he read Quenby Vaughn's series of articles about refugees, he was impressed with her ability to empathize with the tragic loss of the children while condemning those who infiltrated a new country intent on doing harm. It was a wretched line to walk, determining who needed help and who wanted to start a war.

Miss Vaughn was smart and capable, empathetic yet tough. Once his investigator discovered that she was preparing to write an article about Lady Ricker, the employer of Mr. and Mrs. Terrell, it seemed his prayers to find the right person for this job had been answered. And now he prayed that Miss Vaughn would do what no one before her had been able to accomplish.

Together they would rescue Brigitte.

The wind rustled the pine needles again, and for a moment he thought he heard barking in the distance. Instinctively, his body cried for him to run, but his legs were so tired, as if he'd already walked a dozen miles today.

He glanced around at the trees, confused.

He had been walking a long way, hadn't he? All the way from Germany. And he was hungry. Tired.

He lifted the walking stick in his hands. Examined it. Where had he found such a polished piece? Perhaps the farmer had given it to him.

"Brigitte," he called out into the rain, steadying himself against a wet branch as he scanned the trees for her.

She would be nearby, looking for food or a place to sleep. She would never leave him.

Daniel blinked, saying her name again as the rain splashed his face, but this time it was just a whisper. He was back on the island, in the forest near his home.

There was no Brigitte, of course. Hadn't been in a long time.

It wasn't just the walls of the castle that were closing in on his mind. Now the trees seemed to be fogging it as well.

If he didn't find Brigitte soon, he feared he might not remember her at all.

When he emerged on the other side of the forest, Jack was waiting for him.

His driver opened the car door. "You ready to go home, Mr. Knight?"

He nodded slowly. "I believe I am."

"Eileen has a nice cuppa waiting for you."

Daniel closed his eyes in the backseat of the car, trying to think about the tea, but her eyes emerged in his mind again, the vibrant blue of them staring back at him.

Somewhere, Brigitte was waiting for him too.

Chapter 15

Mulberry Lane, December 1940

Brigitte's back was crushed against the closet door, her hands pressed against her ears, but she couldn't block out the yelling. It grew louder and louder in the kitchen below her room.

She didn't understand much English, but the Terrells said one word over and over that she knew well now.

Girl.

They always seemed to be fighting about her.

If only Dietmar were here. He could tell her what else the Terrells were saying. He knew all the English words.

Herr Terrell would leave soon. And perhaps Frau Terrell would as well. Then they'd be gone for hours. Sometimes Herr Terrell didn't return until late at night. Then the fighting would start again.

She reached up and touched her shoulder, her long hair sheared by Frau Terrell's scissors the night she'd arrived. The cuts made by

Frau Terrell's nails had healed weeks ago, but they'd left behind stripes on her skin.

Herr Terrell hated her—she didn't need the words of English to understand that. Frau Terrell tolerated her as long as she did the chores assigned her. The woman would point at the broom and say, "Sweep." Or at the dishes and say, "Wash." So she swept or washed or whatever Frau Terrell asked of her. Just like *Aschenputtel*—Cinderella—from the Brothers Grimm.

She didn't mind the chores. They kept her from thinking about her sweet papa back in Germany. And about her best friend.

Closing her eyes, she pretended that Dietmar was waiting for her below the window, ready to rescue her like he'd done at home. It had all been play back then in the tree house, at least until the enemy really had come and taken her papa away.

Now she needed Dietmar to charge this tower. Climb the vines that led up to her room. Take her with him.

He'd promised her that he would come. A thousand times.

Oh, why had he left her, back when all those people were looking at the children? Why hadn't he stopped the Terrells before they drove out of town?

She'd seen him standing on the curb, his hands to his sides. And she'd thought—hoped—that he saw her in the car. That he would find this house and steal her away.

Weeks had passed—perhaps even a month or two—but still each morning she awoke fresh to the hope that Dietmar would surely come today.

Had Hitler's men found him in England? Had they taken him back to Germany?

The knight clutched in her hand, she looked down at the gardens below the window, as if Dietmar might be rushing toward her. The vegetable garden reminded her of the one at Dietmar's house, except almost everything was brown, dead now that winter had come.

MELANIE DOBSON

One day she and Dietmar would find each other. One day soon, she prayed.

She wanted to sing softly, invite music into her tiny room to ease the aching in her heart, but she would have to wait until the Terrells were gone. They thought her stupid, and she preferred it that way. Instead of talking to them, she reserved her voice for the privacy of this space where they'd set up a cot for her, the day after a woman visited them and apparently said they should.

When Herr and Frau Terrell were gone, for hours and hours at a time, she'd sing songs that Mama taught her long ago. At night, after her chores were done, she'd sit on her cot and gaze out at the moon over the gardens and trees, hoping that Dietmar could see it wherever he was as well. Hoping that perhaps he was sleeping in the forest beyond the cottage.

She never slept on the cot. Each night, she'd crinkle up her blanket on the rug and sleep with her head under the canvas, between the wooden legs. It reminded her of a canopy made for a princess.

There was a knock on her door, jostling of the knob. "Open it, girl!" Frau Terrell called.

Brigitte crept out of the closet and turned the lock.

The woman barged inside, pointing at the door handle. "No. Lock."

She kept her eyes focused on the frayed edges of the rug.

"Come along," Frau Terrell barked, reaching for her wrist. Then she yanked her forward. Brigitte followed, afraid the woman would drag her down the steps if she didn't comply.

Downstairs, Frau Terrell pointed at two eggs in a yellow-and-blue bowl on the counter before handing her a woven basket and scooting her toward the door. As if Brigitte should know where to find the eggs.

She waited another moment for the woman to point her toward the henhouse, but Frau Terrell had returned to washing potatoes in the sink. Brigitte slipped out the door, grateful for the opportunity to roam outside.

The air was crisp, cool as the Elzbach River used to feel streaming between her toes. The breeze brushed over her skin, and she closed her eyes along the lane, savoring its breath.

Sing, it said to her.

But she couldn't sing outside, in the language forbidden here. She'd have to wait until she was safely locked in her room again, the Terrells gone.

A mangy dog stepped up beside her, sniffing the plaid pinafore that the lady from town brought for her to wear. Brigitte stopped to scratch his ears, and he followed her as she ambled across the pathway toward the pasture, between piles of dried leaves and footprints embedded in the dirt.

From her window she'd seen Herr Terrell digging in these gardens. He was younger than her father and a strange sort. He wore a brown cardigan and trousers when he gardened, and each morning he greased his black hair back, as if he were going to a party instead of to work outside.

Frau Terrell wore a straight gray skirt every day when she left the house, under her checkered coat. Her hair was always combed into a neat knot above her collar, a lump on the back of her head.

The Terrells came and went from the house as if they hadn't a care. As if they didn't know that on the other side of the water were men trying to hurt them all.

No one was digging in the garden today, but as Brigitte neared the edge, she saw two men building a wall from a pile of bricks and pail of mortar. Neither of them looked at her or the dog as they drew close.

She ignored them as well, until she heard their voices.

Instead of the language in England, they were both speaking German. They talked in whispers about how far they were from the channel waters. One man wanted to cross back over to Germany on an undersea boat. The other man preferred to wait out the war right here.

One of the men sounded like her father, and her heart raced as she stepped toward him. But it wasn't her father; she could see it now as he picked up a brick. His nose was all wrong, his hair too long.

What if these men were like the ones who took Papa away? What if they would hurt her too?

Her mind screamed for her to run, but her feet froze on the path. And then it was too late. One of the men had already spotted her. He tipped his hat and said something to her in English.

She glanced back toward the cottage. Frau Terrell would be angry if she didn't hurry back with the eggs. And this man seemed kind enough. Perhaps he could tell her the location of the henhouse.

"*Wo ist das Hühnerstall?*" she whispered.

His eyes grew wide, and she knew instantly that it had been a mistake to use her voice. Dietmar had told her not to speak in German. She should have listened.

"*Dort drüben,*" the man replied, pointing to his left.

"*Danke.*"

He asked where she was from, and she told him from a house along the river. Then he asked about her family.

"Girl!" Frau Terrell shouted from the garden.

The dog scampered away as Brigitte turned toward her.

"Stay away," the woman commanded, waving the potato peeler in her hand as she approached.

The man returned to his work, and Brigitte prayed neither man would tell her secret, that she too spoke the language forbidden here. But they seemed to be afraid of Frau Terrell as well. One man dipped his spade into the mortar while the other lifted a brick.

Dozens of words spilled from Frau Terrell's mouth before she boxed Brigitte on the ear. "Fetch the eggs."

Brigitte's head hung as she moved away, her cheeks burning from embarrassment as she found the henhouse to the left of the wall. The chickens scattered when she plodded through the straw, stealing eggs from their nests.

She didn't know much, but Dietmar had taught her how to run. She could leave tonight through her window, climbing down the ladder of vines. The Terrells wouldn't know she was gone, at least until the morning.

But if she left tonight, where would she go? She didn't know this strange country. Didn't know where to find Dietmar or his aunt.

Dietmar knew where she was. He'd promised to come for her, and Dietmar never broke his promises.

The dog joined her side again as she latched the henhouse door.

Just a little longer, and Dietmar would find her.

A little longer, and they could return to their parents.

It wouldn't be long now before they could all go home.

CHAPTER 16

The Tonbridge train station was mostly quiet at a half past one, a direct contrast to the throngs in London. The town center was a paradox as well, modern storefronts mixed with the medieval past. A river ran through town and lapped against the foundations of old shops now housing establishments like Subway and Starbucks. And an abandoned stone castle perched on a grassy hill, overlooking the town.

The public hall had been replaced with an apartment building, three stories tall, but the sidewalk where Quenby stood was the last place Dietmar had seen Brigitte, her nose pressed to the car window. If the Terrells had taken her to Breydon Court, they would have driven north through the town center before leaving town.

With the Uber app on her phone, Quenby requested a ride to Breydon Court. Then she found a bench as she waited for the driver, facing the white bridge that crossed over the river. Its Narnia-like lampposts framed the castle wall behind it.

She'd already spent several hours in the town of Maidstone this morning, searching through records for information. The Elizabethan house at Breydon Court had been built in the 1500s; the owners in 1626 then expanded it into one of the largest manor houses in Kent. The Ricker family inherited it in 1868, and they resided there until Lord Ricker's death in 1944.

After her husband's death, Lady Ricker and her two young children relocated to a town house in the affluent St John's Wood, a district of northwest London. The Dragues, a prestigious family from London, purchased Breydon Court with the contingency that the two Ricker children could keep an apartment in the house for the remainder of their lives if they wished.

Was this why the interviewer had asked Lady Ricker about Admiral Drague during her interrogation? Or was there a personal connection between the Ricker family and the Dragues?

Louise McMann, Quenby had read, married in 1968. After the death of her husband, she'd returned to live in her family's former home.

Quenby couldn't search the census records for the Ricker or Terrell families—those were closed to the public in Britain for one hundred years—but before she left Maidstone, she'd asked the clerk for records of Tonbridge evacuees in late 1940 and early 1941. The woman assured her that she'd e-mail Quenby anything she found in their archives. Thousands of children were evacuated to this area at the beginning of the war, until the Luftwaffe began bombing Kent. Then they had to be evacuated from Kent as well.

A silver Volvo pulled up to a curb near the bridge, and the Uber driver confirmed Mrs. McMann's address before driving Quenby north, past fields with docile cows and brilliant-yellow blooms.

Until the policeman took them to Tonbridge, Brigitte and

MELANIE DOBSON

Dietmar would have walked for miles through pastures and trees like this, searching for the skyline of London. They'd been so close—

But if they had found Dietmar's aunt, both children might have been killed in the Blitz as well.

A jet flew overhead as her driver turned west.

"Is there an airport near here?" she asked.

He nodded. "Biggin Hill is about ten miles north."

"I didn't realize there was an airport so close."

"It's mostly for private airplanes now, but it was an RAF base during the war."

Quenby scooted forward on her seat. "Do you know the World War II history of this area?"

"A little," he replied. "German soldiers and downed pilots were housed over at a prisoner of war camp on Pembury Road. Many of the prisoners worked on local farms to supply the rest of the country with food."

She looked at a half-timbered house outside the window, sitting above a fruit orchard and a field of ewes guarding their lambs. "Are the buildings still there?"

"No, there's a grammar school on the property now."

"Have you ever been to Breydon Court?"

He flashed her a curious look in the mirror. "Most people have never even heard of Breydon Court."

She shrugged. "I'm doing some research for a story."

"I took a passenger there once," he said as he swerved into the other lane to avoid a pack of cyclists. "I had to drop him off at the front gate."

They drove through a neighborhood and then down a quiet street that ended at an ornamental gate made of wrought-iron slats. On the other side, tufts of white-and-fuchsia rhododendrons padded both sides of a driveway.

"There's an intercom." The driver pointed toward the stone pillar on the right of the gate. "Do you want me to wait?"

"No," she said. "I'm hoping to be here for a while."

The gates were locked, so Quenby tried the intercom. When no one answered, she found a seat on the curb, hoping a vehicle would come in or out of the estate this afternoon. In the meantime, she decided to review her notes again on the Ricker family.

In her research, she'd discovered there were dozens of reasons why men and women became traitors—money, power, politics, devotion to a lover or family member. But it didn't seem like the Rickers needed any of Germany's reichsmarks, and they were already powerful in England.

If Lady Ricker had committed treason, why had she risked death by hanging to cripple the country where she lived? Or was her hatred for the Jewish people so extreme that she would do anything to exterminate them? The interrogator had said Lady Ricker's aunt was German. Perhaps her ladyship supported nationalism, like so many others at the time, because of her Germanic roots.

Quenby closed the case over her iPad. She couldn't fault someone for their loyalty, as long as they didn't hurt others under the guise of allegiance. Her own grandmother had been born in 1945, while the citizens of Germany were searching for a new identity, recovering from the catastrophe of hatred and loss. Once, Grammy had told her that she followed no one but her Lord. Germany, though, held sweet memories for her, the innocent ones of a child protected by a loving mother who'd been widowed in the last year of the war.

Grammy had wanted to protect Quenby as well. She couldn't protect her from everything, but she'd introduced her to love and forgiveness, both at home and in a man who'd also felt abandoned as He died on a cross. A man who loved her so much that He gave His very life for her.

She'd forgotten that over the years—that Christ had been left alone in the darkness. He'd suffered horrifically in those last hours because of His love, but instead of bitterness, He chose to forgive.

And it was His forgiveness that changed everything.

A blue coupe pulled in front of Quenby, and she stood as the front gate opened. Sighing, she hurried to the driver's side of the car, hoping that Mrs. McMann was inside. Confrontations like this were her least favorite part of the job, but necessary if someone refused to communicate with her via e-mail or phone.

A woman in her seventies was driving the car, her eyes shaded by sunglasses. She inched down her window as Quenby stepped up beside her.

Quenby smiled. "Good afternoon."

The woman didn't return the greeting. "You're not from this area."

"I live in London."

"But you're from America."

Quenby nodded, sticking her hands into the pockets of her denim jacket. "The state of Tennessee. On the eastern side of the US."

"I know where Tennessee is," the woman snapped.

"My name is Quenby Vaughn. I'm trying to speak with Mrs. McMann."

The woman removed her sunglasses, her eyebrows bowed into two sickles above her glare. "Did you not receive my e-mail?"

"I did, but—"

"Then you will return to London this afternoon and tell your supervisor that there will be no story written about my mother or any other member of the Ricker family."

The car crept forward, and Quenby followed it toward the gate. "Was someone else in your family spying for Germany as well?"

Mrs. McMann braked again before lowering her window farther. "I don't know what fantasy you and your syndicate are trying to create, Miss Vaughn, but there's no story here, at least not one based on facts."

"Your mother was interviewed by an advisory committee in 1948 about suspicions that she assisted the enemy. If she was innocent, then she was the victim of a witch hunt."

"My mother was no witch."

"I'm only after the truth, Mrs. McMann. If you tell me her story, I'll set the record straight."

The woman stiffened. "Don't try and teach me how to suck eggs."

"I've never sucked an egg in my life," Quenby said. "Not here or in Tennessee."

"You know what I mean." Mrs. McMann's finger hovered over the button that powered her window.

"I'm going to find out what happened," Quenby continued. "I just wanted to give your family the opportunity to tell your side of things."

"My mother was an honorable lady who did much good for Britain during the war. There's nothing else for me to tell."

"Did she host evacuees?"

The woman shook her head. "She was focused on raising her own children."

"But you weren't born until after the war—"

"I wasn't an only child."

"Of course," Quenby said, deciding not to add that she knew Mrs. McMann's brother wasn't born either until after many of the evacuees had been relocated. "I read that your mother was from America."

Mrs. McMann reached for her purse and pulled out her mobile. "I assume you are familiar with the law office of Fenton and Potts."

"You familiarized me in your e-mail."

Mrs. McMann lifted the phone to her ear. "They are about to become equally familiar with you."

The woman drove through the gates. Quenby was tempted to follow her but figured she didn't need a trespassing charge for Mrs. McMann or any of her family to discredit her story.

And she was certain now that there was a story. She only had to uncover what Mrs. McMann was trying to hide.

The gate clanged shut, and she took a step back. The blue coupe had stopped on the other side, as if the woman was making good on her threat to call her lawyer right away.

A text popped up on her phone from Lucas.

Have you made a decision?

She returned his text. **I have twelve more hours to decide.**

Seconds later, another question blinked on her screen. **Where are you?**

At Breydon Court. Working on my story for WNS.

Don't move.

She stared down at her phone. **I have to move. Breathing and all that.**

When she looked back up, she saw Mrs. McMann still in her car, watching Quenby in her rearview mirror. The woman opened her door, craning her neck for her final word from the other side of the fence. "If you come tromping on my land, I'll call the police."

Mrs. McMann slammed the door before driving away.

As the dust settled back onto the road, Lucas texted her again.

Do you have a car?

Don't need one with Uber.

I'm south of London. Can drive down.

Lucas might think he could coerce her by his offer to help—and his flowers—but she couldn't let him influence her work or her decision.

She texted back, **No need to come. I'm almost done for today.**

His return text came after she started walking. **I suppose you can breathe then.**

Generous. Thanks.

Where are you going next?

She glanced at the screen for a moment and put her mobile away. She'd send him another text from Mulberry Lane.

Mrs. McMann couldn't stop her from tromping on public land.

Chapter 17

Breydon Court, December 1940

With the exception of black draping the windows, Breydon Court hadn't succumbed to the wartime gloom that billowed across their country and infiltrated the minds of citizens dreary from darkness and fear, from rationed food and the cramped spaces that sheltered them from Germany's wrath.

Electric lights were forbidden at night, but candlelight softened the harsh lines and crevices of the formal parlor in the manor house. Even the ancient portraits seemed to bask in the familiarity of flickering wicks, the faint scent of honey in the melting wax, though they glowered down at the modern furniture and clothing of its occupants with open disdain, appearing quite sinister if one bothered to look long enough.

As Lady Ricker awaited her company in the parlor, Eddie Terrell slipped into the kitchen to find his wife busy preparing for the annual

New Year's Eve party. She, along with three other staff members, had been assigned the task of serving their guests.

"Where have you been?" Olivia whispered as she reached back behind her collar, checking her neatly pinned knot of hair. There wasn't a loose strand hanging from it. Never was. But Olivia still felt obligated to check it whenever her hands weren't occupied with something else.

"In the gardens," he lied.

"You smell like soap."

He shrugged. "I cleaned up."

He hadn't really been in the gardens, of course, but truth was as elusive these days as black treacle at the market. His wartime tasks spanned past his obligatory duties as foreman in the outdoor gardens, like Olivia's. She was a secretary by trade, but Lady Ricker often sent her to work in the kitchen. And now she'd taken on an evacuee for her ladyship as well.

The wooden counter was filled with platters of jellies, chocolates, and cheese. No wonder people came often from London to visit. Between their gardens and dairy—and the cook's sleuthing skills— the residents at Breydon Court didn't suffer the pains of rationing. Here they enjoyed the finest of foods that had seemingly vanished from England at the beginning of the war.

He stole a piece of cheese while the cook was distracted, her wooden spoon circling inside a copper pot on the stove.

The chauffeur, a man named James, stepped into the kitchen. "Lord Ricker has arrived."

"Blimey," the cook snapped. "Where are the others?"

James shrugged. "Haven't seen anyone else."

The cook began stirring the pot again. "The Dragues were due an hour ago."

"Their driver is probably wandering around the dark roads. It's almost impossible to see out there with the new headlamps masking the light, and I know my way."

The cook brushed her hands over her stained apron. "One of these days, I fear you're going to drive right into a den of Nazis."

"There aren't any Germans around here."

"Except those working in the garden." The cook turned toward Eddie as if it were his fault they'd employed prisoners of war to help with chores once done by men who were now fighting or women who'd been recruited by Britain's Land Army.

Olivia motioned Eddie toward the pantry, and they stepped away from the rest of the staff. "One of the Germans was talking to the girl today," she said.

His eyes narrowed. "I thought she couldn't talk."

"Doesn't mean she can't hear."

One of the servants walked by, and they waited until the woman rounded the corner. "Why was the girl outside?" he asked.

"I sent her to collect eggs."

"Maybe we can send her to an orphanage in London with one of our houseguests."

"Then Lady Ricker will require us to take in a new evacuee. Unless another member of the staff can billet a child—"

Breydon Court was required to billet at least one evacuee. Instead of protesting this mandate, Lady Ricker had passed the responsibility down to Olivia, telling her that she would care for an evacuee at home. Her ladyship thought an evacuee would help distract his wife.

Eddie glanced toward the door. "Perhaps I can persuade her ladyship to change her mind."

His words loomed between them, and he waited for Olivia to fuss at him like she always did when he mentioned his friendship with their employer. Instead, she placed her hands on her narrow hips, speaking much too loudly. "Perhaps you can persuade her ladyship to care for the girl herself. The woman is a lazy—"

"Hush," he demanded. "Lady Ricker is one of the most driven women I know."

Her cheeks flushed with red. "You're a fool, Eddie Terrell."

He smirked as she marched out the door. A fool indeed—he was fooling all of them.

Minutes later, a housemaid rushed down to the bottom step with the news that their guests had finally arrived. While the other staff clamored for the platters, he picked up his camera and strung it around his neck. Before the war, he'd been a photographer for a magazine in London, taking pictures of cricket matches and society balls.

The papers these days didn't care much about society, but Lady Ricker still wanted him to photograph her soirees. They must all act, she insisted, as if the war hadn't deterred them from their lives. As if the society pages wanted to print these pictures.

The eight guests were mingling in the room, sipping their drinks, when Eddie walked inside. He heard Admiral Drague talking about the bombs dropped on London, crippling the city and killing more than fifteen thousand people.

Occasionally they heard Luftwaffe planes in the skies above Breydon Court. The Germans were usually flying north toward London or back across the channel after they'd dropped their bombs. They might empty the last of their explosives on any flickers of light before heading home.

Lord Ricker stood by himself near the piano, wearing a plum velvet smoking jacket, a glass of bourbon clenched in his hand. Even though most other Members of Parliament dodged the bombing in their country homes, his lordship preferred London over Kent. And he rarely engaged with their guests or even his wife when he was at Breydon Court.

Lady Ricker's short hair was curled tightly around her oval face, a diamond necklace glittering above her white sequined dress. She leaned toward Admiral Drague on the divan, her gloved hand on his knee as they whispered together. Eddie stiffened. He knew she must entertain multiple men—for the cause—but still he hated the thought of her with this pompous man.

He snapped a photograph of them, the light from his bulb flashing off the somber portraits on the wall.

Admiral Drague's head whipped up. "Put that away."

Lady Ricker gave a sharp nod, acknowledging the man's demands, and Eddie slowly, defiantly, lowered the camera. He was only doing what she'd asked of him.

"Eddie," Lady Ricker said, her voice a dull drone as if she were talking to any of her servants.

He stepped forward. "Yes?"

"Those items we discussed earlier today. Go retrieve them for me."

He glanced at Admiral Drague and saw the sneer of disdain on the man's face. Never would he share the photographs with him on his own accord, but if Lady Ricker thought it necessary, he had no choice except to comply.

"Of course," he murmured.

She shooed him away with her jeweled wrist. "Stop dillydallying then."

The cottage he and Olivia shared was a fifteen-minute walk from the main house, though he could make it in twelve if he hustled. An electric torch in hand, he hurried through the darkness, down the long lane to the cluster of houses built for those who worked at Breydon Court. He didn't dare turn on his light, not unless it was an emergency.

They all must keep their secrets right now, but he hated it when Lady Ricker treated him like one of her subjects. She mustn't show him any favoritism or others, including Olivia, would guess at their scheme, but still it stung.

One day, it would all change. Everyone, including Lady Ricker, would treat him with respect.

His darkroom was in the cellar, but he couldn't risk storing Lady

Ricker's photographs underneath the house, lest rats tear them apart. Nor could he put them in the bedroom he shared with his wife.

Now the evacuee was living in the room where he'd stashed his work.

He pounded on her locked door, heard the girl stir inside, but she didn't unlock it.

He pounded again. "Open this door."

When the girl still didn't comply, he went back down to the kitchen and retrieved the key hanging on a peg by the stove. Minutes passed as he jiggled the rusty key, twisting until the door finally opened.

He shone his torch into the dark room, and it reflected against the glass. Swearing, he yanked the lined blackout curtains across the window before scanning the room with his light. The girl cowered in the corner.

He stepped toward her. "You must keep the shades closed at night or we'll be bombed."

Instead of looking up at him, the girl closed her eyes.

He bent over, whispering to her. "Olivia says you understand plenty. Do not lock that door again and keep these curtains shut."

The girl didn't reply.

"Turn around," he ordered. Lady Ricker would be checking her watch now, wondering at his tardiness. He shuddered to think what she might say to Admiral Drague when he returned. Later, she would apologize for belittling him, but he hated being criticized in front of a man who already thought of him as dirt.

He wouldn't let this child deter him any longer.

"I told you to turn around." He slapped the wall. "Face this."

She slid down to the floor, her head falling into her lap. Olivia was wrong—the girl was deaf. And she certainly didn't talk to anyone, including Germans. His secret would be safe with her.

He glanced at his watch. Twenty minutes had already passed. Lady Ricker was going to be furious.

His back to the girl, he reached for the hammer that he'd hung in the closet and bent down to pry up a floorboard inside the small space. Underneath the plank was a box where he kept the photographs.

After retrieving the box, he pounded the nail back into the board and rushed back out the door, up the lane. No matter what Lady Ricker said now, she'd show him later how pleased she was with his work.

CHAPTER 18

The narrow lane called Mulberry was located outside Breydon Court's sandstone wall. There was another iron gate at the end of the lane, leading onto the property, but the grass around the gate was overgrown, the lock rusted.

It seemed that no one had used this entrance in decades.

Her back to the gate, Quenby looked at the cottages on both sides of the tree-lined street. The walls on some were whitewashed bricks while other cottages were built of stone, their roofs slanted with slate. Behind the cottages on her left was a pasture that appeared to be part of the estate.

Perhaps someone on this street could answer her questions about the Rickers as well as the Terrell family.

There were only four stone cottages on the lane that looked as if they might be at least seventy years in age. Number twelve backed up to the pasture.

The woman who answered her knock was dressed in black yoga pants and a light-pink T-shirt freshly stained. On one hip she was bouncing a baby girl even as she clutched her laptop to her chest with her other hand.

"Sorry to bother you," Quenby said. "I'm trying to track down a family named the Terrells. They lived on this street in the 1940s."

The woman set her laptop on a shoe rack and switched the baby to her other hip. "I've never heard of them, but we've only been here for a year."

"Do you know anyone who could answer some questions about the history of Breydon Court?"

The baby started to cry. "You should talk to Mrs. Douglas. She's lived here her entire life."

Quenby glanced down the cracked sidewalk. "Which house is hers?"

"It's by the wall. Only house with a palm tree planted in the front lawn."

After thanking her, Quenby walked down four cottages. A man wearing blue scrubs answered her knock, and when Quenby inquired about Mrs. Douglas, he introduced himself as Paul before inviting her inside.

"You have a visitor," he called down the hallway. Then he led Quenby into a sitting room cluttered with dozens of frames—some displaying black-and-white photographs, others filled with embroidered sailboats, fruit, and animals. On a hospital bed near the window was a woman propped up into a seated position, wearing a jade dressing gown. She had short gray hair, neatly rolled and styled.

"Please, come in." Mrs. Douglas waved Quenby forward. "Are you from St. Stephen's?"

"No," Quenby said as she sat on a chair beside the woman. "I'm trying to find more information about the Ricker family and a girl who lived on Mulberry Lane about seventy-five years ago."

"I was born in this house, back in 1936, but I don't remember much about the Rickers." The woman glanced out the window, toward the iron gate. Then, turning back, she reached for Quenby's hand and squeezed it.

Quenby held the woman's hand, remembering for a moment how Grammy used to hold her hand as well whenever her thoughts began to wander.

"Did one of your parents work for the Rickers?" Quenby asked.

"My mother was a housekeeper there, though she was often required to serve guests on the evenings Lady Ricker entertained. After Anthony Ricker was born, my mother cared for him."

"I read that Lady Ricker enjoyed entertaining."

Mrs. Douglas nodded. "Mother said she'd charm every man in the room with her elegance and wit."

"But not the women?"

"I don't believe most women appreciated her charms."

Paul reentered the room, carrying a porcelain tea set glazed with peach roses and a matching plate filled with biscuits—some custard iced, others dotted with jam. Mrs. Douglas released her hand, and Quenby splashed milk into both her and Mrs. Douglas's cups before she poured the tea.

"Did Lady Ricker entertain often?"

"She hosted friends from London before and during the war, but there weren't any more parties at the house after V-E Day."

Quenby took a sip of her drink. "I heard that Lady Ricker was anti-Semitic."

Mrs. Douglas blinked. "Who told you that?"

Quenby thought about the file back at the National Archives. The interrogator who had questioned the woman's views. "There are rumors that the men and women she hosted were Fascists. Perhaps they thought Hitler was the solution to what they perceived to be a problem."

"I don't put any stock in rumors." Mrs. Douglas set her teacup on a stand beside the bed, and Quenby saw the concern in her eyes. "Why do you want to know about Lady Ricker?"

She decided to redirect the conversation. "I'm also looking for a family by the name of Terrell."

"Terrell . . ." Mrs. Douglas's voice trailed off; her gaze focused on two robins fighting outside the window. "Do you mean Olivia Terrell?"

Quenby leaned forward. "Did she live on this street during the war?"

Mrs. Douglas nodded. "She was a secretary for Sir Winston Churchill until she got married. Then she came to work for the Rickers."

"As a secretary?"

"Sometimes, I suppose, though Lady Ricker kept her in her place by requiring she work in the kitchen. Mrs. Terrell and my mother were acquaintances until Mrs. Terrell moved away. Mr. Terrell was . . ."

When she stopped, Quenby pressed her. "Mr. Terrell was what?"

Mrs. Douglas shook her head. "It's just a rumor."

"Sometimes these rumors prove true."

Mrs. Douglas patted her hand. "No sense dredging up the past now."

"Do you know where the Terrells moved after the war?" Quenby asked.

"No." Mrs. Douglas leaned back against her pillows. "My mother said that Mrs. Terrell didn't report to work one morning, and she never returned. Mr. Terrell said he didn't know where she or the girl went, though my mother didn't believe him."

Quenby inched closer to her. "What girl?"

Mrs. Douglas shook her head weakly. "I don't remember her name."

Paul stepped up beside them. "I'm afraid she's done for the day."

"Of course," Quenby said, though she was aching to ask more about the girl. Instead she reached for her briefcase and handed the nurse a business card. "Please ring if she'd like to speak again."

As Paul arranged blankets around Mrs. Douglas, Quenby let herself out through the front door.

"Hello again," someone called out from down the street. Turning, Quenby saw the woman from number twelve walking toward her, balancing both her baby and a brown paper bag.

"I don't know if this is helpful, but we did some remodeling a few months ago and I found this tin under a floorboard."

Quenby clutched the bag. "Thank you."

"Why are you trying to find this family?"

"I think a German girl by the name of Brigitte was billeted at their home during the war. One of her friends is trying to find out what happened to her."

The woman smiled, motioning Quenby back toward the house. "Let me show you something else."

An upstairs bedroom had been transformed into a pale-green nursery with flowers painted on the wall and a sketch of Peter Rabbit hopping toward a white picket fence, ears flapping in the wind as if Mr. McGregor was in close pursuit.

The woman pointed toward the flecked carpet in the small closet. "The tin was under there." When she waved her forward, Quenby held up her mobile phone to use the light. "Look at that."

Carved in the wood above the baseboard were the letters *B. B.*

"I couldn't bring myself to paint over it," the woman said.

Quenby smiled as well, snapping a picture on her phone before her gaze turned toward the window, at the acres of pastureland behind it. Mr. Knight's story, it seemed, was true. Brigitte must have stayed in this cottage, carving her initials like Dietmar had done into the tree back in Moselkern.

Had Olivia Terrell taken her when she left, or had Brigitte relocated to another home?

"Did Brigitte come to England on the *Kindertransport*?" the woman asked as they walked back down the steps.

CATCHING THE WIND

"No, she and a friend ran away after the Nazis arrested their parents."

The woman kissed her baby's head. "I hope you discover what happened to her."

"Me too," Quenby said.

She pulled the tin out of the bag and had started to open it when her phone chimed. Instead of Lucas texting her this time, it was Chandler.

We need to talk.

Quenby stared at the screen. Her editor never demanded they talk unless something was wrong.

I can phone now, she typed.

No—come back to London.

Quenby checked the train schedule on her phone before texting back.

I'm still in Tonbridge. Won't be home until almost six.

I'll wait for you at the office.

Quenby read the message twice before sending a reply. **What's wrong?**

As she waited for Chandler's response, the excitement over finding Brigitte's initials and even the tin began to fade.

Louise McMann must have made good on the threat to contact her attorney.

Chapter 19

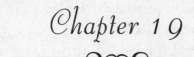

Breydon Court, February 1941

E ddie closed the door behind him and locked it. Snow fell over the deer park outside the bedroom window, the sky darkening. He pulled the blackout curtains over the glass, and then his focus settled on the woman waiting for him on her bed, resting back against satin pillows that glowed in the candlelight.

Lady Ricker smoothed a manicured finger across the gold thread on her bed covering. "Olivia must be wondering where you are."

"She's taking dinner to the girl," he said, slipping onto the pillows beside her.

"I suppose she's too simple to understand anyway—"

"Not as simple as you'd think." Just last night his wife had yelled at him for staying late at the big house again. Lady Ricker, she said, demanded too much of him.

Olivia had no idea as to the extent of his duties for her ladyship, especially when Lord Ricker was away.

He'd met Lady Ricker in London three years ago when he'd photographed her and Lord Ricker's wedding ceremony for the magazine. She'd called him months later, asking him to take pictures at one of her many parties. As the weeks passed, they'd clarified the parameters of their relationship. Lady Ricker was a decade older than him and not wholly unattractive with her ebony curls and slender figure, though he liked to pretend she was beautiful. Attraction was secondary to their mutual passion.

She lifted her hand, smoothing his wrinkled collar. "You've worked hard today."

He smiled. "I always work hard for you, my lady."

"Admiral Drague phoned this morning. He was pleased with your latest photographs."

He stiffened. "I don't work for Admiral Drague."

"Now, now." She clutched his chin between her fingers like he was a child. "You mustn't be jealous."

"You treat me like a dog when he's here."

"If I treated you any other way, they would suspect."

"Let them suspect." He reached across the bed, trailing his finger down her bare arm.

Lady Ricker caught his hand and returned it to his side, focused on the business at hand. And making it quite clear who was in charge of this relationship. "Where are you keeping the pictures?"

"You said you didn't want to know."

"I've changed my mind."

"They're hidden," he told her, cracking his knuckles. "In the cottage."

"What if Olivia finds them?"

"She won't. No one will find them."

"I have plans for you and me, Eddie. Big plans."

He began unbuttoning his shirt. "I know."

"And a new assignment."

He turned toward her, his chest bare. "I don't want to talk about work."

"The girl in your house. What language does she speak?"

He reached for her again. "I don't want to talk about the girl either."

Lady Ricker shook off his hand. "What language, Eddie?"

Sighing, he inched away from her. "She doesn't speak at all."

"Not English, perhaps." She stood up, her dark-blue nightgown trailing behind her as she paced toward the black curtains and peeked outside. "I'm told she speaks German."

"Who told you that?"

She waved her hand. "It's of no matter."

He propped himself up on the pillows. "And you want to use her—"

"You make it sound so crass."

He moved to the window beside her. "You are a crass woman."

She intertwined her fingers in his. "That's our secret."

He kissed her neck. They shared secrets, lots of them. Secrets he would die for.

"No one will suspect her." She wove her fingers through his hair. "We need her help."

"Then you shall have it."

"Olivia won't be pleased."

"Olivia will do what I say," he assured her.

"Very good."

She leaned in to kiss him, but the scream of the air raid siren cut through the room.

"Blast it."

Lady Ricker sighed. "I suppose we must go to the boiler room with the rest of them. Make a show out of it."

Eddie swore as he rebuttoned his shirt.

The sooner this war was done, the better it would be for all of them.

CHAPTER 20

"This makes no sense," Quenby insisted, shielding her chest with her iPad.

"It doesn't have to make sense." Chandler paced across the span of her corner office, waving her cigarette as she moved past Quenby's chair. She leaned forward. "You told me Evan would love this story."

"Apparently I was wrong."

"I thought you'd already told him my idea."

Chandler marched by her again. "I wanted to surprise him."

Evening had fallen across London, and a school of cars and buses swam below the window, streaming between their office building and the department store across Brompton.

Just yesterday Chandler had implored her to do everything she could to secure the interview with Mrs. McMann, saying there wouldn't be any problem revealing a decades-old espionage scheme in print. Then all of a sudden, with a wave of Evan's wand, Quenby's story disappeared.

Chandler edged into her office chair, facing Quenby from across the cluttered desk. As if Quenby were a naughty student, at the mercy of her teacher.

"Did Mrs. McMann's lawyers threaten him?" Quenby asked.

"They called, but I wasn't privy to the conversation."

"Evan's never seemed to concern himself with lawyers before."

"Defamation is a major offense."

"I know that, Chandler." She pulled her chair toward the desk. "I've never defamed a person in my life."

Chandler placed her elbows on her desk. "For the record, I thought it was going to be smashing. Thought it might even win us some awards."

"Let me talk to Evan. I'll explain what I've found so far and all of my documentation from the National Archives."

"I told him what you'd found, but he still shut it down."

Quenby looked back down at the sea of vehicles, trying to make sense of Chandler's words, but there was no sense in them. "I must be close to something big or Mrs. McMann wouldn't threaten a lawsuit."

"It doesn't matter—"

"The lawyers can't stop me from asking questions. I'll write the story and then you and Evan and a whole team of lawyers can read it before you decide whether or not it's publishable."

Chandler crushed her unlit Kent Blue on a tea saucer. A ring of dark-red lipstick coated the cigarette butt. "Evan wants you to take a break."

"A break?"

"You haven't taken leave for more than a year."

Anxiety mounted in her chest. "I don't need a holiday."

"Two weeks, Quenby. Visit the south of France or Spain or someplace where you can sit on the beach and rest."

"I hate sitting on beaches."

"And you hate to rest, but it's good for you," Chandler replied. "If you won't travel south, spend some time with your friends in the States and focus on yourself for a change. When you return, we'll talk about a new assignment for you. Something just as fresh that Evan will love."

"Someone else is going to scoop my story."

"It's not yours, Quenby."

But it felt like it belonged to her. She'd personally vested herself in this story, like she did with every story she wrote. How could she quit, when she didn't know how this one ended?

Chandler opened the door, and when Quenby stepped outside, she looked both ways down the hall as if she were lost. Chandler wanted her to focus on herself, but her work kept her mind engaged, her eyes focused on someone else. Since she'd started this job three years ago, she'd always had a story to work on, even if it was just preliminary research during a public holiday. Old, worn feelings flared inside her again, as if Evan Graham had personally rejected her instead of just her idea.

Mentally, she tried to brush it off and return to the matter at hand. Evan might be able to take away her official work on the Ricker story, but vacation was her personal time. The syndicate couldn't keep her from asking questions on her own, as long as she didn't sell the story to someone else. At least she could find out the end of one story—and perhaps how it intersected with another.

Stepping out of the building, she elbowed her way through the after-work crowds until she reached Hyde Park. The crowds thinned on the other side of the pedestrian gate, mostly couples strolling along the waterfront of the curved lake called the Serpentine. At the other end of the lake were the Italian water gardens that Prince Albert had built as a gift for his wife.

Quenby sat in the small pavilion overlooking Queen Victoria's marble fountain and the stone statues, the briefcase with her iPad beside her and the tin from Mulberry Lane on her lap. Leaning back against the plaster wall, she mentally reviewed all she had learned about the Ricker and Terrell families, trying to fit together the scattered puzzle pieces that spanned almost eight decades now.

She slipped the picture that Mr. Knight had given her from her handbag and examined the girl with braids. The two parents who obviously loved her.

Her answer for Mr. Knight was quite clear now. She had two weeks to find out what happened to Brigitte. And perhaps, in the midst of searching for Brigitte, she could find out what Louise McMann was trying to hide.

A mandarin duck, with his purple breast and red beak, landed in one of the water basins. Then he paddled a wide circle around the fountain's spray before moving toward the statue of the dolphin, as if the creature might come play with him.

Instead of texting Lucas, she phoned him.

"Hello, Quenby," he said when he answered. Perhaps the *Miss Vaughn* ended with dinner last night. "Any luck on Mulberry Lane?"

"I interviewed several people, and I found something else . . ."

"What did you find?"

She hesitated, wondering if she should ask. But they needed to talk about Brigitte, ASAP, and they would both need to eat this evening. "Do you have plans for dinner?"

"Nothing in stone. Are you still in Tonbridge?"

"No, I'm sitting at the Italian Gardens in Kensington. Tonight Chandler mandated that I take a holiday from the syndicate."

"But your story—"

"Has officially been canceled." A female mandarin joined the male, and they began circling the fountain together. "And since I have nothing else to do for the next two weeks . . ."

"Excellent," Lucas said. "Mr. Knight will be pleased. We should go celebrate."

The ducks flew away together, as if they were conspiring for their next venture. "I'd rather pick up something to make back in my flat. Nothing fancy."

"I can do casual."

She smiled. "Are you certain?"

"Quite. Should I bring red wine or white?"

"That sounds fancy."

"How about a French rosé?"

She shrugged. "It's all the same to me."

Chapter 21

Brigitte watched snowflakes fall outside her window until darkness swallowed the theater of white. In her right hand was Dietmar's knight, its smooth helmet and sword pressed against her fingers. She carried it everywhere in the pocket of her cardigan, pretending her friend was with her.

When the Terrells weren't listening, she'd sometimes talk to Dietmar. Ask him if he was hungry or scared or lonely too.

Sometimes, she'd pretend that he talked back to her.

Moonlight parted the clouds, and Brigitte watched as an aeroplane dipped low over the pasture. Then a white canopy floated down from the sky, and she thought she saw legs dangling underneath the canopy before it blended into the drifts of snow.

A great siren blasted through the silence, and she clutched the knight to her chest. But she didn't leave the window. Four silver planes glistened under the moon, and she watched as an ember of light sparked from one of them, like a match struck against its sterling holder. Instead of floating like the canopy, the light plunged toward the ground. Then it exploded in the pasture, shooting flames up into the darkness.

Still she didn't move, and neither Herr nor Frau Terrell were here to demand she unlock the door.

The fire grew, and in the distance, she heard the clang of a fire engine.

What would she do if the flames crept up to the house?

She climbed under her cot and lay on the floor until someone shouted outside. When she looked through the window again, she saw the spray of a hose trying to combat the flames. It reminded her of a broom handle attempting to ward off a lion.

Minutes passed, perhaps an hour, and the flames began to diminish. A door slammed downstairs, and she heard Frau Terrell shout for her. Soon after, the woman unlocked Brigitte's door and stepped inside.

A strand of Frau Terrell's long hair had slipped from its pins and fallen across the shoulder of her wrinkled blouse. "You're supposed to be in the cellar."

Brigitte understood the words but pretended she did not.

The woman stepped toward the window, looking down at the cinders still glowing orange in the darkness. "It's too late for the shelter now, I suppose." She motioned her toward the door. "Come downstairs to eat."

Frau Terrell busied herself in the smoky kitchen, boiling two eggs over the stove while Brigitte sliced pieces of bread to toast. The woman didn't complain about the thickness of the slices. Perhaps she was hungry as well.

Brigitte sat beside the kitchen table, the images of fire still blazing in her mind.

Should she tell Frau Terrell about the canopy that dropped from the sky? Her English was better now—she'd been mimicking the Terrells in the secrecy of her room—but she didn't know the right words to explain what she saw. And if she should speak to this woman at all.

But what if one of Hitler's men had jumped from the plane? What if he'd come across the water from Germany? If he found her, he might take her back. Then she would never find Dietmar.

Frau Terrell spooned the eggs from the hot pan, and as she rolled them in a separate bowl of water to cool, Herr Terrell burst into the kitchen. When Frau Terrell looked at him, her face flushed red. "Where have you been?"

"Lady Ricker is expecting a delivery tonight." He reached for one of the eggs and peeled it. Then he popped it into his mouth. "I was waiting near the toolshed."

"That egg was for the girl," Frau Terrell reprimanded him.

He glanced over. "She won't starve."

Brigitte clutched the bread in both hands lest he take that as well. No need to toast it.

"Did the delivery arrive?" Frau Terrell asked.

"The plans were botched."

"What do you mean, *botched*?"

He glanced at Brigitte again but kept talking. "We can't seem to find it."

Frau Terrell's eyes darted toward the window. "It has to be out there."

As Herr Terrell ate the second boiled egg, Brigitte devoured her dry brown bread. Then she picked up a pencil and paper and began sketching.

Herr Terrell sat down at the table. "Lady Ricker has a new assignment for you."

His wife's eyebrows climbed. "Why doesn't Lady Ricker assign it to me herself?"

"It's a bit more complicated this time."

From the corner of her eye, Brigitte saw Frau Terrell look at her.

"The girl won't understand," Herr Terrell said.

Brigitte drew the rounded edges of a canopy, the body of a man dangling below. An aeroplane, flying below the moon.

"You don't know that—"

"She's not mute, Olivia. She speaks German." He leaned toward Brigitte. *"Sind Sie Deutsche?"*

Her eyes flew up at his question. The words, he pronounced them all wrong, but somehow he'd discovered her secret.

Her gaze dropped back to her paper, and she pulled it down onto her lap. She wouldn't answer his question.

"See." Herr Terrell turned back to his wife. "She can help all of us."

"What does her ladyship want from me?"

"There's a house, about an hour from here. No one will suspect what you're doing there."

"We have to move?" Her voice quivered with her question.

"Not both of us. Lady Ricker needs me to work from here."

Frau Terrell shook her head, and Brigitte watched a tear trail down her cheek. "I'm not going without you."

"The girl will help you with chores. And the messages."

"This is ridiculous, Eddie."

"Lady Ricker will double your wages. I'll bring them to you every weekend along with supplies."

"It's not about the money."

"Then do it for me, love," Herr Terrell said, scooting toward her.

"The girl," Frau Terrell whispered.

He motioned toward the staircase, and like the dog that followed Brigitte across the pasture, Frau Terrell followed him up to their room.

Brigitte finished her picture, and with the paper clutched in her hand, she walked upstairs. Words were softer now behind the Terrells' door, whispered until Frau Terrell's tears turned into laughter.

Inside her room, Brigitte tore her picture into a thousand pieces. Then she opened her window and released them to the embers and snow.

What would the Terrells do, now that they knew her secret?

She plugged her ears so she couldn't hear the laughing next door. For some reason, it seemed to her even worse than the fighting.

CHAPTER 22

Quenby sautéed chopped garlic and slices of red pepper in a pan, simmering it with olive oil. She hadn't made chicken cacciatore in eons, but the dish had been her grandmother's favorite meal. They'd made it together in the cramped kitchen back in Tennessee, Clint Black or Tanya Tucker blaring from the stereo, Grammy twirling around the butcher's block with her spoon in hand like she was boot scootin' across a dance floor.

Lucas arrived at eight with a bottle of pinot noir, wearing jeans and a white polo shirt. "I'm glad we're working on the same team now," he said as he stepped into the kitchen.

She stirred diced tomatoes and capers into the sauce. "Mr. Knight didn't mention being part of a team."

"I'm supposed to assist you in any way that I can."

"I work best when I'm alone," she said before facing him again.

Making the expectations clear now would eliminate any surprises—or distractions—in the weeks ahead.

"Fair enough," he complied, eyeing the vase that displayed his bouquet from last night.

"Thank you again for the flowers."

He smiled. "I'm glad I didn't have to take them home."

"Did you tell Mr. Knight that I'll look for Brigitte?"

"I called him tonight, and he's pleased." He opened a leather portfolio and removed several papers, stapled neatly together. Then he slid it across the counter. "Now we have to make it official."

She handed him the spoon. "I assume you know how to stir."

"I'm an expert." He manned the stovetop while she read through the legalese in the contract. It was simple enough—she was supposed to search for Brigitte over the next two weeks and send a report of her progress to Lucas each evening. Her findings were confidential. There would be no article for the syndicate or book later on, unless Brigitte authorized the story.

In exchange for her work, Mr. Knight would deposit an enormous sum into Quenby's bank account for expenses and a retainer. If she found Brigitte, the contract said he'd double the sum.

She tapped the paper. "That's too much money."

Lucas eyed her curiously. "Take it up with Mr. Knight."

"Seriously—"

"It's fair, Quenby, but if you want to negotiate, you're welcome to do so. This is equivalent to what he paid the other investigators." He slipped a pen out of his portfolio. "Welcome to the team."

"I said I—"

"I know, you work alone. Brilliant."

She snatched the pen from his hand, preparing herself for another fight. "Is this your idea of a truce?"

"I'm attempting diplomacy," he said, but he was smiling this time. Teasing her. Her shoulders began to relax.

"I'll be setting up a password-protected website for you to upload photographs and videos; then I'll add your reports to the website after I review them. Mr. Knight wants to see everything, but—"

"You want to protect him."

He nodded. "I want you to be completely honest with me about your findings, but I may cushion the news I forward to him, at least until all the facts are in place. And I'll leave you alone to your work."

Perhaps she and Lucas would get along during the weeks ahead after all.

She handed back his pen, and then he slid something else across the table. The wooden princess. "Mr. Knight wants you to have this," he said. "So you can give it to Brigitte when you find her."

Quenby placed Princess Adler on the throne of her windowsill, then turned and added the chicken pieces to the pan, coating them with sauce to simmer.

"Look what I found today." Her pulse quickening, she pulled the tin from her handbag. When she'd first opened it on the train, she thought the brown envelope inside was empty. But it contained five tiny photographs, smaller than the tip of her thumb.

Lucas reached for one of the pictures and placed it in his palm. "What are these?"

"Microphotographs," she explained, drawing from the information she'd read online. "The Germans and Allies used them to transmit information during World War II."

He tried to view it in the light like she'd done, but without magnification, the images were only dark blotches on a clear background. "Where did you find them?" he asked.

"In Brigitte's closet."

He slipped the photographs back into the envelope. "How do you know the closet was Brigitte's?"

"Because she carved her initials on the wall."

He smiled at her again, his brown eyes warm. "Impressive."

She propped her elbows on the table. "Did Mr. Knight's investigators find the initials?"

"They did, but not a box."

"What else did they uncover?"

"An evacuee record that said Brigitte was sent to Canada, but her trail ends before she left England. Mr. Knight believes the relocation record was either fabricated or incorrect." He replaced the lid on the box and then handed her a file. "Here's everything from the previous investigations, and there's a profile on Brigitte's family in Germany as well."

"Did the other investigators search in Canada?"

"Every province, but nothing was found." He tapped on the box. "Can you look at these on a microfilm reader?"

"Most of those readers are for light images on dark film. I'll rent a microscope in the morning to view our pictures."

He lifted his phone and began typing. "That is something I can help you with."

"Seriously?"

"There are some advantages to working as a team."

When the chicken was finished, Quenby topped it with fresh basil, and they slipped outside to the small circular table on the patio with their plates. Bullfrogs croaked in the pond below, but the light from her patio drowned out any view of the pond or starlight.

Lucas poured the pinot noir, and she took a small sip like he'd done in the restaurant. It tasted like every red wine she'd ever tried. "What would you do if you didn't like it?"

"Spit it out."

She scrunched her nose. "That's disgusting."

He laughed. "I've never spit out wine before."

She tilted her glass toward him. "What do you taste?"

He took a sip, seeming to contemplate the flavors. "Black cherry. A hint of raspberry. This wine is from the Burgundy region of France."

She chalked up the cherry taste in her mouth to the power of suggestion.

He placed his goblet back on the table. "Listen to that."

An owl hooted from a nearby tree, the one that kept her up at night when she left her window open.

Standing, he stepped toward the railing. "It reminds me of visiting my mother's parents in the summer. I'd spend my daylight hours exploring the forest behind their gardens."

"I didn't spend much time inside my grandmother's house either when I stayed with her. Her neighbor had a boat and a daughter my age."

He smiled as he returned to his seat. "Sounds extraordinary."

"Grammy was my rock after my home fell apart."

"My grandparents were more of the holiday sort," he said.

"They liked to vacation?"

"No, I only saw them twice a year when I was a kid—a few days each summer and then during Christmas." After another bite of food, he tapped the plate with his fork. "This is the best chicken I've ever tasted."

"You're lying."

He sipped his wine. "I don't lie, Quenby. At least not intentionally."

She filled his plate again, and as they continued eating, she told him about her visits with Mrs. McMann and Mrs. Douglas.

"Mrs. Douglas's mother knew the Terrells, and she confirmed that the Terrells housed an evacuee during the war. She also said Mrs. Terrell moved soon after the war began . . ." Her words trailed off.

Olivia—that was what Mrs. Douglas had called Mrs. Terrell.

Lucas set down his fork. "What's wrong?"

She stood. "I'll be right back."

Inside her flat, she propped up her iPad and scrolled through the hundreds of pictures she'd taken at the National Archives. Memos, photographs, newspaper articles, official correspondence. The letter addressed from Lady Ricker to Olivia was among them.

She scanned the seemingly mundane note.

APRIL 1942

Dear Olivia,

You'll be pleased to know the baby took his first steps this week. He seems anxious to move.

He's eating better as well. Last night he woke me up at eleven to eat, but other than that, he is sleeping through the night.

I hope you're enjoying my gift.

Yours truly,
Lady Ricker

The next image was a brown envelope. There was no name on it—of the sender or receiver—but there was an address. Mill House on Kelmore Street. In Newhaven.

Switching to Google, Quenby found the town of Newhaven south along the English Channel, not far from Brighton. An hour from Breydon Court via car.

Lucas was over her shoulder now, looking at her screen, but he didn't interrupt as she searched for the street. There was no record of a Kelmore Street in Newhaven, at least not online. The house had probably been numbered in recent years, the road renamed.

She swiped the screen, moving back to the letter. "I think our Mrs. Terrell went to live in Newhaven after Mulberry Lane."

He didn't say anything in reply, examining her face instead. She brushed her long bangs away from her eyes. "What?"

He shrugged. "Just thinking."

"Wise or not, this time I'm going to ask what you're thinking."

Another breath of silence before he responded. "I was thinking that perhaps Mr. Knight knew exactly what he was doing when he hired you."

She folded her iPad over the keyboard. "Your confidence is overwhelming."

"It's meant to be a compliment, Quenby. If anyone could find Brigitte, I believe it would be you."

She thought he was mocking her, but as she looked at him again, studying his face like he'd done to her, she saw strength in his brown eyes, a genuine smile on his lips.

And it seemed that this time he was telling the truth.

Chapter 23

"Hurry up," Eddie urged, yanking open the drawers in their bedroom bureau, dumping Olivia's blouses and knickers onto the bed. It wouldn't be long before the two detectives up at the big house started knocking on the doors of cottages near the bomb site.

She folded several items of clothing into a suitcase as if the folding were critical. "I'm moving as fast as I can."

He tossed a pile of clothes into her case and clasped it shut. "You must leave now!"

A wet trail streaked across the linoleum and carpet upstairs, starting from where he'd pulled her from her bath minutes ago, but still she didn't seem to understand the urgency of their situation. This was no holiday. Nor was there time to coordinate outfits and such. The basics were all she needed.

She sniffled again, but there was no time for tears either. He'd left the big house twenty minutes ago, soon after two detectives from London arrived. The men were meeting with Lord Ricker, asking about a German parachute the Tonbridge police found after the fire yesterday, hidden in the shed by the greenhouse.

He hoped the officials over in Germany flayed whichever pilot dropped that bomb on Breydon Court. They were supposed to be diverting attention from this property by bombing down south, not marking the spot where their man had landed.

The parachutist was livid as well. He'd run through the snow last night to find a hiding place for himself, no time to stow his parachute.

Now Roger—the name on the man's fake papers—was in Lady Ricker's car, waiting under a canopy of trees with the chauffeur. They needed Olivia before they could leave.

Eddie peeled back the blackout curtain to look outside, but he couldn't see anything unusual in the fading light. Then the telephone rang, and he swore into the receiver.

Olivia whirled toward him. "What is it?"

He hung up the phone. "One of the detectives is driving this way."

"There's no reason for him to stop here—"

"He's planning to interview everyone on Mulberry Lane."

Olivia blanched. "Where's the girl?"

He raced across the landing and found her under the cot. "Get up!"

She actually listened this time, standing as he stuffed the small pile of clothing from her closet into a paper bag. Then he shoved it into her hands. She dropped the bag and bent over to fold the feet of the cot.

"Nein," he said. "You won't need that."

He tried to pull her away, but she clung to the cot.

"Aus." He pointed toward the door. "Get out."

But the girl wouldn't let go of her bed, and he had no time to fight.

"Fine," he shouted, quickly collapsing the cot and rolling it up. "Take it with you."

The doorbell rang below, and for the first time since he'd moved to Breydon Court, Eddie thought their jig was up. Perhaps he shouldn't wait for the investigator. He could go to Newhaven with Olivia and the parachutist right now. Start over again in a new town.

He had already hidden the wireless transmitter, but his camera was still in the cellar, with film inside. He'd been careless, leaving the film, but he hadn't thought someone would be searching his house.

If he ran, the detective would surely suspect him. And the images on his camera would seal his fate. Ultimately they'd discover that he and Lady Ricker were collaborating.

The doorbell rang again, and Olivia burst onto the landing. One suitcase was tucked under her arm, clothing trailing out both sides. The handle of another case was clasped in her hand.

He would stay here and face the investigator, feigning ignorance. Helpfulness, even, if he must. He would tell them that his former wife had been a photographer.

Olivia rushed down the stairs, and he grabbed the end of the girl's cot and pulled her down the steps as well. Near the back door, his wife leaned to kiss him, but he pushed her outside with the girl. There was no time for sentiment when they were all in danger of being shot or hanged.

"Run!" he commanded them.

The doorbell rang for the third time, and he tugged at his collar. What a bally mess. Sweat poured off his forehead, down his neck, and he reached for a dish towel to wipe it off before he opened the door.

A wool topcoat did little to hide the rolls of flesh cushioning the detective's frame. "I'm Inspector Hill." The man tipped his black trilby hat. "Are you Eddie Terrell?"

"I am."

The man looked over Eddie's shoulder. "Does it always take you this long to answer your door?"

"I wasn't expecting anyone."

The detective studied his face.

"You interrupted my bath."

The man gave a curt nod. "I'm from Scotland Yard. And I have a few questions to ask."

He opened the door wider. "Come in."

"Anyone else here?" the inspector asked as he stepped over the threshold.

"No," Eddie said, tugging on his stiff collar again. "I live alone."

CHAPTER 24

The Royal Institution of Great Britain was caged in light—the atrium, lift, even some of the walls were made of glass. In a laboratory, behind one of these glass walls, Quenby waited as Lucas's friend—a pretty technician named Meribeth—connected Quenby's iPad to a camera on the microscope.

After a tutorial, Quenby sat on a stool beside the steel table and removed one of the microphotographs from the envelope with tweezers, sandwiching it between two slides. Meribeth helped her adjust the lighting, eyepiece, and zoom dial until the image grew clear. The picture was of a building with an open front. Like an airplane hangar. Instead of being colored black and white, it was an ivory and brown.

Quenby copied the image onto her iPad before slipping the next photograph onto the microscope stage.

Last night, she'd learned that Lucas worked solely for one client—Mr. Knight and his company, Arrow Wind. This morning, Lucas was at his office writing other contracts, but his text had opened the door for her to use one of the best dissecting microscopes—if not *the* best—in the United Kingdom.

The next photographs captured a lineup of old airplanes, the British roundels on the fuselages distinct. There were no people in these pictures and only the outline of buildings in the background. She saved those photographs to examine later before viewing the last one. A hand-drawn map of an airport. There were no markings of the map's location but plenty of notes about hangars, headquarters, barracks, and runways.

Who had been taking microphotographs of what appeared to be an RAF airfield? And why were they stored in the cottage where Brigitte and the Terrells once lived? The photographer, she suspected, wasn't an amateur.

After thanking Meribeth, Quenby checked her watch. A trip to Newhaven seemed to be the next logical step. Using her new retainer, she'd leave first thing tomorrow on the train and spend the night there.

Her phone chimed when she emerged from the Tube station at Hampstead, informing her of a new text. She figured it was Lucas, but instead it was from Chandler, asking to meet her at Le Pain Quotidien.

She eyed the words curiously. Was her editor going to give her the Ricker story back? If so, what would she tell Lucas and Mr. Knight? She couldn't renege now, not after she'd committed to searching for Brigitte.

Several customers were in the front of the café, drinking coffee as they worked on their laptops. Chandler waited in the back of the room, nursing a pool of bright green—a matcha latte—in an oversize mug.

Quenby ordered the green tea drink as well before taking a seat across from her editor and friend. "Did you decide to take a holiday too?"

"No, I've been in the office all morning." Chandler glanced toward the front door. "And something's not right."

Quenby followed her gaze toward the door. "Are you expecting someone else?"

Chandler turned toward Quenby. "Just a bit paranoid. Evan was obsessing this morning."

"He's always obsessing about something."

"But this something has to do with your story."

"I have no story." The server brought her creamy tea latte, made with almond milk, and she took a long sip.

"At first he asked me to send you away on holiday." Chandler pressed her fingers into a tepee shape, a distinct arc over her drink. "Now he wants to know where you went. I told him I didn't know—"

"I don't have to report where I go on vacation."

"Traditional rules don't apply to Evan."

"It's just basic courtesy."

But she supposed courtesy didn't apply to Evan Graham either. In the past three years, she'd never known him to hesitate before exposing something that needed to be exposed. Even the time Chandler found out through a secret source that one of Evan's associates, a Member of Parliament, was suspected of hiring someone to assault an opponent before the election. The MP was acquitted, but the story ruined his friend's political career and his friendship with Evan.

Chandler straightened her mug. "He also wants to know what you uncovered about Lady Ricker."

"Nothing that isn't already public in the archives. Her descendants have been stonewalling me."

"Evan hasn't been to the archives."

So Quenby rehashed everything she'd learned about Janice Ricker.

"This woman seems like an American version of Lady Mosley,"

Chandler said, referring to the former Diana Mitford, a wealthy British woman who supported Hitler and his regime.

"Except Lady Ricker wasn't imprisoned during the war, and she was quite secretive about her loyalties."

"There must be more to this story." Someone walked by their table, toward the loo. Chandler didn't speak again until the door behind them was closed. "I've worked for Evan for six years, and I've never seen him act like this. Once we've wrapped or canceled a story, he's anxious to move on to the next one, but he can't seem to let your idea go."

"I can't let go of it either," Quenby admitted.

"Even though Evan was the one who killed the story, he might still give you a call. It wouldn't surprise me if he asked you to resume your research."

"Thanks for letting me know."

Chandler took her last sip of the latte. "Are you planning to work with Lucas Hough to find the missing girl?"

"I am."

"Perhaps you could write about her when you return."

She shook her head. "Lucas made me sign a confidentiality agreement."

Chandler twisted her mug. "So it must be a fabulous story."

"One that will remain secret from the public."

Chandler leaned closer. "Is the man as smashing in person as he looks online?"

"I think I'll plead the Fifth."

"The what?"

Quenby waved her hand. "Never mind."

"Does he have a girlfriend?"

"I have no idea." Though she'd wondered if he and Meribeth were more than friends. The woman was stunning, and she was obviously a pro in her field.

"Don't be your prickly self around him."

She squeezed the handle of her cup. "I'm not prickly."

"Not with me," Chandler said. "But you can be quite prickly around any man who dares to like you."

"He doesn't like me, not in that way."

"But he could, if you'd let him." Chandler stood and kissed her cheek. "Either way, try and have some fun on this holiday."

"I'll do my best."

"And don't scare Lucas Hough away."

Chandler left the café, but Quenby didn't move. Lucas was the prickly one, not her. Or at least he had been until he decided to call a truce.

Blast Chandler for making her lose her focus. She and Lucas had moved into an amiable relationship for the sake of their work. Nothing more or less.

Rain fell outside the window. Even though summer was only weeks away, it was still chilly. The warmth of southern France sounded nice at the moment, but she was more interested in pursuing Brigitte's story than seeing sunshine.

Newhaven was on the coast. It wouldn't be warm, but she could work for a few days near the water. And perhaps she'd find out what happened to Brigitte after she left Mulberry Lane.

Chapter 25

Newhaven, February 1941

Brigitte didn't like the man sitting in the motorcar beside her. He smelled like manure and charred meat, and he kept talking to her in German, asking questions about her home, her parents. Inquiring about any family she had looking for her in England.

She didn't answer any of his questions. Instead she kept wiping the fog from her window to watch the darkness lap against their vehicle. If only one of the waves would steal her away.

Hours had passed since Frau Terrell dragged her across the pasture from their house, the muddy snow sucking at both their shoes. Halfway to the car, Frau Terrell tried to wrestle the cot roll from Brigitte's hands, saying it slowed them down, but Brigitte sat on the bundle of canvas and wood, pressing it down in the snow. And she refused to move without it.

Frau Terrell had looked between Brigitte and the bag in her hand as if she were trying to decide which to carry. In hindsight, Brigitte wished that she'd stayed with her cot in the pasture, but when Frau Terrell turned away, Brigitte had followed, shambling behind her toward the vehicle.

The foul-smelling man leaned toward her. *"Wie bist du nach England?"*

She wrapped her arms over her chest, inching as close as possible to the door, the metal rattling from ruts on the country road. It was her secret, how she arrived in England. A secret she would never tell, especially to this man.

When she refused to answer again, the man scooted forward on the seat, speaking to Frau Terrell in English. "Are you certain she speaks German?"

The woman didn't glance back. "I'm not certain of anything."

He looked at Brigitte again, and though she could barely see his face in the moonlight, she shivered. "I'll convince her to talk."

This time Frau Terrell turned around. "You won't convince her to do any such thing."

"I'll do whatever is necessary."

She crossed her arms. "I'm in charge of the girl."

"Of course." The man leaned back, shifting his suitcase on the seat between them. He'd refused to allow the driver to put it into the boot of the motorcar, and anytime Brigitte touched it, by accident, he'd slap her arm.

The bundle with her cot was secure under her feet, Dietmar's knight resting in her pocket. They were her only possessions now besides her clothing. She wouldn't go anywhere without both of them.

Frau Terrell spoke to the driver. "Are we almost there?"

"I'm trying to find the bridge across the river."

"Eddie said the house was only an hour away."

The driver snorted. "Eddie lied."

It seemed they'd been driving forever now, following the cat's eyes reflecting on the road. The same darkness. The same stench inside the car. If they passed villages, Brigitte couldn't see them. Blackout curtains kept any light from trickling out, even to help motorcars find their way.

The driver stopped on the side of the road and examined his map in the light of his torch, shaded by his hand. Her eyes heavy, Brigitte curled up in a ball and leaned against the door. If only she could crawl under her cot to sleep.

How were she and Dietmar going to find each other now, so far away from where they'd parted? But she couldn't give up hope. One day she'd return to Mulberry Lane and search for him.

When she woke, the sound of road under their tires had smoothed, and she realized they were crossing a bridge. In the morning light, she could see the river below, a blue thread woven through chalky white cliffs.

And then there was a small village ahead. A cluster of houses and shops. The man beside her slouched down in his seat as they passed through town, but her nose stayed pressed against the window. No one was on the street, but the houses filled her with a sense of gratefulness, the knowledge that she wasn't alone.

On the other side of town, the driver turned onto another road, and they crept back along a bumpy road that cut through a woodland. The trees grew thick on both sides of the car, spiky arms batting against the windows.

Brigitte closed her eyes, trying not to think about her and Dietmar's flight through the trees. But she couldn't stop the memories. Dietmar holding her hand, urging her forward, then stopping her when they neared a house so he could find them food. Dietmar making them beds of pine straw in the forest. Dietmar covering her with his coat while she pretended to sleep on the rugged floor.

She felt for the knight in her pocket.

How she missed her best friend.

The driver stopped. "There it is."

When she opened her eyes, Brigitte saw a forlorn shack before them, a piece of wood dangling over the front door. The paint had long ago peeled off the sides and a garden of weeds grew tall in the gutter. Across the only front window spread a spiderweb.

The man beside her opened the door. *"Willkommen zu Hause."*

Welcome home.

Frau Terrell began to cry.

CHAPTER 26

O n Friday morning Quenby packed a bag and took a direct train south to Newhaven. By early afternoon, she found herself in the hills overlooking the River Ouse. The wide river flowed through town, severing it into two pieces, and she could see the long break-water that stretched out into the English Channel.

After securing a room and her luggage at a local inn, Quenby located Newhaven Library. The reference section contained a collection of ordnance maps, and she searched through the decades of maps until she found Kelmore Street listed on one from the 1940s. The short road was once north of the library, near the River Ouse.

The map in hand, she greeted the librarian at the reference desk— a woman named Annie—then pointed at the laminated paper. "I'm looking for this street."

Annie lifted the horn-rimmed glasses dangling around her neck and studied it. "The Kelmore family used to own all that property."

"Who owns it now?" she asked.

"It's woodland."

"Public woodland?"

"I believe so, though . . ." Annie examined the map again. "It looks like that road backed up to the Logans' farm."

Quenby snapped a picture of the map on her phone. "How far away is the farm?"

"About three or four miles north on Lewes Road."

"Walkable miles?"

"If you like to play chicken with the traffic." The librarian handed her a card. "Better off to ring for a cab."

"Thank you." She slid the card into her backpack. "Is there a mill near the river?"

Annie pointed to a blue stripe on the map, on the opposite side of the woodland. "Some of the buildings from Camford Mill are still there, but the operations closed down about a century ago."

Quenby stepped out of the library and glanced at the time. There were still several hours of daylight. If she didn't find Kelmore Street tonight, she would set out again to search in the morning.

The cab drove her north on Lewes Road and turned right, into the farm. No one answered her knock at the farmhouse, but a public footpath led through an empty field behind it. Quenby slipped through the turnstile and crossed the muddy land.

She clicked on the picture of the map, but when she enlarged it, trying to determine if the old road was north or south, it was impossible to figure out the direction without any sort of landmark. So she opted to hike east toward the river.

According to Google Maps, there were acres and acres of forest on the other side of the field. And somewhere in those trees was her street.

What an odd place for Olivia to relocate during the war, so close to the English Channel, while Germany was dropping bombs along the coast. Was she desperate for some reason to get away from Breydon Court? Or did she relocate here for work?

She could understand Olivia wanting to leave Lady Ricker's employment, especially if she discovered her boss was helping the enemy, but if she wanted to leave, why would she give her new address to Lady Ricker? It seemed the women continued some sort of relationship through their correspondence.

Mrs. Douglas had said her mother didn't believe Mr. Terrell when he'd claimed ignorance as to Olivia's whereabouts. Had he joined his wife here later? Perhaps this was the only place they could find—or afford—to live after the war.

Mrs. Douglas hadn't mentioned the Terrells having biological children. Perhaps Brigitte and Olivia grew close during their time here, isolated from the rest of the world. If she could find out what happened to Olivia, she might find Brigitte as well.

Quenby stopped at the edge of the trees. The official footpath meandered north, skirting the forest, and several overgrown paths snaked back into the woodland. Perhaps one of them had once been a road, but it was impossible to say.

Taking a deep breath, she chose one of the paths leading east, into the forest. Mud clung to her shoes. Branches scratched her face. And the worn footpath vanished under all the weeds.

Even if she found the house, she couldn't imagine there would be much of it left under this mess. The forest had probably devoured the dwelling and any hint of Brigitte or the Terrells.

Her mobile phone slipped out of service, leaving her with the picture of the useless ordnance map. She was all turned around now in this maze of shadows and trees. Was she walking toward the river or away from it?

Something rustled in the brush, and Quenby stopped. When she ran the trails at Hampstead Heath, there were always people near, swimming in the ponds or hiking through the forest. Here she wasn't certain she wanted to find another person. And certainly not an animal.

She didn't like being out in the wilderness by herself. Hated it, really, this feeling of isolation and vulnerability. The unknown. It reminded her too much of that day she'd spent a lifetime trying to forget.

The sun began to settle behind the trees, and her head began to spin as she lost herself inside her fears. Almost like being trapped on the Dumbo ride when your mom walked away.

It had been the happiest day of her life, back when she was seven. In the happiest place on earth. As she flew through the sky, ribbed with clouds, she thought she was the happiest kid on earth too.

None of her friends had flown on an elephant. Or eaten chocolate mousse under the Eiffel Tower. Most of her friends had never even been to Florida. But her mom, with all her failings, had brought her there. Just the two of them, to play on their own.

She had waved at her mom again as her elephant, strewn with candied pink, circled the carousel. Up and down. Round and round. On the other side of the black fence, her mom waved back. But then, the next time around, she wasn't there.

Quenby had strained her neck as the elephant flew higher, searching the fence for her mother's face. The line for the vendor on the sidewalk. And fear had sparked through her, long before she got off the ride. Her mom liked to play, but like a magician, she was also good at disappearing.

The elephant landed with a thud, and Quenby jumped from her seat, circling the fence on the ground this time. Shouting for her mom to stop hiding. This wasn't fun anymore.

A security guard had found Quenby, hours later, balled up in the passage under Cinderella's castle. She never saw her mom again, and in the years that followed, she doubted anyone, except her grandmother, who said they cared about her.

It was fascinating, really, in a sad way. Her own mother had left, without a trace, and never returned, while Mr. Knight had been searching to find someone he loved for more than seventy years.

She blinked. It was half past six now, and she wasn't at Disney World. Her aloneness wasn't because someone had left her. Still, she didn't want to find herself lost in the maze of trees after the sun disappeared. She'd have to search for the Mill House again tomorrow.

A mosquito landed on her arm, and she swatted it before retracing her steps on the path, passing a weathered plot of gray-and-white gravestones between the trees. Cemeteries usually fascinated her, especially the few words chosen to commemorate an entire life, but there would be no ducking back under the low branches to look at these epitaphs tonight. She swatted another mosquito—she'd be lucky to get back to the farmhouse before she was carried away.

The sky was almost dark by the time she found the pasture and blessed mobile service. No one answered when she phoned the cab company; neither did anyone answer when she knocked for a second time on the farmhouse door. Uber didn't have drivers in this area, and without a vehicle, she had no choice but to walk.

Unfortunately, the librarian was right about the traffic on Lewes Road. Cars were flying by at top speed, and the only place for pedestrians was a thin sliver of weeds on either side of the road. In the dark. Sighing, she tried the cab company one last time and then dialed Lucas's number.

"Hello, Quenby," he answered.

"Did you finish your contracts?"

"Contract work never really ends."

"But for today?" The sky was completely dark now, but the driveway was partially lit by a floodlight hanging on the barn.

"Close enough," he said. "Why?"

She took a deep breath, sucking in air along with her pride. "I might need a team member after all."

Silence.

"And a ride . . ."

She waited for him to tease her, but he didn't. Instead he asked, "Where are you?"

"Down near Newhaven. I came via train, but I can't find anyone to drive me back to my inn tonight."

"I see." She heard the clicking on his keyboard. "I'm almost two hours away."

She glanced around at the farmhouse, then out at the busy street. "I'm not going anywhere."

"Why didn't you rent a car?"

"No one in England wants me to drive on the left-hand side of the road."

"On the contrary." She could hear the laughter in his voice now. "It would be amusing."

"And deadly," she said. "You said you could help me—"

"I'm glad to drive you back to your inn. And I can take you around tomorrow as well, if you'd like."

With Mr. Knight's money, she supposed she could hire a driver, but it would be much easier to have Lucas's help, at least in the area of transportation.

She gave him the address to the farm. Then she climbed up to sit on the low limb of a tree.

Checking her e-mail, she found one from the clerk she'd met two days ago in Maidstone. The woman had found evacuee records in their archives from the end of 1940 and discovered the Terrells' name on the list. The name of their evacuee was simply *Girl*. The log said that the girl had been billeted with the Terrells in October 1940. And she'd left Mulberry Lane in March 1941 to transition to another home. In Canada.

Quenby powered off her screen. It was the same record Lucas had given her when he turned over Mr. Knight's file. Like Lucas said, previous investigators followed this lead to Canada, but approximately seven thousand British children had been evacuated to Canada during the war. They found no trace of a German girl hidden among them.

If Brigitte didn't come to the Mill House with Olivia, did someone adopt her in Canada? Or perhaps something happened to her ship traveling there? Mr. Knight's file contained an article about a ship being torpedoed on its voyage across the Atlantic. The passenger manifest didn't list a Brigitte or an unnamed evacuee girl, but something could have happened on another ship.

It seemed unlikely that Olivia would have kept in contact with a child who only stayed at their house for a few months during the war, especially if Brigitte moved on before Olivia left Breydon Court. Perhaps someone else near Breydon Court would know what happened to Brigitte. A teacher or a friend. If the Mill House was a dead end, perhaps Lucas could take her back to Breydon Court tomorrow to continue the search.

Gravel crackled under tires on the driveway, and Quenby looked up to see the glow of headlamps creeping toward her from the far side of the house. A red tractor parked in a nearby shed, and then a man crossed the driveway before entering the farmhouse.

She hopped out of the tree and moved toward the front door to let him know she was waiting on his property. And ask him if he knew the location of the Mill House.

The man answered seconds after she rang the bell. He was about ten years older than her and had a chestnut-colored beard trimmed above the collar of his T-shirt. With a glance over her shoulder, he searched the driveway for her vehicle.

"I was on the public footpath behind your house," she explained. "My ride's not here yet—"

"Always glad to have company." His gaze fell to her mud-coated trainers. Then they wandered much too slowly back up to her face as if she were a portrait at an exhibition. Or a pint of beer. "I can drive you into town."

She thought briefly about calling Lucas, telling him there was no need to come, but a cacophony of warning sirens blared in her mind. Lucas could tease all he liked. He might annoy her, but he wasn't creepy. Jury was out on the man before her.

"No thanks." She took a step back. "My friend will be here soon." The sooner, the better.

"But you still decided to knock."

She pulled her mobile out of her purse. "I wanted to ask you a few questions about the woodlands behind your farm."

He opened the door wider. "Come on inside."

She eyed the dimly lit corridor behind him. "I need to wait here for my friend."

He leaned against the doorpost, crossed his arms. "What questions do you have?"

She debated asking about the Mill House but decided she didn't want to alert him to her destination in the morning. "I'm searching for an old road named Kelmore."

"There are several overgrown roads near the mill."

"Who owns the mill?"

"The government does now. My family tried to buy the property from the Ricker family, back in the 1930s, but they refused to sell it."

Her head jolted. "Did you say the Rickers?"

He nodded. "Do you know the family?"

"I've heard of them." Her heart raced, but she didn't want to tip her hand. "I thought the Kelmore family owned the property by the river."

"The Kelmores built the mill a long time ago. The Rickers, on the other hand, let it go to ruin."

"When did the mill close?"

"After the First World War," he said. "It was too far gone to open back up during the second war."

The pieces tumbled around in her mind, trying to fit into place. Why exactly did Lady Ricker send Olivia to live on their property here, after the mill closed? Or did Olivia come on her own accord, knowing that the mill was abandoned?

"I can show you the mill tomorrow," the man said.

Before she responded, a car plowed up the driveway, brakes squealing as it stopped in front of the house. At first Quenby thought Lucas had made record time, but when the car door slammed, a woman dressed in a fuchsia blouse and tight jeans marched toward the stairs. When she reached the top, she critiqued Quenby up and down like the man had done, except there was no appreciation in her eyes.

"I'm Kyle's girlfriend," she said briskly. "Who are you?"

Quenby chose the simple explanation. "A walker."

The woman moved around her, kissing her boyfriend. Then she stood beside him, one hand knotted into her hip, as if Quenby were a threat.

Quenby wanted to laugh. There'd be no competition from her.

"Thank you for your help." She backed farther away from the door. "I'll leave you to your company."

Kyle stepped toward her. "Are you certain you don't need a ride?"

"Quite certain."

"Because I need to fetch a few things from town—"

The woman gripped his arm. "She said she was certain, Kyle."

Quenby glanced at her phone. "My guy will be here any moment."

Thankfully Kyle's girlfriend shut the door.

Chapter 27

Mill House, February 1941

Brigitte batted Roger's hand away, not wanting him to touch her, but he kept tugging on her arm in the darkness, insisting that she stand.

Frau Terrell hovered over them with a candle, the light dancing wildly on the wall as if her hands were shaking. Why didn't the woman tell Roger to stop?

"We need you, girl," he said in German, but she rolled over, her nose pressed against the wall.

Last night she'd tried to sleep under the cot, like she'd done in the Terrells' home, but something—a rat or mouse—scampered over her leg. Scared, she'd leapt up and spent a sleepless night on the cot. Tonight she'd had no problem falling asleep.

Wind rattled the window, not far from her bed, and she could hear the rats now, rustling near the wall.

Roger yanked on her sleeve, forcing her to turn toward him again. "Get up."

Her eyes shut, Brigitte clung to the edges of her cot, praying he would go away. Give up. Praying they would both leave her alone.

He swore. "There's no time for this."

"You can transmit yourself," Frau Terrell said.

"No one on this side of the channel can know I'm here."

"I could try—"

"They would never understand your German."

"Perhaps she'll do it in the morning."

"They are listening tonight for my broadcast," Roger clipped. "If they don't know I arrived safely, they won't return to take me home."

Brigitte heard Frau Terrell step up beside him, her voice soft, almost kind in comparison to the German man's. "We need your help, girl."

When Brigitte still didn't respond, Roger stuck something cold into the side of her neck. Steel. Frau Terrell cried out.

Brigitte could block out his face, but not his gun. Or his words.

Roger whispered in her ear, "Do you know what this is?"

She nodded.

"Then you had better get out of bed. And find your voice."

Brigitte slowly opened her eyes, but she didn't sit up. He wouldn't really shoot her, would he? Frau Terrell wouldn't let him.

Something moved in the corner. Another rat. Roger whirled around, and his pistol blasted. Pain fired through Brigitte's ears, all the way down to her toes, and she screamed. The sound echoed around the room like the roar of the gun. And Roger's horrid lips settled into a smile.

At the sight on the wall, blood spattered across the wood, bile flooded her throat. She closed her eyes, plugged her ears, escaping to the tree house. To the laughter in her heart. To the music in the trees.

There was no music in this house. No laughter. There was nothing but sadness and despair.

Roger nudged her again with his gun. "If you don't get up, you are as worthless to me as that rat."

She had no doubt now that he would shoot her. Nothing Frau Terrell could do would stop him.

Shivering from fear and cold, Brigitte sat on the cot, resting her bare feet on the cracked wood floor.

He pointed toward the door. "Let us begin."

His suitcase was propped up on the kitchen table, but instead of clothes inside, she saw knobs and the veins of black wire connected to a box.

"I assume you know how to read German."

She nodded.

"Very good." He passed over a piece of paper with four lines on it. Then he held out a small box and switched a lever.

With a tap of the paper, he signaled for her to read.

"Ich bin—" she began, her voice shaky.

She looked up at Roger, hovering over her. Would he shoot her if she messed up?

Roger's lips pressed together, his eyes narrowing. He was angry at her.

Her eyes back on the paper, she continued reading.

I am safe with a friend and ready for guests. Will meet you next Friday.

Roger clicked off a button and checked his watch. "Right on time."

"Will the British hear it?" Frau Terrell asked as he packed up his case.

"Perhaps, but they won't know where I'm transmitting from. Or who is sending this message."

"And your friends?"

"They heard it," Roger said before he pointed at Brigitte. "Go back to bed."

She slipped away from the table as Frau Terrell moved toward the kitchen, saying she would make tea.

Standing at the doorway into her room, she could see the spatter of blood on her wall, smell the stench that had settled over her cot. Instead of stepping inside, she eyed the front door of the cottage, on the other side of the table.

Lauf.

She could almost hear Dietmar telling her to run.

Somewhere close was the village they'd passed on their drive here. She could find food on her own. A place to sleep. Anyplace was better than this, even sleeping in a shed or on a barn floor. The rats could crawl on her if they wanted, as long as Roger and his gun didn't threaten her again.

Roger swore when she rushed out the door, into the night. She ducked under tree limbs, plowed through the mud and muck, her legs burning. Not once did she look back.

A stream of light shone through the branches around her, but the torch wouldn't find her. Dietmar had taught her how to dodge the evils of light.

CHAPTER 28

"What are you doing up there?" Lucas asked, seemingly perplexed as he stepped out of his car, the headlamps on his Range Rover illuminating Quenby's hiding place among the leaves.

She hopped off the limb. "Thinking."

He leaned back against his car. "Does it help to sit in a tree?"

"People who are scared often do unexpected things," she explained. "Sometimes it helps to do unexpected things as well when you're piecing together their story."

"There's nothing expected about you, Quenby."

She brushed off the seat of her jeans. "Taking that as a compliment."

"As it was meant to be." He opened the passenger door, and she climbed inside.

Fortunately, Kyle and his girlfriend had left earlier, speeding past Quenby's nest in the tree. While she waited in the lamplight, she'd searched various websites for Olivia Terrell in the UK, hoping to find a descendant who could answer her questions about Brigitte.

But Quenby could find no information about the woman who'd once worked for Winston Churchill. So as she sat in that tree, she'd wondered—had Olivia disappeared like Brigitte? Or had she simply been forgotten in the record of time?

When Lucas reversed the car, light from his headlamps shot beyond the house, toward the forest. "Did you find the Mill House?"

She shook her head. "I found the road on an ordnance map, but it's all bracken and bramble around the mill now."

Dozens of cars sped by on the main road before they were able to turn.

"Did another investigator locate the house?" she asked.

"If they did, they never told Mr. Knight."

"The Ricker family once owned Camford Mill." She shifted in her seat. "Even if Brigitte was sent to Canada, I want to search the Mill House."

"So we'll try again in the morning?" he asked as they approached the town.

"If you really don't have to go back to London—"

"I don't."

"Then we'll search together." She wouldn't admit it to him, but she'd be grateful not only for his vehicle but for his company when she went back to explore the woods.

Her inn was full for the night, but Lucas found a motel room a few blocks away. They ate a late dinner of pollack encrusted with chorizo, in a café along a more civilized portion of the river. Lucas's eyebrows furrowed when she ordered a bottle of Coke with her fish instead of a white wine, but he didn't tease her about the selection.

Below them, ferries carted passengers between France and the coast of England, not far from where the Higgins boats launched for Normandy on D-Day.

"Does Mr. Knight own a boat as well as a plane?" Quenby asked as she watched a yacht cruise into the harbor.

"No. I think his channel crossing as a boy cured him of any interest." Lucas took a bite of his spinach salad. "How did everything sort out at the Royal Institution?"

"I'm still working on the report—"

He stopped her. "I'm not angry."

"Meribeth had the microscope waiting for me." Quenby opened her iPad and found the pictures, turning the screen so he could see. "They're photos of some sort of air base."

He scrolled through them at first. Then he returned to look at them again, slowly. "Blast."

"What is it?"

"That's Biggin Hill. See the chapel?" He pointed at the screen before looking up at her. "Probably during World War II."

She studied the screen, then leaned back in her wicker chair. "Biggin Hill was an RAF base," she said, recalling the conversation with the Uber driver.

Lucas searched for more information on his phone. "The Germans bombed it twelve times between August 1940 and January 1941 alone. Took out a teleprinter network and the operations room."

She whistled. "They must have known what to bomb on the base."

"Probably from photographs like these."

Her skin tingled. "So the Terrells or someone else in the cottage might have been helping the Germans?"

"Perhaps, but that would be almost impossible to prove now, especially since the Terrells seem to have vanished along with Brigitte." He watched another yacht cruise into the waterway, rope lights strung from stern to bow. "Then again, I suppose adults leave more of a trail than children, however faint."

"Not all adults leave a trail." The words slipped out, too late to retract. Her mother might have left a trail, but Quenby had never searched for it.

Before Lucas questioned her statement, she changed the subject. "Do you still want me to e-mail a report tonight?"

His eyebrows slid up. "Breaking the contract already?"

"It seems the lawyer who wrote the contract could give me permission to break it, especially since I already told you everything I found."

He sipped his wine. "Mr. Knight will want to read your report."

"Then I'll write up something from yesterday and today."

"You can wait until morning."

"Rule breaker," she teased. "Why don't I dictate it to you right now?"

He laughed as he reached for his phone. "I'll try and keep up."

"Bullet point number one," she began. "I reviewed microphotographs found at 12 Mulberry Lane. They appear to be of the RAF station at Biggin Hill."

She poured Coke into her glass. "Number two, searched for the Mill House on Kelmore Street where Olivia Terrell presumably resided but have located neither a house nor the designated street.

"Number three, received confirmation from an evacuee record that the Terrells did indeed house Brigitte but she left about five months after she arrived, purportedly for Canada. And number four, had dinner with an irritating attorney who—"

"Who rescued you from spending the night in a tree."

"True," she said. "Scratch number four."

He tapped on the screen. "Expunged from the record."

"It's like a superpower," she said, pushing her hair back over her ear.

He laughed again. "The ability to use big words?"

"No—" she rolled her eyes—"the power to expunge. Just think of it. You could expunge anything. Every stupid decision you've ever made or the memories of when someone else has done something wrong to you."

He leaned into the table, searching her face. "If you could erase anything from your past, what would you expunge?"

"I'm pretty sure that's none of your business."

"Said in the nicest way possible," he said, shifting back again at her rebuke.

She took a sip of her Coke. "What would you erase?"

His eyebrows climbed. "And that's your business?"

"You're right." Both hands rose like a shield in front of her. "You don't have to answer that."

"I actually don't mind answering," he said. "I'd erase years eighteen to twenty-two."

She lowered her hands. "Not pretty?"

"Downright ugly." He glanced at the lights along the moorings again, at the white forest of sailboat masts. "Fortunately, I'm learning that God's grace covers even the worst of my sins."

"You believe in a God who forgives and forgets?"

"I believe in a God who forgives when I ask. I'm not convinced that He forgets."

She crossed her arms over her chest. "An almighty being should be able to forget if He chooses."

"It almost makes the grace cheap if He forgets it all. I like thinking, at least in my limited understanding, that in His great love, He remembers and still forgives. Just like we remember when people hurt us, but we can forgive them too."

She'd tried to forget what happened with her mother, many times, but the memories kept flooding back. Was it really possible to forgive even if she couldn't forget?

"Forgiveness is the only thing that truly frees us," he said. "A supernatural power."

That's what she wanted more than anything. To be free of her anger. Wounds.

But she couldn't forgive Jocelyn Vaughn, not after what she had done.

❧

The nightmare woke Quenby and she bolted upright from the lumpy mattress, covered in sweat. In the darkness, all she could see was the blonde-haired girl from her dream, standing by herself. Hungry. Scared.

People had been moving around—even through—the girl, hundreds of them, but not one of them stopped. The girl cried out but no one heard. She was like a ghost. An apparition. And the invisibility hurt to her core.

Quenby turned on the sconce light beside her bed.

She'd had nightmares about this girl before, but she'd never seen her face. This time she saw her eyes, lonely and afraid.

Was it her as a child? Or was this girl Brigitte, lost and alone?

In her mind, their stories were bleeding together.

If only she did have the power to expunge her past, at least part of it, from her mental record. The files in her brain that stuffed things away in a most unorderly fashion, then spilled them out late at night, when she was trying to sleep.

Perhaps finding Brigitte would help put to rest these dreams that plagued her.

She pulled the pillow to her chest, memories that she wanted to forget flooding back to her again.

Twenty-one years ago, when her mother disappeared, the police had searched Orlando. Or so Grammy Vaughn had said. They probably didn't search for long. After her husband died, Jocelyn had a sad history of walking away, leaving Quenby home alone, until child welfare stepped in. When Quenby was six, she and Jocelyn both went to live with Grammy in Tennessee so an adult would be present on those days her mother didn't feel like mothering anymore.

Jocelyn had tried repeatedly to get a job at the Magic Kingdom. She'd wanted to be Snow White, as if she could snap her fingers and become a princess. In hindsight, she was probably wanting to hide behind a costume and makeup, but when Quenby was a little girl, she thought it magical that her mother wanted to be someone else.

On that fateful day, Quenby's seventh birthday, Jocelyn had awakened her after midnight and made a game out of their escape. They'd snuck down the steps, Jocelyn's hand over her mouth, trying not to laugh. Even as a child, Quenby hadn't thought her mother's games were funny, but she'd tried to play along. Anything she could do to please the woman she wanted to love her. The woman who didn't seem to know how to love.

Grammy had done the best she could after Jocelyn left, trying to help Quenby heal. She'd taken Quenby to church and spent a chunk of her retirement fund on a counselor who threw around words like *abandonment* and *attachment disorder*. Words that made Quenby feel as if she could never break free of the cage that adults around her called circumstances. At times, it seemed Quenby and the counselor were playing dodgeball. She tried to duck when these words were thrown her way, but sometimes they hit. When they did, they stung.

She rose from her bed and opened the patio door, overlooking the bay.

Did Mr. Knight know where her mother was? Perhaps when he had researched Quenby, he'd found Jocelyn Vaughn as well. Perhaps he would give her the information if she asked.

She had spent much of her life searching for people, but she'd never even searched Google for Jocelyn. Part of her still wanted to find her mother and ask why. Why hadn't she left her in the safety of her grandmother's care instead of leaving her alone at Disney? Why hadn't she even said good-bye?

But she'd been too scared to inquire, afraid perhaps that this incident that rocked her world hadn't affected her mother at all. That after the Dumbo ride, Jocelyn had gone on with her life freely, relieved she no longer had to care for her daughter. Grateful, even, that Quenby was gone as she started a new family, birthing new children to replace the old one who'd never been able to make her happy.

Brandon might have thought her obsessed with her work, but the truth was she was scared to get close to anyone, man or woman, thinking if they really got to know her, they would be gone too. It was crazy, of course, but it was her own version of crazy. During high school, she'd tried to remake herself into someone much more cool and smart. Likable. Someone different from who she was at the core. Someone people enjoyed being with.

She no longer tried to evolve into someone people liked. Instead she focused all her efforts on her stories. People seemed to enjoy her writing. It didn't matter if they knew or even liked her.

Had Brigitte tried to change her identity as well, stepping into a new one that didn't include the horrible memories of her childhood? Which begged the question—did Brigitte deliberately hide from Dietmar after the war, or was she detained?

Perhaps, after four years as a refugee, Brigitte joined a new family, like Dietmar had done. She could have stayed in Canada, under a new name, or been relocated to the United States, Australia, or even South Africa. Or she could have traveled back to Germany, not knowing whether her father was dead or alive, and stayed there.

Or had Brigitte died, like her father, before the war ended?

The task before Quenby seemed more than daunting. It seemed impossible.

But Brigitte had carved her initials in that wall back on Mulberry Lane. If she wanted Dietmar to find her, at least while she was with the Terrells, perhaps she'd continued to leave a trail along the way. Quenby could only hope time hadn't erased anything else she'd left behind.

For now, like Mr. Knight, she would cling to the hope that Brigitte was still alive.

There were three long hours before she was supposed to meet

Lucas for breakfast. She returned to her bed, yearning for peaceful sleep, but the lonely girl swept back into her mind.

Sitting up, she flipped on the light again and reached for the Gideon Bible in the drawer beside her bed. When she was a child, her grandmother liked to read to her from Proverbs. And Jesus' words in the Gospels.

She found the verse in Matthew.

"For My yoke is easy and My burden is light."

Quenby pulled her knees up to her chest, praying quietly as she'd done over the years that Jesus would do more than help her carry the heavy load of her past. That He would take it away.

She rocked back and forth a few times before resting back against the pillows. As she fell asleep, the pain from her childhood seemed to swallow her again. Rejection. Loneliness. Fear. But this time when she dreamed, there was someone beside the girl. A warm presence. An elderly man holding out his hand. And the girl wasn't scared of him at all.

The man led her through the crowd, and he must have been invisible as well for no one looked at him either.

He guided her to the grassy banks of a stream, to a picnic awaiting them on a crimson blanket. The girl ate the cold cucumber sandwiches prepared for her, gulped the lemonade. Then she swam in the clear waters by the waterfall. Safe. Her stomach full.

The man watched over her while she slept, and when she woke, he held out his hand again.

The alarm woke Quenby, but this time she wished she could slip back into her dream, to see where the girl went. To make sure the man didn't abandon her.

It seemed, in her dream, that he wanted to rescue the girl from her fear and her loneliness. It seemed that perhaps he understood what it was like to be rejected too.

Morning light warmed her room as she leaned back against the headboard. Outside the window, a sailboat drifted toward the channel, preparing to dance with the wind.

Perhaps God did want peace for her and for Brigitte. Not sadness or despair.

Perhaps He didn't want any of His children to be alone.

Chapter 29

Mill House, April 1941

One minute. That's how long it took for Olivia to begin accosting him after he stepped through the cottage door. Instead of greeting him with a kiss, Olivia stood by the kitchen sink, her lips pressed in a firm line. "You said you'd come every weekend."

Eddie shoved aside two dirty plates and dropped the box of food onto the kitchen table. She tore open the box and rummaged through the tins of Spam and tomato soup, pushing aside the dried vegetables and tea until she found a block of government cheddar.

"The dolt from London came back multiple times after you left," he tried to explain. "I couldn't travel until he gave up or he might suspect we'd done something wrong."

"The investigation is done?" she asked, her mouth full of cheese.

He nodded. "Cold as ice. The man couldn't find anything except the parachute."

Truth was that Inspector Hill had returned only once since Olivia left, on his way to investigate another parachute that was found farther south. He'd found no trace of Roger or evidence that anyone on the estate had assisted a German parachutist. Eddie told the man his wife had left him, so he didn't inquire again about Olivia. And the photos were buried safely under the floorboard upstairs, in case the detective searched the house.

"Did you receive my parcels?" he asked.

"The postman brought them, but there wasn't enough food for the girl and me."

"Everyone is rationing."

"There is plenty of food at Breydon Court," she insisted.

"I'll start sending you boxes twice a week."

"Once a week, Eddie. You can bring the second one when you visit on Saturdays."

He glanced around the dirty room, not wanting to stay another minute in this place, much less an entire Saturday. All Olivia had to do was keep house and prepare for the guests that Lady Ricker sent her way. Had she forgotten how to use a broom? Or how to coax the girl to do it for her?

He tested the legs of a rickety chair before he sat in it. "Where's the girl?"

"Locked in her room." She pointed toward a closed door. "She tried to run away right after we arrived, but she returned the next day."

He opened a tin of biscuits and ate one. "I wish we could let her run."

She took her place across the table from him, her hazel eyes grim. "This business is going to be the death of us, Eddie."

Her laziness might be the death of them, but he kept that thought to himself. Lady Ricker had made him swear to keep Olivia as happy as possible, her stomach full, until their business was over. "It won't be long now."

"So you say—"

He reached across the table, pulling her hands into his. "We'll live like a lord and lady when the Germans take over. Think of it—a house of our own, as big as Breydon Court. The prettiest gowns money can buy. A lady's maid, even, to attend your needs."

Olivia's smile was lopsided, but at least it was a smile. Perhaps the idea of being a lady of her own home instead of this dump would keep her engaged.

"Right now, I'd be satisfied with a good meal. Roast chicken or beef Wellington."

"Beef will be the first item on our menu."

She shook away his hands and reached for an apple in the box. "Can you imagine us having our own cook?"

"That's the spirit, Olivia. You'll have anything you want. From jewels to jellies."

"Peach trifle?"

"Of course," he said, growing weary of the game, the talk of food. But everything was dependent on her faithfulness and the work of the girl. Lady Ricker would blame him if anything went awry, rescinding his lordship under the Führer.

"The lady from Tonbridge stopped to register the girl for school," he said.

"What did you tell her?"

"That another woman came after the bombing and accompanied the girl to an evacuee ship traveling to Canada."

"Was she satisfied?"

"I believe so, though she was quite frustrated that someone usurped her authority."

Olivia glanced toward the door. "So the girl is ours."

"Until the end of the war."

She knotted her hands together. "It can't end soon enough, Eddie."

"Agreed." If he left within the hour, he could be back to Breydon Court before dark. "I have more food in the car. Boxes of it."

"Did you bring my coupons?"

"I'm using them to buy food for you."

"I'd rather go into town myself—"

He shook his head. "No one from Newhaven can know you're here."

"The postman knows. And if he can ride his bike out here, I can walk to the grocer."

"It's much too far, and you can't leave the girl." He glanced around the cluttered room again. "It seems you have plenty of work to do here."

She groaned. "I'm bored out of my mind, Eddie."

"You and the girl can plant a garden." He lifted two bags of seeds from his pocket. "I brought you a hoe as well."

If she could grow some of her own food, he wouldn't have to make the journey often over that miserable road.

"I've never gardened before."

"I'll teach you," he said.

She didn't thank him. "We need more candles."

"I'll mail you some, straightaway."

"And another bucket."

No matter what he gave her, she always wanted more. "Why do you need another bucket?"

"To retrieve water from the well." She leaned into the table. "And one more thing."

"There's a war going on, Olivia. We can't have everything we'd like."

"I want some of Lady Ricker's magazines."

He stood up, irritated, but he calmed his demeanor. Lady Ricker certainly had plenty of old magazines stacked by her dressing table, saved from before the war. "I'm sure Lady Ricker would be glad to send you a few magazines with her letters."

Olivia carried the stack of dirty plates to the sink. "This is not what I envisioned when we married."

"It's only temporary," he said, trying to reassure her again. "We have to keep our eyes on the future."

"I can't see past tomorrow."

He handed her a letter for the girl to read over the wireless. "You'll have another guest soon. Next Thursday, if it's foggy enough to bring a boat up the river."

Tears filled her eyes. "I want to come home with you."

"I know you do." He kissed her forehead. "It won't be long now."

She opened the letter and read the words. "Lady Ricker is expecting a child?"

He shrugged. "I don't speak to her about such things."

"But you want me to tell the Germans about her baby?"

"Not you, the girl. But you'll have to translate it first." He pulled a German dictionary out of the box. It was much too risky for him to carry a German letter to her or put one through the post.

"Why must the Germans know about a baby?"

"Trust me, Olivia."

Still she pouted, as if she no longer believed him or in the hope of their mission. Putting down the letter, she walked toward the cobwebs on the window. "I could die out here, and you'd never know it."

"I would know," he said tenderly. "And you can't die. Your work here is going to win the war."

"Sometimes I think you're trying to get rid of me."

"I want what's best for you, for us," he said, pulling her close to him. "But I miss you."

"I miss you too."

Perhaps he'd stay for the night after all. Then he'd go back to Breydon Court at first light. "If nothing else, stay strong for me, Olivia."

"I'm trying—"

"Nothing will ever tear us apart."

CHAPTER 30

They found the abandoned flour mill where the River Ouse flattened and drifted between curtains of reeds along its banks. On the other side of the river, someone was swimming upstream, and Quenby shivered at the thought of being immersed in the murky water, unable to see what was under or beside you. She much preferred venturing on land so she had some visual, even if it was limited in these trees. And she much preferred being here with Lucas to being alone, in case Kyle discovered her on his land again.

Behind the mill, set back in the woodland, was a chimney shaft that towered above a moss-covered waterwheel and a weathered roof striped with rusty corrugated iron. Wild thyme sweetened the breeze as she and Lucas hiked into the forest, but as she scanned the ruined buildings, the rugged piles of wood and brick between the Queen Anne's lace, Quenby feared again that the growth and elements had destroyed the Mill House as well.

"I feel like we're hiking through a jungle," Lucas said as he ducked under a branch.

"Have you ever actually been in a jungle?" she asked. This time she was armed with insect repellent and a pair of rubber wellies she'd bought in town to combat the swarms of mosquitoes and the mud that had stained her trainers.

"I hiked through the Amazon when I was twenty." He lifted another branch and she walked under it. "How about you?"

She shook her head. "There's a reason I live in the city."

"Don't you swim in those ponds behind your flat?"

"I prefer being able to see through the water."

"No surprises?"

"I'm surprised enough in my work." Mud tugged at her wellies as they turned onto a soggy path, but she pressed on.

"I bet you've stumbled over all manner of secrets in your job."

"I don't stumble, Lucas. I search." With that declaration, her toe caught on the root of a tree and she fell forward, plunging into the grass. Her hand snagged on a briar, and she rolled away from the blackberry bush.

Lucas reached out his hand, but she didn't take it. Standing again on her own, she wiped the blood off her hand with a leaf. Her jeans and blouse were now coated with mud.

He reached out and plucked a leaf from her hair, his eyes filled with concern. "Are you okay?"

She held her head high. "Still searching."

"I'm glad you never stumble." His cheeks trembled with his words, a feeble attempt at suppressing his laugh.

"Let's move along."

"Of course, my lady."

She stuck out her tongue.

Lucas continued following her on the dense trail until they reached a cross path. She turned right.

"Look at this," Lucas said, and she stepped back. Intertwined in vines at the edge of the path was an old post. The two of them worked carefully to uncover the rusty sign underneath. *Kelmore Street.* The words she'd been searching for.

"Well done," Quenby said, and he glanced up, surprised at her affirmation. "I mean it."

His brown eyes smiled along with his lips. "Glad you approve."

Weeds paved the forgotten road, and trees on both sides had spread their limbs over the path, as if reaching across to shake the branches on the opposite side. Perhaps long ago this road had been wide enough for a vehicle, but there'd be no driving any sort of car or even a bicycle down it now.

As they walked, she searched the bramble for more ruins, but it wasn't until they reached the end of the lane that they found an old cottage, protected by a canopy of tall oak trees. The front window was shattered, though jagged pieces of glass edged the frame, reminding her of the isolated farmhouse in *Wuthering Heights*.

"This must be it," she said. No nameplate hung near the door, but it was the only house on the entire road.

"For once, I think we can agree."

She eyed it. "What a miserable place to live."

"Not if you're trying to keep a secret."

She took several pictures with her iPad, then tested her foot on the stoop. It held. "Now to find out what secrets the Terrells were trying to keep."

Lucas reached for her arm. "This isn't safe, Quenby."

"Of course it's not safe." She climbed another step. "Watch for nails on the floor."

"I mean the roof. It could collapse at any moment."

She turned back. "You've hiked through the Amazon!"

"With a guide. And there were no falling roofs where we went."

She switched her phone to the flashlight app. The front door was missing its knob, but when she pushed, it swung open. And a bird flew out.

A shriek escaped her mouth before she burst out laughing. Lucas joined her laughter. "Death by kamikaze swallow."

"You think there are more inside?" she asked, eyeing the door again.

He examined the eaves. "Probably."

She groaned. "That's fabulous."

"It's not the birds that concern me."

Quenby took a deep breath, trying to inhale courage. "I'm still going in."

"You want me to go first?"

"Yes, but I'd kick myself for being a coward."

He held the door wide for her. "I'll be right behind you then."

Dull light sifted through a mud-caked window, settling over the room like the bits of plaster that coated the couch, stone fireplace, and crippled kitchen table. The entire room smelled like mold and animal droppings, and tiny footprints, a hundred constellations of heels and toes, were embedded in the dusty floor around the furnishings. Hers was the only shoe print.

There were two plates on the wooden table. No food remained, but it was as if the occupants had rushed away from the house without even finishing their meal.

Lucas whistled when he stepped into the room, the floor creaking under him. "It's like time stopped here, decades ago."

To the right of the main room was a kitchen with a wooden sink, but no oven or refrigerator. No light switch for an electric bulb or pipes for running water. Olivia might have lived here for a season, but she certainly hadn't lived in luxury. Quenby eyed the chipped plates again, hoping that Brigitte had been the one sharing a meal.

Off the kitchen was a sloped tin roof with a toilet seat. An indoor outhouse of sorts. There were two bedrooms along a narrow corridor, one with a window still intact and the other with the broken window. Springs from a bed remained in one of the rooms and the other had an old cot. There were no wall closets in this house, but there was a small wardrobe in the larger room, the one with the bedsprings.

Quenby opened the wardrobe and found several articles of women's clothing. And a dozen British magazines from the 1930s— *Woman* and *Woman's Own*—along with several old issues of the American *Cosmopolitan*.

Instead of a wardrobe in the second room, wooden knobs were screwed into the wall. Quenby crossed her arms, wishing she could climb back up in a tree outside to think.

Why had Olivia moved from a comfortable home to this dilapidated place?

Scratch marks marred the bedroom walls, piles of leaves and debris cluttering the floor. But there was something else, below the middle knob on the wall. She leaned over to see it and realized she was looking at something carved into the wood.

She shone her flashlight on the wall, and her heart leapt when she saw the dual *B*'s etched together again.

Lucas stepped into the room. "We'll probably catch some sort of virus just by breathing this trash."

"That's what vaccinations are for." She held up the light to him. "Besides, one man's trash is another man's treasure."

"I'm pretty sure there's no treasure to be found in here."

"I wouldn't be so certain." Her gaze fell to the floorboards below the initials.

Had Brigitte hidden something underneath her initials? Quenby tapped the board with her toe. It was held in place by a nail, but the rest seemed loose to her.

She knelt beside it. "Think we can pry this off?"

"I thought we were avoiding nails," he said, though he leaned down next to her.

"Changed my mind."

"Typical," he quipped, but she ignored him.

Together they managed to remove the floorboard without injuring themselves. And Quenby's heart began to race. Inside was another tin. "See?" she whispered. "Treasure."

Reaching into the crevice, she pulled out the tin, opened the lid. Lucas shone the light from his phone over it.

Inside was a fountain pen with a silver star on the cap. A German Montblanc, like Grammy used to have. Underneath was a small stack of folded paper. Letters. Perhaps a dozen of them. They were letters from Lady Ricker to Olivia, written in English, but on the back of each paper was a letter in German as well, dated by month starting in September 1941. They looked as if they'd been scribbled by a child, each letter signed with a simple *B*.

Brigitte would have been almost twelve when she was writing these. Perhaps she hadn't been able to practice her handwriting since she left Germany. Or perhaps she was in a hurry. Either way, it was the confirmation Quenby needed. Brigitte had remained in England, at least after her short stay on Mulberry Lane, and her story was intertwined with Lady Ricker's.

She stood up, the tin in both hands. "Brigitte left us a trail."

"Left Mr. Knight a trail."

"Of course," she said, silently chiding herself. She'd already let this search become too personal, thinking the girl was leaving clues for her. "The point is, Brigitte wanted to be found."

"And you'll find her, Quenby."

The girl from her dream flashed back into her mind. "I hope so."

And she hoped the contents of these letters would be life-giving for Mr. Knight.

When they reached the river, Lucas brushed off the leaves on a felled log, and they sat side by side to look at the first letter. Quenby snapped a picture of it with her phone, front and back.

On the front of each letter were Lady Ricker's mundane reports about her baby and the weather and a trip she was planning up to Swindon. On the back sides, the letters were much longer, the German words written in block instead of cursive.

Quenby had learned German from the old fairy tales that Grammy liked to tell her before bed, the ones passed on from the Brothers Grimm. She preferred stories with happy endings, but she'd learned at a young age how a story could haunt you. And teach you about morality.

She opened her iPad case to type the English translation, but before she could attempt to translate Brigitte's words, she had to decipher her handwriting.

"You want me to help?" Lucas asked, scooting closer to her.

"You know German?"

"No, but—" he held up his phone—"Google is fluent."

"As long as nothing is misspelled."

"I'll risk it."

"I can read some German." The breeze fluttered the letter in her lap, and she lifted it. "Perhaps we can figure out what she wrote together."

She read Lady Ricker's letter out loud first—about the stresses of trying to dress her new baby with the clothing rations, about baby's feeding at 5 p.m., about a gift she was sending in a fortnight.

Then she turned to the note in German and scanned Brigitte's first line about Frau Terrell. Slowly, with the help of Lucas and his phone, she began to unravel the girl's words.

SEPTEMBER 1941

Frau Terrell translates Lady Ricker's letters into broken German and demands I read her words into the wireless, even if they make little sense. So I read about a baby boy. Things that interest only L.R. and, for some reason, the Germans. When her boy sleeps. What he wears. When he goes to London with his mother.

I wish I could go to London with my mother. Wish I could go anyplace without Frau Terrell. I tried to run away this spring, but I never found the town. Now Frau Terrell won't let me outside.

She hovers over me when I speak into the wireless that one of Hitler's men left behind. Even though she doesn't understand my words, she tells me I must be precise.

So I am precise. Except with a word or two. Those I change.

OCTOBER 1941

No matter how hard I work, this house refuses to stay clean, as if we are unwelcome guests under its roof. Frau Terrell found a hammer someplace. And a small box of nails. She sent me up to the roof to fix a board that had fallen over the front door.

I kept the hammer overnight—and one of the nails. While she slept, I nailed down the loose board in my room. Now I won't worry that she'll find my letters, buried in the floor.

Frau Terrell only speaks to me when she requires me to work. Like Cinderella and her rotten stepmother.

Girl, fix the roof. Girl, sweep the floor. Girl, read the letter. I hate being called girl, but my name is my secret.

In the old story, Cinderella clung to hope in spite of the cruelness. And she watered the wishing tree outside her home with her tears. Her voice wasn't her own inside the house either, but by her tree, she prayed. And a little white dove brought her what she needed most.

Still, I wish I'd never screamed, that night when Roger was here. Wish Frau Terrell didn't know I could speak.

Frau has my voice when she needs it, but I'll never tell her my name. And I've decided, just this moment, that I'm no longer calling the Terrells by their surname either, even in my mind. From now on, it's Herr and Frau. Names that mean nothing really.

For Herr and Frau are meaningless to me.

NOVEMBER 1941

It's autumn now, and I feel more like Gretel these days than Cinderella, lost in the deep woods. Without a Hansel.

There's no Hansel, but there is a witch in my story. And some days I wonder if she might try to devour me. There's a look in her eyes, of hunger and rage, so I stay in my caged room alone, with the rats.

In the old fairy tale, Gretel and Hansel are abandoned by parents who led them into the woods. Neither my mama nor papa wanted to leave me—they were taken away—but I know what it's like to be alone.

Instead of a wishing tree, Gretel prayed to God in the tale. And God rescued her.

There is no candy house here. No hidden jewels to find. But I believe there is a God who can rescue me. So I continue to pray, every night. But sometimes, on the worst nights, when the darkness coils around me, when my door and window are locked and the rats chatter, my mind turns wicked.

I imagine Dietmar with pieces of bread, leading me to this house before he ran away, wanting to be rid of me. But in the daylight, I refuse to believe that Dietmar led me here. And I refuse to believe God will leave me.

I miss Dietmar so much it aches my whole body. I pray he is well. And I pray he returns to me, before more of Hitler's men come.

When Frau lets me back outside, I'll wait for my Hansel at the edge of the forest.

So the witch won't catch him too.

CHAPTER 31

Quenby tucked the letters back into the tin before glancing up at the riverbank. So Lady Ricker's letter at the archives wasn't meaningless after all. Her letters, it seemed, were meant for someone other than Olivia.

Closing her eyes, Quenby leaned back against a rock behind the log. It was exhausting, not just translating but hearing the story in Brigitte's words.

She and Lucas had been working for hours—stumbling, really—through this translation. Several motorboats and a canoe had sailed past on the river, but no cars had passed them on the rural road leading toward Newhaven. For a moment, she felt as if she'd stepped back into the trappings of Brigitte's world.

In her mind's eye, Quenby could see the house made of cake and sugar, hidden in the bleak forest. A scared, hungry girl. The witch.

In the German tale, the children escaped from the house, their arms full of precious stones and pearls.

Did Brigitte manage to escape? Or had the witch—or Hitler's men—hurt her?

Sitting up, Quenby reached for another letter, but her eyes blurred when she scanned Brigitte's German words, grief overflowing again. Unlike Quenby, Brigitte hadn't had a grandmother left to rescue her.

"It sounds as if Olivia Terrell operated some sort of safe house during the war," Lucas said, dumbfounded by their discovery.

Quenby nodded slowly. "She must have been part of Lady Ricker's network."

"So that's why she moved here. For privacy."

"And she used Brigitte's German to communicate with her friends across the channel," Quenby said, piecing it together. She glanced back at the abandoned mill, the tangled grove of trees around it. At the slow-moving current of the river. Anyone looking for her would have had to search hard to find this place.

"Perhaps the same person who took the pictures of Biggin Hill photographed a map to the Mill House."

"I refuse to believe that Dietmar led me here."

Brigitte's words tumbled in Quenby's mind. How was she supposed to tell Mr. Knight that Brigitte had longed for him deeply but he'd never come?

"She thought Dietmar had abandoned her," Quenby said softly.

"Brigitte didn't know that Dietmar was trapped too. That he wanted to find her."

"It could have changed everything for her to have that glimmer of hope for the future."

"She didn't lose hope, Quenby."

But it seemed to her that the girl's confidence in her friend and any hope for her future was slipping away.

Lucas reached for another one of Lady Ricker's letters in the tin, scanning the English words about her baby. "You'd think a story on the Ricker scandal would be championed at WNS."

"My publisher doesn't see it that way."

"So write it for someone else."

"I signed a noncompete, with you and the syndicate."

He sighed. "Sometimes I hate contracts."

She began to translate the letter in her hands, written in January 1942, but Lucas stopped her. "How many more letters are there?"

She counted them. "Six."

"Seems like we need a break before we read more."

As much as she wanted to continue, he was right. Every lobe in her brain ached. "We could work while we eat."

He nodded. "Then we'll phone Mr. Knight, after we finish the translations."

She smoothed her hand over the top of the tin. The news of finding the letters would be welcomed, but the contents so far might hurt the man. "What happens if the rest of the letters are just as bleak?"

"Mr. Knight knows this story may not have a happy ending. He wants resolution."

"But I want a happy ending for him."

"As we all do." They started walking toward the Range Rover. "Either way, Mr. Knight will want to know about the letters."

"I thought you were keeping these kinds of things from him."

"It's only the middle of the story, Quenby."

She slid into the passenger seat, and as Lucas turned the SUV toward Newhaven, she tried to cling to the dream she'd had last night, of the girl picnicking with a God-like man who cared for her. Was it a premonition? Preparing her for the fact that Brigitte had indeed died as a girl? Perhaps she was with Jesus now. No longer hungry or lonely or afraid.

"Before we go to town . . ." Lucas stopped on the side of the empty road, at the edge of the grassy bank. "I think it's time for you to do something else unexpected."

She eyed the murky river on their left. "Does it involve swimming?"

"No." He turned the car off again and removed the key from the ignition. "It involves steering."

She glanced over her right shoulder at him, horrified. "I'm not driving."

His arm swept across the dashboard as if the woods and river were on display. "No better place to learn than out here."

"I can drive just fine, Lucas. It's the other drivers who won't want me on an English road."

He glanced in his mirror and made a grand show of turning around in his seat. "There's no traffic out here."

She crossed her arms. Silent.

He smiled. "Think of it as an opportunity."

"One that I don't want to take."

"I'm here to change your life, Quenby Vaughn."

Her arms were still crossed, but she loosened them. "It sounds like you're trying to hawk a time-share."

"If you learn to drive, you can borrow my car to explore on your own." He dangled the keys in front of her, sweeping them back and forth like he was trying to hypnotize her.

Her arms fell to her sides. "And leave you in London?"

He tapped the steering wheel's leather cover. "If you master this."

For a split second, the thought crossed her mind that she'd begun to enjoy Lucas's company, but it would be more convenient—for him and for her—if she could travel around on her own. Then he wouldn't have to leave the office to chauffeur.

She eyed the keys. "No wonder you went into law."

"Why's that?"

"You've fine-tuned the art of manipulation."

His face grew serious. "I'm fairly certain that I can't talk you into doing anything you don't want to do."

"True enough." She swiped the keys from him. "I'll try it."

He clicked his seat belt on the passenger side as she restarted the vehicle. Then she pressed the accelerator. It felt strange to be behind a wheel again. Stranger still to be driving a car on the left-hand side.

She steered carefully, tires tracing the edge of the riverbank.

Lucas leaned his chair back. "You're doing it!"

"I guess I am."

They rounded another curve. "Here comes a tractor," Lucas said.

Quenby groaned when she saw the red tractor driving toward them. The same one Kyle had been riding to his barn.

She wished she could duck under the console. Would have, actually, if she hadn't been in the driver's seat.

When Kyle saw her, he waved. Then he swerved his tractor toward her. It was ever so slight but enough to throw her off. She overcorrected to her left, and the tires hit the mud. Then the grass.

"Go right," Lucas urged, but it was too late.

When Quenby pressed on the accelerator, the car just roared back at her, the tires buried deep in the sediment.

In the rearview mirror, she saw Kyle turn the tractor around.

Just great.

Chapter 32

Mama used to sing to her as she fell asleep on Christmas Eve. She had the prettiest voice. A golden thread stitching together each note. Every word.

How Brigitte had loved to hear her mama sing.

There would be no celebrating Christmas in this old house. She wouldn't even know the holiday was tomorrow except she'd heard one of Hitler's men wish Frau a happy Christmas before he left tonight. Then, through the crack near her door, where the wood no longer fit into the frame, she'd watched him kiss Frau on the lips.

How could anyone kiss that woman?

Except for Herr. It seemed they deserved each other. They kissed and they fought and then they kissed again. It was like hearing the bombs in the distance—she hardly registered the bombs or the yelling anymore.

Hitler's man said he was going north. To sabotage an airfield. She didn't know this English word—*sabotage*—but she doubted he was up to anything good. He and his friends might dress like the British, but they meant this country and her people great harm.

One day, when she left here, she would tell someone what the Terrells were doing. That these men knew how to find the house. That they talked about this sabotage and the Third Reich.

Most of them pretended she wasn't there, except when they needed her voice. They laughed with Frau while Brigitte was in her room. Saying it wouldn't be long now before Germany won the war.

Only one man really noticed her, and that's because she stole his black fountain pen so she could write more letters. He searched the cottage for an hour but never found it under her floor. Not that stealing was right—Mama would probably have punished her for it—but she had this burning need to write. Almost as strong as her pangs of hunger when their parcels were late to arrive. Or Hitler's men ate all their food.

On the other side of the channel, someone was listening to her, to know when to send the men. And when the men arrived. The pen, she told herself, was payment for her voice.

Frau thought Brigitte was throwing all of Lady Ricker's letters into the fire, but she was tossing only the German translations into the flames. The English versions she hid inside her blouse before taking them to her room.

Even last summer, Frau made her build a fire for the letters. No matter how hot it was. No matter that she wouldn't let Brigitte outside. She still insisted on burning the words.

But these days, Frau didn't watch her as closely as she used to. Sometimes let her wander in the trees in the cold, almost as if she wanted Brigitte to run again. As if she were the source of Frau's troubles instead of her husband. Or Lady Ricker.

Brigitte was twelve now, and when Frau let her wander, she

searched for a town, for someone like the Belgian monks who could help her escape her prison cell, but it seemed the buildings she saw when they first arrived were all a mirage. Or perhaps it had been a dream. She'd ask the postman, but Frau locked her door whenever he knocked and her window to the outside was still jammed.

She was going to fix the window, so she could breathe in river and pine. And so one day she could run back to Dietmar.

Since there was no place for her to run now, she closed her eyes on these cold evenings and began to dream. Behind the veil of darkness, she could imagine anything. The taste of roast duck and potato dumplings. Gingerbread and *Glühwein*. The sound of singing that poured from the churches. The lights of the Christmas markets at night.

Any light at all.

Stille Nacht! Heilige Nacht!

All is calm, all is bright.

Brigitte sang the words in her head so no one could hear. Inviting the peace birthed that night to settle into her room as well.

CHAPTER 33

Lucas sprayed pink soap out of the wand, covering his Range Rover with foam in the self-service bay. Thankfully, mud seemed to be the only damage done to his vehicle, and the soap and water drained that away.

The wand in hand, Lucas rounded the car a second time, holding it like he was some sort of commander blasting a machine gun. He was still fuming, it seemed, about Kyle Logan's bravado when he helped them extricate the car. The man had embraced his role as rescuer and rural transportation expert, dispensing tip after tip about driving on back roads and how to remove oneself from the clutches of mud.

Lucas was not impressed.

Pink globs bounced off the oversoaped car, landing on Quenby's sleeve streaked with mud from her fall. She flicked them off. "It's already clean," she said from behind him.

Lucas sprayed another round across the hood—or bonnet, as the British called it. "He forced us off the road just so he could talk to you."

"Oh, please."

"Seriously, he couldn't stop flirting with you. Didn't even care that I was with you—"

"Technically, you're not *with* me, Lucas."

"Of course not, but the man doesn't know that," he growled. "What if I *was* with you?"

"Then you'd have the right to be offended."

He flicked the switch on the wall, and a stream of water sprayed from the wand. "I reserve the right to be offended either way."

She crossed her arms. "The right to expunge records. The right to be offended. I need to become a lawyer." When he turned, a plume of water sprayed over her shoulder, sprinkling down on her clothes. "Lucas!"

He turned back toward the SUV, but not before she saw the smirk on his face. "My apologies."

"Not accepted," she said, trying to shake the water off her blouse. "You were the one who asked me to drive."

He released the trigger, the wand dropping to his side. "I'm not mad at you, Quenby. The guy is an idiot. He could have hurt both of us, fanning his tail like that to get your attention."

She laughed at the image of Kyle as a peacock. "I'm glad there's no damage, unless you count my pride."

Then again, her pride had been compromised—completely decimated, actually—when she met Lucas at her door a week ago in ratty shorts and a T-shirt, void of any sort of plumage. Not to mention her bragging earlier in the forest, right before she tripped and landed in the mud.

"I still want to teach you how to drive," he said, sliding the wand into its holder.

"Are you serious?"

"Completely."

"But I ran your car off the road."

"Much better than running into that guy, though I think he would have preferred you left a dent or two in his tractor. Then you'd have to contact him again."

"I'm not the least bit interested in Kyle Logan."

"Glad to hear it. You deserve a man who respects you."

Her face warmed. "Thank you."

He pointed toward the car. "Should we try for lunch again?"

"As long as you drive."

"Fair enough."

They found a café up on Castle Hill, overlooking the English Channel. Lucas ordered two egg and cress sandwiches along with a bottle of San Pellegrino to share. Quenby drank half the bottle of bubbly water before she started thinking clearly again.

Strange that Lucas would trust her to drive after she'd almost wrecked his vehicle. And even stranger that he'd been so ruffled by Kyle's display of feathers this afternoon.

After they finished their sandwiches, and the server brought coffee, Quenby set the tin of letters on the wooden slats of the table. The proprietor had told them they could sit outside all afternoon if they wanted, and it might take them that long to translate the rest of Brigitte's words.

She was anxious to find out what happened to Brigitte, of course, but the anxiety warred with a feeling of dread. What if the remaining letters were more dismal than the others? Their search could end here, in this café, at the base of this tin.

She took out the old wooden princess that Mr. Knight had given her and placed it on the table beside her, as if Brigitte were here with them as well. Then she opened the January 1942 letter again.

She and Lucas began to translate it together.

*Hitler's men only come when the weather cooperates,
meaning that fog is heavy over the trees. The numbers in Lady
Ricker's letters correspond with the times our guests arrive, so
I changed the number in the last letter, from nine to seven, and
waited for a hazy night.*

*I didn't know for certain how Hitler's men arrived, but their
trousers are usually soaked when Frau fetches them, their boots
coated with mud. I snuck out the front door last night, trekking
down to the river in the fog—so like the night Dietmar and
I crossed the channel. Then I hid behind the bars of rush.*

*There was no sound of a motor, but the boat arrived
suddenly, as if emerging from the deep. Like one of the
undersea boats the German POWs talked about at
Breydon Court.*

*In seconds, a man climbed over the rubber side, dressed like
some of the others in a British uniform, his trousers rolled up
high. A backpack was secured over his shoulders, and each of his
hands clutched a boot as he waded through the shallow water,
making him look like a duck flapping its wings.*

*When he stepped onto the bank, the boat vanished back in
the fog. The man looked both ways, seemingly lost below the
mill, before he sat down on a flat rock to tie his boots.*

*I made ticking noises from my fortress of reeds. Like a bush
cricket. Then I couldn't seem to help myself. A shriek escaped
my lips. Wild and strong.*

*Startled, he stood up, patting his side for something that
didn't seem to be there.*

*I wailed again, loud and long like a banshee. Like
a sea monster waiting to devour whoever dared wake him
from his sleep.*

*Hitler's man sprinted up the riverbank, swearing in our
shared language.*

*I doubled over as he ran, in a vain attempt to stop my
laughter. But I couldn't help it. It felt good to yell and laugh.
To watch Hitler's man run the other way.*

*For the first time since Frau and I arrived, my voice chased
evil away instead of inviting it through our front door.*

*Frau went to find the man at nine that night, but all she
found was a pair of leather boots.*

Quenby put down the letter, but her eyes didn't wander from
the writing. Not only was Brigitte's story linked to Lady Ricker, but
here was proof that linked Lady Ricker directly with the espionage
mentioned in the National Archives file, her letters orchestrating the
delivery of Nazi agents onto England's shores.

Her fingers drummed on paper, itching to write the lead for
a story piecing together in her head. If only Evan would let her write
it, she could leave Brigitte's name out of the story. Her sources would
remain confidential, for Mr. Knight's sake.

"You still with me?" Lucas asked.

Blinking, Quenby looked over at him.

"You've gone back again, haven't you? About seventy years ago?"

She shifted in her chair. After she found out what happened to
Brigitte, she'd ask Chandler to speak with Evan about moving forward with this story. Or if Evan did call her directly, she'd try to
convince him herself.

She slipped the letter to the bottom of the stack. "Good for
Brigitte for fighting back against the evil the best she could."

"I wonder if the Terrells ever discovered that she was working
against them," he said.

"If they did, they would have tried to silence her for good." The
Terrells or Lady Ricker couldn't have let her live, especially after
the Germans lost the war. Traitors were killed, and Brigitte knew
the secrets that could convict all of them.

There would be some sort of grim relief in knowing Brigitte escaped from the Terrells' abuse, yet in her heart, she hoped Brigitte had survived this, even thrived. For Mr. Knight's sake.

Lucas poured cream into his coffee. "Her resilience is exemplary."

"She kept thinking that Dietmar was coming for her."

"And he did."

She looked down at the next letter. "Where did you go?"

MARCH 1942

Herr rarely comes now, but a box of food arrives each week from Breydon Court, along with L.R.'s letters. At least he doesn't let us starve.

Frau seems to think he will love her forever, but Herr loves her as much as he loves the hoe he left in the shed. Both are useful to him. For now.

I fear what will happen when he has no need for her or me anymore.

SEPTEMBER 1942

The letters stopped coming for several months, so I had no paper to write. But then a letter. And a week later, another of Hitler's men.

Lothar ate. A lot. And he stayed much too long before he went wherever these men go.

After he left, I had to scrounge for berries and nuts and what was left in our garden since nothing remained from our box.

Lothar also came into my little room before he left, late at night. But he wasn't like Roger. Instead of shaking me, he slithered up to my cot and touched me. Where no one should touch.

When I screamed, Frau ran into the room. I didn't think she would help, but she coaxed Lothar to leave. Said he could come back in a year or two.

Then she locked my door. I heard them laughing on the other side.

She thinks I still don't understand much English, but I understand the important words. From now on, when the men come, I will sleep with my cot against the door. And wish I had Roger's gun.

OCTOBER 1942

Herr finally came, and he was angry. The postman directed Frau to town.

Herr said she shouldn't have registered for coupons there. Frau said if she hadn't, both she and I would have starved. And frozen to death since he'd forgotten to send matches for our fire.

Wood and water we have aplenty, but food is scarce, the boxes coming infrequently now. At least with Frau's coupons we have something to eat. And with the matches we are warm.

I tried to follow Frau to town once but realized I couldn't go. Can you imagine? Frau has new clothing, but mine is tattered and stained, like I've been digging through cinders. And I smell worse than Roger on that night we came to this place that can hardly be regarded as a home. The people in town would run me out, as if I were a wild cat.

Bombs fell last night, not far from here. I looked outside for flames, like I'd seen back in Breydon Court, but there was nothing except black.

Were Hitler's men dropping bombs nearby? Or was it the British, trying to bomb our house?

Herr says Germany is winning the war, though we have no other news of it except when Hitler's men come.

I pray the good men win.

I pray they let me go free.

I pray I never have to talk again.

DECEMBER 1942

Today I turned thirteen.

I took Dietmar's knight into the forest and sat on a log by the river, surrounded by the company of birds. I pretended to eat cake and toast myself with wine. Pretended I was back home under my father's magnolia tree, wishing like Cinderella that everyone I loved was celebrating with me.

It's been more than two years now since Dietmar and I left home. I can no longer remember Papa's face, but if he were here, he would toast to my thirteen years. He would say he was proud of me. And Dietmar would carve me something special to commemorate the day.

Dietmar's not coming for me. I know that now. And even if I ran from here, I wouldn't know how to find him.

If he's still alive, Dietmar would be fifteen. A man.

I pray that my friend is safe, wherever he is. That he's warm and fed.

That someone celebrated his fifteenth birthday with him.

JANUARY 1943

The wind changed again today, blowing from the east.

And I think, perhaps, that I've found a new friend.

Chapter 34

Breydon Court, January 1943

"Oh, Eddie," Lady Ricker sighed as she rested back on the satin pillows, her curls coiling around her face. "I must get dressed for the party."

He twirled her dark hair in his fingers, examining the lace on her negligee as he leaned on one arm. "But you look smashing just the way you are."

She laughed as she always did when he complimented her. "Admiral and Mrs. Drague will be expecting lipstick and jewels for New Year's."

"Admiral Drague is always expecting something."

She traced her finger along the edge of his chin. "Thanks to you, our little operation on the hill was successful again."

"What did they take out?"

"The barracks and at least two hangars."

Lady Ricker had assured him that he would be rewarded handsomely for his loyalty and work. Still, he'd made five extra photographs and hidden them under the floor for collateral, so he could prove his allegiance after the war. Just in case her ladyship tried to cross him.

After kissing him, Lady Ricker inched to the opposite side of the bed, taking a cigarette from her gilded case. "How is Olivia making out?"

"I don't want to talk about her."

She lit the cigarette. "It's a dreadful shack," she said, clearly ignoring his desire not to discuss his wife. "I fear for her health."

"She's not happy, but she's well enough."

She took a long drag of the cigarette and the smoke settled over the bed. "You must work to keep her happy, Eddie."

"I send her food and supplies, but nothing pleases her."

"I will have Cook make some nice cakes to take with you when you visit this weekend."

"I wasn't planning a visit—"

"Is Olivia still caring for the girl?"

"Of course." Except the girl wasn't so much of a girl anymore. Over the past months, she'd developed into a woman. A pretty one, even with her tattered clothing.

Perhaps next time he'd bring a frock for her instead of Olivia. Perhaps she would show him a little appreciation for his efforts.

Lady Ricker crushed her cigarette in a tray. "We must keep the girl happy too."

"I will ensure her happiness."

"Very noble of you."

"I have another job—"

The telephone interrupted her, and when she answered it, Eddie heard a man speaking rapidly on the other end, saw her face pale.

"How long ago?" she demanded before hanging up the phone.

"Who was that?" he asked.

She reached for her robe. "You must leave here."

"But the job—"

She waved her hand. "We'll discuss it later."

He wasn't worried. Her bedroom door was locked, and the corridor would be clear. Lady Ricker demanded all of her staff stay away while she enjoyed her afternoon naps.

When the doorknob rattled, Lady Ricker swore. Eddie swiped his trousers from off a chair, trying to devise some sort of story if Lord Ricker had returned early from London or the nanny needed something yet again for the baby boy.

But a young woman glided into the bedroom, dangling a key in one hand. She eyed his bare chest, laughing. "Well, hello there."

Eddie rapidly buttoned his shirt.

"Apparently the New Year's party has already begun." A mink fur was wrapped over her bare shoulders, across the low sleeves of her shimmering blue dress, but her most prominent feature was her protruding stomach. Clearly the woman was expecting a child and had no qualms in letting the world know.

"Who are you?" he demanded.

A smile slid smoothly across her lips, glistening from a fresh coat of gloss. "I'm a secret." The woman walked toward the bed. "Hello, Mummy."

Her ladyship straightened her shoulders like a soldier preparing for a battle. "Hush, Rosalind."

When the woman saw Lady Ricker's attire, she looked back at Eddie. Then she laughed again. A gut-wrenching, awful laugh that echoed down the corridor.

His gaze shuttled between the two women. Was Rosalind really Lady Ricker's daughter?

Eddie closed the door so none of the servants would hear.

"The maid said you weren't to be disturbed. I can see why." Her

CATCHING THE WIND

gaze traveled from the top of Eddie's head down to his toes. "Where'd she find you?"

Lady Ricker responded. "He was a photographer for *London Life*."

Rosalind cocked her head. "And now?"

It was none of her business what he did now.

"Let me guess." She eyed him again. "You were pressed into the service of agriculture so you won't be called up."

"I manage the gardens," he said, refusing to let this woman humiliate him, even if she was Lady Ricker's daughter.

Rosalind turned back toward her ladyship. "Stop looking at me like that, Mummy. I thought you'd welcome me home."

Lady Ricker tied the cord around her robe. "We have friends coming soon. And Lord Ricker."

Rosalind shrugged. "I'm not the one sleeping with the gardener."

Lady Ricker studied her stomach. "You've been sleeping with someone."

"A distinguished gentleman. To make you proud." Rosalind collapsed onto a chair, looking out over the deer park covered in a fresh snow. "It's been a long journey."

Eddie wasn't certain what to say. He'd known Lady Ricker had been married before she'd moved to England. Her first husband, the staff had whispered, owned half of Boston. But Eddie had been working here for almost four years now and no one had whispered about a daughter.

Rosalind tossed off her leather pumps. One of the heels was missing. "Papa sends his love."

Eddie looked between the two women before settling his gaze on Lady Ricker. He'd known she had other lovers over the years, but thought she'd ended all of her relationships, except perhaps with Admiral Drague. "Who's her father?"

Lady Ricker lit another cigarette and then took a long drag on it. "No one of significance."

Rosalind swept her hands around the upholstered arms of the chair. "He'll be thrilled to hear you say that."

Anger boiled inside him. The women were playing some sort of game, and he wasn't going to play along with them. "Where's your father?" he asked.

"In Paris at the moment, meeting with Goebbels." Rosalind leaned back on the chair, closed her eyes. "I'm famished."

"Eddie will fetch you some food."

"Oh, would you, Eddie?" She glanced over, winking at him.

"Don't say anything to the others about her," Lady Ricker commanded.

"Of course not."

He looked away, deciding right then and there that the sooner Rosalind was gone, the better it would be for them all.

CHAPTER 35

Quenby chugged down a cup of Colombian coffee made in her room's Keurig. She'd been up much of the night, rereading the translations of Brigitte's letters on her iPad, trying to piece together any hint of where Brigitte might have gone after the abrupt ending of her story in 1943.

Maybe she ran away with her new friend in spite of her fears. Or maybe another one of Hitler's men had broken into her room, and she'd decided to run from him.

God forbid that any of those men had their way with her. The thought of it made Quenby's stomach roll.

If Brigitte had left with an acquaintance, it meant someone else knew where she went, but nothing in her letter hinted at the age, nationality, or even gender of this mystery friend.

After showering, Quenby dressed in cropped jeans and a taupe blouse, switching her clumsy wellies to summer sandals since they had no plans to trek back into the forest this morning. She and Lucas would return to London today, though she wasn't anxious to go home. Some days she liked getting lost in the crowds, but other days, like today, she didn't want to be lost at all.

Back in her flat, she would read through the letters one more time, along with her notes, before she continued her search.

At a quarter till eight, she met Lucas down in the small library on the bottom floor of her inn. After closing the door behind her, she joined him on the formal settee. His laptop was propped up on a stack of books, the screen facing them as they waited for Mr. Knight's morning call.

Mr. Knight's face was darkened by shadows on the screen, the windows behind his desk black. It was almost midnight in the San Juans.

"Hello, Lucas," he greeted, as if the man beside her were his nephew or grandson.

"Good evening, sir." Lucas reached to adjust the brightness, and Mr. Knight's wild white hair filled up most of the screen.

Mr. Knight leaned forward, squinting. "Miss Vaughn?"

She leaned closer to the camera. "I'm here."

"Very good." He looked down at the desk beside him and picked up a stack of papers. "You've uncovered quite a bit already."

"It appears that Brigitte left a trail for you after all."

"My earlier investigators should have found the tin in Newhaven," he said.

She glanced at Lucas before turning back toward the screen. "You mean the one on Mulberry Lane."

"No." Mr. Knight shook his head. "At the Mill House."

"Your investigators knew about the Mill House?"

"Of course."

When she looked at Lucas again, he didn't look back at her. Heat crawled across her skin. Why had they been withholding information from her? And how much more did they know?

"Why didn't you—?" she started, but Lucas stopped her. Not with a word, to her or Mr. Knight, but he gently placed his hand on her knee, signaling her not to probe. At his touch, a tremor rocketed through her.

Clearing her throat, she decided to change direction. Later she would ask about the Mill House. It was completely unproductive for her to unearth a trail that had already been blazed.

"Did you read the letters we found?" she asked, not knowing whether Mr. Knight had found the letters as well in years past.

"Not yet." He looked down, and then his eyes returned to the screen. "Is she well?"

Quenby hesitated. "She was hungry and worried. She missed you."

"Any idea where she went?"

"Not yet."

"The Terrells, sir," Lucas said, inching closer to the camera. "It seems as if they were helping the Nazis."

Something flickered in his eyes, and Quenby wished she were on the other side of Mr. Knight's desk instead of studying a screen. "I suspected as much, with those photographs in their house."

"Mrs. Terrell moved to Newhaven to assist them during the war."

"With Brigitte?"

"I'm afraid so."

Sadness lingered on his face, and she guessed this was new information for him. Information she almost wished they hadn't found, for his sake.

It was too late to redeem Brigitte's life. Why dredge up this sadness when they had no influence on the outcome? Unfortunately, justice was too late in coming for people like Eddie and Olivia Terrell.

But then again, perhaps justice had already been served.

"I want you to keep searching," Mr. Knight said.

"Of course."

His eyes grew wide as if something had alarmed him. "But you must be careful, Brigitte."

Confused, Quenby wasn't certain how to respond.

Mr. Knight's screen shook, his head bouncing up and down on their monitor. "They'll try to stop you."

Lucas leaned forward, stealing away Quenby's view of the camera. "She didn't forget you, Mr. Knight."

There was a long pause before Mr. Knight responded. "I told her I would find her."

"We know, sir."

"And I will find her yet."

Lucas inched away from the screen, and Quenby saw Mr. Knight again, the man's hand pressed into his chin. "I pray God leads us to her, before it's too late."

Lucas ended their conversation, and then he disconnected the video chat.

Quenby turned toward him. "Too late for what?"

Lucas shrugged, closing the computer screen.

She scooted up on the upholstered seat. "Why wouldn't you let me ask about the Mill House?"

"Mr. Knight was confused."

"I'm confused! He called me Brigitte."

"I don't believe any of the past investigators came to Newhaven."

"But he said—"

Lucas's gaze trailed to the morning light that streamed through the window. "Sometimes his mind slips and takes him back to his youth. He's trying to stay present."

She paused. "How confused is he?"

"A little more each day. Some days there's more absence in his mind than presence."

"Hence the urgency," she whispered.

Lucas nodded. "He wants to find her now, before he forgets that he was looking."

"Poor man."

"He's a fighter, Quenby. Always has been."

"But he can't fight the battle against his brain."

"He has a team of doctors, the best in the world, fighting alongside him. And he has people like us who'll remember for him."

"Perhaps it's better for him to just remember the good."

"The good isn't what he usually remembers." He slid the laptop into his black messenger bag. Then he checked his watch. "I have to leave for London before noon."

"Can I catch a ride?" she joked.

He picked up his bag, and when their eyes met, a smile returned to his face. "Perhaps."

She stood beside him. "Perhaps what?"

"If you'll try driving again."

Quenby followed him out of the library, stopping beside him at the bottom of the steps. "I might actually damage your car this time."

"I'm willing to take that risk."

Courageous or stupid—she wasn't quite sure what to make of the man standing in front of her. "I'll drive—if you'll let me take back roads."

"As long as you stay on the pavement."

She tilted her head. "All four tires?"

He nodded. "Preferably no mud or grass or men named Kyle today."

❖

"We're going to be late." Lucas glanced at the clock on his dashboard as they circled a roundabout in Lambeth, wedged into the crush of London traffic.

"Late for what?"

"The concert," he said.

They'd traveled country roads most of the way up, stopping near Tonbridge so he could see the Terrells' former cottage and in Westerham for lunch. He'd taken the wheel once they reached London proper, an hour ago. Until then she had managed to keep all four tires on the road and a fair distance from any other vehicles, though she couldn't make any promises about mud or grass on the tires. Either way, she was quite proud of her feat. They'd had a good day together. Fun even.

"You should come with me to the concert," he said as he turned left onto Westminster Bridge.

"No luck finding a real date?"

"I didn't say that."

They crossed over the Thames, the London Eye circling above the river on their right, Big Ben standing stalwart on their left.

She pondered his question, her mind wandering. What kind of woman would Lucas Hough ask out on a date? Someone like Gwyneth Paltrow or more like Princess Kate? Probably a woman who knew all the rules of British etiquette, dating back to King James.

After they passed Westminster Abbey, Lucas turned left and parked on a side street.

"Please, Quenby." He flashed a puppy dog–esque look. One that was almost impossible for her to refuse.

"Please what?"

"Come with me."

He hopped out of the SUV as she reviewed her options. He couldn't drive her home, at least not until after his concert, but she could easily call for a ride or hop on the Tube a block away.

But then again, if he really wanted her to attend a concert, why shouldn't she accompany him? She might actually enjoy the music.

He opened her door.

"I'll go," she said, stringing her backpack over her shoulder. "But no promises that I'll stay."

"Fair enough." He locked the door behind her. "I think you'll enjoy it."

They walked down the street, and he turned toward the plaza that led into Westminster Abbey. An outdoor board said there was an evensong at three.

Quenby glanced at her watch. It was five minutes after.

The stained glass glowed inside the Gothic cathedral, the warmth of light filtering up to the tip of the vaulted ceilings, raining down on the solemn stone statues and marble floors. A chorus was singing at the other end of the abbey, their voices echoing off stone and glass. She and Lucas hurried across slabs inscribed with names like Sir Isaac Newton and David Livingstone, along an aisle flanking the immense nave as they rushed toward the music on the other side.

Had her mother visited this abbey during her childhood in London? Perhaps she'd even sung here in a choir.

Quenby remembered well the music that seemed to smolder somewhere deep inside Jocelyn, surging up through her lips on the best of days into the most beautiful songs. She even remembered, in choppy clips, her mother and father singing together. Their laughter as they stood hand in hand onstage to perform for a crowd. That's all she really remembered about her father. That he'd enjoyed laughing.

She and Lucas emerged in a tiled annex between the sanctuary and quire. Dozens of children sang from the tiered choir stalls, their young voices blending in with all things old, brightening the somber space.

Rows of folding chairs lined the annex, most of the seats filled with families listening to the children's song, the women all in smart casual with their dresses or a skirt and jacket. Quenby glanced down at her jeans and blouse and wished she'd had an opportunity to change.

Lucas placed his hand on her back as they walked up the side aisle. They slipped into two chairs near the front, about three rows from the choir.

"There's my date," Lucas said with a grin.

Date? Quenby froze as the word ricocheted through her mind. Then she began to panic, scanning the rows around them for the woman who belonged with Lucas. All she saw were irritated glances from several parents, annoyed at the interruption.

Right now, she was more than annoyed at the man next to her. She wanted to clobber him. "You're meeting someone?"

"Of course."

She scooted to the edge of her seat. "I'm outta here."

"She won't mind."

"I'm fairly certain that she will." Her voice was much too loud, but at the moment, she didn't care.

Lucas reached for her hand. "It would be ungentlemanly of me to let you walk home alone."

"It would be unladylike of me to tag along on your date!"

He glanced at the chorus and raised his other hand, waving toward the two tiers of children. A girl about seven or eight lifted her arm in return, her white-and-red choir robe dangling like a flag.

The girl's smile seemed to radiate across the annex when she waved a second time.

Lucas released Quenby's hand. "She's stunning, isn't she?"

"That's your date?"

He nodded. "My niece."

Someone hushed them as Quenby moved back into her seat. She stopped the nervous laugh that almost escaped her lips, but she couldn't stop the pounding of her heart. Lucas said she did unexpected things, but she hardly compared to him.

The children sang in Latin. Beautifully. Lucas's niece kept smiling toward them, clearly glad that her uncle had made it to the evensong.

It was a man of contrasts sitting beside her. Proud and irritating at times. Then funny and endearing, though she'd never tell him that.

When the singing ended, the girl raced toward Lucas, arms outstretched as she gave him a hug. He picked her up and twirled her around once before setting her back on the ground.

"I didn't think you were coming," she scolded.

"I wouldn't miss this," he said, tweaking her nose. "Layla, this is my friend Miss Vaughn." He glanced back at Quenby. "Miss Vaughn, I'd like to introduce you to my favorite niece."

The girl put one hand on her hip, tilting her head up toward Quenby. "I'm his only niece."

Quenby laughed. "It's nice to meet you, Layla. You have a lovely voice."

She scrunched her face. "My brother doesn't think so."

"Boys can be like that. I think God created them to keep us humble."

"Do you have a brother?"

"No, I have your uncle." The words spilled out, and she wished she could stuff them back in, but it was too late. Lucas was beside her, trying—unsuccessfully—not to laugh.

"That's not exactly what I meant," she insisted.

"I take my humility responsibilities quite seriously," he said.

"Hello, Lucas." A polished-looking woman stepped up to his side. She was dressed in a tailored black pantsuit and wore a silver necklace. Her long hair was a dark brown, perfectly straight. "Who is this?" she asked.

"My colleague and friend," he explained. "Quenby Vaughn."

"I'm Anabelle," the woman said, shaking her hand. "Layla's mum and the sister Lucas likes to keep humble as well. I'm glad he's decided to turn his attentions elsewhere."

Quenby wished the floor of the annex would open up and swallow her. She hadn't meant to say that about Lucas, especially not with his sister nearby.

Layla held up her arms to display her choir robe. "I have to change."

Anabelle took her hand and guided her away. Quenby watched them for a moment before she turned back toward Lucas. "Please tell me that your parents aren't here too."

"Actually—"

She groaned.

"They wouldn't miss hearing Layla."

She crossed her arms. "You should have told me I'd be meeting your family."

"But if I'd told you—" he leaned down, his voice low—"you would have run."

Chapter 36

Mill House, January 1943

Rosalind blew into the cottage like a summer breeze, dusting away the winter gloom that had settled over the house, shaking branches so a bit of sun could radiate through.

Brigitte first saw her from her bedroom window, riding in the front seat beside Herr. The moment the woman stepped out of the car, her hand resting on the hump of her belly, Brigitte knew everything was about to change.

She watched the three of them through the crack by her door. Instead of fear, Rosalind radiated confidence and sophistication. An air of indifference to the miserly furnishings around her.

"She can't stay," Frau hissed even though Rosalind sat poised on a kitchen chair, right in front of her. The red polish on the younger woman's fingernails matched the color of her tailored coat, and the sitting room seemed to cower in her presence, the dullness of it blurring away.

Even Herr was rattled. "We have no choice," he said, pacing beside the women.

"Of course we have a choice. I can hardly feed the two of us as it is, Eddie. I've no food for her or anything for a baby."

"He'll bring us food and supplies," Rosalind said, examining the nails fanned out in front of her, bored instead of worried about their discussion. "Won't you, Eddie?"

Frau's eyes pierced like darts, but Herr ignored the woman completely, speaking to his wife instead. "I've brought plenty of food in the motorcar."

"But what about next week? Or next month? We've gone for weeks at a time without a single box from you or her ladyship."

"I can't help it if the Royal Mail loses a parcel."

"You could drive it here yourself, like you promised."

"Not without raising suspicions. They're keeping their eye on us." Herr glanced at Rosalind.

She rolled her eyes. "Don't sugarcoat it for my sake. I've seen and heard plenty in the past five years, and one thing I've learned— when you're the one holding the secret, you're either dead or fed. The Nazis feed their people well, as long as you stay in their good graces. Fortunately, Mummy needs all of us right now, so we'll have food."

Frau seemed to be considering her words.

Rosalind stood, patting Herr on the arm. "Eddie, I'm certain, will make sure we're fed. He and Mum are on the best of terms."

Brigitte covered her mouth to suppress her giggle. She liked how this woman stood up to Herr. And how Herr had no retort.

Rosalind glanced around the room, holding the handle of a suitcase. "So where shall I sleep in this stately pile?"

"I'll bring you a cot," Frau said.

"Oh no," Rosalind said, moving toward Frau's room. "I need a bed."

"That's mine—" Frau began.

But Rosalind had already disappeared inside. "Baby and I will sleep just fine in here."

After Rosalind closed the door, Frau turned slowly toward her husband, her wide eyes narrowing. "This is ludicrous."

"We have no choice. No one knows that Lady Ricker has a daughter, not even Lord Ricker. He and the servants will wonder where she's been."

Frau's knotted hands flew to her waist. "Where has she been?"

"In Berlin and then Vienna, with the man she says she's going to marry."

"A German officer?"

"That's what she told Lady Ricker. She acts all high and mighty, but she wouldn't have come home unless she's in danger."

"You don't know that," Frau said. "If she finds out what we've been doing here, if she tells a single person besides her mother, you and I will both be dead."

"Rosalind supports Hitler."

Frau shook her head. "That girl supports herself. I wouldn't trust her for a second to keep our secrets."

"You don't have to worry, Olivia. She doesn't know what we've been doing."

"The moment one of the men shows up—"

"Lady Ricker will make alternative arrangements. Until Rosalind is gone."

Brigitte's heart leapt at that news. If Rosalind stayed, perhaps Hitler's men would never come here again.

"How do you suppose we're going to care for a baby?"

"Lady Ricker will send you some of her things."

"The woman likes to make promises that she doesn't keep."

"The war is almost over," he said. "And we're winning."

"That's what you always say."

"Just a few more days. Then we can celebrate. Perhaps even before the baby is born."

❄

"What will you name it?" Brigitte whispered in German, sitting beside Rosalind on the edge of the bed. There was no reason, she'd decided, to hide her language from her new friend. Rosalind knew it too.

"I suppose I can't call him Fritz. People will wonder."

"Was that the name of your—?" She searched for the right word but wasn't certain what to call the father.

"He was my lover, Brigitte. No more or less." She rubbed a white cream into her hands, and Brigitte was fascinated by her assortment of jars. "If it's a girl, I'm naming her something simple. Not stuffy like Rosalind."

"You have a beautiful name."

Rosalind studied her for a moment. "I think I just might like you."

She pulled her legs up to her chest. "Nobody likes me."

The front door slammed outside, and Rosalind glanced toward their bedroom door. "If you're referring to Olivia, she is a nobody. And I doubt she likes anyone. Eddie, on the other hand—"

"That man hates me."

Rosalind gave her that look again as if she was trying to determine if she could trust her. "It doesn't mean he won't take advantage of you."

"What advantage?"

Rosalind sighed. "Just stay away from him. Tonight you can sleep in my room."

Brigitte looked at the bed with its covers. The mattress underneath. She hadn't slept in a real bed since leaving home. "Are you certain?"

"Quite," Rosalind said before she opened the door. "Eddie, fetch me my luggage."

The man actually did what Rosalind bade although he clearly wasn't happy about it. Minutes later, he returned carrying two large suitcases—filled with items Rosalind said she'd pilfered from her mother—both of which he deposited on the bed.

Then he lingered in the room, staring at Brigitte. The hatred was still there, but there was something new in his eyes. Something she didn't like. They wandered this time, tracing the holes in her ratty pinafore, studying her bare feet. And she felt naked before him. Sick. The same way that man—Lothar—had made her feel when he'd touched her in bed.

Was this the advantage he had?

"That will be all, Eddie," Rosalind said, waving him away, clearly secure in her station.

He still stared.

"Eddie," she snapped.

After he left the room, Rosalind tossed Brigitte a dress, a slender pleated one with white polka dots. It fell on the edge of the bed. "Wear this," she commanded.

Brigitte didn't touch it. "Are you certain?"

"You must stop asking me if I'm certain."

She lifted it gingerly, assessing it. The collar was rounded and it had large white buttons down the front to match the dots. She held it up in front of her, and even the gown Cinderella wore to the ball couldn't have been more beautiful.

At the stroke of midnight, it would probably turn back into rags, but she would enjoy it while she could. Just like Cinderella.

Herr and Frau drove away in the car, which was just fine with Rosalind and Brigitte. They pumped water from the well and heated it in a kettle over the fire. Then they sponged themselves with the warm water and even washed their hair in the basin, drying it in front of the flames.

Rosalind let Brigitte borrow a nightgown from among her treasures, and they laughed as Rosalind rolled her hair in curlers.

Herr and Frau returned late. The door to Rosalind and Brigitte's room rattled once, but then she heard Frau's voice, calling out to Herr.

Before they went to sleep, Rosalind locked their window. And Brigitte helped her push the dresser in front of the door.

CHAPTER 37

As the sun rose over Hampstead, Quenby tied her muddy trainers and left to run through the eight hundred acres of heath behind her flat. Swimmers were already immersed in the ponds, stroking their way back and forth across the water. Others, like her, were jogging in the hills.

She'd wanted to dislike the Hough family last night, wary of their pomp and circumstance, but there wasn't much pomp involved and the circumstances were awkward enough to take off the edge of formality. Lucas's parents had been quite gracious to her as they exchanged stories over dinner in Anabelle's terrace home, across the Thames in Greenwich.

Quenby had answered their questions, all of them friendly enough, but mostly she'd just observed, not sure exactly what to do. They all teased each other, like Lucas had teased her. And they all seemed to enjoy one another's company.

She'd watched Anabelle and Mrs. Hough working together in the kitchen, laughing as they'd peeled potatoes. A mother and daughter who loved each other.

Not everyone had a family who liked being together, she knew that, but sometimes she'd wondered what it would have been like to grow up surrounded by people she loved, who loved her as well. A family to visit when she was on holiday.

She raced up the heath, her lungs burning in spite of the cool air.

Grammy had been her only family after Jocelyn left, and after she died, the concept of home went with her. One didn't just invent a new family. They were either born or adopted or married into one.

Even though she longed to be loved as strongly as Daniel loved Brigitte, for someone to pursue her like they were pursuing this woman he'd lost, she couldn't imagine trusting a man with her heart and her future in marriage. Or risking getting hurt again.

Her mobile rang a few minutes after eight, and she glanced at a number she didn't recognize. Perhaps Evan was contacting her about the story. She hoped so. With the new information she'd unearthed in Newhaven, she was hoping she could change his mind.

She slowed to a walk. "Hello?"

"Is this Miss Vaughn?" a man asked. She didn't recognize his voice.

"It is."

"This is Paul, Mrs. Douglas's nurse. I met you at her house."

"Of course."

She heard something slam in the background, perhaps a door. "Mrs. Douglas asked me to contact you. She would like to speak with you again."

"Did she mention what she'd like to speak about?"

"A man named Eddie Terrell."

"What about Mr. Terrell?"

"She wants to tell you in person."

Lucas had said she could borrow his car today if she needed it.

The streets of London still intimidated her, but after his lessons and her practice yesterday, she felt confident enough to drive around Tonbridge alone.

But if Lucas needed his vehicle after all, she would take a train back down. "I could visit her this afternoon."

"Mrs. Douglas will be relieved to hear it. She's been having trouble sleeping the past few nights."

"Please tell her that I've had trouble sleeping as well."

Back in her flat, Quenby called Lucas before she showered and changed. He agreed to let her borrow his vehicle, though he offered to drive her to one of the boroughs south of London before she set off on her own. She readily agreed to this plan.

The Tube delivered her to Canary Wharf in East London, and she found Lucas's flat in a silver tower, overlooking the Thames. When he answered her knock, he leaned over to kiss her cheek, but she backed up, stunned, as if he were a porcupine who might pierce her. Though Chandler would probably say Quenby was the prickly one.

Red splashed over his face, drowning his smile. "It's customary among friends to kiss on the cheek."

"I know that," she said, trying to absolve herself from her awkwardness. "Where I'm from, we shake hands."

Or give hugs, but she wasn't about to hug him. The professionalism between them had already slipped over to personal, and she was grasping to rebuild the wall that once kept them apart.

He opened the door wider. "One day I hope you can trust me, Quenby."

She stuck out her hand in response, shaking his stiffly. Then she stepped into the open reception room of his flat with its kitchen, dining table, and sitting area—the furnishings black and white with clean lines and orderly shapes. There were only two pieces of artwork on the wall—photographs of the rain forest, palettes of a thousand green lights to burnish the gray outside.

Outside the sliding glass, a silver-railed patio extended over to what she assumed was a bedroom or two. The stormy expanse of the Thames stretched below the windows, barges furrowing through its slate waves, docked boats banging against a pier.

Lucas slipped up beside her. "I like to watch the boats when I'm working."

"I'm afraid I'd be too distracted to get any work done."

"You don't seem like the type to be easily distracted. Except, perhaps, when a certain red tractor forces you off the road."

She laughed, grateful for the familiarity of his teasing. She much preferred it over the cheek kissing. "I expunge distractions."

He took a step away. "Now I'm afraid."

"You don't distract me, Lucas."

His nod was curt. "Glad to hear it."

And with that, everything was back in its place.

"My family liked you," Lucas said as they drove away from the wharf.

"I liked them, too, though you still should have told me they were at the concert."

"Would you really have come if I had?"

She wanted to say yes, but it wasn't true. She wouldn't have run away from them, per se. She just never would have stepped into Westminster Abbey.

Sunlight broke through the gray, and Lucas slipped his sunglasses out of their holder. "I'm glad you stayed, for the concert and for dinner."

"Me too. It's a gift, you know, to have a family as normal as yours."

He glanced over at her. "You think we're normal?"

"Comparatively."

"We've had plenty of angst over the years, but I guess we've sorted it out."

"Do you still regret being sent away to school?" she asked as they drove south through the endless city, rows of brick houses and church steeples, glass skyscrapers and railway stations.

"Immensely. I didn't feel particularly close to either of my parents until I was fourteen. That year I begged them to let me attend a public school near home, and they finally conceded. I missed so much in those earlier years, being away."

"Will you send your children away to school?"

He flashed her a smile. "Assuming I have children?"

"I suppose I was assuming. Don't you want to have kids?"

"Eventually, though I'm a bit concerned for my children."

"I think you'll be an excellent father, Lucas. And you'll have great kids, like your niece and nephew."

"Don't let them fool you. All Houghs are unruly at heart."

She laughed. "I doubt it."

"Layla texted me this morning. She wants to know when you're coming back for a visit."

Her heart twinged with his words, happy-sad. But she knew she couldn't get involved in these people's lives, no more than she'd already done. She might have the gift of reinventing herself, but the reinventions didn't last for long. They'd eventually see through the chinks in her armor, to the rough edges underneath.

She didn't want to disappoint Layla. Or her uncle.

"I'm glad I went," she said, her eyes falling to the safety of her phone. A barrier to mount between them. Something that she could control.

Instead of continuing the conversation, she checked her e-mail. Then she whistled.

"What is it?" he asked.

"Listen to this."

Dear Miss Vaughn,

I've learned that you are trying to contact the Ricker family about a story. I'm glad to speak with you but this is not a conversation to have via phone or e-mail.

I'm available to meet tomorrow in Jacksonville, Florida. If
this is acceptable, please reply so we can work out the details.
I'll tell you all about my mother.

Alexander

She set down the phone. "Who is Alexander?"

"No idea."

"Seriously, Lucas. If his name is somewhere in Mr. Knight's files, I need to know about it."

"I'll ask." He reached for his phone. "And I'll arrange a flight for tomorrow morning."

"I can't go to Florida," she said, speaking to herself.

"We have to—"

"We?"

"You can't go alone. You don't know who this man is."

"He's contacting me about the Ricker family, not Brigitte."

"Brigitte's story is so intertwined with the Rickers', I'm not certain which is which anymore."

Quenby stared out the window, at a colorful mural of children flying kites in a park. She couldn't tell Lucas, but even on a corporate jet, even with the carrot of a story dangling in front of her, Florida was the last place she wanted to go.

Chapter 38

Mill House, March 1943

Rosalind and Brigitte laughed as they strolled up the rutted path from the river, their legs damp from a morning spent splashing in the water.

The day was warmer than usual for the end of March, and they'd been anxious to escape the house, away from Frau's low mood. Somehow the woman had obtained rum, either as payment from Lady Ricker or a gift from the postman.

Brigitte had shown Rosalind all her secret places. The rooms she'd found in the old mill. The reeds along the water. The cemetery hidden in the trees. And she'd told her that her name was Brigitte—sworn to secrecy of course.

Rosalind told her about her family. Her father—a man named Oskar—was a high-ranking officer in the Wehrmacht, and her mother had been madly, hopelessly in love with him when she was nineteen. Lady Ricker was already married to her first husband when Rosalind was born in Boston, though she'd been traveling in Europe, alone, when Rosalind was conceived.

After Lady Ricker divorced her American husband, she'd sent Rosalind to Germany to be with Oskar, planning to join them later, but Oskar decided that Lady Ricker would be much more useful to him in England. Even after her marriage to Lord Ricker, Lady Ricker had visited Rosalind and Oskar in Germany. Until two years before the war.

Apparently Oskar was married as well but Rosalind didn't tell her much more about him, only that she was terrified of the man. And he didn't know she was expecting a child.

Brigitte didn't tell her about Lady Ricker's letters or her botched translations. Not with Rosalind's father looming in the background.

Her friend stepped around a tree branch, but then she froze, holding out her arm to stop Brigitte as well. A strange motorcar was parked beside the house. Black with four doors.

"Follow me," Brigitte said, directing Rosalind to the side of the house.

Cigarette smoke wafted through the sitting room window, and she could see two men inside with Frau, clinging to a cigarette.

Brigitte glanced at Rosalind. She didn't look surprised.

"We know what you've been doing, Mrs. Terrell," one of the men said. "We picked up a man near Swindon last week, by the name of Lothar. Do you remember him?"

Her voice trembled when she denied it.

Brigitte peeked over the windowsill again as the man leaned closer to Frau. "Too many men for you to remember?"

"You're insulting me."

"Lothar is quite a talker. He said you hosted a number of his friends here. He also said that he was sent by Hitler himself, to wreak havoc on the railway works up north." The man stopped for a moment, and when he turned, Brigitte ducked down. "Do you know what that makes you, Mrs. Terrell?"

"I want to speak to my husband."

"That makes you a collaborator with the enemy." Silence reigned before he spoke again. "A traitor."

She still didn't speak.

"Where is your husband?"

This time she didn't hesitate. "He's in Manchester."

"Manchester?"

"He found a position there on a farm."

"I thought he was working at Breydon Court."

"Not any longer."

"Lothar said you had a daughter living with you. She helped in your work."

Brigitte braced herself, waiting for her answer. Would Frau tell the men that she and Rosalind were in the woods?

"She's not my daughter."

"What's her name?"

"I don't know. We called her 'girl.'"

"Lothar said she's German."

"She's a mute. And she ran away, months ago."

At first, in her wistfulness, Brigitte thought Frau might be trying to protect her, but she was probably terrified of what Brigitte would say if they found her. And she had plenty to say.

Her feet turned toward the front door, but Rosalind caught her sleeve and started to whisper. Brigitte put her finger on her lips, hushing her as she glanced up into the window again.

The men inside were probably police. British Gestapo. They hadn't believed Frau's lies. They probably wouldn't believe Brigitte's story either, even if she spoke the truth. At least not when they discovered that she was German and that her voice had been broadcasting back to the enemy.

They would brand her a traitor as well and probably put her in the hold of another boat traveling straight back across the channel. Or hand her over to Hitler's men the next time they floated up the river.

"Brigitte," Rosalind said, squeezing her arm. Then she groaned.

Brigitte almost hushed her again, but as she turned, she saw the panic on Rosalind's face, her hands pressed against her abdomen.

Moving away from the window, she and Rosalind stumbled toward the woods until Rosalind stopped and doubled over, the house still in sight. Then Brigitte began to panic as well. "You can't have your baby here."

"Baby's ready to come, whether or not we are."

The front door opened, and she pulled Rosalind back into the trees. The policemen marched toward their car, Frau secured between them. Her head was down, resigned, it seemed, to her fate.

Brigitte probably should have wondered what would happen now that Frau was gone. Would they continue receiving their boxes of food from Breydon Court? The food rations from town?

But as the car drove away that afternoon, all Brigitte could think about was Rosalind and the baby about to be born.

CHAPTER 39

Quenby brought an orchid for Mrs. Douglas, the petals a dark shade of plum. The woman had dressed in a neat peach-colored suit for their meeting, and she wore a strand of pearls and polished ivory pumps.

"You look lovely," Quenby said as she extended her gift.

The woman smiled from her high-back chair next to the hospital bed, placing the flower on the tray beside a blue ceramic teapot, steam curling from its spout, and a plate of digestive biscuits. "Thank you for returning, Ms. Vaughn."

"Please call me Quenby." She gently shook the woman's hand, mindful of her tender translucent skin.

"I hope it wasn't too much trouble."

Quenby thought about her first venture alone on England's roads and was quite pleased with herself. She'd left Lucas an hour ago, at the train station in Bromley, and her confidence was bolstered by the time she reached Tonbridge. "It wasn't any trouble at all."

"I can't stop thinking about Olivia Terrell," Mrs. Douglas said as she dashed each cup with milk and then poured the tea. "Could you please remind me why you're trying to locate her?"

"I'm searching for the evacuee girl who lived with the Terrells," she explained. "When Mrs. Terrell moved away, Brigitte went with her."

Mrs. Douglas scooted toward the edge of her chair. "Do you know what happened to Mrs. Terrell?"

"Lady Ricker sent her to live in a house near the coast, but I don't know where she went after the war."

Mrs. Douglas shook her head sadly. "So many people were killed in those days. My father died at the Biggin Hill aerodrome in December 1941."

Quenby set her biscuit back on her plate. "Did he work at the airfield?"

"Yes, he was an instructor."

"I found some photographs of the airfield at the Terrells' house."

"What sort of photographs?" Mrs. Douglas asked.

"The sort that might have educated the German military."

Mrs. Douglas closed her eyes briefly and then opened them. "I suppose that doesn't surprise me. Mother suspected Eddie Terrell was up to no good. He was curious about the RAF and even went with my father several times to visit the base. Eddie told my parents he was interested in joining the RAF, but he stayed at Breydon Court."

"Did your mother continue to work at Breydon Court?"

She nodded. "Lord Ricker died before the war ended, and then Lady Ricker took her two children to live in London."

"And your mother was out of a position—"

"Oh no. Lady Ricker kept her on the payroll as a housekeeper until the house was transferred to the Dragues. My mother followed the lives and careers of the Ricker children as they grew. Kept lots of clippings and such from the papers." She smiled. "My mother liked to keep things."

In Quenby's work, she had a fondness for people who kept things, especially pictures and papers. "Why did your mother tell you so much about Eddie Terrell?"

"Come with me." Mrs. Douglas leaned forward on her walker and motioned for Quenby to follow her. They walked around the kitchen, into an office next to it.

The room was filled with boxes and stacks of papers, one pile of boxes looking like a tower of Jenga blocks, ready to tumble onto the floor. Mrs. Douglas's walker maneuvered precariously close to the tower, but she moved smoothly around it. Then she knocked on a box with the leg of her walker. "Would you be so kind as to open this?"

"Of course." Quenby removed the cardboard boxes from the top of the stack and placed the selected one on the desk.

Mrs. Douglas peered inside; then she riffled through the manila files. "Here it is." She pulled out a file. "Eddie was usually behind his camera, but someone must have borrowed it."

Quenby studied the black-and-white picture of a man leaning against a polished newel post, his legs crossed casually as if he didn't have a care in the entire world. Beside him was a prim-looking woman, probably in her late twenties, but she looked a decade older than her husband with her lips pressed firmly together, her hands clasped in front of her straight skirt.

"Is this Olivia?"

"It is. Quite an unhappy-looking woman."

Quenby agreed. "How did you get her picture?"

"My mother found it in Lady Ricker's bureau, years after the family moved out." Mrs. Douglas opened a drawer and took out a clear cover with newspaper clippings inside. "I don't think she had any qualms about taking it. She said no one was left to appreciate the beautiful things anymore. The Dragues, she feared, would dispose of it all."

Mrs. Douglas plopped one of the newspaper articles onto the desk. Eddie Terrell was on the front page, smiling back at them. The date was May 1965.

Quenby glanced between the glossy photograph and newsprint. "He looks almost the same—"

Mrs. Douglas tapped the paper. "Read the caption."

Quenby read it twice.

It wasn't Eddie Terrell in the photograph. It was Lord Anthony Ricker, the Rickers' only son.

"I see," Quenby said before looking up again. Apparently Eddie Terrell had known Lady Ricker quite well.

Mrs. Douglas's gaze was intense. "Do you?"

"Indeed."

"Well, then." Mrs. Douglas shuffled toward the door. "Shall we finish our tea?"

"When did Eddie pass away?" Quenby asked as she returned to her chair.

"I'm not certain, but Mother said there were rumors that he died before the war ended. He went on an errand for Lady Ricker in 1943 and never returned."

"Perhaps he went to live with Olivia."

Mrs. Douglas picked up her teacup and took a sip. "The driver took Lady Ricker to find Eddie, but they returned without him or his car. There were whispers that Eddie had been murdered."

"What did the driver say?"

"Nothing, to my knowledge. Apparently he died a few weeks later as well."

Quenby shivered. "Did your mother think Eddie was helping the Nazis?"

"I wouldn't accuse anyone . . . ," she began, tea splashing over the side of her cup.

"I'm not looking for accusations, Mrs. Douglas. I'm trying to find the truth so I can locate the girl who lived with Olivia and him."

Mrs. Douglas set her teacup back on its saucer. "Mother didn't know if Eddie was a Fascist, but his grandfather was German. That's why Olivia lost her job with Churchill. Everyone was suspect at the time."

"Perhaps Eddie was suspect for good reason," Quenby surmised.

"At the time, many British people thought Hitler was going to win."

Had Eddie lost his life on one of his trips to Newhaven? If so, did one of Hitler's men kill him or had Olivia finally had enough? Maybe she was tired of living in that dump of a house, of being Eddie's pawn.

Quenby's mind flashed back to those tombstones she'd seen, tangled up in the weeds near the Mill House.

Was it possible that Eddie was buried there? If so, what happened to Olivia and Brigitte after he died?

❖

Quenby cruised south toward Newhaven on the A26, a file filled with photographs and newspaper articles from Mrs. Douglas on the seat beside her. The Mill House was the last place where Brigitte was known to be alive. And the place, Quenby suspected, where Eddie Terrell had died.

Olivia had given up her job for Eddie. Was it worth giving up her entire life to become a traitor with him? This Eddie must have been some charmer. Married to Olivia but sleeping with his boss while Olivia operated a safe house for them. Almost as if he and Lady Ricker had sent her away so the two of them could carry on their affair in private.

A real hero of a guy.

If someone had murdered Eddie, would Olivia have stayed with Brigitte at the Mill House? Quenby doubted it, unless Lady Ricker paid her handsomely to cooperate—and she never found out about the affair.

Then again, Quenby was assuming Olivia was a victim here. She could have supported Hitler's cause on her own. Perhaps she'd even married Eddie because he was a Fascist. It was entirely possible that she knew about the affair and didn't care.

Her phone rang, and she glanced down and saw Lucas's number. "You're not talking while you're driving, are you?"

She pulled into the parking lot of a Shell station. "Of course not."

"Very good," he said. "The plane will be waiting for us tomorrow morning at Biggin Hill. We'll fly back on Wednesday."

"We don't need to stay in Florida an entire day."

"Yes, we do. The pilots need to rest at least ten hours before we fly again."

"What are we going to do for ten hours?"

"I say we go to Disney World."

Her stomach rolled. Surely Lucas must not know what happened to her there. "I've already been."

"But I never have."

"Why not go to Disneyland in Paris?"

"Because I'm not going to be in Paris tomorrow," he said. "This will be fun."

Fun for him, perhaps, but not so much for her.

"Are you headed back to London now?" he asked.

"No, I decided to detour down to Newhaven."

"Newhaven is hardly a detour."

"Fair enough," she said before telling him about the conversation she'd had with Mrs. Douglas. "There's a cemetery near the Mill House. I thought Eddie Terrell might be buried in it."

"You think someone murdered Eddie and then gave him a funeral?"

"I know it's a long shot, but I want to check."

"Kyle's probably waiting to run you off the road again so he can rescue you."

"I doubt it."

"Should I take the train down to meet you tonight? We can visit the cemetery early in the morning and then drive to the airport together."

"I'll be fine," she insisted. Venturing into the woods north of Newhaven was nothing compared to going back to Florida. "Do you mind if I keep your car overnight?"

"I don't mind, but—"

"Yes?"

"Please be careful."

"I will."

It was almost six o'clock now. She wouldn't race against the setting sunlight again to find the cemetery or risk having to knock on Kyle's door after dark. But if she hurried, she would be able to visit the library before it closed. Eddie Terrell might not have had a formal burial, but if he had been murdered at the Mill House, perhaps the local newspaper wrote a story about it.

After hanging up with Lucas, she phoned Chandler to tell her she was returning to Newhaven. Evan hadn't contacted her, she reported on her boss's voice mail, but the more she searched, the more complicated—and disturbing—the story about Lady Ricker had become.

As she drove south, the realization of what the Terrells and Lady Ricker had done almost overwhelmed her. They had conspired with the Nazis to kill people like Mrs. Douglas's father. Promoted the hatred and annihilation of an entire race of innocent people. How could they justify what they had done, supporting a man who was slaughtering innocent men, women, and children?

Perhaps they didn't know the extent of what was happening in Germany during the war.

But perhaps they did.

Chapter 40

Mulberry Lane, April 1943

"They have Olivia," Lady Ricker whispered, tipping her straw hat closer to her eyes with her gloved hands, perusing the gardens beside him.

Eddie stabbed the hoe into the soil and glanced both ways. Lady Ricker would never come out to the gardens unless it was urgent.

Two lads were planting seed for him nearby. They were from the village, hired for a few months to help him and the two POWs they retained. It was necessary to hire outsiders to maintain their food supply, but they had to be even more cautious with their words outside the house.

"I'll come to your room to discuss it," he replied, glancing over at the boys. "This afternoon."

It would be a double advantage for him. He hadn't been invited up to her room since Rosalind arrived.

"You can't," she whispered. "Lord Ricker is coming from London."

He took her arm, motioning her away from the curious eyes of the workers. Lady Ricker didn't put much stock in the lips of the lower class. No one, she thought, would believe the gossip of a farmhand, but Eddie knew well the power of a workingman to light a match of speculation. These days one didn't need much more to start a wildfire.

As they walked along the stone pathway, he pointed at the pond strewn with lilies as if he were giving her a tour of her land. "Who has Olivia?" he asked.

"The investigators from Scotland Yard."

He groaned. All it would take was the slightest twist of his wife's arm, and she would spill everything about their work. And she'd take down Eddie and Lady Ricker with her.

He opened a gate, and they slipped into the secluded woods of the deer park. Only the herd and birds were behind these gates, both too busy rummaging for food to care about them. If anyone asked about their walk, he would say that Lady Ricker wanted an account of her animals.

But he doubted anyone would ask. Most of the staff knew he and her ladyship had a relationship that crossed a line or two. If the truth came out, he guessed none of them would be surprised.

In the seclusion of trees, he turned toward Lady Ricker. The lines fanning out from the woman's eyes had deepened, her skin a gray pallor in the forest light. "Are you certain they have Olivia?"

She nodded. "A friend phoned this morning."

He wrung his hands, pacing between the mossy trees. They must come up with a way to stop her from talking. "Perhaps your friend—"

"He's already taken care of it."

His nod was firm. Brisk. Olivia had soldiered alongside them for four years, attempting to gather information from Winston Churchill himself before he became prime minister. Then she'd reluctantly agreed to help Lady Ricker. Her work the past few years had proved to be invaluable.

But sometimes soldiers had to be sacrificed for the common good.

He'd never intended to continue on as a married man after Hitler invaded anyway. He'd sacrificed much for the cause as well and was ready to reap all that he had sown without a wife in tow.

Eddie leaned back against the trunk of a tree. "Our work is compromised."

Lady Ricker nodded. "An investigator is planning to return here in the morning to search for you."

He ripped off a spindly branch and broke it into pieces. The man had already said, the last time he met with Eddie, that he thought Eddie as guilty as men like Oswald Mosley and William Joyce. It was only the small matter of time and facts, he'd said, before he uncovered the truth.

Lady Ricker reached for his hand, her voice light again. "You needn't worry, Eddie."

"What if Olivia already talked?"

"The only significant thing she said was that you'd left Breydon Court. You're supposed to be working at a farm near Manchester now."

He pushed away from the tree. "Good girl," he muttered. Olivia had been faithful until the end. "If I'm supposed to be in Manchester, why is an investigator coming here?"

"Because he had no luck finding you up north, just as he'll have no luck finding you here." She paused. "But we still have a problem."

"There's always a problem."

"The investigator is planning to search the Mill House as well. My acquaintance said no one mentioned finding Rosalind, but if she's still there, I suspect she'll be glad to talk to him, as long as the spotlight is shining on her."

"Why didn't you tell me about Rosalind before she arrived here?"

"I can't tell you every detail of my life."

"That's more than a detail." He kicked the dirt. "She's like one of those delay-action bombs. Heaven help us when she detonates."

Lady Ricker removed a cigarette from her reticule, her hand shaking ever so slightly when she lit the match. The fug of smoke curled around her neck like a gray stole, and she looked up at him in the familiar way he knew before she asked him about taking on another job.

"She's not going to detonate." She took another drag on the cigarette. "At least not publicly."

"How do you know?"

"Because you're going to pay her a visit early tomorrow, before the inspector arrives. And not the kind involving biscuits and tea."

"You want me to—"

"Hush," she snapped.

Unbidden, his feet paced to the tree across the knoll and back again. He was an innovator. A photographer. And a gardener for Lady Ricker. But an assassin?

Plenty of people had died as a result of his work, but he was much more comfortable in his role as an accomplice. Even if he despised Rosalind—and he did hate the woman for her utter disdain—he'd never directly taken a life before.

"It's imperative that you do this, Eddie," Lady Ricker implored. Then she removed a brown bag from her reticule and held it out to him. "Here's enough money for you to disappear until the war is over."

He stared at the bag. Blood money.

"If you don't stop her, Scotland Yard will have more than enough evidence to hang you and me."

Eddie sighed, resolute. He had no other choice. "I'll leave at first light."

Lady Ricker patted his face, not like a lover but as a mother would do for her child. And in that moment, he knew she was saying good-bye. At least for now. They would keep each other's secrets until they celebrated together under Hitler's reign.

"I will find you, after the war."

"Perhaps you will," she said, but her words lacked conviction.

They'd had plans for their future, to share the bounty of treasure from Hitler's cache. He wouldn't be dismissed with a bag of pounds sterling for killing her daughter.

"I will find you," he repeated so she would understand. He expected much more for all he'd done—and was about to do.

When she turned to walk away, he called out. "What should I do with the German girl?"

She glanced back. "Whatever you'd like."

Leaning against the tree, he glanced into the bag at the stack of crisp new banknotes.

At least there was a lining of silver in this situation.

After Rosalind was gone, he could do exactly what he wanted with the girl.

CHAPTER 41

Annie, the Newhaven librarian, yanked out a long drawer from the catalog file and began searching through hundreds of cards for a reference on Eddie Terrell. "Did you find your street?"

"I did," Quenby said. "It was close to the River Ouse."

"You never know what you're going to find along that river. Or in it, for that matter."

"I prefer to stay above the water."

"I don't blame you. Did you know Virginia Woolf drowned in the river, up near her home in Rodmell?"

Quenby shook her head.

"She filled her pockets with stones during World War II and stepped right into the current."

Quenby shivered. She'd known the writer had committed suicide, but not the details. The thought of it only added to the creepiness of the river, the ghosts that lingered.

"Here." Annie plucked out a card. "What name did you say again?"

"Terrell. Eddie Terrell."

"There's no Eddie recorded in here, but I have a card on an Olivia Terrell." She held it out. "Would you like to see it?"

"Very much." Quenby took the handwritten card. In 1943, it said, there was a newspaper article recording Olivia's death.

Had Eddie and Olivia died together that year?

"Do you want me to retrieve the microfilm?" Annie asked.

"Yes, please."

"It will take me a few minutes."

As Quenby waited in a chair, she checked her e-mail again. Alexander had replied to her note, confirming that he could meet her tomorrow, early afternoon, at a tearoom near the riverfront in Jacksonville. Seconds after she replied, Annie returned with a reel containing the *Sussex Express*.

"Do you want me to set up the reader for you?" she asked.

Quenby shook her head. "I can do it." She might not know how to operate a microscope, but she had plenty of experience with microfilm.

"The article ran the second week of April."

After threading the film, Quenby turned on the light and began ticking through the pages. It didn't take long to find the story. Three paragraphs to commemorate the life and death of Olivia Terrell. It was longer than an epitaph, she supposed, but it still didn't seem nearly long enough to remember someone's life.

According to the article, Olivia had been residing at a house near Camford Mill. She was taken into custody on suspicion of treason, though she was never convicted of this charge. Several days after she arrived at London's Holloway Prison, she hanged herself in her cell. No one knew how she obtained the rope.

Mr. Williams, the postman, said Mrs. Terrell had been living at the Mill House for approximately two years while her unnamed husband was soldiering for the British army. She received regular parcels, packaged with no return post. And he told investigators that, to his knowledge, she never sent any mail.

According to Mr. Williams, Mrs. Terrell had a daughter living with her, though upon inquiry, a child was never found. Police requested any additional information as to Mrs. Terrell's activities be directed to them.

Perhaps Mrs. Douglas was confused, like Mr. Knight. Perhaps she'd remembered her mother's story wrong, and it was actually Olivia who'd died instead of Eddie that year.

Yet Mrs. Douglas said that there were rumors Eddie had been murdered. And Lady Ricker, Quenby felt certain, would put up an ironclad curtain between her and the woman suspected of betraying Great Britain.

Did Olivia—like Virginia Woolf—really choose to kill herself, or had someone helped her along?

Quenby turned off the machine, rubbing the chill that crept up her arms.

Lady Ricker, it seemed, would do anything to keep her secrets. Would she also kill the German girl who had translated her words?

Fog veiled the River Ouse early the next morning as Quenby drove back up the road where she'd dodged Kyle Logan and his tractor.

Last night, the innkeeper had eyed her curiously when she walked into the lobby with two plastic bags, filled with a fresh change of clothes and toiletries from Boots chemist, and requested the same room she'd had two nights ago. But like all good innkeepers, the woman kept her questions to herself and handed over a key to the room.

Quenby waited in the SUV by the river until the fog lifted. When sunlight finally made its debut, she sprayed herself one more time to repel, she hoped, both bugs and men, though she kept her phone in hand as she trekked into the forest.

When she texted Lucas last night, he'd promised to keep his phone beside him this morning. Not that it would help if she slipped out of service again, but it made her feel better knowing that she could contact him near the river.

In and out of the trees. That's all she had to do. The cemetery had been along one of the overgrown paths, and if she found the pasture for the Logans' farm, on the other side of the woodlands, she'd turn back.

The running app on her phone traced her steps past the mill, along the winding path. When she got to the Kelmore crossroads, she hiked left instead of right. And about twenty minutes later, she found the cemetery.

Scraps of wooden gravestones were scattered in the weeds, but five slate stones were still intact. She brushed aside the weeds on the stone closest to her, a weathered gray slate engraved with a cross, to read the epitaph. It was the grave of a Kelmore man who'd died in 1882.

She ducked under the crawling branch of an elm tree and read the inscriptions on four more Kelmore family graves, each one including a Bible verse or kind sentiment in recognition of the man or woman buried there. But Lucas was right—there was no grave for Eddie Terrell.

And no marker among the trees for Brigitte, either. Not that Quenby expected the Terrells to put a stone on her grave, but she was still clinging to the hope, for Mr. Knight's sake, that the girl's life had extended far beyond the Mill House, blossoming into womanhood.

She snapped several pictures of the cemetery, of its raw beauty and isolation. Nature sprouting new life to replace what had been lost. Then she hiked back to the Mill House and took a panoramic picture encompassing the broken house, the limbs of beech trees, and what appeared to be an old garden nearby.

Something cracked in the branches behind her, and Quenby jumped. As she scanned the trees, Lucas's words from yesterday seemed to hammer in her head. The ones he'd said about taking care.

She couldn't tell what was in the forest. Perhaps one of the cows had wandered beyond the pasture. Or was it Kyle, watching for her?

At the moment, it didn't particularly matter. She wasn't staying here any longer.

Chapter 42

Baby girl had cried for hours last night. Rosalind's body, Brigitte feared, wasn't giving her the nourishment she needed, but they had no milk in the house or even a bottle. The baby sucked on Brigitte's finger for comfort, but it didn't soothe the pain in her belly.

When Brigitte was a child, Mama used to send her outside to play, saying the fresh air would do her some good. So she and baby girl went on a walk this morning, and as they strolled in the forest, Brigitte told her stories about her childhood in Germany, sang her the German songs that Mama used to sing.

She wished the baby had a proper name like other children, but Rosalind hadn't concerned herself yet with a name. It wasn't Brigitte's place to name her, but she pretended the baby had a beautiful name, a name with wings. Like Princess Adler.

Soon, she prayed, they could all fly far away from here.

The girl was four days old now. After Olivia left, Brigitte and Rosalind had labored together to deliver her. Brigitte had never seen so much blood before and then—the miracle of life. The scream of a child no longer harbored in Rosalind's womb.

But Rosalind had retreated into her own shell after the birth, not sure, it seemed, what to do with a baby. She'd been reluctant even to feed her, as if she wasn't certain that she wanted the child to live.

Baby finally slept as Brigitte carried her toward the cemetery. The markers there, with their Scripture verses, reminded her of the yard around her father's church in Moselkern. God might not be in the Mill House, but she hoped that His presence lingered here among His saints.

So she stopped by the tombstones to pray, begging *Vater Gott* to save this baby's life. For the baby must live. Before they left the cemetery, she knew what she must do. Defy Rosalind, if necessary, to make sure her daughter survived.

As she and baby drew close to the house again, beside the garden plot, Brigitte paused. There was a motorcar in the drive, but unlike the investigator's vehicle, this one she recognized. It was the dark-blue Wolseley that Herr drove.

What would the man do when he realized his wife had been taken away?

Even though Frau didn't like her, she'd been a sliver of a shield between Brigitte and her husband. Now that she was gone, Brigitte feared he wouldn't have any use for her or Rosalind. Or for a baby.

"Wait for me," she whispered, laying baby girl in a tuft of grass beside the garden. The baby stirred but slept, exhausted from her sleepless night and hunger pangs.

Brigitte wouldn't let Herr touch this child.

"I'll return," she promised, like Dietmar had done with her long ago. Then she reached for the mud-caked hoe beside a tree, the one Herr had brought them to plant a garden.

Clutching the handle, Brigitte crept through the front door and past the fireplace. Herr was talking to Rosalind inside the bedroom. His voice was calm, and it scared her more than his yelling.

"Where were you in Germany?" he asked.

"I wasn't in Germany. I was in Austria." Rosalind wasn't commanding this time nor did she seem scared. She sounded bored, as if she'd already tired of talking. "With the father of my child."

"I don't care about the child's father. I want the name of the man who fathered you."

Her laugh was hollow. "Are you going to kill him too?"

"Tell me his name," he repeated, the calm in his voice tightening into a demand.

"Ask your lady."

"She won't tell me."

"That's because Mummy loves him much more than she'd ever love you."

Brigitte stood at the bedroom door, her fingers washed purple as they clenched Herr's hoe. But he didn't turn around. His eyes were fixed on Rosalind, and in his hands he had something as well, pointed at her friend. Like Roger when he'd pointed his gun at Brigitte.

Herr stepped closer to her. "Too bad your mummy wants you dead."

"Dead or fed," Rosalind said with a shrug. "It won't be long before she wants you dead too."

"Lady Ricker needs me."

Rosalind laughed again. "She doesn't need anyone, except my father."

"Where's the girl?"

When he glanced toward the window, Rosalind signaled Brigitte forward with her finger, ever so slightly. "Which one?"

"The—"

Brigitte cringed at the vile word on his lips, but in that moment she found her English voice. Rich and strong. Calm and controlled. "I'm right here."

When Herr swiveled, she hammered him in the head with the hoe, and he fell like one of the toy knights in Dietmar's army, crashing onto the wood floor.

Rosalind swept the gun out of his hand, and as he groaned, Brigitte raced out of the room, out of the cottage, and retched in the brush. A blast of gunshot reverberated through the trees, and in that instant, she knew she'd been fully liberated from the Terrell family and this miserable house.

Rosalind stood at the front door, her black dressing gown whirling like a storm cloud around her. "We have to leave."

Wiping off her mouth, Brigitte followed her back into the house, stepping over Herr's body as she reached for the sack with cloth diapers in the bureau and the extra layette Lady Ricker had sent before the birth.

Her hands shook as she packed Dietmar's wooden knight and a change of clothing for herself, but Rosalind didn't seem to tremble at all as she slipped the key for the Wolseley out of Herr's pocket.

"Should we bury him?" Brigitte asked, unable to look at Herr again.

Rosalind shook her head. "The rats can have his body."

Brigitte felt as if she were drowning in the rusty smell of blood, the lingering smoke from Herr's gun.

"We must hurry," Rosalind urged, her suitcase in hand. "My mother will kill us both if she finds us."

Apparently Lady Ricker no longer wanted to feed any of them.

Brigitte froze on the doorstep, images swirling in her mind. For more than two years, this cottage had been her den. An unsafe place, and yet she could hardly remember the world on the other side of these trees. The outside seemed large and looming. Impossible and terrifying.

How was she going to live out there?

Rosalind was in the driver's seat of the car, starting the engine. And Brigitte heard baby girl crying in the garden.

Lauf.

She could almost hear Dietmar whispering to her again. And she knew she had to run, for her life and for this baby.

Gears grated as Rosalind began reversing the car, and Brigitte pounded on the hood.

"Wait," she demanded before rushing to the garden.

If she hadn't stopped her, Rosalind would have driven off, without Brigitte or her daughter.

CHAPTER 43

A steel-colored Porsche was parked along the river road, beside the Range Rover. As Quenby stepped out of the forest, the door opened and a man in his early sixties emerged. She stared at him in shock.

"Mr. Graham?" No one at the syndicate called him Evan to his face.

He rounded the car, dressed in jeans and a short-sleeved plaid shirt. She'd never seen him wearing anything except a business suit.

"Good morning, Quenby."

"What—?" She forced her words to form. "What are you doing in Newhaven?"

"I was over in Brighton," he explained. "Chandler said you came here on your holiday."

She opened the door to Lucas's SUV and tossed her backpack

inside, trying to recover. Then she turned back to the man who could make or break her job. "Do you typically check in with your employees on vacation?"

"Of course not." He slid on his sunglasses. "It's just that I have a particular interest in the story you've been working on."

"Chandler said you killed it."

"At the time, there didn't seem to be enough information to run an article."

"And Mrs. McMann's attorney called you."

He leaned against the car, a casual position more forced than natural. "Mr. Fenton wasn't very pleasant about the whole business either, but I'm not afraid of a lawsuit. As long as you do your job right, there won't be any litigation."

"I was doing my job—"

"You're a brilliant journalist, Quenby."

"Thank you," she said, though her words sounded more like a question. He was leading this conversation, and she wasn't certain to what end.

"I'm reconsidering this story." He drummed his fingers on the door. "Chandler said that your research is focused on the Ricker family."

Quenby nodded. "Lady Ricker organized a network of people who worked for Hitler during the war."

"But you need proof."

"I have plenty of proof."

When his eye twitched, she decided to take a step back from her allegations. "I'm still working to gather all the facts."

"So nothing concrete yet?"

"I'm verifying what I've found."

"I'm intrigued, but your article has to be different from any other story written on German espionage."

"It will be," she said. "It's about an American-born woman who operated a safe house for German infiltrators. She opened up the door to England and invited the country's enemies inside."

"This network," Evan said slowly. "Are you still gathering information about them as well?"

"I am."

"And you think there's some proof at this abandoned mill?"

She hesitated. "I've been doing some hiking during my holiday."

"Of course," he said, though he didn't seem to believe her.

"I'll ring Chandler if I find anything pertinent before I return to work."

"Please contact me directly if you have any new leads," he said before giving her the number for his mobile. "Are you staying in Newhaven for the next week?"

With that question, he crossed the line. Quenby loved her job, but she was on a mandated holiday, free to do what she liked whether it was walking the woodlands or searching for a lost woman or flying off to Florida.

She climbed into the SUV, the door propped open. "I'll be around," she said as she started the engine.

"I don't suppose I need to remind you about the confidentiality in your job."

The reminder sounded a whole lot like modern-day blackmail to her.

"I know all about confidentiality."

But there was nothing in her contract about staying mum on a canceled story.

She closed the door and drove north, toward the Biggin Hill Airport to meet Lucas.

Like Louise McMann, Evan was worried about something, and she intended to find out what it was.

Chapter 44

River Ouse, April 1943

Rosalind's hands were clamped over the wheel of the Wolseley, her gaze fixed on the ruts in the bumpy road. The laughter was gone from her lips. The quick wit that could put even Herr in his place. The two of them, together they'd put Herr permanently into a place where he'd never trouble them again.

Neither of them shed tears over the man as they fled the Mill House, but baby girl cried, kicking against Brigitte's chest. She was hungry and probably just as scared.

When they emerged onto the narrow road beside the river, Rosalind turned north. And Brigitte ventured a question. "Where are we going?"

Rosalind didn't answer. It was as if she couldn't hear.

They would travel far away from here, the three of them. Go someplace where Lady Ricker would never find them. Wherever the wind led.

Farmland was on their left, the river on their right until the road turned west toward the farms. As the road meandered through pastures and woodlands, Brigitte realized that Rosalind had no destination in mind. No plan. She was just driving away from the house, until their petrol was gone.

For so long she'd wanted to be free from the oppressive hand of the Terrells, but this was not what she'd imagined. A dead man and a friend who'd slipped out of her mind.

There was no door to hide behind now. No words to twist or change. She and baby were both exposed and at the mercy of Rosalind.

"We can drive to London," Brigitte said. "My friend's aunt lives there."

Silence.

"Or you and the baby can go back to Germany. Her father could take care of both of you."

Rosalind shook her head, her gaze frozen forward. But this time she spoke. "Her father is dead."

Baby squirmed in Brigitte's arms as farmland transformed back into forest. Rosalind turned right onto a bumpy path and the Wolseley began to climb a wooded hill toward the river.

"She's blessed, Rosalind. She has a good mother to care for her, no matter where you live."

Rosalind's lips pressed together in a steely silence as she accelerated the car. Brigitte braced her feet against the floorboard, her fingers clutching the handle. Their tires hit another rut, and her head slammed against the metal roof.

"Slow down," she demanded, but Rosalind was lost to her again.

And Brigitte knew—she had to get the baby out of here.

Baby was crying louder now, but the cries only seemed to propel Rosalind to drive faster, as if speed would swallow the car and the noise. The wand on the fuel gauge dipped toward empty, and Brigitte prayed the petrol would run out before Rosalind killed them all.

A cow stepped into the path ahead of them. Brigitte screamed, and Rosalind braked, the car shivering as it swerved through the branches. Brigitte yanked on her handle and the door swung open, its hinges rattling behind her. Then she jumped out onto the forest floor with baby clutched close to her chest. She rolled into the brush, away from the car.

The crunch of metal ripped through the trees, her door torn from its hinges. And the cow, it snorted at her before strolling back into the forest.

Baby girl was quiet in her arms—too quiet. As she sat on the moss, stunned, Brigitte thought the impact might jolt Rosalind back to reality, that she would turn around at least to check on the baby, but minutes passed, and Rosalind didn't return.

Adrenaline rippled through Brigitte's body as she stood, the earth beneath her still trembling, branches bobbing in the wind. When baby began kicking again, the realization hit her. She had nothing to care for an infant. No food or clothing or diapers. She could survive in the woodland until winter, if she must, but the baby could not. Without milk, baby girl might not survive the day.

A blast of sound raked through the forest then—the squeal of brakes, skidding of tires, the crash of metal against rocks.

Brigitte raced with the baby through the trees, until she reached the cliff above the river. Wind gusted up from the chalky canyon, blowing past her, rustling the trees. In the grass strip between trees and cliff were black tire marks, leading straight over the edge.

Below she could see the blue Wolseley in the water, the boot standing on end as if it were the mast on a sinking sailboat. She couldn't see inside the vehicle—the front was completely immersed.

"Rosalind!" she shouted over the edge. The name rolled and coiled and sprang back to her.

There was no answer to her pleas. No sight of her friend.

Her stomach turning, Brigitte scanned the cliff for some sort of path, but a rock wall blocked her from the river. It would be precarious climbing down there by herself, and she certainly couldn't do it with a baby.

There was no sentiment for losing Herr, but Rosalind . . .

How could she bear to lose her only friend?

Brigitte called her name again and again as if she might be in the water, waiting for her.

Finally she turned back toward the forest. When she did, she swore she saw a shadow shift in the trees.

"Rosalind!" she called one last time, but the shadow was gone.

Welcher Mensch ist unter euch, der hundert

Schafe hat und, so er der eines verliert,

der nicht lasse die neunundneunzig in der Wüste
und hingehe nach dem verlorenen, bis daß er's finde?

LUKAS 15:4, LUTHER BIBLE (1912)

What man of you, having an hundred
sheep, if he lose one of them,

doth not leave the ninety and nine in the wilderness,
and go after that which is lost, until he find it?

LUKE 15:4, KING JAMES VERSION (1611)

CHAPTER 45

"It's very odd," Lucas said as the jet prepared to take off from Biggin Hill. He was across the aisle from Quenby in a leather recliner the color of silver birch.

"Evan didn't seem to think our visit was odd at all. He was spending a few days near Brighton and wanted to speak with me about the story."

Lucas continued his rant. "But how did he know you were in Newhaven?"

"Chandler told him."

"Brighton was just an excuse. He came down to see you."

She took one last sip of her London Fog before Samantha swept the cup away. "Chandler said he'd taken an unusual interest in this story."

"*Obsessive* might be more accurate."

"Like Mr. Knight?"

"No—Mr. Knight's interest is more like a calling. I think you uncovered something that's worrying Evan Graham."

"*Intrigued* is what he said. He asked me to report what I find directly to him instead of Chandler."

"Which you're not going to do—"

"Of course not. Until my story's reinstated, I won't be reporting anything about it to him."

"If it is reinstated, how are you going to write it without mentioning Brigitte?"

"I don't know," she said. The lines between the Terrell story and the Rickers had blurred in her mind now, Brigitte like a zipper holding them together. "It's all so confusing."

"Indeed," he said. "You once told me I had to earn your trust, and I think you're absolutely right. Evan needs to earn your trust as well."

"Do you know Evan?" she asked.

"I've never met him, but I know about him. He's from an old London family."

She'd never heard Evan talk about his family in their meetings, but he certainly had the air of one who'd been rooted in superiority, like Lucas had acted when she first met him.

Evan's father, Richard Graham, had started a small newspaper called the *London News* after the war to support the recovery of their country. Back then, Chandler once told her, the Graham family hadn't been as concerned about making money. They'd wanted to stitch back together what had been frayed by the war.

Quenby glanced out the window, at the brick chapel near the terminal. It was a memorial, Lucas had told her, for the RAF and civilian men and women killed here during the war. How strange to think that bombs were raining down on this place seventy-five years ago. That some people today could still remember them falling.

The plane sped down the runway and the wheels lifted. In seconds they were climbing above the outskirts of London and then soaring over the gardens and woods of Kent.

"Look out this window," Lucas said, motioning for Quenby to join him across the aisle.

When she scooted to the seat opposite him, Samantha scolded her from the front of the plane. "You'd better find that seat belt right away."

"Yes, ma'am." Quenby snapped it. "Seat belt is on."

"Splendid." Samantha looked back down at the magazine in her lap.

The jet flew low over trees until the forest flattened into lawn. They were above a grand house now with its austere stone facade, a dozen chimneys, and two wings that rambled down each side of the main house, the slate roof sloping down toward garden walls and a swimming pool with a stone pool house.

"Is that Breydon Court?" Quenby asked, glancing at Lucas. He was grinning.

"The very one."

"It's bigger than I imagined."

"The Rickers were quite influential in their day," Lucas said.

"I read that Lady Ricker stopped coming here after the war. She settled into their town house in London and became somewhat of a recluse."

Lucas placed his laptop on the coffee table between them, the screen open. "How many children did she have by then?"

"Two—Anthony and Louise. Louise was born a few months after Lord Ricker died."

"Perhaps she decided to focus on raising her children?"

"Perhaps . . ." But Lady Ricker didn't seem like the type of woman who would prize motherhood. "Mrs. Douglas showed me a picture of Anthony Ricker when I visited her. When he was younger, he looked exactly like Eddie Terrell."

"You think they were having an affair?"

"I'm fairly certain of it."

Lucas sighed. "I wonder if Anthony Ricker ever found out."

"That's not a conversation I'd like to have with his children."

"Was Lord Ricker the father of Louise?"

"Mrs. Douglas didn't mention her when we spoke."

Samantha stepped up beside them. "Would you like to fly over the house again?"

"Yes, please."

After Samantha spoke with the pilots, the plane circled above Breydon Court one more time. Then it headed west toward the Atlantic.

"Are you going to sleep this trip?" Quenby asked.

"Only the second half, and you should sleep too." He pointed at his laptop screen. "Do you know they have special passes so you don't have to wait in line for Space Mountain?"

"Everyone knows that."

Her sarcasm didn't deter him. "Will you ride Space Mountain with me?"

"You're like a kid."

"Will you?" he persisted.

"I'm not big on theme park rides."

He sighed. "I suppose we can stick to Winnie the Pooh."

She shook her head. "I'm not going into the park."

"Dream slayer."

She'd let him think she was only trying to douse his dreams instead of avoiding her own nightmare.

They flew out over the coastline of England, above a lineup of wind turbines twirling like the batons of a majorette troupe—owned by Arrow Wind, Lucas informed her. Then he unbuckled his seat belt. "Mr. Knight wants to conference with us."

Quenby followed him back toward the leather couch. "Does Mr. Knight travel very often in this jet?"

"Not anymore, though his executives use it often to meet with other companies around the world. I think . . ."

"What?" she pressed.

"I suppose having a plane makes Mr. Knight feel more secure, as if he can escape quickly if necessary."

At the press of a button, a television screen slid up from a bureau across from the couch. Seconds later, Lucas had connected them with Mr. Knight, and the older man's greeting boomed through the cabin. It was three in the morning on the Pacific coast, and Quenby wondered when the man slept.

He greeted both of them and then called out, "Hello, Samantha."

"Good morning, Mr. Knight."

"Are you treating my passengers right?"

"I'm planning to spoil them, sir."

"You better warn their waistlines," he said.

"They could both stand to gain a pound or two."

When he returned the laugh, Quenby rested back against the cool leather. Not only was his mind clear; Mr. Knight seemed to be in a jovial mood. And it comforted her, knowing that the man had surrounded himself with employees who were like family to him. Samantha, she suspected, had worked for him for a number of years, like Jack and Eileen.

The aroma of strawberries and espresso drifted through the cabin as Quenby recapped what she'd discovered about the Terrells. Mr. Knight didn't speak until she was done.

"Where did Brigitte go after Olivia died?" he asked.

"I'm trying to find that out," she said, but it was like the ocean itself had swept over Brigitte's trail now, erasing it from the sand.

"If Mrs. Douglas was right, who do you think killed Eddie?"

"I suspect either Olivia or Lady Ricker asked one of Hitler's men to do it."

"You don't think Brigitte—"

"Only if she was in danger," she assured him.

He leaned back in his chair, his eyes sad again. "Whoever killed Eddie could have taken Brigitte's life as well."

The sadness of that thought lingered for a moment before Lucas spoke. "Quenby took some pictures of the cemetery and the Mill House this morning."

She reached for her iPad and typed in the password for their private website. "I'll post them right now."

As she worked, Lucas told Mr. Knight about her odd visit from Evan Graham. Mr. Knight inched toward his computer, his face ballooning on their screen. "You have to be careful, Quenby. There are still Fascists in England today."

"Mr. Graham isn't a Fascist," she said.

"But the Ricker family might go to great lengths to keep Lady Ricker's secret."

In her work, she knew that people did indeed try to cover things up, but she didn't want to be paranoid. "The only way the Ricker family has threatened me is through legal action."

"Then you'll need a good lawyer." Mr. Knight glanced between them. "In fact, I'd like Lucas to accompany you wherever you go this next week."

When she looked at Lucas, he winked at her. Neither of them told Mr. Knight that he was already accompanying her almost everywhere she went—and that she had accompanied him to a Hough family dinner.

"Anything else before you enjoy Samantha's cuisine?" Mr. Knight asked.

Lucas's eyes were on her, and she fidgeted under his gaze. "Do you have anything else, Quenby?"

She swallowed hard, knowing she needed to ask Mr. Knight another question before they landed in Florida. One of the hardest questions she'd ever asked before.

"When we met at your house, you read from a file about me," she said slowly. "Does that include more information on my mother?"

"It does."

She took a deep breath. "Could I read it?"

"Certainly. Lucas should have the file with him."

She cringed. Did Lucas already know what happened to her? If so, he was being extremely cruel in trying to coax her to visit Disney World.

When they disconnected, Lucas dug a white catalog envelope out of his messenger bag and held it out to her. Quenby stared at the sealed envelope like it was sprinkled with poison. Or bits of candy, leading right up to the witch's front door.

She glanced out the window, at the blue wash of sea below them. "Have you read it?"

"No. Mr. Knight told me you're the only person allowed to open it."

She took the envelope and clutched it in her lap. "I'm not quite ready . . ."

He closed his eyes. "I can pretend to sleep."

"No sleeping yet," Samantha said beside them. "Not after I went to the effort of making these." She held out two strawberry and yogurt parfaits in glass mugs, each one topped with Oreo Mickey Mouse ears.

"Very clever," Quenby said, though she wished her stomach didn't turn with every reminder of their destination.

"Would you like a latte with yours?"

"I believe I would. Decaf, though, if you have it."

"Of course I have it."

Samantha placed each parfait on a plate, both of them centered on the coffee table. Then Quenby dipped her spoon into the concoction and took a bite. It was as rich and sweet as it appeared with the layers of strawberries and honey. "You're a master craftswoman."

"And you're my new best friend."

Lucas laughed. "Quenby collects friends wherever she goes."

"Along with a few enemies."

After Samantha moved up toward the galley, Lucas searched Quenby's face. "Why don't you want to open this file?"

"It contains a minefield of memories."

"About your parents?"

"About my mother," she said, and in that moment, she decided to trust him with the ugliest part of her own story. "Her name was Jocelyn, and she left me alone when I was seven."

"Left you at home?"

"No, she left me flying on Dumbo."

He shook his head. "I don't understand."

"She buckled me onto a ride at Disney World and then walked away."

His mouth gaped open as if a bomb had dropped on his head. A hundred questions, she suspected, were clamoring in his lawyerly mind, trying to connect logic and motive. "She left you for good?"

She nodded. "It was the last time I ever saw her."

"That's . . . ," he started. "Well, there's no words for it, Quenby."

She tried to smile. "I didn't think you'd ever be at a loss for words."

"There's nothing funny about abandoning a child."

"I suppose not." She dipped her spoon into the yogurt again.

"No wonder you don't want to visit Disney World. I'm sorry—"

She intercepted his apology. "You didn't do anything wrong."

"What if something happened to your mother?"

"Unfortunately, she had a history of leaving. I don't think the police ever suspected foul play."

Leaning back, Quenby closed her eyes, remembering it so clearly again. In the minutes after climbing off Dumbo, she'd thought surely her mother must have gone to get them ice cream or a pretzel. That if she'd wait, her mother would appear soon, frazzled and apologetic, wanting to surprise her with the treat.

Then she had thought her mother had gotten lost or injured or taken against her will, but adults didn't get kidnapped in Fantasyland. And if she'd gotten lost or hurt, Jocelyn would have called Grammy, at least once in the last ten years of Grammy's life.

When she was younger, Quenby had often wondered if Jocelyn had been angry with her. If somehow it had all been her fault. But it was completely irrational. No child should be abandoned, for any reason—her counselor had reiterated—even if the parent was mad.

She turned toward the window, the strands of sunlight fading as the clock slipped backward. What would her counselor think of her now, all these years later and still afraid to find out what happened to her mother?

She curled her fingers around the edge of the envelope. Baby steps.

Samantha stepped back into their space, carrying two drinks. "A latte for each of you."

They both thanked her as she set their drinks beside the parfaits. "Would you like anything else to eat?" she asked. "The galley is full."

They shook their heads.

After she left, Lucas picked up the remote and turned the TV screen back on. "Would you like to watch a movie?"

Quenby stared at the menu of options, her mind wandering again. She shouldn't have confided in him. He had the perfect family, and he must wonder—what was wrong with her that made Jocelyn want to leave?

"Quenby?"

His voice jolted her back to reality. "Yes?"

"Do you want to watch a movie?"

"Please." Perhaps a movie would take her mind off the file that was now on the table beside her.

He scrolled through the options. "You pick."

The movie featured at the top of the screen was an older one about Queen Victoria, filmed thirty years ago. The actress who played Queen Victoria was dressed in a beaded ivory gown with orange blossoms in her hair.

Quenby pointed at the image. "I interviewed her earlier this year."

"Queen Victoria?"

"Very funny," she said. "Hannah Dayne."

"I thought she stopped giving interviews years ago."

"I talked with her via phone. She asked me to write about refugee children."

"Brilliant of her."

"It was," Quenby replied. "She's been quietly assisting refugees in Yorkshire, but if readers found out about her involvement, they might be more interested in her reappearance than the plight of the people she wants to help."

"You want to watch her movie then?"

"I think we need something more whimsical." She pointed at another icon. "Like *Pride and Prejudice*."

He groaned, but without much conviction.

She smiled. "You're a closet fan, aren't you?"

"I admit to nothing."

"Right. Superpowers."

He started the movie, but before the Bennet sisters began dancing at the ball, his mobile rang. It was Mr. Knight.

"He wants to speak with you again," Lucas said before turning on the speaker.

"Hello, Mr. Knight."

"Do you have your computer?"

Quenby flipped her iPad screen up from the keyboard. "It's right here."

"Look at the panoramic picture of the house again," he instructed.

She pulled the picture up on her iPad, and she and Lucas studied the tangled web of branches, leaves, and vines surrounding it.

"That tree," Mr. Knight said, almost breathless. "The one to the right of the Mill House."

She enlarged the photo and examined the dying yellow leaves, the emerging green to replace them. And she realized it was like no other tree in the forest around it. Where the sunlight hit the branches, the waxy new leaves glowed.

"Magnolia," Mr. Knight said.

The words in Brigitte's letters flooded back to her. The tree in her father's yard. The tale of Cinderella.

Eyes wide, Quenby glanced at Lucas. "It's a wishing tree."

Chapter 46

London, February 1953

The girl clung to her mummy's hand as they skipped over puddles on the pathway that threaded through Kensington Gardens. Rosalind watched them closely, mesmerized by their camaraderie. It was an anomaly to her—a mother and daughter who actually enjoyed one another's company. Not once, in her memory, had Lady Ricker wanted to be with her.

Rosalind visited the garden nearly every Sunday and sat on a bench by the Long Water, even on days like this when the clouds drizzled a winter rain. Her umbrella and Burberry trench coat were the stoic color of stone, though she longed for a brash red, emerald, or sapphire to pierce through the gray.

But neither she nor her coat could stand out in London or anywhere else in England. Her role for the moment was to be like everyone else, one of a thousand raindrops blending smoothly into the lake before her. Not making any waves. Even her string of boy-friends had been as bland as the autumn sky.

The narrow stretch of water, dividing the gardens from Hyde Park, transported her back a decade, to that fateful spring afternoon when she'd jumped out of the blue Wolseley and watched her old life plunge over a cliff. It was so surreal that sometimes she thought she'd dreamed it.

But it had been no dream. Eddie Terrell, the fool, had left a bag of banknotes behind in the car. She'd discovered it before they left the Mill House, when she was throwing her suitcase into the boot. The moment Brigitte had leapt from the car, the baby in her arms, Rosalind knew exactly what she was going to do.

She'd stopped the car before the edge of the bluff, removed the money. Then she'd snapped her life in two.

The past behind her, she opted to embrace her new existence in shadows of her making. Lady Ricker, she felt certain, would want her dead, even in this decade after the war. Rosalind knew far too much about her mum's dealings with the Nazi dreck. The secrets she had to keep.

If her mum was able to change her colors, acting as the loyal wife of a British MP even as she supported Fascism, then Rosalind figured she could be a chameleon as well. Changing her colors until Lady Ricker died—from a vibrant modern woman into the drudgery of browns and grays.

She didn't regret what she'd done all those years ago. Brigitte might have thought she was much older, more mature, but Rosalind had only been sixteen when she'd parachuted into Breydon Court. And she'd known little about how to survive on her own.

Brigitte was three years younger, but she already knew how to care for herself and for someone else.

The mother and child in the park drew closer, both laughing as their umbrella bobbed overhead. Her eyes should remain on the lake water—staring was akin to making waves—but she couldn't seem to help herself. The woman with her short brown hair brushed back over her ears, wearing an olive jumper over her plain dress, looked like an older housewife version of Brigitte. If it was Brigitte, the girl clinging to her hand might be Rosalind's daughter.

Rosalind stayed frozen on the bench, squeezing the wooden crook of her umbrella as the two walked by her, seemingly unaware of the stone lady on the bench.

It wasn't Brigitte—or at least, she didn't think so. Nor was it Rosalind's child. Baby would be nearly ten now, and this girl looked to be no more than five or six.

Almost every week, she spotted a mother who reminded her of Brigitte, though she never pursued her inquiries. If she ever did find Brigitte, she wasn't sure what she'd say. Probably she would do exactly what she'd done long ago and walk away.

Just because Rosalind had carried the baby in her womb didn't mean she was the right one to care for her into adulthood. The baby had deserved a fresh life where no one would try to harm her. And a mum who knew how to mother well.

When the rain clouds took a respite, Rosalind closed her umbrella and propped it beside her. A boy stopped by her bench, a stack of newspapers tied up in a cord under his arm. He eyed her plain coat. "Two pennies for a paper?"

She studied his plain clothes in return. "I'll take one," she said, wanting to contribute to the boy's welfare more than read the words on his paper. The world and its news moved rapidly around her, but Rosalind didn't—couldn't—waver.

The woman and girl were near the reeds around the water now, feeding something to the ducks. She turned her attention to the *Times* in her lap.

February 8, 1953.

Then she read the headline near the bottom of the page. Twice.

The paper boldly announced what she'd been waiting for. Lady Ricker was finally dead, the enemy of influenza taking her life.

According to the writer, Mum had left behind two children in London—a boy named Anthony and a girl named Louise. There was no mention of Lady Ricker turning traitor during the war. And more importantly, no mention of her oldest child.

Rosalind slowly lowered the paper, her hands trembling as a shell of stone seemed to crack near the top of her head, shooting down the seam and crumbling in a thousand pieces at her feet. Then she smiled.

She'd thought it would be many more years before she was free, but finally her life was about to begin.

CHAPTER 47

A chauffeur sped Quenby and Lucas toward the tearoom to meet Alexander. Quenby had suggested Lucas rent a car at the Jacksonville airport, but he'd refused to drive in the States. And he insisted that she rest.

As they'd crossed the Atlantic, she and Lucas had forgone their movie and launched into a new discussion about Brigitte and the possibility of her planting a magnolia tree near the garden, like Cinderella's wishing tree.

But how did Brigitte obtain seeds for a magnolia? The beautiful trees grew across England, just like they did in the States, but acquiring magnolia seeds near the Mill House, during the war, seemed an impossibility.

After Lucas fell asleep, Quenby had chipped away at that question until she realized that Brigitte, the refugee, wouldn't have access to magnolia seeds or the money to purchase them. But Brigitte, a young woman after the war, could have returned to plant it.

That thought revived her.

If Brigitte had left the Mill House after Olivia's death, why hadn't she tried to find Dietmar? Or had she tried and failed after Dietmar changed his last name? And most important, had Brigitte hidden something under this magnolia like her father had done all those years ago?

The answers, she hoped, were back in Newhaven.

Humid air clung heavy on her skin as she stepped out of the car and into the elegant tearoom. Palladian windows overlooked a floral garden, and bouquets of summer flowers decorated every table.

A gentleman in his fifties crossed the floor and welcomed them. He was taller than Quenby by a solid foot, his brown hair thinning, and he wore a taupe linen suit over his lanky frame.

"Thank you for meeting me here," Alexander said, motioning them toward a table.

Quenby chose a seat by the window, and Lucas held it out for her. "I have to admit my curiosity," she replied as she hung her handbag on the chair.

"And I must admit mine as well." Alexander sat across the table, resituating his crooked fork into a perfect line. "My aunt says you are writing a story about the Ricker family."

Quenby wove her fingers together, rested her chin on their nest. "Who is your aunt?"

"We'll get to that," he said with a warm smile. "Please, tell me first about this story of yours."

She dropped her hands onto the marble tabletop. There were no warning signs flashing, like there'd been with Evan, though she knew well that she couldn't rely solely on intuition to judge a man's character. But if Alexander was willing to tell her his story—and she hoped he was—then she needed to tell him the basics of what she'd found.

"I'm afraid there's not much of a way to cushion this," she said. "I believe Lady Ricker operated a safe house for Nazis during World War II."

His face didn't register the sort of shock she'd imagined. "That's not new information for the family."

"The Rickers know?"

"Of course," he said with a nod. "Janice did a lot more than just operate a safe house."

Before he expounded, the server stepped up to the table with a plate filled with fruits and cheeses. Then he brought a pot of Darjeeling tea. Alexander, it seemed, had already ordered for them.

She smeared the creamy Brie on flatbread while their host poured the tea. "I come here often," he said, splashing milk into his cup. "It reminds me of home."

"You're from England?" Quenby asked as she stirred a cube of sugar into her tea.

"Kensington. I lost the British accent during my freshman year at an American high school."

"Did the other kids beat it out of you?" Lucas asked.

"They teased it out of me, I suppose. I wasn't confident like my parents at that age. My mother, on the other hand, clung to her accent until she passed away."

Quenby waited, hoping he would expound on his mother, but instead he said, "My dad stayed back in London when we moved to the States, but his absence didn't make much of a difference in our lives. My parents separated when I was very young, and I didn't see much of him after that."

Over English tea and finger sandwiches, Alexander began to tell them his story.

"My mother kept me so entertained that I hardly missed my father. She worked as an actress in London, but she always wanted to leave England."

Perhaps Brigitte became someone else in her adult life. An actress who could move people to laughter and tears. Perhaps the stage took away some of her own pain. For the Brigitte in Quenby's mind had grown into a woman who was fiercely courageous and strong. Mr. Knight had said she loved to pretend. With a new name, perhaps she'd hidden herself in plain sight on the West End.

"My mother hated the cold of New York and the drudgery of the movies in Hollywood. She ended up performing on the stage at Disneyland for a season. When Disney built the Magic Kingdom, we moved to Orlando."

Quenby's heart beat faster. "What was your mother's name?"

"In London, she was known by her stage name, Eliza Cain." He took another sip of the milky tea. "But her real name was Rosalind."

He looked across the table as if Quenby should recognize the name, and she tried to hide her disappointment, wiping the crumbs off her lips with a cloth napkin.

"Was Rosalind related to Lady Ricker?" she asked, feeling foolish for not knowing where this woman fit into the Ricker family.

He nodded slowly. "Rosalind was Janice Ricker's oldest daughter."

Quenby blinked, processing this new information. "I've read extensively about Lady Ricker and no one ever mentioned Rosalind."

"That's because Janice didn't tell anyone about her. In fact, she tried to kill her."

Quenby shuddered. "Why would she try to kill her daughter?"

Alexander glanced out the window as a couple clothed in matching tennis outfits walked by. "Janice didn't work with just anybody in Germany, you see. She collaborated with Rosalind's father. The man who became my grandfather."

Quenby blinked, stunned. "Lady Ricker had a lover in Germany?"

He nodded. "She and Oskar met when she was touring in Europe, while she was still married to her first husband. She became a devout, albeit secret, Fascist who was focused on helping Oskar first and then

Hitler and the Third Reich at any cost. Unfortunately, when Rosalind returned to England, she knew too much. My grandmother couldn't risk having anyone find out what she was doing."

"How did Lady Ricker and Oskar communicate?" Lucas asked.

"Through a wireless."

"And perhaps through the letters." She told him what they'd found under the floor of the Mill House. "Brigitte believed the letters were coded."

This time he looked stunned. "I didn't think anyone else knew about Brigitte."

❖

Foamy waves lapped the beach outside Jacksonville as Quenby buried her toes in the warm sand, her jacket doubling as a towel underneath her. Lucas leaned back on his elbows beside her, bare feet crossed over his jeans.

Two boys raced through the surf in front of them, battling the string of a ladybug kite that dipped toward the water. The older boy pulled back on the string before it clipped a wave, and the kite soared again in the breeze.

Over tea and sandwiches, Alexander had told them what happened after Rosalind arrived at the Mill House and then after Eddie Terrell died. How she'd tried to fake her own death and left her daughter with Brigitte. Rosalind had followed Brigitte and the baby, he said, until they reached a village nearby. Then she ran north and folded herself into the crowds of London. After Lady Ricker's death, Rosalind had embraced life as a new woman, released from the chains of being the daughter of a German officer and an American aristocrat turned British. After joining the theater, she'd married a man her mother would never consider respectable. In a few years, Rosalind didn't consider him respectable either, but she stayed in the marriage for a decade before she relocated herself and their son to California.

Rosalind had passed away five years ago, but before she died, Alexander had pressed her to tell him all of her story. She talked at length about the theater, the costumes and glamour and opening nights, but he said he wanted to know about the years before the West End.

Finally she told him about the Rickers. About her mum and the safe house and about Brigitte. Brigitte, his mother had told him, was a hostage as well, but if Rosalind knew where she'd gone after the war, she never told her son.

Rosalind never met her half sister or half brother—Anthony Ricker had preceded Rosalind to the grave, and she had no desire to meet Louise. After his mother's death, Alexander connected with his aunt. In fact, after Quenby e-mailed her, Mrs. McMann was the one who'd called him, warning him not to talk with her, but Alexander said he'd never seen eye to eye with his aunt. In small part, he wanted redemption for his mother. To tell the world that she was an over-comer in spite of what Lady Ricker had tried to do.

Neither Lucas nor Quenby told Alexander they were searching for Brigitte. But if they found what happened to her, perhaps they would find Rosalind's daughter as well. She and Alexander could meet at last.

Quenby asked Alexander if Rosalind had any regrets about leaving her daughter, but if she had, she'd never told him. He said she'd left her baby behind because she thought Brigitte could take better care of her. And if Lady Ricker had found Rosalind and the child, she would have killed them both.

Or at least, that's what Rosalind thought. Somewhere in her mind, perhaps polished and justified over the years, she'd come to the conclusion that she had done what was best under the circumstances.

Quenby nudged Lucas's leg, and he glanced over at her. He looked so handsome, lying on the sand. *Eye candy* was what Chandler would call him. Anyone else on the beach would probably think he was full of himself in his confidence. She'd certainly thought, in her own insecurity, that he was arrogant when they first met, but now she wondered if he hadn't trusted her, like she hadn't trusted him.

She'd seen far past his facade in their time together and had come to appreciate much more than his features. He was a man who spoke his mind about his family, his doubts, his faith. A man who seemed to want what was best for her.

She took the envelope containing Mr. Knight's file from her handbag. "I think I'm finally going to open it."

He sat up. "And you need some space?"

"For just a few minutes."

He didn't look irritated at her request. In fact, it seemed that he understood.

"I won't go far," Lucas said as he leaned toward her. "Call me when you're ready."

When he kissed her cheek this time, there was no awkwardness between them. One friend caring for another friend.

Then he left her.

The children before her laughed as they flew their ladybug kite, and she flashed back to her Dumbo ride again. Back then, with her mother watching, she'd felt as if she really could fly.

She closed her eyes, remembering the smile on her mother's face when, in hindsight, she shouldn't have been smiling at all. But Quenby had known something was wrong even though she couldn't put it into words. Wrong because her mother was happy.

Had the thought of leaving her daughter filled her with joy?

Her stomach turned as she opened the envelope and saw the neat stack of corporate paper, stapled together. A dossier. Whoever Mr. Knight hired to research had done their job well.

The first page was polished and precise, lifted from the biography on the syndicate's website. It was the kind of description one used to portray a life neatly put together, every piece in perfect place. College, writing credentials, her love of English literature and all things British. Of course, no one's life was perfect, and no one could truly contain a synopsis of twenty-eight years on one page.

The next page dug a little deeper into her childhood. Where she was born (Nashville). The short background on her father, Trevor Vaughn, an aspiring country music artist who'd died in a motorcycle accident when he was twenty-three.

A brief background on her mother, Jocelyn Vaughn, a flower child growing up in the decade after being a flower child was cool. Quenby had never known her mother's maiden name, and the dossier didn't mention it.

Trevor and Jocelyn had met at a country music festival in Atlanta, their mutual passion for music solidifying a bond that lasted six years. And the story began to unravel from there, chock-full of details that Quenby hadn't known.

There was the story of Grammy, who'd left Germany two decades after World War II with her American husband, a soldier stationed in Berlin before he went to Vietnam. About Grammy's father— Quenby's great-grandfather—a devout Nazi who had fought for the Wehrmacht. About Grammy's uncle who'd died when his plane was shot down in Poland in 1939.

Quenby closed her eyes for a moment, processing the words on paper. Grammy had told lots of the Grimm stories, but she'd never talked about her own childhood. And no wonder. The shame from her family's devotion to Hitler must have been overwhelming for a woman who loved almost everyone, except perhaps Jocelyn.

Grammy had tried to hide her contempt for her daughter-in-law when Quenby was young, but there was no hiding it after Jocelyn abandoned her. As a girl, Quenby remembered being glad that someone understood her pain, even as part of her heart still yearned for love and approval from a woman who could never give it.

There were three pages left in the report. The top of the next page was a photocopy of a newspaper article that ran in the *Orlando Sentinel*, two days after Jocelyn disappeared. Beside the column of copy was a picture of Quenby's mother on her wedding day, wearing a crocheted dress, white cowboy boots, a wreath of flowers around her head.

Quenby tentatively flipped the page. Mr. Knight's file followed Quenby's life from college to England; then the final page began to detail her mother's movements after she stepped away from Dumbo.

Her fingers brushing over the top of the page, she tried to steady her breath. Then she lifted her gaze and watched the tail of the kite as the boys rushed away. Finally, after all these years, perhaps she would finally find out what happened to her mother. Courage was what she needed. An internal strength as she sought truth about her own story.

As she prayed for that strength, her gaze fell back to the paper.

According to the investigation, Jocelyn left Disney World that Thursday afternoon and drove to a man's house in a place called Narcoossee. Her boyfriend's house, the record said, though Quenby hadn't known her mother was dating anyone. The last few lines in the profile sounded so impersonal, an outsider's sketch.

When she finished reading, Quenby slammed the file shut, her chest void at first, and then tears began falling down her cheeks.

Seconds later, Lucas slipped onto the sand beside her again, waiting quietly at first before he spoke. "Are you okay?"

She pulled the file to her chest. "I will be."

"Does it say what happened to your mother?"

Nodding, she took a deep breath. "My mother's dead," she said simply, her words seeming to come from someone else's mouth.

"I'm sorry, Quenby."

"The police told Grammy, but she never told me."

"She was probably trying to protect you."

"I know." Grammy had loved her dearly. She wouldn't have done anything purposefully to hurt her.

"How did your mother die?" he asked.

Her gaze fell back to the paperwork, her stomach churning. "She overdosed on methamphetamines."

He reached for her hand and gently covered her fingers. Instead of fighting him, she sat quietly beside him as sorrow streamed down her cheeks, neither of them moving again until the tide swept salty tears of its own across their toes.

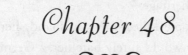

Chapter 48

Rodmell, April 1953

Lily Ward lived in the village of Rodmell, five miles north of Newhaven. She'd lost her husband during the Battle of Britain, and then she'd lost their only child, a six-year-old daughter, when a bomb dropped on her school's playground. Much later, Lily told Brigitte that God gave her two new daughters, not to replace her first one but to redeem what had been lost.

It was in Lily's house, years after they arrived, that Brigitte finally began to believe that God might indeed be good. That He gave each person the opportunity to cultivate His creation and care for those in need. And that He sacrificed His Son to redeem hearts laden with bitterness and hatred. Some of His children still chose evil, but He was even willing to forgive those who'd murdered the people Brigitte loved, if they would repent and turn from their sins.

Mama Lily was like Jesus to her. She chose forgiveness when, in those early years, Brigitte could not.

After the war, Brigitte ate sparingly as her stomach began to adjust to the regularity of food—bacon and eggs and Lily's black pudding. She adored the woman who became like a mother to her and the sister who followed in her footsteps. But still she slept with her bedroom door locked, the night lamp turned on. And she never spoke German in Lily's house, terrified as to what the older woman would do if she discovered Brigitte's heritage.

The German people killed Lily's husband, her beloved child. Brigitte thought Lily would surely hate her, a German girl, and she couldn't blame her for it. Her people had killed millions in their hatred, and she didn't want to add to Lily's grief.

Now she knew differently. In hindsight, Lily surely heard the accent that Brigitte had tried to stifle as a child and chose to love her anyway. Even as she grieved, Lily refused to hate the men who'd killed her family. If she did, she said she would be just like them.

Lily adopted the two orphaned girls after the war, and those who knew her rejoiced that God had given her a family after losing those she'd loved. The girls' presence helped bring healing to Lily. And her little farmhouse, all neat and clean and comfortable, saved their lives.

When Brigitte had first stumbled toward Lily's house, a decade ago, she'd feared there would be another witch inside, but two cows resided in the pasture beside the Wards' house and baby girl had stopped crying. The baby, she'd realized, would never cry again if she didn't get milk.

Long ago, Dietmar had rescued her, and Brigitte knew that she must rescue Rosalind's child like he'd done with her.

Thankfully, Lily Ward was no witch. She'd known exactly what to do with a baby, feeding her fresh milk from bottles, milk that revitalized her cries. Then the cries turned into laughter and the war was over. Mama Lily and Brigitte began to smile, too, when baby girl blew bubbles or purred like the cat she adored.

The spring following her twenty-third birthday, Brigitte borrowed

Lily's car and followed the river south. To the Mill House. She didn't dare go inside the house, fearing that Eddie's corpse might still be there, but in her hands was a pot sprouting the tender leaves of a magnolia tree, purchased from a local nursery.

Her own prayers had been answered. She had a mother who loved her. A sister who was becoming a friend. And neither Olivia Terrell nor Lady Ricker knew where she had gone.

She dug a hole for the tree, then a second one nearby to hide her final letter for Dietmar, enclosed in a metal box. If he searched for her, he would find this tree. He'd know she was well and that, like her, he was free.

CHAPTER 49

The houses around Narcoossee were a mix of high-end mansions and mobile homes, surrounded by swampy wetlands and neatly swept orange groves. Quenby had closed her eyes on the drive down from Jacksonville, but there'd been no sleep for her after reading the file on her mother.

Their driver found the address for Chase Merrill—the boyfriend—on a dusty lane flanked by knobby roots of cypress trees, Spanish moss draping over the branches like sleeves on a wizard's robe.

She thought they'd find a dilapidated cottage at the end of the road, like the Mill House, but instead there was an elegant yellow lake house, trimmed with white to match the picket fence around the lawn. In the driveway was a Jeep.

Lucas eyed the house. "You want to talk to him alone?"

"I do."

"Take as long as you need," he said. "I'll wait for you here."

She guessed it wouldn't be a long discussion, but while she was in Florida, she wanted to meet the man who'd stolen her mother from her. Or at least, that's what she'd gathered from the file. Chase Merrill was the last strand to Jocelyn.

Stone pavers led to the front door, and as she moved toward it, she tried to steady the racing in her heart, breathing deeply, in and out. Tension knotted her left shoulder, and she massaged it as she stood in front of the doorbell. It felt as if she were about to interview a hostile contact, as if he might throw her out on her backside when she explained her intent.

This visit didn't really change anything about her current life, and yet it seemed everything had changed.

The window to the right of the door was cracked open. The blinds were closed, so she couldn't see inside, but she heard the loud thump of music behind them. Taking another deep breath, she rang the bell.

A man fully entrenched in midlife answered the door, dressed in a black rash guard, wakeboarding shorts, and flip-flops. A dark beard, salted white, covered his chin, and his skin was a leathery tan.

"Are you Chase Merrill?" she asked.

"I am." He glanced at the sedan waiting in the driveway. "Do I know you?"

"No, but you knew my mother."

His laugh made her cringe. "I've known a lot of women in my life."

"Her name was Jocelyn."

He stopped laughing. "Jocelyn's been dead for twenty years."

"From a drug overdose, I'm told."

"How did you find me?"

She shrugged. "Everyone leaves a trail."

He stepped forward, his hand pressed against the doorpost. "What do you want?"

"I want to know—"

"Money?"

"No." She paused. "I just want to know the truth of what happened to my mother."

"My wife and I have been married for twenty-five years." He narrowed his eyes. "Do you understand?"

She didn't have to be a genius at math for those calculations. "Clearly."

He glanced at the stretch of windows behind him, at the expanse of lake outside, palm trees perfectly framing the view. "The truth is messy."

"It usually is."

"Are you Quenby?" he asked.

She nodded. Perhaps Jocelyn had told him about her after all.

"Stay here," he said, as if she might lift a memento from his house to take with her.

The room beyond the entry was decorated nautically with a wooden ship's wheel, pictures of sailboats, glass bottles filled with seashells. And a large photograph of Chase Merrill and his wife.

Had Jocelyn known he was married?

She stepped through the propped-open front door into the Merrills' house. A boat flew by on the lake, hauling a wakeboarder who rode up a ramp, then flipped when he reached the top, landing in perfect form on the other side.

If only they could all ride up the ramps of life, twisting and turning and landing without injury on the other side. But in real life, often the person who was being towed ended up getting dragged underwater.

The boat turned toward the dock behind the house as Chase returned, carrying a dust-coated storage box. He dropped it on the floor and riffled through papers before he pulled out a thin album. "I was with her in the hotel room when she died. I called for the ambulance—"

"Noble of you."

"This was in her things." He held the album in his hands. "She wouldn't have wanted her mother to have it."

Quenby flinched. "You knew my grandmother?"

"Not personally." He gave her a curious look. "You don't know her?"

"No."

He glanced toward the back windows and then shoved the album at her as if he were handing her an envelope stuffed with cash, exchanging it for her silence. "For what it's worth, I didn't know Jocelyn had a daughter until I found this."

Bitterness bubbled in her throat. "She left me for you."

He didn't seem to be fazed by her words. "She was addicted to meth, Quenby. That stuff makes people do crazy things."

"Who gave her the meth?"

Instead of answering, he glanced toward the windows again, at the woman and two teenagers strolling up the lawn. Then he pointed to the front entrance. "You have to leave."

She didn't move. "Who was Jocelyn's mother?"

"I don't remember her name."

She crossed her arms. "I don't believe you."

The woman called for Chase from the patio, and he shoved Quenby back outside, the album clutched to her chest.

"The truth might be messy," she said, "but it tends to come out in the end."

"It's not the end for me."

"For me either," she replied, but he'd already slammed the door behind her and slid the bolt as if she might burst inside and ruin his life like he had ruined hers.

Instead of moving away from the stoop, she opened the worn album.

There were pages of baby pictures, each one labeled in a flowery script. Quenby's first steps. Quenby's first Christmas. Quenby with

Mommy and Daddy, riding in a boat on Old Hickory Lake. Then there were pictures of her parents' wedding and some silly ones after it, at a carnival and a concert.

There weren't many pictures after Quenby turned four, the year her dad died. On the last page was a picture of a girl waving as she circled around on her elephant. Smiling as if she really could fly.

Through the window, she heard a woman's voice. "Who was that?"

"A solicitor."

The woman groaned. "I hate it when people come begging."

"Me too," Chase replied.

"Did you give him anything?" the woman asked.

"Of course not."

"Hopefully he won't come back again."

"No," Chase said. "He's gone for good."

Quenby closed the album. Chase Merrill was right. She wouldn't be knocking on his door again.

❖

The golden turret on Cinderella's castle blazed like a torch in the setting sunlight, and the realm below smelled like dark chocolate and caramel corn. Hundreds of children crowded Main Street, ice cream dripping from their cones, balloons dipping and soaring. The cheery music overhead and clanging bell of a train welcomed Lucas and Quenby into the kingdom.

But the scene didn't bring the same joy to Quenby as it did to the kids around her. Instead the magic cut through her heart.

As she stared up at the castle, Lucas reached for her hand and together they rounded the castle moat, walking toward Fantasyland.

Lucas hadn't insisted they visit Disney World, but when he suggested they make new memories here, to replace some of the old ones, she'd agreed.

On the car ride over, she'd shown Lucas the photo album. He'd stared at the picture on the last page alongside her.

"My mother took that, right before she abandoned me."

"It's almost like she wanted you to be happy for life. Like she had this image in her mind and in this album of how she wanted your future to be."

"I stopped smiling the moment I got off that ride," Quenby said. "And it was a long time before I smiled again."

"She loved you, Quenby."

"But she loved Chase even more. And perhaps the drugs."

"People sometimes do terrible things when they think they're in love."

"Chase said something about Jocelyn's mother," she'd mused. "Perhaps I still have family. . . ."

Now Lucas stopped on the path, interrupting Quenby's thoughts. "There it is."

Lifting her eyes, she saw a yellow-and-red circus tent. Two Dumbo rides with carousels turning in opposite directions. The flying elephants were ablaze in color, the lights reflecting in the pools below them. The carousels seemed larger than she remembered. And the old fence was gone. The ride, in its essence, was the same, but it had changed in the past two decades. Like her.

"I think we need to take another flight together," Lucas said.

Her eyebrows slipped up. "On the Global?"

"No, on an elephant."

She took a step back. "I don't think so."

Lucas reached for her hand, trying to inch her toward the circus tent. "New memories, Quenby."

She hesitated at first, but Lucas wasn't trying to harm her. He only wanted the best. One more ride on Dumbo might do her some good.

She climbed into the seat of an elephant clothed in orange,

wide enough for a kid and an adult. Lucas began to climb in beside Quenby, but she stopped him. "I like my personal space, Lucas."

He smiled. "I happen to like your personal space too."

She eyed him again before scooting toward the far side. Truth was, she didn't want to ride this without him.

His arm rested casually behind her, her back rigid as they rose from the ground.

"Let's fly, Quenby," he shouted over the music.

She took the joystick and flew high above the park, above the lights. And it felt . . . magical. As if she could do anything.

They spent the evening riding the mountains of Space and Thunder. Then they dined in the Beast's enchanted castle before Quenby talked Lucas into taking a cruise around It's a Small World.

The sky was pitch-dark when they emerged from the trip across the continents, the song looping in her head. But it didn't annoy her. It made her happy instead. They did share hope and fears, laughter and tears, with people all over the world.

Night cooling the air, they stood by a waterway and watched sprays of golden fire, a spangle of color, turn the dark sky into a parade of light. When Lucas pulled her close, Quenby didn't resist. She leaned back against his chest, and he wrapped his arms around her.

The strength of his body anchored her; the touch of his hands, overlapping hers, sent a tremor of warmth through her skin. The snide remarks, cutting comments, came easy to her, the keeping him at an arm's length, but what was she supposed to do now?

As she rested against him, she knew they needed to discuss this, whatever *this* was. Or maybe there would be no discussion. By the time they landed back in London, he would probably change his mind; then he would leave like everyone else.

A fountain of a thousand lights rocketed up into the air and cascaded down, glittering like pixie dust. The warmth of it, the beauty, mesmerized her. Oddly enough, in this park where she'd lost everything, perhaps she would begin to find again what was most important to her.

The finale ended, but she didn't want Lucas to let her go.

He stepped back, clearing his throat. "Ready for an overnight back to London?"

She didn't want to step away, but it was time to return to Newhaven and find Brigitte's wishing tree.

He smiled. "It's a good thing we have Samantha to chaperone tonight."

She nudged him. "You're the only one who needs a chaperone."

"Quenby—" he started, his voice much too serious.

She stopped him. "Let's not break the magic."

"This isn't about a place," he said, the crowd behind them swarming toward the exit.

"I know." At least she thought she did. Places were powerful.

"It's about people. Namely you and me."

"Tomorrow, Lucas."

"I thought, when I first met you, that you were arrogant—"

"I wasn't the arrogant one!"

"But now I think—"

She shook her head. "We'll talk tomorrow."

"Do you need me to write a contract?"

"No—"

"We can seal it with a kiss."

Quenby shivered. "A handshake will do just fine."

Chapter 50

When Lily Ward first asked for the baby girl's name, Brigitte had called her Hannah after her mother, so that the woman who'd loved Brigitte as a child would never be forgotten. A Hebrew name meaning "favor" or "grace."

It was a miracle that Hannah had survived her early days of starvation and the filth at the Mill House. She'd grown into a striking young woman who entertained her sister and mother and ultimately the entire village with heart-stirring melodies that teemed from her lips.

Hannah didn't fear like Brigitte. She'd grown up in a home filled with love and laughter. Plenty of good food and clean clothing and a personal tutor in her younger years since Lily had refused to send her to the village school.

No one told Hannah that she hadn't been born a Ward, but still she suspected. When she was eleven, she'd asked Brigitte if she was adopted. Brigitte told her about Rosalind and the little she knew about the man who had fathered her. Lily might not have birthed either of them, but the woman had rescued them both.

Brigitte attended nursing school up north to learn how to care properly for children. After graduation, Lily fell ill and Brigitte returned home to nurse her as well.

Mama Lily lived two more months at home, and then one night she slipped away. Brigitte grieved the loss deeply. In her twenty-six years, she'd loved and lost two mothers.

Lily left all her worldly goods to her daughters, though there wasn't much to give them after she poured her widow's pension and the small income from the farm into rearing Hannah and sending Brigitte off to school. Brigitte had found a position in Yorkshire, and her new income was enough to enroll Hannah in a public school nearby.

A week after Lily died, while Brigitte was still putting their affairs in order, a stranger knocked on the door. Hannah didn't trouble Brigitte in her work until after the stranger was gone.

The man, she'd said, was searching for someone named Brigitte, and Hannah knew no one by that name. Which was true. Brigitte had changed her name to Bridget Ward years ago. It meant she was British. Safe. And thanks to Lily, her English was as polished as any of her classmates' in London.

But the moment that man showed up, the illusion of safety was gone. Somehow, it seemed, one of Lady Ricker's people had found her. For her ladyship was the only one left who knew Brigitte's secret. And perhaps Brigitte was the only one who knew hers.

She heard her old friend's voice, whispering to her to run one more time.

So she and Hannah had packed their bags quickly, cramming everything of value into her little Fiat before fleeing to their new home in Yorkshire. It wasn't until much later, when she was unpacking, that she realized Dietmar's knight, the one she thought she'd shoved into her purse, was gone.

CHAPTER 51

Pink stars were bursting from the yellow-and-green magnolia, a galaxy of blossoms to transform the forgotten garden into a place that whispered the promise of new life.

Quenby traced the tree's bark with her fingers, but she didn't find initials carved into it. "I wish Mr. Knight were here."

Lucas smiled. "We'll phone him the moment we have news. Where's your mobile?"

She slipped the phone out of her pocket and opened the metal detector app they'd downloaded on the plane. Hopefully Brigitte had buried a letter far enough away from the trunk that the sprawling roots hadn't destroyed it.

The app whistled as she scanned the ground; then the sound turned into a piercing scream. Lucas reached for the shovel he'd brought and stomped on the edge of it to dig between the roots. He persisted until his shovel hit metal. "There's something here."

She rubbed her hands together. "Brigitte knew what she was doing."

Instead of a tin, they found a rusted metal box, buried within the web of roots. Quenby brushed off the dirt and lifted the clasp. Inside was an envelope.

She carefully peeled back the flap and removed a single piece of paper, handwritten in English instead of German. Then she began to read it out loud.

Dearest Dietmar,

If you're reading this, you have kept your promise. After all these years, you have returned.

I wish I were there to greet you. I waited so long for you, hoping that you would come. Praying I would be able to find you one day. I know now how many were detained during the war. How many died. Yet in my mind's eye, you are still very much alive.

My father died in 1942, and I suppose your lovely father and mother died as well. Sometimes I think I can see them, waiting with arms outstretched for you and for me.

Did you return to Germany? Or did you run someplace else?

It seems like a dream, the years you and I had together. Our autumn in the fields of Belgium, the time we closed our eyes and pretended to be blind. How I wish I could go back and thank those monks for rescuing us.

Now I want to rescue others, like those monks—and you—rescued me.

I listened to the soft wind breathing through the grass, Dietmar. And like the eagle, I've decided to catch it this time.

> *With a grateful heart,*
> *And forever yours,*
>
> *Brigitte,*
> *Your Princess Friend*

Quenby dropped the letter to her side. "She doesn't want to be found."

"You don't know that."

"It's her good-bye to Mr. Knight. The end of their journey." Quenby reread the last paragraph. "'Soft wind breathing through the grass'—that's from *Wuthering Heights*, when Lockwood is passing by the graves of Catherine, Edgar, and Heathcliff. He thinks they will be peaceful in death—"

"But the reader knows differently," Lucas said. "There will be no peace with Catherine and Heathcliff together in the grave."

She glanced up at him, startled. "How do you know?"

"Required reading at secondary school."

"I'm impressed you remember."

"I'm here to impress you," he quipped. "How did you remember that last line?"

She shrugged. "English lit minor and Brontë aficionado. It's like Brigitte was burying her life to start anew."

"She's conflicted, but I think she still wants to see him."

She folded the letter and put it back into the box. "Some people really want to disappear."

"She isn't your mother, Quenby."

"I know, but perhaps there was a good reason that she wanted to start again. Perhaps Rosalind's daughter thought that Brigitte was her mother."

"You'll have to ask Brigitte when you find her."

She took a blossom from the magnolia tree and placed it in her handbag along with the letter. It didn't particularly matter whether or not she should continue searching for Brigitte as the letter in her hand was another dead end. A soft wind left no path. Someone might have felt it rustling once, but they would never remember.

She and Lucas hiked out of the forest as Brigitte's words replayed in her mind. She'd said her good-byes and left to live her life. Saying good-bye to Dietmar—her past—probably freed her to embrace her future.

Had Brigitte forgiven those who'd wounded her?

Quenby needed to do the same thing as Brigitte, this letting go of her own past, but she knew she couldn't do this on her own.

Jocelyn had been addicted to a drug that made people do strange things, and in her craziness, she'd probably thought she loved Chase Merrill. It wasn't an excuse for what she had done, but it helped Quenby understand.

If she truly forgave her mother, would God take away her pain even if her memories remained? Perhaps that was the superpower she needed most. The power to let go. And the power to love again.

Shivering, she glanced at the man walking beside her.

She needed to finish this assignment for Mr. Knight and say good-bye to Lucas. At first he'd gotten on her nerves, but somehow he'd maneuvered his way under her skin, precariously close to her heart. He'd been a friend to her, a good one. Like Mr. Knight had been to Brigitte. But like Brigitte, Quenby had to step into the wind and let it take her wherever she needed to go.

"Should we call Mr. Knight?" she asked when they reached the mill ruins.

"I suppose."

"At least he'll know she was safe after she left the Mill House. Perhaps that will keep him from worrying."

They stopped beside the waterwheel, and Lucas dialed the number, putting it on speakerphone so Quenby could hear. Eileen answered the call.

"He's too ill to speak tonight, Mr. Hough."

Lucas shot Quenby a look of alarm. "What did Dr. Wyatt say?"

"For him to rest, but he isn't resting well. He keeps asking for Brigitte."

"I'm afraid we may not find her," Lucas said. "But she left him a letter telling him that she is well."

"Can you read it to him?" Eileen asked. "I'll hold the phone to his ear."

Lucas glanced at Quenby. "Will you read it?"

She lifted the letter and read Brigitte's words before she folded it back into the metal box.

There was a long silence on the other end, and then Eileen spoke to them again. "I think he heard you. He opened his eyes for a moment."

Tears spilled from Quenby's eyes as Lucas reached over, taking her hand. She clung to his.

"Thank you, Eileen," he said.

"It's good for him to know that she survived the war. It will give him comfort."

After he disconnected the call, Quenby wiped her tears with the back of her hand. "I wanted to find Brigitte for him."

"You gave him the gift of her words."

"But where did she go from here?" A motorboat sped up the river, and she glanced up the rural road to the north.

She didn't want to stop searching yet. Not when they were so close to finding her. Perhaps Lucas was right—they could continue looking, and if Brigitte still didn't want Dietmar to know her location, Quenby would keep her secret. "I'd like to visit the cliffs where Rosalind last saw her," she said. "And then I want to stop in Rodmell."

But even as she said the words, her eyes began to grow heavy. Unlike Lucas, she hadn't rested well on the airplane in either direction, not with everything racing through her mind.

He tucked his phone back into his pocket and held up the keys as they walked toward the car. "You want to drive?"

She shook her head. "Wake me up when you find the cliffs."

The sunroof open, they began driving north. The road was flat here, but according to sat nav, it curved away from the river a few miles up and climbed between farmland and trees. Then they would have to hike to the cliffs.

Her eyes closed, she thought about Mr. Knight locked away in his fortress. He had the best of care, yet his body wouldn't hold on forever. He'd been hanging on, it seemed, until she brought him word about Brigitte. Perhaps this final letter was what he needed to let go as well.

"What in the——?" Lucas blurted, and he swerved suddenly to the left, toward the trees.

Quenby's eyes flashed open, and she saw a gray lorry on the road ahead, barreling toward them, stirring up the dirt into a blinding cloud. At first she thought it was Kyle, trying to flare his feathers again, but the driver, it seemed, had lost control, racing toward a head-on collision. If he didn't stop, he'd kill her and Lucas both.

"Hold on," Lucas shouted.

He spun the wheel right, toward the river, and she heard the grating of metal as they plunged over the bank. Then there was an awful ripping sound, the car shuddering.

Her air bag exploded, flinging her back against the seat.

Lucas shouted her name, and then she heard someone else. A woman.

She tried to open her eyes, but they were glued shut. And her toes, they were soaking wet.

Swim, that's what she needed to do, out of this murky water. Rush away.

Lucas said something else, but the last voice she heard wasn't his. It was Brigitte's, whispering her name.

Chapter 52

London, 1961

Theater called to Hannah like a mockingbird, mimicking the cry of her heart. She craved an audience enraptured by her talent, and adoration—the theater's song of promise—lured her into a nest that turned prison cell in her later years.

It's impossible to really love someone hidden behind the armor of costumes and makeup and lights, but Hannah didn't care about love back then. Lily and Bridget had spoiled her with it when she was a child, cushioning her from the pains of hunger, loneliness, and fear. Perhaps they'd spoiled her too much.

For her eighteenth birthday, Hannah had begged to attend a musical in the West End, and they went together to London to see *Brigadoon* in Her Majesty's Theatre. Hannah soaked in the grandeur of velvety reds and brilliant golds, the aroma of expensive perfumes, the buzz of a well-dressed audience waiting eagerly for the curtain to rise. And when it rose, Eliza Cain took the stage.

Bridget recognized her immediately, though eighteen years had passed, though she wore a powder-blue Celtic dress and a wig with a hundred blonde curls.

She was magnificent as Fiona. Headstrong and beautiful. Larger than life as she sang about being in love. She captured the hearts of her loyal subjects until she disappeared into the darkness. For a moment even Bridget forgot that Fiona was really Rosalind.

Tears streamed down Bridget's face as she thought about Rosalind so long ago, vanishing by the cliffs. But unlike Fiona, Rosalind never returned. Her path took her away from the one person who needed her most.

When the curtain dropped, Hannah was holding Bridget's hand, tears smearing her mascara, streaking her flawless cheeks. And Bridget knew right then that she'd never be able to contain her. Hannah was too much like Rosalind. Bold and rash and afraid of nothing, except perhaps being tied down.

She didn't love her any less knowing this, but she worried for her. And she feared that Hannah, too, would one day walk away.

CHAPTER 53

L *isten to the wind, Quenby.*

And so she had. She'd lain down on the lawn by her mother, the sticky grass poking her arms, tickling her ear. And Quenby had listened.

It's breathing through the grass, her mother had said. *Across the dales.*

There were no dales in their apartment complex, at least none that she'd ever seen, but she'd imagined the dales in Yorkshire, where you could hear the soft wind instead of sirens, feel its coolness instead of the summer heat.

But then Henry, the bully from the apartment next door, began throwing rocks at them, and it broke the magic.

Her mother had only been to Yorkshire a few times, to visit her auntie, but she'd told Quenby about a grand house there, the color of buttercream. It was like Wuthering Heights except the stories in that house were only allowed to have happy endings.

The grass, Quenby remembered, had smelled sweet that morning with her mother, but all she could smell now was disinfectant. Instead of wind, there was a beeping noise that wasn't close to soft, sheets chafing her skin. Still she wanted to believe that her mother was alive. That there was a place they could find healing.

When she opened her eyes, a doctor was standing by her bed, asking her questions. Her head, she told the woman, hurt the most.

"Where's Lucas?" she asked.

But the doctor had already stepped away. When she tried to sit up on the pillows, the room whirled.

"There now," a nurse said, patting her hand before attaching something to the fluid bag above. "This will help you rest."

In minutes, Quenby was gliding across the dales again.

The next time she woke, soft light filtered through the glass in her hospital room, though she wasn't sure if the sun was rising or setting.

Memories flooded back to her—Lucas driving his car, the gray lorry, the river. That terrible sound of metal against metal.

"Lucas?" she whispered, praying he was okay.

"I'm right here." She felt him take her hand.

His left eye was black, his cheek bruised. "Your eye—"

"The air bag left its mark." He kissed her forehead. "And it saved your life."

"How long have I been in the hospital?"

"Two days. You had a concussion, so they did a CT scan in Lewes and ran some other tests, but they concluded that rest is what you need most to recover."

"Who was driving the lorry?"

"I don't know yet, but the police are trying to find him. He rammed into the back of us after we went off the road."

She leaned against the pillows, her head aching. "Your Range Rover?"

"It's trashed."

"I'm sorry," she said.

"It wasn't your fault, Quenby. It's my fault for wrangling you into this mess. I'm calling it off."

"Calling what off?"

"Our search."

"You can't cancel it. I have a contract."

"You'll get your money," he started, an odd coolness in his words.

"I don't want the money, Lucas. I want to find Brigitte."

He smiled again, pushing her hair away from her forehead. "You've searched with your heart, Quenby."

"I suppose I have."

"I'm afraid you won't be telling any more stories if we continue our search for this one."

"Did you get Brigitte's box?" she asked.

"I did. Along with your purse."

"What if Brigitte's letter wasn't actually a good-bye? What if it was a clue?" Her mother's words came back to her again, how she'd loved to talk about the wind in the grass. "There's something else, Lucas."

She closed her eyes again, trying to remember her dream. It had been based, she thought, on a happy memory with her mother, one that had been stuffed deep. Her head ached, and it wasn't solely from the accident. There were new pieces to the puzzle, poised to fit together, but she couldn't even make sense of the frame.

"In the car . . ." He clung to her hand. "For a moment, I thought I'd lost you. It's not worth it, Quenby, to find someone who disappeared long ago."

He did care for her, as more than just a colleague. Enough to call off the search for Mr. Knight. He couldn't cancel it, not for her sake, but his kindness eased some of the pain.

"How's my patient?" The woman who walked into the room reminded Quenby of a fairy with her snowy hair and elf-like body under her pale-blue shirt. The wrinkles fanning from her eyes flared with her smile.

"My head aches."

"A side effect, I'm afraid, of playing chicken with a lorry."

"This is Dr. Eaton," Lucas said as the woman scanned her chart. Then she took Quenby's blood pressure and listened to her heartbeat with a stethoscope, asked Quenby to wiggle her fingers and move her feet.

"Everything appears to be in working order," Dr. Eaton said, taking off the stethoscope. "But no playing sports until after you see a neurologist in London."

"Or climbing trees," Lucas added.

"And no electronics, for at least a week."

Lucas leaned forward. "When can she travel?"

"I'd like you to stay at least one more night nearby, just in case."

"In case of what?" Quenby asked.

Dr. Eaton slipped the chart back into its box. "In case you miss me."

❖

There was only one bed-and-breakfast in the village of Rodmell, and the owner—Clara—had two rooms available, with an interior door between them. Lucas made Quenby promise to keep the exterior one to the hallway locked and barricaded, just in case the man in the lorry decided to show up for an encore.

Her bedroom was painted a warm olive color, and there were white hydrangeas in a large vase on her nightstand. At the foot of her bed were two curtained windows and a case made of ash wood and glass, filled with dozens of trinkets.

She fell back asleep quickly, as if she hadn't slept in days, and when she woke again, the clock beside her bed blinked 6:45. Her headache was finally gone and she was itching to use her iPad, but she followed the doctor's orders and took a shower instead.

Lucas tapped on the door an hour later, looking vastly relieved to see her out of bed and ready for the day. He kissed her cheek. "How is your head?"

"A hundred times better."

"I'm glad."

"I think I could climb a tree."

"Not on my watch," he said before escorting her downstairs to the breakfast room.

With her ban on electronics, she carried the stack of files about Brigitte and the Rickers to review with Lucas over breakfast. Clara already had sausage, grilled tomatoes, and fresh fruit waiting for them along with coffee that she'd roasted in the barn.

Quenby placed her files on the table beside her food and set Princess Adler on top. Then Clara pulled up a chair at their table. "What brings you two to our little village?"

"We're trying to find someone who might have lived here near the end of World War II," Quenby explained. "A woman named Brigitte."

Clara shook her head. "I've lived here my entire life, and I've never known anyone by that name."

Quenby reached for the top file, moving the princess to the side of her plate. "I have her picture here."

Clara examined the photo of the girl with the braids and bow. "I'm afraid I don't recognize her."

Quenby returned the picture to the file and placed Princess Adler back on top.

"That's strange," Clara said, reaching out to touch the wooden princess.

"What is it?"

"Where did you find this toy?"

"Brigitte's best friend gave it to me. He made it for her when they were children."

Clara stood. "Let me show you something."

They followed her upstairs, to Quenby's room. Clara moved toward the glass case and opened it, rummaging through the trinkets. Then she pulled something off the top shelf.

When she turned, Quenby and Lucas both gasped. There was a knight in her hand, about three inches tall, carved out of the same wood as Princess Adler.

"Extraordinary," Lucas said.

Quenby took the knight, rolling it in her hand before passing it along to Lucas. "Where did you get that?"

"Would you believe it was once Hannah Dayne's toy? I like to think she left it for me."

Quenby's and Lucas's eyes met briefly before they looked back at Clara. "Hannah Dayne, the actress?"

"Yes, except she was known as Hannah Ward when we were children. She lived right outside Rodmell."

Quenby's mind raced. She'd only spoken to Hannah once for their interview, over the phone, and when Quenby asked about her own childhood, she'd said it had been a happy one, living with her single mother in a village south of London. "I didn't realize Ms. Dayne grew up here."

Clara nodded. "Her parents were killed during the war, but Lily Ward raised her and her sister. After Lily died, the two women left Rodmell and never returned. I found the knight when I helped clean out their home." She paused. "What was the name again of the woman you're searching for?"

"Brigitte."

Clara's voice trembled. "Hannah's older sister was named Bridget."

Quenby glanced at the knight in Lucas's hand. Could Hannah Dayne be Rosalind's daughter? Alexander had said that Rosalind left Brigitte and the baby near Rodmell, at the cliffs along the river. Brigitte must have taken the baby to Lily Ward's house.

Had Hannah followed in her mother's footsteps as an actress without realizing who her biological mother was? Or had she somehow discovered that Eliza Cain was her mum? Her chosen surname was eerily similar to the one her mother used on stage.

Quenby retrieved the knight from Lucas. "Where did Bridget go?"

"Last I knew, she was going to work as a children's nurse up in Yorkshire, but that was back in the 1950s. Lily Ward left her house to the girls, but they never returned to claim it."

Pieces began to click together in Quenby's mind. The knight. The soft wind. The story of Hannah Dayne.

She looked toward the desk. "I need to look up something on my iPad."

"I'll do it for you," Lucas said.

A bell rang on the floor below, and Clara moved toward the door. "Take the knight when you leave, in case you find either Bridget or Hannah."

Lucas propped up Quenby's iPad on the desk and opened her web browser. She told him exactly what to search for, and he began reading off the names of the country homes in Yorkshire. Abram Park. Acklam Hall. Adler House.

Quenby smiled. "Princess Adler."

"The woman who wanted to fly."

Lucas continued searching, but there wasn't anything else about Adler House online. No images or stories or links.

"We can take the plane into Leeds this morning," he said.

"Can you check my e-mail first?"

"Of course." He tapped on the keyboard before scanning the screen. "You have two e-mails from Chandler. In the first one, she says she's been trying to contact you on your mobile."

"Tell her I've been swimming in the River Ouse."

"In the next e-mail, she says that Evan has changed his mind and wants you to finish the story on the Ricker family. He'd like to meet with you in his office, first thing tomorrow."

"Tell her—" Quenby paused, her head starting to ache again. "On second thought, don't tell her anything at all."

Chapter 54

H annah gave birth to her daughter in the summer of 1967. She'd managed to hide her pregnancy, all the way up until the opening night of *Cinderella* in London's Adelphi Theatre. The director was furious when he discovered her secret. Ian Levine demanded that she get rid of it, the very next day, but she refused to visit the man who made babies disappear.

Hannah left the West End for three years, but the stage kept calling her back. Her audience of one rewarded her hard work with cries instead of applause. Sleepless nights without any praise. She missed her beautiful costumes and the lights that poured down on her. The appreciation of an audience cajoling her onto the stage for a curtain call.

When Ian showed up at her door, he said he'd forgiven her, as if she'd done something wrong. That he wanted her back for *Gone with the Wind.* Years later Hannah told Bridget that he'd never even asked about their daughter.

She returned to the West End. Not because she wanted to work with Ian, but because she wanted to be Scarlett O'Hara.

After Jocelyn was born, Bridget had saved up enough money to take a long holiday from her work. She offered to come to London, to stay with her niece in the evenings while Hannah was performing, but Hannah assured her that she'd found a governess who watched over Jocelyn while she was onstage.

So Bridget had stayed at the children's hospital, working with some of the most courageous children she'd ever met, not knowing that Hannah's child was suffering alone.

Bridget traveled to London twice a year and took Jocelyn out for afternoon tea at the elegant Palm Court. She was a lively girl, just like her grandmother and mother. And she loved beauty and joy. When Jocelyn was eleven, Bridget asked Hannah if she could spend the summer with her, and for those months, they'd hiked over the dales, sung songs, and pretended to fly. She was what Bridget might have been if she'd stayed a princess for a few more years.

Childhood is fleeting, and she'd wanted Jocelyn to dream like she and Dietmar had once done.

As she and Jocelyn played, Bridget wondered again what happened to the boy who'd helped her in spite of her fears. The boy who'd saved her life.

Though Dietmar, like her, had probably changed his name, she still searched the phone books whenever she was in London, but she had never found a listing for Dietmar Roth. She'd stopped letting herself think that he'd died during the war. Instead she imagined him with a houseful of his own children, spread out on the floor with dozens of the wooden toys he'd liked to carve, charging the grand castle he'd built for generations of Roths.

Autumn of 1979, Hannah was offered a part in *The Music Man* on Broadway. New York City. Bridget had said good-bye to the two people most dear to her, not knowing what the future held. Then she counted down the days until they returned home.

But those weeks turned into years. Each time Hannah thought she could bring Jocelyn home, another commitment delayed them. Hannah invited Bridget to New York, but her old fears flared, chaining her to England. She'd even stood one morning at the door to a Jetway, pilots and passengers alike encouraging her to walk down the corridor, but between the narrow walls, all she saw was the dark hold of a fishing trawler, the walls caving and crawling over her, waves hurling her and Dietmar back and forth.

She couldn't move. Nor could she breathe. An attendant wheeled her back to the ticket counter, and the plane left for New York without her.

Her body betrayed her when she so wanted to be strong. If she'd known what the future held, she would have forced herself to fly across the pond.

Seventeen years passed before Hannah's stilettos stepped back onto British soil.

Jocelyn never returned.

Fame for Hannah had been like the apple for Snow White: one bite and she was hooked again. After New York, she answered the call of a Hollywood producer. Her career on the silver screen flourished at first, four films that gave the illusion of success. But somewhere in her rise to stardom, she misplaced her daughter.

All it took was one bad film to kill Hannah's film career. Hollywood rejected her, and while she was still recovering from the loss, she received a call from a hospital in Orlando. Jocelyn had died from a drug overdose.

Bridget's heart broke at the news. She could have been there, should have been there, to rescue Jocelyn before she ran away. Then to protect her from the anonymous man who'd given the ambulance driver Hannah's name.

For years she'd hated herself for not intervening, and Hannah hated herself for abandoning her child, like Rosalind had done to her.

But God can redeem even the bleakest of situations. After she returned, Hannah never left England again. The two women—sisters—partnered together in their regrets and redemption.

God could still love, they discovered, even when they'd failed.

CHAPTER 55

L ucas carried two new suitcases into his parents' stately home in Brentford, the brick walls of the old house a pale pink. They'd spent the day driving through the dales of Yorkshire, asking about Adler House.

When they didn't find it, Lucas suggested they fly back to London and stay at his parents' house for the night—the police in Newhaven hadn't located the gray lorry, and he didn't want Quenby to spend the night in her flat.

Until police found the lorry driver, she didn't want to spend the night alone either.

Mrs. Hough greeted them warmly, and Quenby thought the woman looked quite regal with her tailored blue suit and white scarf tied neatly around her neck.

"Welcome," Mrs. Hough said, shaking her hand.

"Thank you for having me."

"I'm pleased you came. Please roam wherever you'd like."

Lucas held up their bags. "Right now, we'll roam upstairs."

Quenby climbed the winding staircase behind him, and he placed her bag beside a bed in one of the guest rooms. The bedcovering and wallpaper were striped with a tangerine color, and two oil paintings hung at the end of her bed—an austere-looking man with a white wig and a pretty woman wearing an elegant mauve-and-gray gown with a lace bonnet and satin bow.

Lucas pointed toward the portraits. "My great-great-great-grandparents . . . or something like that. They lived here more than a century ago."

What would it be like to have a family heritage that stretched back for centuries? A story that was beyond yourself?

He reached for her hand, holding it as he'd done the entire flight and the car ride here. He blamed himself for the accident, though she'd told him repeatedly he'd done nothing wrong.

Outside the dual windows, twilight made the pool behind the manor glow pink and orange. "It's lovely," she said.

"Indeed."

But when she turned, Lucas wasn't looking outside. His eyes were on her. Nervous, she released his hand and reached for her handbag before scooting toward the door.

"Quenby—"

But she was already out in the corridor. She'd been avoiding this conversation since their evening in Florida, and she had no desire to start it now. Her heart was all wrapped up in this man, and she was terrified that it was some sort of mirage. When she blinked, he'd be gone.

Beside the kitchen was a breakfast nook that contained a small table walled in by windows. She removed Mrs. Douglas's file from her bag along with her phone and iPad, placing them on the table.

Mrs. Hough walked into the kitchen and glanced at the items spread across the table. "Would you like some tea?"

"I would love some."

"With milk?"

"Please."

Mrs. Hough filled three mugs with hot water and dropped a tea bag into each one. Once they steeped, she added fresh milk to the mugs and brought them to the table, sitting down beside Quenby. "You're immersed in some sort of project," she said, tapping the file.

"Lucas and I have been working to find someone lost during World War II."

She nodded. "It's been a long time since I've seen Lucas so—so engrossed."

Her words seemed to hover between them and the steam from their mugs. Was Mrs. Hough talking about her son's interest in this case or his interest in Quenby?

She propped her iPad up, uncertain how to respond.

Mrs. Hough patted her hand. "It's good for him."

"He's a loyal man—to Mr. Knight."

Mrs. Hough smiled. "He's always been loyal to the people he cares for."

Quenby glanced back at her computer screen.

"What are you searching for?" Mrs. Hough asked.

"A house in Yorkshire called Adler." She turned the screen so Mrs. Hough could see the reference online.

"Lucas's grandparents might know where it is. They spend a few weeks up there each summer."

"I tried to ring them," Lucas said as he stepped into the room. "They aren't answering their phones."

"They're holidaying in Porto Cervo at the moment." Mrs. Hough inched one of the mugs toward her son. "I'll contact a few of my friends up near Yorkshire to see if they know of it."

Lucas reached for Quenby's iPad, pulling it away from her. "You're not supposed to be on that."

"Bossy," she huffed.

He shrugged, winking at her. "Doctor's orders."

Mrs. Hough cleared her throat.

"I'm allowed to look at photographs," Quenby said, opening the paper file.

She spread the articles and photographs from Mrs. Douglas out on the kitchen table, looking at the various pictures she assumed were taken by Eddie Terrell. Photographs of dinner parties and of people sunning on beach chairs by a swimming pool and bathing hut. Some of the photographs had been taken inside an elaborate parlor that reminded her of the one used for *Downton Abbey*, Lady Ricker trimmed with a jeweled necklace, opera gloves, and a tiara.

"Where is this?" Mrs. Hough asked, picking up a photo of Lady Ricker sitting on a settee.

"Most of them were taken at Breydon Court near Tonbridge. At the home of Lord and Lady Ricker." Quenby inched the photographs toward her. "Do you know any of these people?"

Mrs. Hough turned over one of them as if searching for writing on the back, but it was blank. "I recognize this man."

Lucas leaned forward. "Who is it, Mum?"

"Drague," she said, pointing at an older gentleman with Lady Ricker. "Admiral Drague. He was quite the charmer in London society after his wife died."

"Was he a commander during World War II?" Lucas asked.

"No, it would have been the First World War. He came home a hero."

Quenby looked at Lucas, and she knew he was wondering as well why this hero from the war was socializing with Lady Ricker. And why he had later purchased her home.

"Didn't you say you worked for the World News Syndicate?" Mrs. Hough asked.

"That's correct."

"Admiral Drague's daughter married Richard Graham, back in the 1940s, I think. Around the time he founded the syndicate."

Quenby's eyes widened at this revelation, stray pieces of this puzzle snapping into place. She turned back toward the iPad, her fingers itching to start researching the man.

"I'll do it for you," Lucas said as if he'd read her mind.

He typed as Quenby and Mrs. Hough sipped their tea. Then he whistled.

Quenby dove toward the iPad, but he pulled it out of her reach. "I'll read it."

He'd found an editorial written by Richard Graham—Evan's father—in 1948, about the late Lord Ricker and his wife. It was a seething condemnation of anyone absurd enough to think they'd been part of an aristocratic espionage network. The Rickers, he wrote, were loyal to Great Britain and the efforts of the war.

"This story must have run around the time Lady Ricker was interviewed," Quenby said. "If she and Admiral Drague were acquaintances, he would have wanted her name cleared so no one would suspect him of being a traitor to his country as well."

Lucas nodded. "A marriage between his daughter and Richard Graham was collateral for the future. With Graham as his son-in-law, any other questions about the Rickers could have been circumvented by the papers."

"Spoken like a lawyer," Quenby teased.

He sat back in his chair. "It's the power of your press."

"If they were collaborating in some way, why would Lady Ricker keep a picture of him?" Mrs. Hough asked.

Lucas's smile was grim. "Probably to use for blackmail."

"A smart woman, I suppose," Mrs. Hough said as she pushed away from the table, her mug empty.

"Where does Richard Graham's son play into all of this?" Lucas asked.

The light on Quenby's mobile blinked. The name on the screen was the one she'd keyed in days ago by the river. "Perhaps we are about to find out."

CHAPTER 56

"Will you walk with me?" Lucas asked after Quenby emerged from the library, shaken from her conversation with Evan Graham.

Quenby glanced toward the corridor, but Mrs. Hough had conveniently disappeared. "It's late."

"Does your head hurt?" he asked.

"No."

"Please—we won't be long."

When she nodded, he gently took the phone from her hand and placed it on the table. "You won't need a phone out there."

She followed Lucas outside, onto the stone pavers of a patio. The burr of crickets accompanied them as they walked toward a pool surrounded by flowers and ornamental shrubs. Starlight reflected in the still black water, and the aromas of jasmine and rose perfumed the evening air, wind rustling their leaves.

"What did Evan say?" he asked, pausing beside the pool.

"He wants to know what I've uncovered in my research."

"And you said——"

"That his grandfather was a friend of the Rickers."

"I bet he loved that."

"I didn't say it *exactly* like that, but I told him I'd found a photograph of Admiral Drague and Lady Ricker together before Admiral Drague purchased Breydon Court. I told him I had no desire or even evidence to implicate his family, but still . . ."

"What?" Lucas asked.

"He offered me a tremendous amount of money to return to work in the morning and hand over my research. Then he wanted me to start writing a different story."

"I hope you told him you're not motivated by money."

"That's exactly what I said."

"You are an amazing woman, Quenby."

She shook her head. "Not so much. Not after you get to know me."

He reached for her other hand. "I think I know you pretty well."

"There's much that is still unbeknownst to you," she said, trying to make a joke, lighten the intensity in his eyes, but he didn't laugh.

"You are worth fighting for." He stepped closer. "You and I both know I'm far from perfect, but I would like the opportunity to love you as you should be loved."

She swallowed hard, basking in his words. "I——" she started, faltering. If only she could ride on the breeze, travel far away from here. "You're using your superpowers again."

"Which power is that?" he asked.

"Manipulation."

"That's not a superpower." He stepped back. "And I'm not trying to manipulate you."

Disappointment laced his words as if she were accusing him of the worst sort of crime. Now he would surely run.

"I'm being completely honest with you," he said, still holding her hands though he was losing grip.

Could she do the same? Be completely honest with him?

Daniel had spent his whole life trying to keep his promise to return to Brigitte, and it seemed as if Lucas kept his promises too. He'd certainly kept his word with her. Perhaps she could learn again to trust the people who wanted what was best for her.

Perhaps she could love him in return.

"Lucas," she started again, taking a deep breath.

"I'm not going to leave you, Quenby."

Before she replied, Mrs. Hough called out to them from the patio. Quenby stepped away.

Lucas looked at Quenby a moment longer and then called over his shoulder, "We're out here."

"Oh, good." She hurried forward, finding them by the pool. "You said Adler House, didn't you?"

"That's correct," Lucas said.

"The provost at a secondary school in Yorkshire said some of his best students come from there."

"Students?" Quenby asked, her voice a strange squeak.

Mrs. Hough shrugged. "He didn't expound, but he gave me the address."

"Thanks, Mum," Lucas said.

She glanced between them. "I'll leave you alone, then," she said, backing away.

But the magic was already gone.

❖

Adler House was hidden among the dales of North Yorkshire. It was a place, Quenby guessed, where knights triumphed over evil. A place where princesses could fly.

Like Breydon Court, iron gates blocked the lane into the property, but there was no intercom button to press. And a For Sale sign hung crooked from one of the gates. Quenby feared that once again, Brigitte had slipped away.

An unkempt hedgerow, made of yew, extended from the gates, and the limbs of several large trees dangled over it. Quenby eyed the branches. "Should we climb it?"

"You're not climbing anything," Lucas said as he stepped out of the rented BMW. He hurried around the car to open her door.

She stood up beside him. "My head feels fine now."

"Thanks to the ibuprofen."

Quenby lifted her fingers to her lips, glancing toward one of the trees. "Listen."

Someone giggled, up under the cover of leaves, and Lucas stepped toward the hedge. "It sounds like a monkey."

"Hello," Quenby called out.

A boy somersaulted over the lowest branch like an acrobat and dangled off it from his knees, his head hanging precariously close to the ground. Quenby held her breath as he flipped like the wakeboarder back in Florida. Thankfully, he landed on his feet as well.

"Bravo," Quenby said with a clap, stepping toward the tree.

He held out his hand to shake hers. "I'm Elias."

"I'm Quenby, and this is Lucas."

The boy didn't acknowledge Lucas.

"Do you live in Adler House?" Quenby asked.

He studied her face as if he was trying to decipher her words.

The curtain of leaves parted again, and a girl with blonde pigtails stuck her head out between them. "He doesn't know much English."

Quenby smiled at her. "We're looking for the woman who owns Adler House."

"Ms. Hannah?"

Her pulse raced. In her interview with Hannah Dayne, the

woman had never mentioned that she actually cared for children in her house. "Yes, is she here?"

"She's always here." The girl dropped to the ground and shook her hand like Elias had done. "I'm Maya, from Syria."

"It's very nice to meet you, Maya. How long have you been in England?"

"A year and four days. Ms. Hannah said I could stay here as long as I'd like."

Quenby pointed back toward Lucas. "My friend and I are trying to find a girl who was lost a long time ago."

The girl said something to Elias in another language. Then he jumped up and grasped the bottom branch of the tree, weighing it down. He pointed at Quenby and then at the tree. "Come."

"Wait a minute." Lucas moved forward. "The doctor said—"

"Technically, you said it, but I'll be careful."

"Quenby—" His words faltered. They were so close to finding Brigitte. Nothing, he seemed to realize, was going to stop her from climbing over to the other side.

Lucas reached for the branch. "I'll go first."

But Elias scowled at him. "No man allowed."

Maya apologized. "Some men . . . they hurt him before he left home."

Quenby couldn't imagine what both of these children had been through. Nor could she understand what evil drove a person to hurt an innocent child . . . or abandon one. Thankfully, it seemed these children had found safety here.

"Lucas is a good man," she told Elias. "A kind one."

She didn't know if he understood, but she felt Lucas's hand on her shoulder.

"Be careful, Quenby," he whispered. "You might start liking me."

She glanced back at him. "I'm afraid it's already too late for that."

She thought he might kiss her right there, but he eyed the tree instead. "I don't want you to go over that wall alone."

"I won't be alone," she said softly. "Elias and Maya will be with me."

"But—" he started to protest again.

"If I don't go now, the children will surely tell Brigitte. And she might run again."

Lucas glanced at Elias. "Take care of her."

Elias didn't stop scowling, but he nodded.

"Do you have your phone?" Lucas asked.

Quenby checked her handbag. "I do."

"If I don't hear from you in thirty minutes, I'm phoning the police and an ambulance."

"Give me forty-five."

Maya and Elias pressed down on the lowest branch with the strength of their feet. Quenby secured the strap of her handbag over her shoulder and then, with Lucas's help, pulled herself up onto the branch. She climbed the tree and then over the hedge to the other side.

When her feet touched the ground, she shouted to Lucas that she was fine. Then, turning, she glimpsed the expanse of the park in front of her. It was blooming pink, white, and magenta from a host of magnolia trees.

Maya was on one side of her, Elias on the other, and together they paraded through the color, toward a roof in the distance.

Moments later, when they emerged through the trees, Quenby felt dizzy. Standing before her was a house of buttercream.

"Just a second," she said, bracing herself against one of the magnolias.

Surely there was more than one house in Yorkshire that used the honey-colored stone, but . . .

Was it possible her mother had visited here when she was a girl? Or even been raised here, as one of the fostered children?

Ivy covered part of the stone front, and the lawn around it was overgrown. The house had been expanded with a wing of a darker-colored stone that bustled toward a garden and greenhouse. It wasn't derelict by any means, like the abandoned Mill House, but it could use some care.

Maya motioned her toward a side door as Elias raced away. Quenby and Maya both brushed their shoes off on a rug inside the house.

The floor of the narrow hall was wooden, rugged and unpolished, but neatly swept. Another child glanced out a door, a toy knight clutched in his hand.

"I'll find Ms. Hannah," Maya said, dashing down the corridor.

Quenby turned right into a formal library, paneled with knotty pine and filled floor to ceiling with the colorful spines of books. She picked one of the books from a low shelf, titled *The Amber Light*. It was a fairy tale, illustrated with watercolors, but she didn't know the author. *Sir Vincent* was all it said.

Outside the window, divided by a dozen panes, she saw a woman sitting on a wooden bench, surrounded by five or six children, a dark-pink scooter parked at the edge of her bench.

Quenby replaced *The Amber Light* and moved out of the library, into the sitting room next door. There she lingered beside a set of open French doors, listening to the woman read a story.

One of the older children, standing behind the bench, turned toward Quenby. When the girl saw her, she tapped the woman's shoulder. And the woman turned as well.

Her pale skin was wrinkled, her blue eyes clear and kind. And strong.

Quenby stepped down the flat ramp leading out of the house. "Brigitte?" she asked.

The woman looked terrified.

CHAPTER 57

Children were scattered across the garden and park, playing on a swing set and climbing trees. As Quenby slid onto the bench, she removed the metal box from her handbag. The woman glanced down at the rusted box, but she didn't say anything.

"Brigitte—" she started again.

"Please call me Bridget. There's no joy in that old name."

"I think it's a beautiful name."

"Only a handful of people know it, and most of them want to bring me harm."

"Not me," Quenby said. She opened the box and took out the photograph first, of Brigitte and her parents.

Bridget clutched the old picture in one hand, the other hand over her mouth. "I'd forgotten what they looked like."

"They must have loved you very much."

She nodded.

Quenby took the wooden princess out of the box and set it gingerly in one of Bridget's palms. "Do you recognize this?"

Bridget folded the toy between both hands before clutching it to her heart. "Where did you get her?"

"From a friend who's been looking for you."

"Dietmar?" she asked, and in her voice, Quenby heard a thread of hope.

Quenby nodded slowly. "Except his name is Daniel now. Daniel Knight. And he's been worried about you for more than seventy years."

Bridget lowered the princess to her lap. "Long ago, he said he would find me."

"After you left with the Terrells, Mr. Knight was sent to the Isle of Man," she explained. "He was interned there until 1944, and then after the war, he searched relentlessly but couldn't find you."

"I looked for him as well, but I thought he'd died in the war." Bridget glanced out at the children. "In my heart, I knew he would keep his promise, if he was still alive."

"Would you like to see him?" Quenby asked.

Bridget fidgeted with her hands, rubbing them across the book in her lap. "It's been too long."

"And yet not so long between friends."

"Do you believe in a God who saves?" Bridget asked.

"I do."

"I believe God uses our pasts, even our regrets, to help us and other people find Him."

"You think God kept you and Dietmar apart?"

"No, but He used our time apart to tear open my heart and fill it back up again."

Maya sailed up beside them. "Ms. Hannah said she'll be out in a moment."

"I need to speak with Ms. Hannah before she meets you," Bridget told Quenby. Then she held up the book to Maya. "We were just reading your story."

Quenby could see the cover now with its fierce dragon, blowing fire at a little girl. The title was *Dragons & Ash* by Princess Maya.

Bridget handed the book to Maya. "Could you read it to our guest while I speak with Ms. Hannah?"

Maya looked quite pleased to do so.

When Bridget pushed herself up on the arm of the bench, Maya reached for one of her arms, helping her move onto the scooter, and Quenby reached out to help as well. Then Bridget maneuvered her way toward the house.

Maya settled back down on the bench beside Quenby.

"Did you write this?" Quenby asked, tapping on the cover.

Maya nodded. "With a little help from Ms. Bridget."

"When did you become a princess?"

"When Ms. Hannah and Ms. Bridget invited me to live here."

Quenby smiled with her until her phone chimed. "Just a moment," she said as she dug it out of her handbag.

Should I phone the police? Lucas texted.

She sent him a message right back. **No.**

Did you find her?

She sent back a smiley face and then dropped the phone into her bag.

Maya opened her book. The first illustration was of the fierce dragon from the cover, more charcoal black than green.

And Maya began to read her story.

Fire flared from the dragon's breath, his throat and cheeks seared with burns. He was ugly and fierce and tortured the villagers who tried to fetch water at the town well. Each night he paced through the streets, searching for anyone who dared to leave their home. Some nights he sprayed fire on the houses and the residents were forced to run.

Maya turned the page, and Quenby saw the little girl dressed in a simple brown cloak, her hands clutching the handle of a cup.

Maya continued reading her story, turning the pages slowly so Quenby could appreciate the artwork. As she read, the children began bringing Quenby flowers and she bundled them together as a bouquet.

One little girl lived in town all alone. She'd waited for days to fetch water, and now she was so thirsty, she thought she would surely die without a sip.

All she had was a tin cup, dented from the dragon's heat. On a cloudy night, she crept through the narrow alleys until she saw the well ahead. As she tiptoed forward, she prayed the dragon was asleep. Or that he'd left their town.

When she reached the well, she uncoiled the rope with the bucket, dipping it down into the water like her mother used to do. Her first sip of water was cool and sweet on her tongue. There was life in her tin cup, streaming down her throat, filling her empty stomach.

When the cup was empty, she refilled it and began to drink again.

But then the dragon rounded the corner, its beady eyes searching the broken buildings around the square until it found her.

The girl trembled at the dragon's roar, water spilling over the sides of her cup. It tromped slowly toward her, and she knew she should run, but the fire would find her, no matter which direction she fled.

She was terrified of the dragon, but the creature had taken
her mother and her father and her beloved brother. It had stolen
away her grandparents and auntie and her sweet dog.

No weapon could kill the dragon, but she would fight back,
the best she could.

She flung the drops of cold water toward the dragon
and braced herself for its fire. But the most marvelous thing
happened. The dragon reared its head, blew out of its nostrils,
but no fire came. Instead it was only smoke.

The little girl filled her cup again and threw it toward the
dragon.

The creature began to shrink, and other villagers rushed out
into the street, escaping their shuttered windows and doors. They
filled their cups and buckets and began drowning the dragon
until the creature was so small, a gust of wind swept into the
town and blew the ashes away.

As Maya closed the book, she looked up at Quenby with expectation.

Quenby blinked back her tears, quickly slipping on sunglasses so the girl wouldn't see her cry. "That was a beautiful story."

"I dedicated it to my brother."

Quenby didn't ask about her brother's whereabouts. The sadness in her voice made it clear that he wasn't here.

Maya passed the book to Quenby, and she held it in her lap, the dragon and the girl staring back at her, until the door slid open behind them. Bridget drove her scooter back outside, trailed by a thin woman of timeworn beauty, a woman Quenby recognized from the movies as Hannah Dayne.

"May we speak with our guest?" Hannah asked Maya.

"Her name is Quenby," Maya told her. "And her boyfriend is waiting outside the gate."

"Is that correct?" Bridget asked.

"Lucas is a friend," Quenby replied. "And Mr. Knight's lawyer."

Bridget shooed Maya off the bench with her hand. "Go let him in."

Maya kissed Quenby on the cheek before she raced around the house.

"Her story is remarkable," Quenby told both women.

Bridget reached for her hand, squeezing it like Mrs. Douglas had done. "There's power in story," she said slowly. "We may be powerless at times in this life, but on paper, we can chase our demons away."

"Do all the children here write their own stories?"

"Most of them do," Bridget said. "There is a lot of healing to be had, and we think it helps."

Quenby slipped off her sunglasses. "Where are their parents?"

"Many of them died on their journey," Bridget said.

Hannah motioned back toward the house. "Could we talk inside, Miss Vaughn?"

Quenby blinked, surprised at the woman's use of her last name. "You know who I am?"

Hannah nodded. "I saw your picture with the series on refugees."

Bridget stayed on her scooter, watching the children play, while Quenby followed Hannah toward the house. She'd already admired the woman for advocating for refugees, and her admiration grew as she saw the private work they were doing here, far away from the spotlight.

"My sister is very old," Hannah said as they walked through the sitting room, into the library. "She's lived a good life, helping me when I was young and then caring for a number of children. There's no need to exhume the past."

Quenby sat in a chair across from her. "It's not about exhuming. It's about redeeming what has been lost."

Hannah looked over at the window. "Redemption comes in different forms."

"It's wonderful what you're doing here."

"The work has transformed all of us, but unfortunately, our funds to keep up a house like this are diminishing quickly."

"How long have you been operating this house?"

"My sister has been living here for fifty years."

Quenby took a deep breath before asking. "I believe my mother might have visited here as a child, perhaps even lived with the other children."

"What was your mother's name?" Hannah asked.

"Jocelyn."

Hannah reached for the arm of the couch, steadying herself as if she might faint.

"She used to talk about a house of buttercream."

Hannah leaned forward. "You're Jocelyn's daughter?" she asked as if she hadn't quite understood.

"I am."

"I—I didn't know she had a girl."

Quenby's heart skipped. "Did she grow up here?"

"Oh no," Hannah said slowly. "She grew up in London."

"How do you know her?"

Hannah's eyes focused on the shelves of fairy tales before looking back at Quenby. "Jocelyn was my daughter."

And with those words, Quenby thought she might faint as well.

CHAPTER 58

Raw tears funneled down Quenby's cheeks as she climbed into the rental car. She didn't even care that Lucas was sitting beside her. Their work was done. She'd come here to find Brigitte for Mr. Knight, and yet it seemed as if two lost girls had been found.

Dietmar had rescued Brigitte from the Nazis long ago, but in their afternoon together, Hannah explained that Bridget had spent her life rescuing her and a host of children. Bridget was worried, saying she still needed to protect Hannah from Lady Ricker's descendants, but Hannah assured her that she didn't need protection anymore.

The truth unfolded like a shaky ladder in Quenby's mind.

Lady Ricker wasn't just some aristocratic woman bent on harming her country. Janice Ricker was the mother of Rosalind. And Quenby's great-great-grandmother by birth.

She grieved deeply in that car, for the people who'd died at Lady

Ricker's hand, for the children during the war who'd lost their parents, for children today who continued to lose them. This wasn't someone else's story any longer. This was her story, rooted in a muddy reality. And she couldn't make peace with her past, she realized, until she cried. Couldn't love again until she grieved her loss.

Lucas didn't try to stop her. Instead he reached out and pulled her close to him. She wanted to say something witty, something smart to keep him at bay, but the strength of her aloneness seemed to siphon out of her. And in its place was a weakness—not of character or physical power but of a deep heart's desire to have someone there next to her, someone who wasn't afraid of her tears. Or her story.

He kissed her hair, kissed the tears from her cheeks.

She leaned back. "I know God has forgiven my sins, but there are so many ghosts roaming around in my past."

"A clean slate—that's what you and I have in Christ, Quenby. Whiter than snow."

And she saw it in her mind, the powdery snow of a ski slope, waiting to be forged. Everything was changing for her. After today, she was no longer alone. She had family left in this world—a grand-mother who'd been racked with guilt as well over Jocelyn's leaving. A grandmother who said she'd welcome Quenby into her life and her home.

She couldn't change her past, like any of the children here, but it didn't define who she was today. Nor did she have to hide behind someone else's script, play a role like Hannah and Rosalind had once done.

She had the power to write a new story from this moment for-ward. Her story. One where the past molded and then empowered and strengthened instead of crippled her. A new story filled with strong, healthy relationships with people she loved and a heart open to trusting God and Lucas as well.

A heart willing to forgive.

She prayed silently that God would help her forgive her mother for what she had done. She'd never forget what happened, but she wanted to let go of the bitterness that she'd kept locked inside her, stop using it as a weapon against anyone who wanted to love her.

Lucas rolled down the window, and images fluttered into Quenby's head with the breeze, pictures of a new story. She and Lucas together, following wherever God led. A smile when she thought of the good memories with her mother. Prayers for those trapped, like Jocelyn, in an addiction.

She glanced out the window, at the tree branches fluttering in the breeze. "What do we do now?"

"We fly to Solstice Isle for the reunion of a lifetime."

Quenby nodded; that's exactly what she'd hoped he would say. "Are you going to call Mr. Knight?"

"I tried, but Eileen said he still couldn't talk on the phone."

"We need to leave soon."

He nodded. "Quenby, you don't have to be afraid of me."

She almost told him that she wasn't, but it would be a lie. She was terrified.

"If you'll have me," he said, "I won't leave you."

She looked into those dark-brown eyes that had captured her days ago. "You can't promise that."

"I won't run or walk away—how about that?"

"You hardly know me, Lucas."

He smiled. "It's been a pretty educational two weeks."

"Indeed it has."

"The real question is, would you dare to take a chance with me?"

Quenby thought back to that meeting with Chandler before she met Lucas—at the pictures her boss had pulled up online. She'd thought Lucas arrogant, but she had built the same type of wall around herself. And yet here they were, hearts exposed.

"I think I just might," she said.

His kiss was quite gentlemanly, but she felt it all the way down to her toes.

❊

Bridget Ward drove her scooter right up to the jet at Leeds Bradford, eyeing the flight of steps that led into the craft. Before they left Adler House, Hannah had warned Quenby about the last time Bridget had tried to fly, of her sister's fierce claustrophobia.

But there was no Jetway leading onto this plane. No pilots on a strict schedule. They could wait all day and night, if they must, for her to overcome her fear.

"We'll have a scooter waiting for you on the island," Quenby promised, her hand resting on the woman's seat back.

"Is it pink?"

"I have no idea."

Bridget's smile was strained. "I suppose any color will do."

Quenby patted her shoulder. "You can do this."

Bridget gave a sharp nod. "I'll regret it if I don't."

"Would you like a hand?" Lucas asked, stepping up beside them.

"More like two feet."

Lucas flashed her a winsome smile. Bridget had already fallen for him, back at Adler House when he'd complimented her on her beautiful voice. And Quenby was thoroughly smitten as well.

Lucas leaned over and swooped Bridget off her chair. "How about feet and hands?"

The woman's smile was genuine this time. "My Prince Charming."

A modern-day knight without the armor.

Quenby carried the woman's handbag up the flight of steps behind them. When they were near the top, Bridget cried out, "Please stop."

Lucas obeyed.

"Put me down."

"Are you certain?" Lucas asked as he lowered her.

"Quite."

Quenby glanced at the five steps behind them, leading down to the tarmac. For a woman of Bridget's age, a fall from here could be fatal.

Samantha was waiting inside the doorway as Bridget stood on the top step, staring into the jet. Would she refuse to get on board?

Lucas stood below her, on the step alongside Quenby, both of them creating a wall to protect her.

"I can do this," Bridget whispered.

"Yes, you can," Quenby said. "You're writing a new story too."

Bridget gave another brisk nod and then she walked through the door.

CHAPTER 59

Bridget dabbed a cool washcloth on Dietmar's forehead. Of the hundreds—if not thousands—of times she had thought about him over the years, of their reuniting one day, she'd never imagined that she'd find him like this, living in the stalwart castle of a knight yet not able to fight any longer.

He tossed on the pillows, his white hair thrashing from side to side. Now it was her turn to fight for him.

Days passed in quiet solitude, only her and Eileen and occasionally Jack taking turns to care for him. It was so different from her house full of children, but it gave her time to think. And to pray.

Dietmar had saved her life as they fled from Germany, and she thanked God for giving her the strength to board that plane back in England, grateful for this opportunity to be taking care of Dietmar for a change. She'd been so silly in her youth, relying on him like he was an adult when he was only three years her senior. Instead of acting like a princess, she should have discarded her make-believe crown and, for heaven's sake, tried to milk that cow alongside him back in Belgium.

He tossed again and threw off the covers.

"It's okay, Dietmar," she said, uncertain if she should call him by his German name. But Daniel Knight was a man she didn't know. Dietmar had been her best friend.

"Brigitte?" he whispered, his eyes closed.

She kissed his forehead. "I'm here."

When he rested against the pillow, she leaned back in her cushioned chair as well and looked out at the waves battering the rocky coast.

She would stay right here with Dietmar in his fortress, for as long as he needed her.

❖

Dietmar heard bells, ringing from the necks of cows. And he smelled mowed grass and honeysuckle and roasted meat. But he and Brigitte couldn't go into the farmhouse. The woman there, she would turn them over to the police.

His head thrashed back and forth. He needed his armor. His sword.

"*Lauf,*" he wanted to scream, but the word came out as a whisper on his lips. Why couldn't he yell anymore?

"It's okay, Dietmar."

His eyes flew open, and he glanced around the dark room.

Had they trapped him in the farmhouse already, the farmer and his wife? He struggled to get up from the bed. To find Brigitte. They wouldn't send him or Brigitte back to Germany.

A light shone beside him, and there was a woman, holding his shoulder. He shouted at her, the words jumbled together—English and German. Told her that she couldn't have him.

"Brigitte!" he called again.

And then she was there. Standing beside him, smiling down. She looked older than he remembered, but it was of no matter. He was older too.

He glanced around the room, searching for the woman with the coat of teeth. "I won't let them take you," he said, reaching for her hand.

"Don't worry, Dietmar." She kissed his forehead. "Now it's my turn to take care of you."

"No—" he started, but his eyes began to close. This time, though, he wouldn't let go of her hand.

Later, when the sunlight began trickling into his room, he opened his eyes. Brigitte was still there, stretched out on the bed beside him, asleep. Her hair was gray now, but she was so beautiful, content in her rest. Finally she was well again.

He was still watching her when she woke, and she inched up against the walnut headboard, looking out from the tower room at the whisk of wind stirring the sea.

"I tried and tried," he said. "But I never caught the wind."

Brigitte took his hand, smiling at him again.

"I caught it," she assured him. "And it blew me right back to you."

EPILOGUE

Seven months later

Precious stones and pearls, that's what Hansel and Gretel took when they ran from the witch. But when Bridget ran from the Mill House, she took a baby, and her life was forever changed.

As Quenby sat on a rug in front of the fire, inside the eagle house, she reminisced on the lives of two very different sisters, writing down thoughts for their memoir while Bridget and Hannah both read books nearby. It was a story they'd decided to tell together, with Mr. Knight's permission. One that was partially Quenby's to share as well.

Months ago, she'd told Hannah that Rosalind, her biological mother, had another child—and that her brother, Alexander, now lived in Jacksonville. Uncle Alexander. It was strange to Quenby. She'd never had anyone to call aunt or uncle before.

Hannah and Quenby had flown to Florida several months ago to visit with him. Bridget had thought Lady Ricker sent someone to knock on her door, back in Rodmell, but Alexander said it was actually his father, asking about Brigitte. Rosalind, swept up perhaps in the early days of romance, told her husband about the daughter she'd birthed and then lost near that village. Alexander didn't know his father's intentions, beyond confirming whether or not Rosalind's story was true, but he said it was probably good that Brigitte and Hannah had moved north.

Each of Lady Ricker's children, it turned out, had a different father, and it seemed that none of them was Lord Ricker.

Rosalind's father had been Oskar, the German officer whom Lady Ricker had loved. He had been killed in Normandy on D-Day.

Anthony Ricker's father was probably Eddie Terrell, confirmed only by Mrs. Douglas's photograph. Quenby thought it best to keep that speculation to herself.

Alexander said that Louise McMann's father was actually Admiral Drague. Only a few people knew about Lady Ricker and Admiral Drague's affair, but Louise was privy to the information, as was Evan Graham, Admiral Drague's grandson.

Quenby wouldn't be writing an exposé on the Rickers, and Evan didn't even have to pay her to suppress it. He didn't have the money anyway. The news had come out recently, unreported by the syndicate, that Evan's finances were in the tank. An article exposing the Ricker family, and ultimately Evan's family as well, would have discredited him as a publisher and completely ruined his financial state.

Also, the police in Newhaven were questioning Evan after they found the driver of the gray lorry. The man had directed them to a tourist visiting Brighton, a man who'd promised to pay him a substantial sum to scare Quenby and Lucas away.

Her work at the syndicate was done, but this memoir, she hoped, was only the beginning of stories she could help people tell.

The twelve children housed in this home were all asleep upstairs as snow fell on the lawn. Lucas was supposed to come tonight, but she guessed he'd have to wait until tomorrow.

Bridget rubbed her arms. "I miss Dietmar."

"Me too," Quenby said.

Warming her hands on her tea mug, she thought back over the summer and then autumn months. Bridget had stayed true to her word. She'd spent five of those months helping care for Mr. Knight, alongside Eileen. When he passed away, they discovered that he'd written Brigitte into his will long ago, hoping he would find her one day. After his death, Bridget and Lucas became partners at Arrow Wind.

Bridget didn't really know anything about wind, except it could bring people together or tear them apart. But Lucas had learned plenty over the years about the company, and Quenby had no doubt that their farms would continue to thrive.

Part of Mr. Knight's income had restored Adler House into a beautiful estate. The For Sale sign was gone, and Lucas and Bridget had begun investing in other houses across England to help unaccompanied children and refugee families who needed a home.

Quenby looked up from her iPad screen, her gaze finding Hannah. She'd learned much about forgiveness in these months, but still one question remained for her. "How do you reconcile that our ancestors were Nazis?"

Hannah glanced at Bridget, as she often did when Quenby asked questions about their story, gaining a silent sort of permission from her older sister before she spoke. "They weren't all Nazis."

Quenby tilted her head. "Of course not, but—"

"Quenby," Hannah said, stopping her. "I took a genetic test a few years ago and discovered that I'm of Jewish descent as well as German."

"From your father's side?"

"No, from my mother."

Quenby leaned back against a chair, stunned by her words. "Rosalind was Jewish?"

She nodded slowly. "Passed down from *her* mother."

"Lady Ricker?" Quenby whispered.

"Precisely."

Which meant that Quenby was of German and Jewish descent as well. "I wonder if she knew . . ."

"It was a grand cover-up scheme if she did. Perhaps she was afraid of what Hitler would do if he took England. She wanted to be known in Germany as someone who supported him."

Jack ducked under the open doorway and stepped into the room, holding up a porcelain teapot. "Would you ladies like some more tea?"

All three women readily agreed, and he began filling their cups with the steaming brew.

Jack didn't need a job—Mr. Knight had taken good care of both him and Eileen in his will too—but he'd asked Bridget if he could accompany her to England. And then he'd stayed. The children loved him, and Quenby thought there was a spark between him and Hannah, though they'd probably both deny it.

Her phone rang, and she saw Lucas's number on the screen. The other two ladies pretended to be engrossed in their books, but she'd learned they were both quite nosy. And they both adored her guy.

"Will I see you tomorrow?" she asked when she answered his call.

"How about tonight?"

"The weather is terrible," she said, but then she saw headlamps outside the window, and her heart filled with joy.

Hannah excused herself to help Jack in the kitchen, and Bridget pretended to have fallen asleep in her recliner, though Quenby saw her peeking through her eyelids.

"How's my fiancée?" Lucas asked when he walked into the door. He liked calling her that, ever since she'd agreed to marry him. And each time he said the word, it made her smile.

"I'm much better now."

He kissed her lips instead of her cheek and handed her a winter bouquet with red roses, white calla lilies, and glossy magnolia leaves.

"What are these for?"

"Just because," he said as he settled down on the rug beside her as if he belonged here. "Because I love you, Quenby Vaughn."

When she kissed him this time, the winter wind rattled the glass, but it didn't startle her. Finally she, too, had found her way home.

Author's Note

More than a year ago, I sat down with a mug of green tea in my favorite coffee shop, scribbling down my ideas for this novel. Outside the window stood an old tree, a weeping cedar with its sturdy branches and dangling leaves that ballooned like a giant umbrella over the people drinking coffee and tea below.

In my mind's eye, I saw two German children—the best of friends—playing high among those branches. In a tree house. They were in danger, though at the time I didn't know what threatened them. I just knew the boy and girl had to run. And the girl would be lost along the way.

As I sipped my drink, the plight of Dietmar and Brigitte began unfolding. It was a gift to me, this story. Given by the Master Creator, who, I believe, works powerfully through stories to redeem His children.

My journey to research this novel took me north to the misty San Juan Islands, across the Atlantic to visit the historic streets and heaths in London and the beautiful gardens and villages of Kent, then down to Switzerland to tour the medieval fortress Château de Chillon.

Years ago, my husband and I hiked in a forest of bright green behind Moselkern to visit another medieval castle called Burg Eltz.

I drew on my memories of touring both Germany and Belgium and then living in Germany for a season to tell the story of Dietmar and Brigitte's escape. The Disney scenes were from my own childhood—and adult—fascination with the magic of story in Orlando.

While in London, I spent an entire day at the National Archives reading through a stack of recently released top secret files as well as older documents about German espionage in the United Kingdom. Many British citizens sympathized with Nazi Germany for a multitude of reasons, and I read account after account of men and women who either gathered information for Hitler or attempted to wreak havoc on England's facilities. There were handwritten letters from suspected spies; documents about microphotography, invisible ink, and secret codes; a worn file about a Nazi parachutist who became a double agent; and the transcriptions of interrogations conducted during and after the war.

Before World War II, hundreds of German agents gathered information in England about airfields, military bases, and factories, but hours after Great Britain declared war against Germany, British agents apprehended many of these men and women. They were either detained or deported back to Germany. Still the Nazis continued sending men over during the war via plane or boat to gather information and sabotage the country.

England has a grand tradition of documenting the normalcy of life through volunteers who submit their diaries to an organization called Mass Observation. These accounts from the 1940s were an invaluable reference for me as the diarists recorded their fears about espionage, the preparations for war, and the explanation of how the resentment toward Nazis spread to a hatred of all German people, many of whom already lived among the British.

While the threads of espionage stitched this novel together, my heart was not to expose those who betrayed their country—or those who came to a country bent on destruction—as much as to celebrate the redemption and resiliency of children removed or evacuated from their homes and sent to live in another place around the world. So many children today need to begin writing new chapters of redemption and love in the stories of their lives. *Catching the Wind* was written with a grateful heart to all those who've helped abandoned, orphaned, and refugee children begin a new story.

If you're interested in more information about helping children who need a home, here are five extraordinary organizations that care for kids around the world: remembernhu.org, hearthecry.org, worldorphans.org, runministries.org, and worldrelief.org. Also, prayforthem.com is an excellent resource if you'd like to pray specifically for refugees.

As with all my novels, writing this story was a personal journey, but a host of people partnered with me to help straighten up my facts and encourage me along the way. I've had to change minor points for the sake of story—like relocating chalky cliffs from the eastern bank to the west along the River Ouse—but I've tried to remain as accurate as possible with my facts. Any and all errors are my fault.

A special thank-you to:

My editors—Stephanie Broene, Sarah Rische, and Shaina Turner—and the entire staff at Tyndale House Publishers for welcoming me so graciously to your team. It's a privilege to partner with you. My agent, Natasha Kern, for your constant support and the wisdom you pour boundlessly into my life and writing career. Your heart to fight for those in need inspires me and so many others.

Kevin and Amanda Bates, Jacob Pflug, and all the baristas at Symposium Coffee for allowing me to sit for hours, nursing a green tea as I write in the old house you've turned into a beautiful shop, and for inspiring me with your faith and your love of story as well. Amanda—there are two lines in this novel taken straight from your lips. They still make me smile. . . .

The delightful Peter and Anne Cook for sharing your home in

Greenwich and your many wonderful stories with me. Caroline Watts, travel agent extraordinaire, for helping me get exactly where I needed to go and for sharing your own stories of England. Ed and Jitka Peacock for graciously rescuing me after I toured the remote Scotney Castle in Kent and delivering me to a train station near Tonbridge so I didn't have to spend the night in the forest alone.

Aunt Janet Wacker for embracing our family's heritage and for inspiring me with your many stories. Pinn Crawford and all the librarians at my local library who not only helped me find the resources I needed, but did it with such joy. My engineer brother-in-law Jim Dobson for brainstorming plot and my scientist brother-in-law Dr. Steve Dobson for teaching me how to use a modern-day microscope. Thanks to each of you for sharing your expertise.

My cousin and airline pilot extraordinaire, David Ransopher, and my friend and corporate flight attendant, Ann Menke, for educating me on corporate aviation. My critique partners—Dawn Shipman, Kelly Chang, Nicole Miller, and Mesu Andrews—for sharing your wisdom and allowing me to step into your stories even as you step into mine. Michele Heath, my friend and first reader, for your insight and encouragement. You always cut to the heart of what I want to say and help me communicate it better on the next version. Sheila Herbert for your gracious gift of time and wisdom as I continue learning about life in England both past and present. Tamara Park for inviting me into your journey and for your courage and passion as you interview refugee children and families around the world.

My Sistas—Mary Kay Taylor, Diane Comer, Julie Kohl, Ann Menke, and Jodi Stilp. You show me love in abundance, and I love each of you back. Thank you for linking arms and praying for me, empowering me with your kindness, and sharing your own stories. And to Jodi's sister-in-law, Quenby, for letting me borrow your very cool name.

My friend Tosha Williams, to whom I dedicated this book. I'm grateful for every one of the thirty years that we've journeyed together arm in arm as sister friends. I savor your prayers and every encouraging word.

My entire family, who are an endless fount of encouragement as I write, including my parents, James and Lyn Beroth; my sister, Christy Nunn; my husband, Jon; and my daughters, Karlyn and Kinzel. Each of you keep me grounded (in the best sense of the word) and God-focused. I love you to pieces.

The power of story has transformed my own life, and I'm incredibly grateful to Jesus Christ, the author and finisher of faith, for enduring pain and humiliation and ultimately conquering the evil in this world, redeeming and healing because of His boundless love for His kids.

About the Author

MELANIE DOBSON is the award-winning author of sixteen historical romance, suspense, and time-slip novels, including *Chateau of Secrets* and *Shadows of Ladenbrooke Manor*. Three of her novels have won Carol Awards; *Love Finds You in Liberty, Indiana* won Best Novel of Indiana in 2010; and *The Black Cloister* won the *Foreword* magazine Religious Fiction Book of the Year.

Melanie is the former corporate publicity manager at Focus on the Family and owner of the publicity firm Dobson Media Group. When she isn't writing, Melanie enjoys teaching both writing and public relations classes at George Fox University.

Melanie and her husband, Jon, have two daughters. After moving numerous times with work, the Dobson family has settled near Portland, Oregon, and they love to hike and camp in the mountains of the Pacific Northwest and along the Pacific Coast. Melanie also enjoys exploring ghost towns and abandoned homes, helping care for kids in her community, and reading stories with her girls.

Visit Melanie online at www.melaniedobson.com.

Discussion Questions

1. At the beginning of the book, Dietmar's heart is torn. He wants to rescue his parents, but he's not strong enough to overpower the Gestapo. Have you ever been in a situation where you wanted to help but could not? How did you reconcile this?

2. As Quenby struggles with insecurity and fear of abandonment, she tries to escape her feelings by immersing herself in someone else's story. What are other ways people escape from either past memories or present conflict? What do you think is the best way to heal from emotional wounds and fear?

3. Mr. Knight believes that many people don't understand or honor faithfulness. What does faithfulness mean to you? How are you faithful to the people in your life? How has someone been faithful to you?

4. When Dietmar and Brigitte are in the public hall, Dietmar believes he must walk away in order for Brigitte to find a home. Does he make the right decision? Was there a time in your life where walking away was the best or only choice?

5. Brigitte identifies with fairy-tale characters and stories while she lives with the Terrells. How has a book or movie changed your life? What are some stories or characters that have stayed with you over the years? Why have they stuck with you?

6. This novel slips between historical and contemporary stories. How do actions in the past affect the present-day characters? What was a seemingly small decision from your past that had a significant impact on your future?

7. Rosalind thinks of herself as wise and perhaps courageous to leave her daughter with Brigitte, in order to protect the child. Do you think she made the right choice? How did her decision change the future for multiple characters in this story?

8. The magnolia tree is common in England today but would have been rare during World War II. What does the magnolia represent along Brigitte's journey? If you had Cinderella's wishing tree, what would you wish?

9. As they get to know each other, Lucas and Quenby discuss "superpowers," including the abilities to forgive and to expunge things from the past. Do you think we can forgive and forget things that have happened in the past? How do you process hurtful things that happened to you as a child or as an adult?

10. Quenby believes that the death and forgiveness of Christ have the power to change her life today. Do you believe that God can heal both the past and present through forgiveness? If so, what does this look like in your life?

11. Mr. Knight is fascinated by heroic knights from the past, but Lucas thinks Mr. Knight is a modern-day hero. What is your definition of a hero or heroine? Has someone served as a hero or heroine in your life?

12. Quenby wrote an article comparing the *Kindertransport* during World War II to the flood of refugees in our world today. How does the portrayal of Brigitte, a young refugee, influence your perspective on the current crisis? How do we balance caring for the needs of refugees while stopping those intent on doing harm?

13. What does the wind symbolize throughout this novel? How does it bring the characters together?